Praise for the action-packed fantasy
of
LINDA ROBERTSON

Arcane Circle

"[Each book in this series] can be read in one sitting with hours of enjoyment as I linger in the alternate world of Cleveland that Robertson has created."

—Fresh Fiction

"Took the various aspects of urban fantasy I love, threw them all together, and created a masterpiece of discovery, devotion and desire. . . . Make sure you don't have anything planned for a few days when you pick this up because you will not be able to put it down."

—Bitten by Books (5 Stars)

"Urban fantasy at its best, with lovable characters and the perfect mix between action, romance, and magic."

—Book Lovers Inc. (5 Stars)

"A great addition to this incredible series. I can't wait to get my hands into the next book."

—Fiction Kingdom

"Action filled, sexy, and full of promises for future installments."

—Scooper

Fatal Circle

"The third in Robertson's Circle series won't disappoint fans who've come to expect lots of romance, mystery, and intrigue from her books."

D0190593

Vicious Circle

DON'T MISS THESE OTHER
PERSEPHONE ALCMEDI BOOKS . . .

Vicious Circle

Hallowed Circle

Fatal Circle

Arcane Circle

Available from Pocket Books

WICKED CIRCLE

LINDA ROBERTSON

Pocket Books

New York   London   Toronto   Sydney   New Delhi

Pocket Books
A Division of Simon & Schuster, Inc.
1230 Avenue of the Americas
New York, NY 10020

This book is a work of fiction. Names, characters, places, and incidents either are products of the author's imagination or are used fictitiously. Any resemblance to actual events or locales or persons, living or dead, is entirely coincidental.

First Juno Books/Pocket Books paperback edition January 2012

JUNO BOOKS and colophon are registered trademarks of Wildside Press LLC used under license by Simon & Schuster, Inc., the publisher of this work.

POCKET and colophon are registered trademarks of Simon & Schuster, Inc.

For information about special discounts for bulk purchases, please contact Simon & Schuster Special Sales at 1-866-506-1949 or business@simonandschuster.com.

The Simon & Schuster Speakers Bureau can bring authors to your live event. For more information or to book an event contact the Simon & Schuster Speakers Bureau at 1-866-248-3049 or visit our website at www.simonspeakers.com.

Cover illustration by Don Sipley

Manufactured in the United States of America

10 9 8 7 6 5 4 3 2 1

ISBN 978-1-4516-4695-5
ISBN 978-1-4516-4699-3 (ebook)

DEDICATION

For my agent, Don, who recently
embarked on the path of fatherhood.

May your journey be blessed.

ACKNOWLEDGMENTS

Red-Caped Hero Thanks to:

My nephew Evan for letting me use his name;
and also to Doug Kusak and Matt Grabski at the
Great Lakes Science Center for answering all my
questions about the steamship *William G. Mather*.

Java-and-Chocolate Thanks to:

My writing groups, OWN & CNW,
to the gals at word-whores.blogspot.com,
and to my beta-readers
Shannon, Beth, Missy, Jon, and Andrea.

Margarita Thanks to:

All the readers that blog and review
who took the time to read and spread the word!
I called you out by name last time,
but you are far too many to list now. *SQUEE!*
My appreciation is truly heartfelt.
Cheers!

Geek Hugs for:

S. A. Swann—for an invaluable critique.
Michelle "Swann"—for the most
incredibly scrumptious brownies EVER.

REVERENT GRATITUDE FOR:

The Many-named Muse. Rock on!

WICKED
CIRCLE

CHAPTER ONE

Heldridge Ellington opened the small crypt door from the inside of the musty hole that served as the Wirt family's final resting place. Although not a unique place for a vampire to shelter for the day, it did not suit Heldridge's particular taste. But as it had been raining and dawn fast approaching, the place had met his specific needs at the time.

Cold rain spattered his blond hair as he emerged. The vampire swore under his breath.

Making every effort to keep his clothes clean, he wriggled free. If his luck held, he'd soon be meeting with the Excelsior—the highest authority in all of the Vampire Executive International Network —to reveal the immense secret Menessos and his court witch were hiding. Heldridge didn't want to be discredited by arriving covered in cobwebs and grime. It was bad enough that he would smell of moist earth and old death.

He trudged toward the Congressional Cemetery gates. Washington, D.C.'s persistent rain had made a monstrous marsh of the ground—it sucked at his every muddy step.

Heldridge soon traded the mucky path for a solid sidewalk. He couldn't meet the Excelsior with filth on his shoes, so he stopped and kicked a homeless man curled in a storefront alcove. When the man groaned and sat up, Heldridge showed him a twenty-dollar bill. "Get the mud off my shoes."

The homeless man twisted onto his knees and shrugged out of his jacket. He tugged off his shirt and wiped the shoes with it, exposing his emaciated body to the rain and cold. When he'd finished, Heldridge inspected the job and walked away with the money still in his hand.

"Hey," the homeless man cried, scrambling to his feet.

Heldridge wadded the cash and tossed it over his shoulder. He laughed as the man scampered into the rain to claim the paper before it was swept down the gutter and into the storm drain.

Hunger gnawed at him, but he dared not try to feed at the local blood bar; that was exactly what the area vampires would expect him to do. Instead of risking recognition and capture, he would feed unlawfully.

In an alley a few blocks away, Heldridge sated his hunger with a mesmerized donor in a dapper hat. It was illegal and dangerous, but this risk was necessary.

As he thought of how easily he had fed for the last decade at his own bar—the Blood Culture, which catered to the vampires of Cleveland—his outrage swelled.

Menessos had transferred his headquarters to Cleveland! Heldridge had barely gotten away from him, barely established himself as a legitimate vampire lord, and his night-father had followed him to measure his every move.

He thinks he's found his Lustrata. His witch queen. If I can't have autonomy in my own haven, then he can't have her. If I can't part them, once I tell the Excelsior what I know . . . VEIN will.

Heldridge wiped his mouth on his coat sleeve, immediately realizing the mistake. The scent of blood would linger. He shuffled his small packets of home earth from his coat to his pants pockets, then traded overcoats with the unwitting donor. This new coat reeked of cheap cologne, but that would be a benefit. Snatching the man's fedora as well, he fled.

He flipped the collar up and lowered the hat brim so it mostly hid his flaxen hair. Hopefully, this was enough to conceal his distinctive features; Heldridge could have modeled for comic book artists. His chiseled jawline and broad-shouldered body had brought him much admiration.

Tonight, however, being easily recognized was a problem.

On K Street he strode directly toward the massive building where VEIN was housed.

With an easy gait he passed the building, examining the security. Two vampire sentries stood under the awning on either side of the revolving door, chatting. Though they scented him, it was a superficial effort. They detected the terrible cologne and dismissed him as a mortal.

Behind them the lobby inside was empty except for the receptionist at the desk. Relying on cameras, they kept the real security forces out of sight. This maintained a nonaggressive appearance in the nation's capital— where lawmakers would be more than pleased to have an excuse to deem VEIN a threat.

Heldridge snapped his fingers and turned as if he'd forgotten something, then hurried back the way he had come. At the last second, he rushed toward the revolving door with inhuman speed.

He walloped the vampire on the right, grabbed his shoulders, and dragged him into the space of the spinning door. The unconscious sentry suffered a secondary impact with the floor as Heldridge used him as a temporary doorstop to block the other vampire from entering.

Inside the scarlet and dove gray interior, the lovely receptionist picked up a phone and pushed buttons. Heldridge sped by her, running directly to the elevator in the rear of the lobby, discarding the hat and overcoat on his way.

The doors parted, revealing a sentry vampire in a stark white shirt, black dress pants, and shiny shoes. His collar had been loosened. He was posed to keep whatever he was holding hidden behind his thigh. Smiling, he said, "It must be my lucky night."

Heldridge was taller and broader than the guard, but vampiric strength was based on age rather than size. With immortals that was never easy to tell at first glance. "Escort me to the Excelsior."

"Gladly." The sentry showed fang as he produced a machete from behind him. "Part of you, anyway." He stepped out of the elevator, advancing toward Heldridge.

Heldridge widened his stance, preparing for an attack. "I am a haven master and I demand to see the Excelsior!"

"Dunno what you'll see, but I promise to keep your eyes open for you, traitor. There's a bounty for your head. The rest of you is optional."

Heldridge hissed, "I want an *audience* with the Excelsior."

The elevator doors began to close. Heldridge surged forward. He blocked the vampire's machete-swinging arm and hit him in the solar plexus, knocking him backward into the elevator car. Momentum carried Heldridge in also, and the doors shut them in.

The guard didn't have room to effectively swing the long blade and resorted to jabbing with it. Heldridge caught the vampire's arm, twisted, and felt the elbow break. The machete clattered to the floor and Heldridge slammed the guard's head against the elevator wall, denting the shiny metal.

When the doors parted on the next floor up, Heldridge wedged the machete in the opening to keep the doors from closing and, more importantly, prohibit the car from picking up reinforcements. There were other elevators and stairs, but he didn't have to make it easy for his opponents.

He dragged the unconscious vampire by his unbroken arm. The hall was nondescript gray with a slate floor and plain wall sconces for light. At the next checkpoint, six sentries blocked his path.

With minimal effort, Heldridge sent the body sliding to the sentries' feet. "I want an audience with the Excelsior. He told me no."

"Do you think our answer will be different?"

Heldridge could have torn both the door guards and the machete-wielding sentry apart, but he'd hoped his restraint would gain him a measure of consideration instead of indicating he was weak. They had been individual foes, however. With six vampires before him, his options were fewer.

He was willing to kill his way through the building if it became necessary, but as it would undermine his claims of acting in the best interests of VEIN, he preferred to consider slaughter only as an emergency exit strategy.

He gauged his adversaries as he calmly resettled his suit jacket. "I do not wish permanent harm to anyone, but the information I have for the Excelsior is worth any risk."

More sentries burst from a stairwell behind him.

Heldridge was surrounded. *Stairs to the rear. Focus to the front and they'll all think you're going forward. Let them get a little closer, then make a break for it.*

The wall speaker crackled. A voice ordered, "Conference Room Two." The vampires stepped away from Heldridge.

Minutes later, a sentry opened a heavy black door with a scarlet "2" on it. Heldridge entered with a confident stride. The door shut loudly behind him.

A single forty-watt bulb glowed in the overhead fixture. Beneath it sat a plain stool. An array of video cameras, red lights blinking slowly, all out of sync, focused on the seat.

Heldridge couldn't confine his irritation. He glowered into the centermost camera. "How do I know the Excelsior is receiving this transmission?"

Five floors up, in a darkened theater with six rows of executive seating, various viewpoints of Heldridge's entrance played across the many screens mounted to the main wall.

"An imprudent endeavor, coming here." The deep voice of Meroveus Franciscus thrummed like distant thunder. Except for the plain elastic band restraining the curls of his waist-length black hair, his appearance was that of a handsome thirty-something businessman in a Rolex advertisement—and he did wear an exquisite timepiece with his bespoke suit.

"He's still annoying." Giovanni Guistini's voice was also distinctive, but not for a mellifluous quality. Giovanni's every word scratched the ear in a painful rasp. Beneath his pointed chin an ugly scar gnarled the flesh of his neck. In life, his throat had been torn open. "Note his stance, his lifted chin. He is our prisoner, yet conceit pours from him. The young masters are always intolerable. They think they know so much."

Mero countered, "Sometimes they do."

"Sometimes they're just overconfident fools," Giovanni retorted, melting into a pose that might have been an attempt to appear thoughtful in counterpoint to the fierceness his shaven head afforded him.

Mero was familiar with his counterpart's contemptuousness and had long considered Giovanni a deliberate egotist who dressed in black V-neck shirts and collarless jackets so no one would ever miss seeing his scar.

Both provided advice to the Excelsior, but Mero often found himself choosing words and opinions that would balance Giovanni's typically stubborn and pitiless claims. The trick was guessing what opinion the other advisor would choose, then expressing his own opinion first, so that Giovanni sounded like a squabbling child.

On the screens, Heldridge cried, "Do you hear me? I demand to speak to the Excelsior!"

Speaking of children, Meroveus thought.

Sitting in the back of the theater, where the gentle radiance of the screens could barely reach, was the Excelsior. He wore an ink-dark suit, and the matching shirt and tie both had the sheen of polished obsidian. His black hair was loose and hung straight, framing his angular face with ferocity. Despite the pallor of his skin his hairstyle imparted a Native American quality, but Mero knew the vampire was descended from ancient Franks—indeed, from mortal kings.

The Excelsior touched a button on the arm of his

chair, which activated a microphone. "I hear you," he said crossly. His words echoed, slightly delayed, into the room with Heldridge. When he finished speaking he released the button so anything his advisors said would not be piped into the conference room.

"You will put a bounty on my head but you won't meet with me directly?"

Giovanni chuckled. "Please let me kill him for you, my lord."

The Excelsior pressed the button. "You attempted to strike down your superior. You've brutalized two of my sentries. Why should you not be drained to a husk?" The accented lilt of his voice did not soften the iciness of his words.

"On these premises I have only defended myself. As for the other matter, you have received misinformation. I did not attempt to strike down my Quarterlord, but his Erus Veneficus."

The Excelsior triggered the microphone again. "You freely admit to this crime?"

"The witch has hexed him, bound him by witch-mark into her service."

"Ha!" Giovanni laughed. "Never!" He paused. "Unless . . ." He cast a glance toward Mero beside him, then over his shoulder toward the Excelsior.

Mero had to concede that fact. "The Quarterlord made no secret of his long search for the Lustrata."

The Excelsior did not respond.

His silence, to Mero, was a sign. "Do you have information about this?"

Nonplussed, the Excelsior said, "She claims to be

the Lustrata, though the witches remain divided in this matter. She must not be slain. At least, not yet."

Why didn't he tell me this? Mero wondered.

Heldridge paced impatiently away from the camera. He spun back. "Do you still hear me? A witch has sway over your Northeastern Quarterlord." His countenance was a confident mask, but his pacing and tone belied apprehension. His arms spread wide. "You do understand that my actions were merely to protect my Quarterlord and release him from her grasp?"

"He would have us see him as a defender, and be blind to his lawbreaking," Mero mused.

"He would prefer," Giovanni added, "advancement of his position. Exposing a weak Quarterlord who begs replacing creates a chain of repositioning."

On-screen, Heldridge shifted his weight nervously. "My Lord Excelsior?"

Mero could see that Heldridge was about to do something desperate. Or stupid. He opened his mouth to make his own suggestion—

"I beseech you!" Heldridge blurted. "Release the shab-bubitum. Send them to the Northeastern Quarterlord. You will find that my claim is true."

Meroveus could not believe his ears. Heldridge had risked his own destruction to plead his case, but making this absurd proposal demonstrated only panic. Mero swiveled his chair toward the back of the theater and made a steeple with his fingertips. "Heldridge is of Menessos's line," he offered, "yet the young master has not spoken the name of his Maker. It suggests disassociation between them. Menessos allowed Heldridge to leave him and become his own master, but recently Menessos transferred his haven from Chicago to Cleveland—"

"A matter he told this court of only after the fact," Giovanni interjected.

"He is now based only a few miles from the location of Heldridge's haven," Mero continued. "Perhaps Heldridge seeks distance, as many sons seek from their fathers. It seems a matter between the two of them. I suggest you remove the bounty on Heldridge, set him free, and let Menessos deal with him."

"Ha!" Giovanni barked. "It was Menessos's Erus Veneficus that was the target. He will not be impartial if he is to judge Heldridge!"

"Heldridge has admitted his crime. What need of impartiality is there?"

Giovanni cleared his throat, a sound like gravel in a blender. "It has been centuries since anyone has dared invoke the name of the shabbubitum to this court, and according to the old accounts, over two millennia since they walked the earth." His eyes flicked downward and he frowned thoughtfully.

Mero knew the dramatics were a bad sign. He started to interrupt, but on-screen Heldridge was screaming and waving his arms. The Excelsior had obviously turned the volume down.

"Their truth-finding abilities are legendary," Giovanni said. "Perhaps we need the rectitude attributed to those three bitches. Perhaps it is time we recover the precision our justice had in antiquity." He lifted his gaze. "I say send for them."

"You're mad," Mero whispered.

Giovanni spoke, but not to Mero. "Give Heldridge

what he wants. Unshackle the shabbubitum. Subject him to their methods, then, if he's honest, send them to Menessos."

Mero shifted, uncomfortable in his chair. "Your eagerness gives me caution, Giovanni. The shabbubitum were bound for a reason."

"This young fool has requested it!"

"It seems overindulgence to exploit their unique skills upon a task such as this." Mero had to regain the advantage. Nothing good would come of the Excelsior consenting to this ludicrous idea. "Heavy-handed wastefulness would not reflect well upon our Lord."

Giovanni tilted his head. "This is an opportunity. Heldridge has opened the door, Mero, and I long to see what the great Menessos has hidden behind it." Giovanni leaned forward. "Don't you?"

"I do not wish to tread where the shabbubitum run free." Eager to drive his point home, Mero sat straighter and said, "They are dangerous, sentient beings, not domesticated animals that can be made to perform tricks. Treating them as such would be very unwise. Better to leave them where they are."

Guistini stood, facing the darkness surrounding the Excelsior. "For long decades Menessos has puzzled us all. He refused the very position you fill so well, Excelsior." The vampire maneuvered his thin frame between the seats one section closer to his lord. "Do you not want to know why? Do you not want to know if he regrets that decision?"

"You reveal your true motive: revenge against the one who tore your throat." At that, Mero expected Giovanni would explode in anger, but he did not.

Giovanni mounted another step. "Revenge? No. I

am merely thinking of the Excelsior's safety. If Menessos believes his witch is the Lustrata, he will bond with her in order to unite their power. If he's found her, the Domn Lup won't be far behind. A triumvirate of power merging the Wolf King, the Witches' Messiah, and the vampire who could have been Excelsior . . . what will they seek, once they are united, my lord?"

Mero tried once more to stop the madness. "Your manner suggests guilt, yet you have only minimal facts." He glanced at the screen again; Heldridge was pounding on the door.

"They could not have yet recognized their full potential." Giovanni made a fist as he said, "This trio is yet within your grasp, Excelsior. The shabbubitum are at your beck and call. Do you dare keep your hand at your side?"

The Excelsior's eyes gleamed in the darkness.

Giovanni had won this time. The danger of inaction outweighed the danger of action.

Bowing low before the Excelsior, Giovanni whispered, "Summon the shabbubitum. Let us have all the secrets Menessos would hide."

CHAPTER TWO

The day's meager light was nearly gone as I stood enshrouded in fog at Point State Park in Pittsburgh and yanked the white sheath dress over my head. Nana placed a circlet of ivy on my head.

"The bell sleeves are nice," said my mother, Eris, as she smoothed my dark hair. "You're going to make a beautiful bride."

Those words furrowed my brows. "Someday," I retorted, envisioning Johnny standing before an altar. Then, in my imaginary scene, Menessos stepped up on the other side. What would I do if I had to choose between them? "Maybe."

Besides, it wasn't like I was wearing a *silk* gown. My attire was simply meant to be symbolic of the maiden aspect of the triple-goddess. This was a plain cotton chemise I bought on eBay from a seamstress who could have independently costumed a Renaissance fair.

Having always been more tomboy than prom queen, I'd always had an extremely low tolerance for dresses. However, this plain gown was reminiscent of those worn by the women in the art of John William Waterhouse, and for that reason alone, I was thrilled to be wearing it. At least until Eris's romantic notion spoiled the mood with implied lifetime commitments.

Shoes were another story. I'd not thought of them

when ordering, and by the time I realized my error, it was too late for even overnight shipping.

My mother supplied me with a close imitation of the appropriate footwear: ladies' slippers from Isotoner.

"You'll be a bride someday soon, I'd bet. I've seen how Johnny looks at you."

Words like "mom" and "mother" didn't yet roll off my tongue with any ease, so my reprimand was blatant name-calling. "Eris."

"What? Mother said he's been sharing your bedroom at the farmhouse."

Disapproval for Nana's gossip-mongering darkened my expression. As she presented me with the silver belt I whispered, "Traitor."

"And who was it that told her I was trying to quit smoking?" Nana shot back.

"She has you there," Eris quipped. "And she's hoping for great-grandchildren, though she doesn't want you to . . . how did you say it, Mother?"

"Don't put the cart before the horse," Nana answered.

"Wæres can't breed," I reminded them.

Nana smiled optimistically. "Yeah, yeah, but with him being the Domn Lup, a lot of those wære rules don't apply to him."

That hadn't even occurred to me. Fear must have shown in my expression, because they both giggled.

Irritably, I wrapped the belt around my waist, my glare snapping back and forth between Eris and Nana. "I'm certain the molecular science behind the 'non-viability' of wære reproduction is something not even the Domn Lup can defy."

My anger, however, was all for Eris. She knew that a

calm mind-set was essential pre-ritual, but she'd had to get that crack in. She couldn't resist exerting some type of control over me.

I bit my tongue to keep from saying anything else. I'd gone to a lot of effort for this ritual, and I wasn't going to let her mess it up.

Part of that effort included drawing a pentacle with black chalk earlier on the concrete near the fountain. Because of the dark powder, Nana had brought the dress with her to keep it from getting dirty, but that meant my wardrobe change had to be done on-site. Though the park was seasonably abandoned, I had expected to have to use the quad-cab of my mother's newly purchased used truck as a dressing room. The fog provided adequate privacy, however, and I opted to switch my clothing beside the fountain.

When I finished adjusting the silver belt, I glanced at my mother.

All in all, Eris seemed to be remarkably accepting of the loss of her limb. She'd even gone so far as to say, "Losing my arm was a fair price to pay in order to have you in my life again, Persephone."

It seemed like the simple show of a positive attitude. *At first.* After hearing it for the fourth or fifth time, the passive-aggressive tone became obvious. That sentence, as in "grammatical unit," was becoming my sentence, as in "judicial determination of punishment."

In a single afternoon I'd brought the two biggest regrets of her life into her tattoo parlor: me and Johnny. After sixteen years of separation, on the first day I'd spent with Eris, her home had been invaded. The top dog of the wærewolves, the Rege, had followed us to her home—led by a tracer he'd planted in my phone. In a hail of bullets, he'd forced his way inside, where the spell to unlock Johnny's tattoos had been under way. The Rege had hoped to kill Johnny and eliminate the threat a Domn Lup would have on his power base, but Eris had caught two bullets playing human shield and protecting Johnny. That had led to the loss of her right arm.

For all her recent heroics, she'd also been the villain who, eight years ago, had tattooed Johnny in the first place. She'd used her magic and sorcery to hide and constrain the power of the Domn Lup. A mysterious man had paid her to perform the magic and create the tattoos, but she could remember nothing about him. Or that was what she claimed.

After my messy reentry into her life, she should have told me to get the hell out, to drag my dangerous destiny with me and never come back. Yeah, she should have abandoned me again. This time, at least, she had a legitimate reason.

Instead, she was using these events—and her consequent loss—as a means to keep me around. It felt like I'd been condemned for life, and my prison was the unending inclusion in her world. *What is it with mothers and guilt trips?*

I'd truly forgiven her for the awful childhood she'd provided. I'd even let go of my resentment for the subsequent abandonment. She'd protected my boyfriend from certain death, and I had made sure the damage to her apartment was repaired pronto. I'd also agreed to stay and help her adjust to life without her arm and get to know her again.

But that was before I realized what she was doing. And what she *wasn't* doing.

Tonight, November 16, was the Night of Hecate, and that particular goddess had shown me great favor. There was no way I would miss honoring Her. But I didn't have to include Eris and Nana in it. I'd involved them because the guilt trip my mother was determined to send me on felt like a brand-new wedge between us, and I wanted it gone. I wanted her to get into a circle. I wanted her to see that she couldn't perform ritual tasks like she did before. I wanted her to eat that knowledge and get angry. I wanted her to cry. Not in order to satisfy some vengeful side of me; those days were gone with the absolution I'd sincerely offered her. These things would be healthy for her. She had to grieve her loss in order to accept it. Instead, she was disguising the truth—and I was the camouflage.

That kind of self-deception wouldn't help anyone.

But in this ritual she had been charged with specific duties, and she'd have to figure out how to perform them one-handed or admit defeat. Either would force her to begin dealing with her loss.

Since we were in Pittsburgh, I had selected a park where a triangle of land jutted between the Monongahela River and the Allegheny River. The tip of the triangle pointed toward the Ohio River, and on it sat a fountain celebrating this liquid confluence by spewing water high into the air. Or it did in warmer weather.

The fountain and its pool had been drained for the coming winter, but there was no lack of moisture in the air. With the mist embracing us so thickly, we were going to have to rely on Menessos to determine when the sun sank beneath the horizon. Not that he was here, but I would feel when he awoke, and at that exact moment, the Night of Hecate would commence. That was when we were to begin our journey to the river's edge.

Nana pulled a white-lidded bowl from a cloth satchel and passed it to me. The standard supper offerings were eggs, bread, cheese, and fish. As she removed the lid and replaced it in the bag, I saw I had, as expected, the eggs. Once standing in position, I quieted my mind and tried to purge the not-so-calming effects my mother had on me.

Nana put a red bowl into the crook of Eris's only arm. "Good?" she asked.

"Good," Eris replied. Representing the mother aspect of the triple-goddess for our ritual, she was dressed all in red: scarlet jeans and a tight-fitting crimson tee that said TREMENDOUS under a flannel-lined red jacket. She'd insisted that Nana cut off the sleeve and sew the hole shut. This alteration made it obvious that nothing of her right arm remained. She'd even had a pair of red leather cowboy boots in her closet to complete the scarlet head-to-toe.

Lastly, Nana, who signified the crone aspect of the triple-goddess for our ritual and therefore wore black polyester pants and a thick black sweater, drew out a black bowl and dropped its lid into the satchel before taking her place in our line. The smell of delicious fish wafted to me and reminded me how hungry I was. We'd fasted all day for this ritual.

And we waited.

I had time to notice the pair of black combs with little silver owls in Nana's hair. She'd found them at a local sundry store.

My fingers drummed on the edge of the white bowl.

I checked on the candles behind us. After I'd drawn the circle earlier, I'd placed and lit short black pillar candles at each of the five spots where the lines of the star met the circle. Because of the constant wind here, the candles were topped with glass hurricane globes. They flickered but didn't seem in danger of going out.

Abruptly, my body felt like it was being inflated with hot air—Menessos was awake. My insides resonated with his screaming as if the waves of sound were vibrating from within me. Returning to life must be a horrific experience. I pitied him because of it.

When the resonance faded I breathed deep and exhaled with purpose to counter the sensation.

Then, I began walking. Eris and Nana fell in behind me, and we made a single-file trek toward the river's edge. The light of the candles we were leaving behind would disappear into the fog as we strode further away, but hopefully I could maintain a straight line back until we were in range of the glow that would guide us unerringly to the circle to complete the ritual. Parading all over the park, lost in the white air, would be embarrassing.

Another part of my earlier on-site preparation had included hiking down to the river's edge to stick two oil-burning bamboo torches into the ground. When the torches glimmered into view, my nostrils filled with the smell of the cypress I'd scented the lamp oil with. Pausing on the last piece of level ground, I waited as Eris and Nana re-formed the side-by-side line.

"I am the maiden," I said, ceremoniously hoisting the bowl of eggs skyward. The fog gave this ritual an ambience of mystique and majesty, so it felt appropriate to try to display a formal and serious demeanor.

As I surveyed the embankment, though, I realized I was in trouble.

This slope had been no problem earlier, when I'd worn my hikers, but the Isotoners were soft-soled. With my first step, sharp rock points jabbed into the bottom of my foot. I wished my boots would magically reappear on my feet.

Compensating and shifting my weight onto my heels led to the discovery that the slippers had zero traction. The rocks shifted under my feet. Two quick steps kept me from tumbling down, but I was certain that something had pierced the sole and cut into the arch of my foot. The eggs clacked roughly in the bowl, but when I inspected them, none had cracked.

Trying futilely to regain my solemn demeanor amid the giggling from Nana and Eris, I proceeded between the torches. Crouching before the water, I found my bell sleeves made placing the bowl into the river tricky. Not willing to let anything further dampen the mood, or my sleeves, this problem was solved by wrapping the draped length around my forearm and tucking the edge under. "I offer this food for the Supper of Hecate, for the Lady of the Crossroads." The bowl quickly floated out of sight in the mist.

"I am the mother," Eris said.

She awkwardly surrendered the red bowl to me. In the transfer, I couldn't help seeing the red ink now embedded in Eris's palm. That, too, had happened when she'd reversed the spellwork on Johnny.

The red bowl contained a round loaf of bread and a fresh log of goat cheese. As I placed it into the river Eris said, "I offer this food for the Supper of Hecate, for the Queen of Witches."

"And I am the crone," Nana croaked.

When she placed the black bowl in my hands I saw that it bore three Filet-O-Fish sandwiches.

The drive-thru contribution lacked the charm an offering should have. Rolling my eyes up at her I whispered, "Really?"

"I wasn't about to stink up the apartment cooking fish." She flapped her hand at me. "That'll do just fine."

I took the black bowl to the water.

"I offer this food for the Supper of Hecate," Nana said, "for the Dark Mother of the Underworld."

The river carried Nana's offering away. Finished, I held the hem of my skirt up, put my foot on the slope, and dug my toes in. It felt secure, so I took the step.

The loose gravel shifted and gave way. My balance was ruined. I flailed my arms trying to steady myself as I backpedaled. My forearm smacked against one of the torches, and something sharp pierced my already injured foot. The torch fell toward the water. I tried to catch it, pivoted wrong, and my ankle wrenched.

Pitching backward, I kept the falling torch in my view, aware it had a burning wick and a container full of lamp oil. Landing on it would be very bad.

It smacked on a rock protruding from the water. The edge cracked. Lamp oil spilled, and light flared as the flame caught it. A gush of heat shoved me, then I was down, too, and I briefly felt the river's cold embrace just before the agonizing pain of my skull striking stone.

CHAPTER THREE

I stood on a mist-shrouded shore in the dark. Not the shore of the rivers in Pittsburgh, however. The willow tree to my right meant this was the shore of my meditation world.

My view was limited to about a dozen yards in any direction. I made a full revolution, searching the thick white air for a telltale sign of Amenemhab, my totem animal, but the jackal was nowhere to be seen.

What am I doing here? I couldn't remember slipping into what I called my "alpha state" and prompting this visualization. The white dress I wore didn't help clarify anything for me. *Am I dreaming?*

A strange, trumpeting bellow made me spin toward the water again. It was not a sound I could readily identify.

The heads of two black dragons materialized from the mist before me. They floated side by side with their necks arched like swans, wings tucked down. Nothing like the eel-ish and smooth-skinned creatures at home in the barn, these dragons had scales and horns and gills. Silver crowns adorned the bases of their horns, and I saw a flash of crimson embedded in the metal. Strands of rubies and diamonds draped to a ring hooked on their rhinolike snout horns. A silver yoke linked them to a wide plank that ran between their long bodies.

It was connected to a tree they towed through the

water. Not a log floating behind them, but a branched tree, upright. Squinting, I tried to make sense of what I saw. The trunk was dark, gnarled and angled, as if it had grown in shadow and had had to reach for light. As it neared I saw it was actually a cluster of trunks. In some places, the trunks were like stacked drainpipes, in other spots the bark had smoothed over like scarred skin.

By that, and the evergreen foliage, I identified it as a yew tree. The branches stretched twice as wide as it was high, and enclosed lanterns were hung along the outer perimeter. In their soft glow, black veils hung closer to the trunk and fluttered eerily, defining the base of the rectangular boat.

I noticed a woman sitting on the sloping tree trunk. Her somber pose reminded me of Waterhouse's *Ophelia*. Her head was down, the gray hood of her cloak raised. Dark hair spilled down her chest like ink. Her fingers trailed in the water beside her, and her pale, smooth skin had the barest trace of phosphorescence.

The dragons neared the shoreline and lurched suddenly. As they sloshed forward I realized that in addition to their wings, they had four limbs! The dragons I knew didn't have legs.

I retreated three steps as they brought themselves— and their passenger—right to me.

When they stood ankle-deep in the river, the wide plank plowed into the sandy mud and they halted. One shook his mighty head, and the gemstones flashed in the dim light. The other one warbled in response. The teeth in that mighty maw were as long as steak knives.

I went stock-still, thinking stupidly of the *Jurassic Park* movie. *These aren't tyrannosaurs, these are dragons.*

Movement behind them caught my attention as the woman drew away from the water. Her dress, like mine, had long bell sleeves, but hers had been dragging through the water. They dripped as she gestured for me to join her in the boat.

The plank, it seemed, also served as a gangway, but the mere idea of walking between the dragons with their rows of sharp teeth wasn't a notion that snuggled up to my sense of well-being.

Guardedly, I went forward. The beasts did nothing but benevolently watch me, so I dared onward. The plank creaked under my weight, and once past the dragon's long necks, I raised my arms for balance.

Ducking under the foremost branches, I got a better view of the boat bottom. It seemed the tree roots had crawled free of the earth and woven together to form this slender, watertight vessel. At the bow I waited for my host to indicate if I should sit down or come closer.

Her hair had faded to gray. The skin on her hands was like spotted parchment. Her hood shifted slightly as her head rose and her chin jutted toward me. Her smooth cheeks had wrinkled and grown sallow. Her eyes remained hidden in the shadows of the hood.

Even so, I knew her. I had been witness to this transformation before and wasn't surprised when the cloying fragrance of raisin and currant cakes filled my nostrils.

"Hecate." I sank to my knees.

The dragons backed the boat onto the lake once more. I tried not to think of the shore that was getting farther and farther away.

For minutes we remained with me on my knees, the

world silent except for the gentle splash of water as the dragons swam. When finally She spoke, Hecate said, "The company of men can be warm and pleasant, but men are willful where women are involved. More so when she is a woman of power. Like you."

The Goddess brought me here to give me dating advice? Dumbfounded, I simply nodded.

"The vampire wizard marked you once, but here in this place, we reversed it onto him. When you showed him you would wield the power you had over him, when you put him on his knees before you, it prompted his planning."

"Planning what?"

"Another way to control you."

My brows lowered.

"In signum amoris. 'A sign of love.'" She spat into the bottom of the boat.

In signum amoris, the spell Menessos had performed on Johnny and me. He had not asked permission, he'd just acted as he'd seen fit. At the time of the offense, he'd cooled the heat of my fury by explaining that it had created an important link between Johnny and me. "Because of that spell, Johnny and I have been able to communicate telepathically when touching."

Hecate rose from Her seat and shuffled toward me. "A nice benefit to be sure, child, but the vampire did not tell you what else he did." Her misshapen fingers gripped my chin and forced me to look at Her just as the breeze lowered Her hood.

The goddess's eyes were the eyes of the moon, eyes that had stared into the sun for eons. They were the most bizarre color—the color I see in the dark after staring too long into a candle's flame. I focused on Her face, which was haggard and hard but not unkind.

"*He* was a part of that binding. *He* can also hear your thoughts when he touches you . . . and yet he can shield you from his own thoughts."

Bastard. He'd claimed that spell amped up the imprinting bond that already existed between Johnny and me. He'd said it was all for my safety, so Johnny could feel my strong emotions and ride to my rescue if necessary. The bond hadn't been any help when the Rege had kidnapped me, but the concussion I'd suffered had probably interfered.

"It is vexing that he waited until there was nothing you could have done to oppose him. Disguised in your intimacy, the spell was complete before you knew it was happening." She released me and made a flicking gesture that caused the tree roots to form a seat behind Her as She sat. "He knew the *sorsanimus* would become necessary. Because the three of you are now additionally bound tight with that soul-sharing, he can use his 'sign of love' to read you. Through it, he can learn what you would otherwise hide, and therefore, his words can manipulate you to his aims more efficiently."

"Are You saying that his goal isn't the same as Yours?"

"I see the past that was, the present that is, and all the possibilities that the future holds, but Menessos travels a road unlike that of any other man. His path is unceasing, like that of a god. His choices are bold and yet unavoidably bound to the slaking of an unquenchable thirst. His purpose is difficult to define."

"I thought he was Your servant. At the Eximium, You told him he was forgiven."

She cocked Her head. "Menessos serves no one but himself. Sometimes even that selfishness can become a path that aligns with the goals of a goddess."

"What were You forgiving him for?"

Hecate's cackle of laughter echoed across the lake. She made no effort to answer.

That didn't surprise me. We weren't here to discuss Menessos's past. We were here to discuss what he'd done without my permission. Including Johnny in it made it doubly wrong—even if Menessos's intentions had been pure, and he was evidently incapable of pure intentions.

"The triangular power base the three of you have formed now binds you to each other, but it will not be pliable forever."

"What do you mean?"

"Like an infant's bones, such constructs harden as they age. Your triangle will break if each side is not equal to the others."

"It could break?"

"You are all striving to adjust to the pressure put upon you; should one grow too fast, it burdens the other sides. The sides of the triangle stretch as each of you grow. This forces a matched pace upon you all. If one stumbles or fails to meet your challenges, you risk collapse and the failure of all."

I considered this. "So you're saying the *in signum amoris* has to go."

"Indeed." She added, "The sides must be equal. Not even your side can dominate."

"How do I get rid of it?"

Her strange gaze was a physical touch upon me, raising the hair along my arms and up the nape of my neck. "The *sorsanimus* binding is virtually impervious. That shielding links the three of you together. It is a protection like thick stone walls." She sat forward and clenched Her hands to characterize strength. "And you will all need that. By comparison, the vampire's 'sign of love' is but a wooden fence." Her pose relaxed and though She sat back, Her chin remained elevated. "Yet even that could destroy you all."

"And there's no way for Johnny and I to grow to match this?"

"It gives the vampire an unfair advantage. Rather than try to re-create it for yourself and the wolf, remove it."

"How?"

"You must unmake it. Burn his fence to the ground, so to speak."

I stood, ready. "It's here? A physical fence in this world?"

She motioned for me to sit. "You passed the test of fire here," she said. "Passed the test of water."

Fire was represented by the south. I'd witnessed my own burning at the stake in that test. Water corresponded to the west. I'd nearly drowned during that test. A deosil path around the pagan elemental compass would mean that earth was the next element, yet something in my gut nagged at me. She'd hauled me out on the water and away from land, away from *earth*.

"Air?" I asked.

"Air," she said.

CHAPTER FOUR

Eris Alcmedi saw her daughter stumble and she laughed—until the torch fuel exploded in a blast of white light. Seph lay in the water, and she wasn't getting up.

Stunned, immobile, Eris thought, *Get up, Persephone. Get up.*

Beside her, Demeter started forward, then halted. "My knees," she said. "I can't get her. Go!" She pushed Eris forward, panic in her voice as she commanded, "Go, the river's taking her! She'll drown!"

The alarm in Demeter's tone triggered Eris into action. She charged down the slope in her slick-soled cowboy boots and immediately lost her footing. Without two arms to pump and swing for balance, she lurched and fell on her behind. She scrambled up too fast, tripped over her own feet, and then dropped to her knees. Momentum pitched her forward. She thought to catch herself on the heels of her hands, but her brain forgot what her body was missing and she toppled to the right, smacking her face and shoulder into the rocks and mud. Cold pain shot over her cheek and she saw stars.

Stunned, she found her thoughts speeding in circles; she was strangely unwilling to make the usual instinctive self-recriminations.

"Get her, Eris! Quick!" Demeter shouted.

Eris scrambled up, keeping the white of Seph's dress in sight as she plunged into the river, but the mist was determined to obscure her view. She sloshed in up to her knees. Her boots filled with water—*So cold!*—and her feet became leaden weights. Each step was a burden. *Why am I doing this anyway? She's the Lustrata. The goddess won't let anything happen to her.*

Eris halfheartedly pressed on. When the frigid water was thigh-deep, she stretched and groped for the dress hem. *I can't do this. I can't dive for her. . . . I can't swim one-armed! I'll be lost.*

Without warning, she slipped on a slimy rock and went down. She heard Demeter call her name just before the water closed over her head. The current tugged at her, impeding her effort to stand. She fought with the current, kicked her feet into position and planted them.

Finally, gasping, she broke the surface only to hear Demeter screaming. Eris wiped her eyes and searched around for a sign of Seph's white dress.

Persephone was yards away now, so far out of reach. Eris stared in disbelief as the powerful flow of the river swept Seph away. The mist closed in.

Seph isn't the Lustrata. This wouldn't be happening if she were. She's going to die. . . .

Eris turned and struggled back to the shore in a panic. "I couldn't get to her, I couldn't get to her! I couldn't!" Demeter was sitting on the shore. She tried to get up, grimaced, and rubbed her knee.

"Mom? Are you okay, Mom?"

"Where's Persephone?"

"I couldn't get to her."

"She'll drown!" Contempt, blame and disappointment flashed in Demeter's eyes.

"The river carried her away."

The lap of the water taunted Eris, laughing at her weakness. The silence between them was a crushing weight.

Demeter pushed her fingers down into the mud on either side of her and chanted. "Poseidon, naiads, hippocampi! Protect my granddaughter and bear her to the shore . . . that she may come to rest where she belongs. Bear her to the shore. Bear her to the shore."

Eris felt useless. Seph, her daughter, was out there right now in the water. She could imagine her sinking, drowning. *She isn't the Lustrata after all.* Eris had wanted to believe it. She wanted to believe that she'd done something right, that she'd brought someone special into the world. Her tears spilled.

"Knock off that crying," Demeter croaked.

"I lost her!"

"Crying won't help right now."

Eris sniffled and wiped her nose. "I can't even put my will into the ground, like you just did. I can't create the circle of energy you just created."

"You have feet, don't you?"

It's just like Demeter to sit there all imperious and tell me what to do after I've ruined everything. Eris glared. "Feet?"

"Your feet aren't as good as your hands for focusing and directing energy, but that's what you have, Eris. So buck up and start figuring out how you're going to be a one-armed witch."

Eris turned her back on her mother, but that left her looking at the water that had just swept Seph to her doom. She choked on a sob she didn't want Demeter to hear.

"Your feet have carried you all your life," Demeter

said. "You just need to figure out a new way of walking."

Spinning back, Eris shouted, "Don't lecture me! Persephone is"—she swung her arm and pointed, and it was so *not normal* to do this with her left arm—"*out there!*"

"And you couldn't—"

"Don't you dare lay this on me!" The tears sprang up again. "I tried. I did the best I could." But she hadn't. She hadn't believed this could happen. She hadn't believed the goddess would allow it to happen.

Eris saw her mother's pained face. "You're lucky you didn't break a hip." She reached out to Demeter, ready to lever her up.

Demeter accepted her hand and tried to stand, but she cried out, "Let me sit, let me sit!"

Eris noticed the shallow trenches in the embankment mud. "You didn't scoot over the edge and ease down. You fell."

"Everybody else did tonight. Why not me?"

Eris invoked the Norse healing goddess. "Eir's sweet mercy, Mom!"

Demeter rubbed at her knee. "I could use some of Eir's attention right now, but I'd settle for an OxyContin."

CHAPTER FIVE

Hecate's dragon-drawn boat dropped me off at the island in the middle of the lake. It was comprised of a narrow, muddy shoreline around a sun-bleached stone that, when viewed from the opposite shore, seemed like a giant's spearhead rammed into the earth.

I walked to the backside of the huge rock, searching for the crevice I'd entered when Hecate, in the form of a mustang, had led me here during the *sorsanimus*. This time, there was no crevice.

My shoulders slumped. She'd delivered me here, so what was I supposed to do now?

The fog shifted and swirled. A thunderous cry heralded me.

A griffon limped into view. He was missing a few talons on his right foreleg, and his gait identified him as much as his sleek black feathers and tiger body did. "Thunderbird!" He was missing his right eye as well, so he kept his head slightly aslant to monitor me. "How did you get *here*?" He was supposed to be in the barn at my farmhouse in the real world.

"The goddess," he said.

I stumbled, then froze. "You. Talk?"

"Your totem animal can speak in this place. Why shouldn't I?"

He sounded unnervingly like the actor Patrick Stewart. "Right." Still, the shock felt like a kick in the chest.

He positioned himself facing the water and stretched the wing nearest me back toward his haunches. With a nod he indicated that I should sit astride him. "Shall we?"

A test of air obviously included flying. Still, I hesitated. "What are we supposed to do?"

"I do not know."

"That makes two of us."

He wiggled his wing insistently. "Get on."

He wasn't quite the size of a pony. No grown-up in her right mind would expect him to ably carry her. "I'm too big."

His one eye tilted in its socket, up then down. "No, you're not."

I gave him the once-over, assessing the muscular tiger body. *This has to be done. This destiny of mine depends on the three of us.*

Hauling my skirt up, I straddled him in front of his wings. I sat—tiger backs are not comfy—and wrapped my arms around his sinewy, feathered neck. He cantered along the shore, beating his wings. As his muscles flexed his great strength was remarkable, and suddenly we were rising in the white air.

We burst through the fog, and now, flying above it, I was glad for the clear air . . . until a flash in the distance drew my attention to the clouds. Ahead of us was a massive cloud formation. The edge could have been a snapshot of stormy seas, freezing the frothy water in motion. The "crashing waves" ascended in asymmetrical jumbles, puffy and beautiful. Atop that, layers of smooth-edged clouds jutted out as if a layer cake with thick icing had been placed atop that curling wave.

"That's the mother of all storm clouds," Thunderbird said.

Again, lightning flickered within the depths of the formation, a reminder that such beauty was often dangerous and wrathful. "We have to fly inside it, don't we?"

"To confront the most powerful air we do."

"You won't be able to see inside it, will you?"

"Don't need to. I just need to feel the current and ride it without you falling off."

This test couldn't be just about the ability to hang on, but my fingers burrowed under his feathers for a better grip anyway.

"Wind shears spiral around, up from the ground, then back toward it. Young griffons play in them often, but that involves much twisting and would increase the risk for you, so I'm going to skim the top."

Sounded like surfing. "Do the young griffons ever carry extra weight when they play in wind shears?"

"No."

"Do you think it will make a difference?"

He craned his neck regally. "I am strong enough, Persephone. Are you?"

Considering the previous tests, this one was stirring up significant unease. "I have to be."

Leaping from a plane without a parachute might prove easier than what I was going to have to do.

Thunderbird pumped his wings faster, gaining speed. Griffons could be incredibly swift if they wanted to be. Beneath us, miles of ground elapsed at amazing speed.

Thunderbird's path had us pass in front of the formation. Clouds, I learned, were deceptive. They gave the appearance of being close even when they weren't. As he angled back to approach from the southwest, we were dwarfed by the storm.

He caught the wind shear on the western side. It pulled us across the top toward the north, but before it threw us over the downward eastern side, his wings arched and his whole body tensed as he fought to ride the top of the shear. Doing this propelled him—*us*—even faster.

For me, a pair of goggles would have been nice.

We were rising again. "Updraft," he shouted. "Hold on!"

Thunderbird let the spiral sustain us, twisting his body to keep me as vertical as possible as we rose up into the cloud. The temperature was dropping rapidly, and it was hard to breathe. Swallowing to release the pressure in my ears, I wondered how high we had flown. With the way he could cover distance, I was sure our altitude would have petrified me if I could have seen the ground.

The frigid ascent lasted for long minutes, including brief bouts of rain and hail—during which I buried my nose in his feathers. Finally we seemed to peak, to break over the updraft's edge and spiral downward, again detecting the precipitation in the air. The temperature was warming and my ears popped again, but the wind was tugging at me as if it were cognizant and seeking to snatch me from Thunderbird's back. I squeezed as much with my legs as I did with my arms.

Then the lightning flashed again and a rumble filled the air around us. In seconds, the sound had escalated, roaring like a jet engine just inches from my skull. Caught in a rushing wind, we were tossed outside the cloud as a funnel formed beside us, and I saw the tornado's tip lunge toward the ground so very, very far below.

My stomach heaved like I was on a roller coaster. I felt a static charge, then lightning flashed. A heat wave throttled me as thunder boomed with a metallic clang.

Thunderbird spread his wings wide, tilting to slow us down, but the buffeting winds were too powerful. He adjusted and pumped his wings as if trying to break free of the downward spiral. That didn't work either.

We were dropping fast, and I knew my added weight was keeping the griffon from breaking free of the storm.

We looped around three more times and then the hair on my arms lifted. In seconds lightning struck just beyond Thunderbird's flank. In the instant before it became blindingly bright, the erratic illumination was beautiful, as it always was in the sky. It had even been beautiful when it crawled over Menessos when I'd called my power up out of him.

Aha.

My grip loosened on the griffon.

"Persephone! Hold tighter!"

I barely heard him over the freight train rumble of the tornado, so I didn't even try to answer him. When I felt the next flare of static, I threw myself off the griffon.

As we tumbled head over heels through the air, the charge flooded my body, reaching through fabric, scouring my skin, searching me. Fingers splayed, my palms felt it most, like the friction from sliding down a rope. I clutched at that rope, squeezing as a thread of light formed.

In the milliseconds that it took for my core to open—as it did when I accessed the power of a ley line—the bright thread swelled in my hands, becoming a thick bolt. Every molecule of oxygen inside my body jolted as if joined with the lightning, scalding me, fighting my grasp, rejecting my will.

But I held on.

Bound with burning, itching pain, I ground my teeth together. I had burned in the heat of fire. I had drowned in the depths of water. This explosive bolt was the creative and destructive power of air. I *would* harness it. No matter how much it hurt.

I free-fell toward the earth, dragging the lightning, my instincts screaming, *"Let go!"*

But I held on.

Element encounters weren't about obeying instincts. I had learned that much.

Arcing electricity crawled over me. It forced my head back. It choked me. It pried at my grip with electric fingers. It beat upon my forearms with a swordlike arc that raised welts on my skin.

But I held on.

The sword image made me think. In Tarot, air was linked to the suit of swords.

My intention of harnessing this element by bullying it into submission wasn't going to work. Air was far more aggressive than little ol' me would ever be. I'd never defeat it, and I didn't need to. I had simply to embrace this gale force like the lightning that had already crawled inside me.

My fingers slackened, relaxed. I embraced the lightning like a long-lost friend.

Air. Glorious air. Atmosphere of earth! You are the breath of life!

The arcing arms of lightning hugged me back. Electric fingers stroked my hair.

My body exploded with sensation. I breathed every breath of my life in a second. I sighed and I sang.

The lightning flickered and sizzled and flowed continuously into my palms.

And still I was dropping.

Air gusted past me. The tornado threw me around like a speck of dust. I curled into a ball. I felt full, so terribly crammed with energy that my skin might split open.

Thunder trumpeted nearby, but softer.

Thunderbird.

Wings flapped up around me as his body flew under me. I stretched out and clung to his neck.

Beside us, the tornado dwindled and the wind died down, the roar falling into near silence. The griffon glided to the ground beside a white picket fence.

Here, there was no fog, or the storm had blown it away. I could see the pale barrier stretching endlessly across the land of my meditation world, penetrating the surface, an obstruction that divided this place that needed no separation.

Why, Menessos?

With my hands hovering above the white wood, I reached into my core again. Electricity crackled across my knuckles and I grabbed the fence, letting the energy and heat flash out of me.

Sparks crackled from the pickets, stretching in either direction. The wood blackened. Smoke wafted up. I opened the conduit as wide as possible and shoved all that I'd absorbed into this fence.

> *What binding there was is about to fade.*
> *The spell is broken, magic unmade.*
> *What binding there was is burned and scorched.*
> In signum amoris *is no more.*
> In signum amoris *is no more.*

The fence exploded, shattering pickets into little more than splinters one by one for as far as I could see. When the energy of the bolt was used up, the land on either side of the fencing was unaffected, but what remained of the posts was reduced to ash.

I was awestruck by what I'd accomplished, but horrified by the ease of destruction.

"It's done," Thunderbird said. "And time for you to go home." Behind me, he flapped his wings, and the talons of his foreleg wrapped around my arm.

I awoke from the meditation to a cold world of wetness and fog and pain. I threw my arms, splashing and thrashing, caught in a swift-flowing river.

The fog above me swirled and parted. Thunderbird descended through the mist, talons out. He gripped my arm and dragged me through the water. In minutes, I could hear voices, and weeping. My heels bounced over rocks and I twisted toward the shore.

Nana was sitting on the bank. Her cheeks were red, but she was silent. My mother stood a few feet away, sobbing, with her arm clutching her stomach, as if she were about to be ill. The griffon dragged me ashore, released me and flew away.

Both turned as I scrambled to my feet.

"Persephone," my mother blurted in a choked voice. "Is it really you?" Her eyes were wide and watery with disbelief.

"Yeah." As I shivered and rubbed at my aching head, everything that had happened snapped into place and I realized what they must've thought. "Yeah. It's me." I glanced from her to Nana. "What are you doing on the bank?"

CHAPTER SIX

After crawling up the embankment—swearing all the way over the ruined dress—I hurried into the fog. Just as I was sure my feet had veered to one side, the light of the candles brightened the mist. On target, I was able to locate the parking lot.

In the days that had followed my mother's accident, we'd all understood that Eris wasn't ever again going to drive the old stick-shift Corvette. So, partially as a pity-present and partially as a thank-you-for acting-to-save-my-boyfriend, I offered to buy her an automatic vehicle that she would be able to drive when the doctor gave her the okay.

She'd picked a ten-year-old Dodge Dakota SLT from the third car lot we'd visited. It was a high-mileage vehicle, but neither the rust edging the wheel wells nor the American flag and eagle decorating the rear window had deterred her decision.

I think she decided the candy-apple-red vehicle was perfect when she saw the SLT emblem on the side. She laughed and said, "Get the salesman. Tell him I want to take the *Slut* for a test drive."

Of course I hadn't repeated that to the salesman, but the truck's name had stuck.

I ended up driving the Slut here tonight. That left Nana to drive the Corvette—the image kept me amused the whole way. Zhan, my personal bodyguard from

Menessos, had been reluctant to let me out of her sight; I'd only been able to get her to stay behind by giving her orders to obtain some sneaky cell phone video footage of Nana getting into the low-riding sports car.

By the time I made it to the Slut, I was limping. My foot ached where it had been sliced by rocks.

After changing into my jeans and T-shirt, I donned the hoodie. The solidity of my hikers was reassuring. Once the hood covered my wet hair, I felt warm enough to function.

Despite being certain this was illegal, I drove the Slut into the park itself, jumping the curb and rolling slowly through the fog. Past the circle I veered around and backed the Slut to the edge of the embankment, where I cut the engine. Outside, I rolled under the truck's back end.

Eris asked, "What are you doing?"

"Getting the spare tire."

As I tried to loosen the rusty bolt holding the tire on, Eris checked both sides of the truck. "The Slut doesn't have a flat."

My fingers slipped and I scraped a knuckle. "Damn it," I muttered. The bolt was rusted in place. Louder, I said, "I know."

"Then what the hell are you doing?"

"You'll see."

I squeezed the metal nut holding the bracket and concentrated, moving a little energy into my hand. "Loosen, loosen steel I hold, must get Nana out of the cold." I pushed the energy into the nut. Pain zapped through my thumb. I jerked away and swore.

When I tried again, the rusted-on nut turned easily. I

figured the jolt meant I had a little lightning left over.

With the huge tire loose, I dragged it to the edge of the embankment and heaved it down.

Nana gawked at the tire. "What's that for?"

"Getting you up to the parking lot." I retrieved a rope from behind the extended cab's backseat and returned to Nana, silently praising the glorious traction of the average hiking boot.

She said, "I'm not going to like this, am I?"

"Would you rather I call the emergency squad?"

"No," she snapped.

I unwound the rope, looped the middle of it through the center a few times and hauled the tire closer to Nana. "C'mon." I offered her my hand. "Sit on the tire."

"What?"

"Give me your hand. I'll pivot you onto it."

She assessed the all-season radial, then the rope. "Are you shitting me?"

"Just hold onto the tread. It'll be fun."

Nana glowered but gave me her hand. "It better be."

Once she was maneuvered into the center of the tire, she said, "I'm relieved I got to play the crone tonight."

"Why?"

"If I'd played the maiden and worn all white, I'd look like the Michelin Man on this thing."

I laughed, proud of her for finding some humor in the situation. Our three-generational trio was a kind of triangle, too. I didn't trust Eris, but I could always count on Nana.

Perception hit me harder than the river rock that had knocked me unconscious: With all I had to do, knowing Menessos and Johnny would be there for me gave me strength. Hecate was right. If either one of them faltered . . . none of us could succeed.

"Keep your legs straight." I tossed the rope's length onto higher ground and gave Eris my arm. "Your turn." My mother's teeth were chattering. "You're soaked! Why aren't you in the truck and out of the wind?"

"I'll get the seats wet."

"The seats will dry." We trudged cautiously up the bank.

"Are you seriously going to do what I think you're going to do?"

Feeling like an ass for not noticing sooner that she was wet and shivering, I studied her and saw the cut and bruising on her cheek. "Yup. Unless you have a better idea."

She snorted in answer.

"Just one more minute in the cold for you," I said as I tied the rope around the trailer hitch. "I won't be able to see Nana with my mirrors, so you have to watch her. Signal me when she's level."

Eris nodded.

In the truck, I twisted the key in the ignition. The engine rumbled to life, and I smiled to myself. When I'd brought this thing to Eris's apartment, Lance had teased her that it was only a gun rack shy of being officially redneck. I hadn't argued.

With the brake fully depressed, I put the Slut in gear. I slowly let off the brake, and the vehicle inched forward. When Eris gave me the signal to stop, I put it in park and cut the engine.

"That was *not* fun," Nana proclaimed. "But it wasn't terrible," she added with a wink.

Once I had completed the not-so-easy task of getting Nana in the passenger seat, I put the spare tire in the truck bed and the rope in the backseat. "You're going to have to drive," I said to Eris. "Get her to the hospital."

"I'm *not* going to the hospital," Nana grouched out her open door. "It's just a sprain."

"It may be more than that."

"It isn't. Eris needs to go home and get warm and dry. All I need is some ice and Aleve. I'll be fine." She dangled the Corvette keys from her finger, then tossed them to me.

I caught the key ring. "How are you going to get up the stairs?" Eris's apartment was on the second story, above her tattoo parlor.

"Lance will help me." Nana slammed the truck door.

"And she has spoken," Eris said through chattering teeth. "I may not have been around her for years, but I still know when her mind is made up. That hasn't changed."

She was right. "Drive the Slut home."

Eris barked out a laugh. "I'm telling Nana what you called her."

"Her knee's sprained and I can still run. I'm not scared." And besides, Nana knew the joke behind the truck's name.

"I was scared." Eris reached up and stroked my hair, pushing a wet tendril off my brow and under the hood. "I tried to get you. I swear I did." Tears plunged down her cheeks again.

I wanted her to realize the magical impact of having lost her arm. I wanted her to get creative and figure out how to work around it. She had tried to save me, but

Hecate had intervened, and Eris had failed to get me. That failure had frightened her more than I could gauge. I worried the failure had emphasized what she couldn't do in a way that would make her withdraw to an inward and needy place instead of standing up and fighting to retain independence.

Eris wiped her eyes and asked, "What about you?"

"I'll gather up our stuff here. Fifteen minutes. I'm right behind you."

She didn't budge. She simply stared at me, as apologetic and guilty as was humanly possible.

"Go." I spun her gently toward the truck. "You can do this." I was mindful of her awkward climb into the cab, and how she settled into the driver's seat. Securing the seat belt was tricky, but it was easier than turning the key and putting the truck into gear.

Neither the doctor nor the Pennsylvania Department of Motor Vehicles had cleared her to drive, but we had no options just now and I was sure she would manage the actual driving just fine. Driving herself and Nana home was something she could do.

I didn't offer to help; Eris was going to have to learn she could do these right-handed things for her left-handed self.

CHAPTER SEVEN

I want you to be the one to free the shabbubitum." The
Excelsior spoke in a language no living human had
spoken in centuries.

In the antechamber of the Excelsior's private rooms,
Meroveus sat in a comfortable chair with a fire blazing
in the wide hearth. The environment was a cozy—albeit
aristocratic—setting of French antiques shrouded in
shadows and subdued colors, but Mero was not at ease. Even
as the advisor to the most politically powerful vampire in
the world, he had only been in this room a few times before.

Those other occasions hadn't been good, either.

"Mero."

Refusing the Excelsior was unwise, so he said nothing.

Opposite him, the Excelsior vacated his seat and stood
staring into the flames. The flickering illumination cast
across his visage seemed to catch on his high cheekbones
and smolder there.

The Excelsior's mother in life, Chlo, had often said the
mesmerizing dance of the fire called forth the best of her
thoughts like moths, illuminating them in her mind. His
features so favored hers. . . .

The Excelsior reached into a bucket on the hearth and
tossed a fistful of some granular substance into the flames.
The scent of hazelnuts filled the air. "I know this is not
what you wanted," the Excelsior said, reclaiming his seat.
"But I need you to do this."

Mero would not meet the gaze he knew was upon him. There were three adept-level vampire wizards capable of this spell. Menessos could certainly not assume the task, but there was still another option. "Send Konstance instead."

"No." The Excelsior's answer was soft but firm. "You were there when they were sealed in stone. You know how to break the spell."

"I can tell Konstance how."

"You are my representative. It should be you."

Mero finally looked up. "I beg you, Deric. Do not make me do this." Speaking the Excelsior's given name was a trump that he rarely dared to use.

"Konstance is tending to a matter in China that I cannot call her away from. There is no one else."

"Then, do not do this at all. It is not right."

The Excelsior played *his* trump. "Father."

The word was a stake in Mero's heart, pinning him to the chair. The man he had fathered was asking something of him. It did not happen often, but when it did, Mero could not help seeing Deric as the sad boy who'd lost his mother when he was nine, and as the boy who would be a king in dangerous times. *Some things never change.* "If they read me, they will know of Giovanni's suggested course of action. Worse, they will see the absence of your disagreement with his sordid idea. I would not wish myself into such a predicament, but even more, I would not wish you into it. Konstance is unaware of these things, and it makes *her* the best choice."

The Excelsior kneeled before his advisor's chair. His hand rested on Meroveus's knee. "I trust you will not let those unfortunate things happen."

Mero's son had kept from him the intelligence concerning the Lustrata, and now he was willing to risk the existence they both clung to in order to gain intelligence about Menessos. "Menessos Made me because I asked him to. When you made your request, he did not refuse you either. Do you hate him now?"

"No," the Excelsior replied. "But there are things he did not tell me, things he did not tell you. For that, I question whether or not I trust him." The Excelsior resumed his spot before the fire. "After this, I will know if I can, or if I can't. Because of her ties to him, if she truly is the Lustrata, I need to know more than ever if he is worthy of my trust."

What the Excelsior wanted from him was not unlike many instances that had occurred when Deric had yet lived and reigned as a mortal king. Mero had not refused him. Though he understood what the Supreme Vampire longed to know, he also understood that Giovanni had expertly planted that seed of doubt about Menessos and his intentions.

Mero could not refuse Deric now, either.

Mustering his resolve, Mero stood. He gripped Deric's shoulder. When next he spoke, it was not to the Excelsior; it was to his son. "As always, I will do as you wish."

A grateful smile rounded the Excelsior's lips just slightly. "The plane leaves at eleven thirty tonight. Your arrival will coincide with the setting sun in Athens."

Mero was at the door when his son added, "I will have the official order drawn up for Menessos. It will be delivered to you when the plane arrives in Dulles for refueling."

"What of the woman? What if she is the Lustrata?"

"If she is, she must be subdued and brought here."

"And if she is not?"

The Excelsior hesitated. "Eliminate her."

Meroveus emerged from the limousine and crossed the tarmac. His dark curls were unbound, and the wind tossed them into his face as he scrutinized the jet. It was the big one, the Gulfstream V-SP. It seemed ostentatious to transport a single traveler on a plane that could comfortably seat fifteen. Athens, however, was a twelve-hour flight. Of VEIN's fleet, only this larger jet had the fuel capacity to make the trip.

Halfway to the aircraft, he paused and dug a small cellular phone from his pocket. This was not his usual phone. For emergencies, he always carried a prepaid disposable—one not traceable by VEIN. The display gleamed brightly when he opened the phone to dial. He punched numbers from memory.

On the third ring, he heard Goliath Kline say, "Talk to me."

"Heldridge Ellington gained audience with the Excelsior. In a little more than twenty-four hours, I will bring the shabbubitum to serve their libations to your master." Mero then shut the device, squeezing it until the pieces popped and cracked, crushed in his palm. He reduced the phone to dust, letting it sift to the ground.

Let us see how you respond, Menessos. It will tell me much.

CHAPTER EIGHT

As Eris drove away, I jogged behind, heading for the fountain where our ritual supplies rested. The taillights weren't out of view when my satellite phone rang from my back pocket. I jerked it free and a name flashed on the little screen to identify the caller.

Menessos.

Mr. Manipulator himself. Do you know what I did already? I swallowed my anger and answered sweetly. "Hello?"

"Persephone," Menessos said. "Are you well?" Something about his voice was different.

"Absolutely." I arranged the glass hurricane globes into the cardboard box I'd placed beside the fountain. "And yourself?"

"I am fine."

No, he wasn't. He was hoarse. Ever since I'd staked him and applied a second hex to him, I'd been aware of his death every morning and his regained life every evening. While he tended to die gently, his sunset awakenings were violent. I'd felt him screaming his way back to life before the ritual started. Even so, the pity I'd felt earlier was in short supply now. "Liar."

"You are correct in refuting my statement," he said sullenly, "but mortals often downplay their replies to such questions. It is unnecessary for you to impugn my character over it."

If I could have reached through the phone, I'd have smacked him.

"Persephone?"

"Hmmm?"

"Our fears have been realized."

Unmoving, I felt like I'd been kicked in the gut. "Heldridge?"

"He gained an audience with the Excelsior. You need to come home. Immediately."

With one box of supplies on the passenger-side floor and the other on the seat, I arrived at Eris's apartment over the Arcane Ink Emporium. The Slut wasn't here.

There were, however, lights on upstairs. So, retrieving my wet clothes from the narrow crevice that Corvette owners call a trunk and lifting the boxes stashed up front, I hefted it all up the metal steps.

Going home had been my desire even before Menessos had called, and now I had a good excuse. Knocking on the door and hoping they heard me over the music playing inside, I had time to rehearse my announcement once more before the door opened.

Zhan relieved me of the boxes. I put the Corvette keys on top. She carried the supplies toward the black door of Eris's "woogie room," where she kept all her magical materials.

Nana and Eris sat in dining chairs near a table lamp missing a shade. My mother's wet hair clued me in that she'd just showered, and she wore only sleep pants and a bra. Nana jabbed a needle into Eris's shoulder joint, stitching the flap of skin where her arm used to be. Eris winced.

My horror must have been evident. After a shallow but

derisive snort, Nana explained, "Her stitches broke." Eris squirmed as Nana sewed, tightened the thread, tied it off, and cut it.

The wound was ugly enough before. I shut the door behind me and approached.

"I felt them pop when I fell down the embankment trying to get you," Eris said.

Crap. Here we go again.

Nana smeared Neosporin on a gauze pad and placed it over the wound, securing it with medical tape. "Bled all over the place, but her wet red outfit didn't exactly show it."

"Did you—"

"Sterilized the thread and the needles." She passed Eris a T-shirt. "I'm not stupid, Persephone."

Nana was more than her I-need-a-cigarette cranky. That meant she was in pain. "Did you—"

"Took Aleve. I'm icing my knee every fifteen minutes and am in the off-phase right now." She tugged the back of the T-shirt down as Eris struggled into it.

Zhan returned. "How are you?"

"Knocked my head, but it isn't bad." Before anything else could be said, I blurted, "I have to go to Cleveland. Right now."

"Why?" Nana demanded, going from cranky to pouty.

With both of them injured, I felt guilty about leaving them. "Bad stuff," I said. Without a word, Zhan was in motion, gathering her things and mine, packing.

The Slut's distinctive motor roared outside, pulling up. "What kind of bad stuff?" Nana pressed.

Pounding footfalls outside gave me reason to avoid answering. I opened the door. Lance lugged two large pizza boxes and a pair of two-liters inside.

He must resemble his father, I thought. With sandy blond hair, he didn't get his looks from our mother. Lance was also trying to grow a goatee without much success. He sort of resembled Shaggy from the Scooby-Doo cartoons.

The smell of the pizza instantly reminded me of how hungry I was.

Lance rounded the table and set the boxes down. "Does weird shit happen around you all the time?"

"Lately it does."

He gave me a reproachful glare as he strode into the kitchen. I helped Nana and Eris twist their chairs back to the table. Lance brought cups, an ice bucket, paper plates, napkins, and two wet rags. "I put some soap on these," he said. After he'd put the other items down, he gave one rag to Nana. Sitting down next to Eris, he washed her hand.

She protested, "I just got out of the shower."

It would have been better to let her figure out how to do it herself, but he was reacting as any good son would, coddling her. He wasn't thinking about the future, a few years from now, when he'd want to be on his own. If he made her dependent on him now, it would get ugly then.

Or maybe he was doting on her because Eris was so focused on me these days. He'd had her to himself all his life, and tending her was a way to maintain her attention.

At least I had one reason to *not* feel guilty about leaving.

Nana must have caught the accusation in his tone; she didn't press me about the "bad stuff." Eris, however, wasn't aware of all the nuances where Menessos and I were concerned. "So what's going on that you have to leave?" she asked.

Lance perked up. "You're leaving?"

I nodded. "Zhan and I have to go to Cleveland as soon as possible."

"What's happened?" Eris asked.

"An already existing problem seems to have escalated." The irony that those words could mean the situation in Cleveland *and* mean the situation here wasn't lost on me.

Eris wrenched away from the washing Lance was providing to stand and curl her fingers around mine. "Don't be so vague. Tell me."

"I can't."

Sorrow dimmed her. "So you're just going to leave me like this? You said you'd stay and help."

Behind her, Lance stood, too. I could feel the anger he was trying to hide. *Damn it.* "This is important or I wouldn't be going. Eris . . . you'll be fine."

Lance openly glared at me.

"You're in good hands. Lance is here. Nana's here. I have to do this."

"I understand." She sank into her seat. "Your life doesn't shut down because of my wounds."

Oooo. My eyes narrowed with resentment at her brilliant guilt-trip statement. It didn't matter. Nothing she could say would make me revise my plans.

Lance gathered up the washcloths and made for the kitchen. He motioned for me to follow.

I was certain that this was going to be bad.

"How are you going to get to Cleveland?" Nana called as I followed Lance out.

I was grateful for the delay. "Dunno. Zhan and I could get a rental car, I guess."

The moment of silence that followed wore thin as

Nana dug into the food and my excuse to stay out of the kitchen dissipated.

A polite five feet away from Lance, I spoke so as not to be heard over the music in the other room. "What did you want?"

Plucking the Corvette keys from the counter where Zhan had obviously set them, he threw them at me. "Leave now."

The keys hit me in the chest. I winced but caught them before they fell. "What did I do?"

"Do you see her?" he whispered hotly. "All that she's already suffered for you isn't enough. Because of you, her stitches were ripped. Because of you, she went into the damn river! Fully under the surface! She came in here shivering cold. What if she gets pneumonia? Her wound was open in the river water. What if it gets infected?"

"Lance—"

"Save it. The doctor gave her specific orders, and because of you, all that's blown to hell. Just leave before you do her any more damage."

He left the kitchen, plastering on a fake grin as he shunned me. "Hey, Mom, I told Seph she could take the 'Vette. It'll save them some time. You don't mind, do you?"

With arms crossed, I trailed him into the dining/living room area. Eris, chewing on a piece of pizza, said, "Not at all."

I was glad that Lance continued on to his room. I hugged Nana good-bye. "You're going right this second?" she asked. "Don't you even want to wash up and eat?"

"I'd love to, but this is critical, Nana." I raised an eyebrow and hoped she'd understand I didn't want to say too much. Of course we could easily have stayed longer, but between Lance's anger and my mother's inquisitiveness, it was best to leave immediately. Zhan and I could grab some dinner once we were on the road. Then I embraced Eris.

When I stood up, Lance was back. "I'll carry your bags, sis, and get my hug by the car."

Sis? He was laying it on thick. He swiped the bags from Zhan's arms and exited first.

"Persephone," Nana called.

Please have understood I don't want to talk about Menessos in front of Eris. "Yeah?"

She opened her mouth, then shut it. "I don't need to wish you luck. You always work things out."

Zhan was just outside the door. "How about I drive, Seph?"

I gave her the keys. I'd left it unlocked, so Lance had already shoved the bags into the mini-trunk and was leaning on the car, arms crossed, waiting for me.

"Why did you stop calling her Mom?"

"Because she started with the guilt trip."

"Well, it *is* all your fault."

I'd known this argument was brewing. Resigned to it, I said, "She dove in front of those bullets. I didn't make her. I wasn't even in the circle with her."

"The doctors could have saved her arm if she hadn't stayed to finish the spell."

"She made that choice too! Or have you forgotten her threatening Zhan with a knife to keep the medics back?"

He pursed his lips, then snapped, "Saving your boyfriend from a spell or two was more important to you than saving her arm! She did it for you."

"Yeah. She. Did. It."

"It wouldn't have happened if not for you. You don't have any sense of responsibility, do you?"

I dropped my head down. *If you only knew.*

He read my lowered chin as some kind of concession. He pushed away from the car. "Get going. Take this." He shoved something at me. I dropped it and had to pick it up.

He was three paces away before I had a grip on the little book. "Lance."

He kept walking. "Got no time for you, sis. Mom needs help."

"Yeah. As long as you do everything for her she won't learn to do anything for herself."

He spun back at the bottom of the stairs. "You'd like that, wouldn't you? If I quit helping her? That would punish her good, right? Well, one of us needs to physically help her. Maybe I can't buy her a big-ass apology truck, but I can be here."

"You're absolutely right." That shut him up. I continued. "And in a few years, Lance, what then? What happens when you meet someone you want to spend your life with? What happens when you've made Mom dependent on you and you want to leave?"

"Like you're leaving her now? Is this a good enough payback for her leaving you, sis? Are you satisfied now?"

"This isn't about me, Lance. It's about her. You're not helping her if you don't help her learn to do things for herself."

"You are so twisted! Maybe she abandoned you, but she's always been there for me. I won't leave her."

It seemed he had mastered the snotty little brother routine. "Of course you won't leave her. Not tonight. Not next week or next month, either, but unless you are ready to give up your whole life and have yourself surgically attached to her, you're not her new right arm either."

"I've got nobody else," he snapped and pointed at the book. "You do."

As he stormed up the metal stairs, I examined the book in my hands. It was a small photo album. Inside were pictures of my father.

On our way out of the city Zhan asked, "Why did Menessos call us back?"

I shut the photo album. It was too dark to see it clearly and my head was reeling anyway. I was glad to have her distract me. "Heldridge met with the Excelsior."

She didn't know I had mastered her master, but she knew we'd been hoping Goliath found Heldridge before he made it to VEIN. "Oh." Her reply wasn't a light, airy vowel sound. It was the kind that was launched in a normal tone but dropped into the lowest of her alto tones, transforming it into an *Oh-ewww.* "Did he elaborate?"

"No."

Zhan checked the rearview mirror again and changed lanes. It was nearly eight o'clock on a Thursday evening. Luckily the Steelers' game was an away one, so traffic was light. I could guess the information I'd just given her had put her into alert mode. She would be aware of the vehicles behind us, maybe pull off a few times to see if we were being followed.

She understood the kind of bad things happening to cause our sudden trek home.

She was silent for several heartbeats. "We should find a restaurant, since you haven't eaten all day."

"Wonderful idea." My stomach growled at the thought of food. "Afterward, I want to go home and shower, then head to the den."

"Does Menessos know that? He may intend for us to—"

"*I* intend to see Johnny before I go downtown."

I didn't need to say more; she would do what I said. As the Erus Veneficus of his haven—the fancy title of a court witch—I outranked her and could make such decisions. Good thing, too. It was best if no one at the haven knew I was farther up the chain of command than they thought.

CHAPTER NINE

We arrived home just after midnight. Lingering over dinner and staying away from major highways—a tactic Zhan claimed would make it easier to tell if we were being followed—made the trip take almost twice as long as it usually would have. It also meant I slept in the car for the ninety minutes it took us to reach my farmhouse in rural Ohio south of Cleveland.

The first thing I did upon arriving home was stash the photo album in my desk drawer. I'd looked through it at dinner, but I wanted to snatch all the pictures out and see if anything was written on the backs. I'd deal with *that* later.

Despite the nap, after a hot shower I was ready for bed, but that was a luxury I couldn't afford. The night was far from over. I donned a fresh pair of jeans and layered two tank tops, white and peach, under a black scoop-neck sweatshirt that had the habit of slipping over one shoulder. My hair would be dry by the time we arrived at the den. "Let's go."

Zhan chose a direct route to the Cleveland Cold Storage building (CCS), the giant, mostly windowless structure at the heart of the disputes of the new I-90 project. The real reason the old building continued to exist was that it secretly housed the Cleveland wærewolf pack. The advertising painted on the sides made it a big money-maker for them; they refused to sell and relocate. The city couldn't afford to forcefully tear down the one place that kenneled ninety percent of the local wærewolves. Bad things would happen if they didn't have a den.

Apparently, bad things were happening anyway. It was one thirty in the morning and the parking area underneath the structure was packed like a Best Buy at dawn on Black Friday.

"There's nowhere to park and the moon isn't full for another twelve days." Zhan stopped the Corvette in front of the rickety freight elevator.

"Wait for me over by the University Inn," I said.

"No way. You don't know what's going on up there."

"Wæres aren't fans of Offerlings." The term referred to a twice-marked member of a vampire's court, and that's exactly what Zhan was.

"I'm not a spy."

"I know that. I'm not comfortable pulling E.V. rank on you, but if you need a direct order to remain behind, consider it given."

She crossed her arms. "Text me that you're fine in ten minutes or I'm coming up."

"Deal."

Having little trust in the elevator, I headed up the stairwell as the Corvette rolled out of the parking garage. The wæres had increased the security, and though there was no one seen here, that didn't mean they weren't watching. They should all be familiar enough with me that they weren't alarmed by my presence.

A young man and an older man were waiting atop the first-floor landing. I hadn't seen either of them before. "Miss Alcmedi," the older man said. "I'm George. This is Renaldo."

"Hello." I paused halfway up and out of reach. "I called earlier, and Johnny said I could meet him here, but he didn't mention there was anything going on. Has something come up? Can I see him, or is he too busy?"

"He said to bring you up when you arrived," George said.

Renaldo added, "And he said to tell you the elevator's safe."

Johnny knew I was leery of that elevator; that he'd thought to tell them to assure me helped me believe these strangers—but not totally. "Lead on," I said.

Without hesitating, Renaldo proceeded to the waiting elevator. It could have transported a car, but I wouldn't have dared such a thing. George held the gate for me. The second-floor gate wasn't as bad as the termite-damaged garage-level gate. Still, small pieces of wood splintered to the floor.

Renaldo lifted the dirty control panel, revealing a pristine and high-tech one underneath. He pressed his thumb to the button. A light flashed under his print. The gears shuddered, and we were heaved upward. Good thing I hadn't tried the elevator. I would have fiddled with the fake cover forever.

I glimpsed the dark open expanse of the third floor as we rose past it. Only dim bulbs in steel fixtures at each corner of the elevator illuminated us. On the eighth floor the main doors parted. Renaldo led us out.

The halls in the upper floors of the CCS were off-center, leaving smaller rooms on one side and larger ones on the other. In the days when this place was the cold storage center of Cleveland, there was probably a reason for it. Now, however, it meant I didn't have a clear view down the hall from the elevator. It made me nervous.

I relaxed when Johnny's voice wafted down the hall. He was talking to someone in slightly loud but formal tones, then he fell silent. He was here and these two were truly escorting me to him.

As we entered the head of the hall, however, a wave of energy hit me like an explosion. I staggered. Shock waves rolled through the walls. Johnny's yell of pain followed.

I bolted.

Renaldo grabbed my arm as I passed him and he jerked me back. "He's just transforming." He released me.

I'd never felt such a surge of energy when any wære changed near me. "Didn't you feel that?"

"Feel what?"

Guess that was as good an answer as any.

I knew things might be different for Johnny since we'd unlocked the power bound in his tattoos. That, and the fact Renaldo did let me go, made me more inclined to keep on believing him, but wære strength is not to be underestimated. My skin stung under my sleeves and a bruise was forming.

"There's cameras in there," Renaldo said. "Running live via satellite to the Zvonul. Allow me to lead so you don't disrupt the confirmation meeting?"

"Of course." Johnny had to prove to the Zvonul that he was the Domn Lup, and though they'd sent the Rege to confirm him, the Rege was now dead. It appeared that the Zvonul were moving forward in spite of the loss of their head honcho.

"Remain quiet when we enter," he added.

George and I followed.

Inside, a throng of bodies stood between us and the

corner, where bright lights were illuminating the dingy block wall. Some of the rooms, I'd learned, still had the old steel panels with the piping underneath that had once contained coolant. In this room, all of that had been discarded. Mobile work lights were the only light source in the room, but they had wattage to spare.

Three cameras were also aimed at the corner, and the red lights atop them meant that they were broadcasting.

A howl erupted from the corner and resonated off the block walls so loudly that I covered my ears. Renaldo clasped me by the arm, more gently this time, and led me through the throng to the front. Gregor, the head of the Omori—the Zvonul's version of the Secret Service—adjusted his bulk to give me a spot.

In front of me a large, familiar black wolf paced. The animal sniffed in my direction, blinking as if the bright lights made it hard to see the crowd.

But this was not the wolf I'd seen before. The fur was still jet-black, and the size and conformation were the same visually, but he *felt* different. Power continuously radiated from the beast to the point that I wouldn't have been surprised if sparks shot off of him.

When Eris had released him from the bonds she'd placed upon him long ago, I'd been aware he was different. He'd returned to Cleveland before I'd been able to get a real sense of the "new" him. Now, all the power that had been locked away blazed around him like a nimbus only my core could feel, completing him in a way I hadn't previously realized had been lacking.

Sideways to the camera, the wolf stilled and the transformation reversed. In under a minute Johnny crouched, naked, before us all.

He was on his fingertips and toes, his knees an inch from the floor. His body, lean and muscular, was beautiful. In that position he rolled one shoulder, then the other. He twisted his neck side to side and arched his back. I could see every muscle ripple, and then he stood, his thighs flexing as he assumed a square-shouldered stance and faced the camera.

I felt more in awe of him than I'd ever felt before.

Power radiated from him still. It was heady and invigorating, with a touch of recklessness. It was unreservedly masculine.

He was unquestionably a power-equal to Menessos, in his own unique way.

He said, "I am your Domn Lup."

Something flickered beneath the camera lens, and Johnny's focus dropped a few inches to see it. On the far side of the room, a larger screen also flickered. I hadn't noticed it before because of all the bodies in the way. The whir of a motor sounded as the screen mechanically lifted so those in the back could see it as well.

The screen was a field of black with a crowned wolf rampant in two shades of red: one the bright color of fresh blood, the other darker. The two shades of red meant not only energy, but vigor; not only strength, power, and determination, but leadership and courage. The wolf had his claws out, holding a shield divided into eight triangles of either dark blue or gold. Emblazoned on the shield was a silver and black helmet with spikes rising from its crown.

The crowned rampant wolf was the symbol of the Zvonul; the shield was indicative of the local den. Each pack had its own coat of arms.

The screen faded, showing an array of seating. One grand throne was elevated; other thrones were arranged to either side of it in three rows of five. A short pillar loomed in the foreground; atop it sat a wooden box that appeared to have a small opening in the top.

Within seconds, men started strolling past the container and dropping something inside before finding their seats.

I tried to text Zhan. It wouldn't go through. Renaldo leaned over. "You can't get a signal in here."

"Then you're going to have another woman coming up your stairs." I put the phone away and thought apologies to Zhan.

After long minutes of men walking by the box, the studious group assembled in the seats on the screen. Two seats were empty, one of which was the elevated throne. Lastly, a man in a long black cassock strode past, ignoring the wooden box. He placed three stones upon the empty throne: white, red, and black. Then he ceremoniously took his place on the remaining seat.

"They've replaced the Rege already?" I whispered.

"Taine Vega," Gregor whispered back.

The new Rege had dark hair in a style that would have satisfied any drill sergeant. The tribal tattoos on his square face began between his dark eyes to mimic the arch of his brows. Lines defined the bridge of his nose and pointed to his high cheekbones. Accentuating his thin lips, a pair of swirls graced his chin.

A shirtless young boy scurried into view on the screen. He set three small plates before the pillar where the camera and those assembled could see them. He opened the box and retrieved a small white stone from within.

Over the next minute he sorted twenty-nine stones. "Eight black. Six red. Fifteen white," he said.

The new Rege stared into the camera. "Eight of my brethren oppose you, Mr. Newman."

"Fifteen do not," Johnny said.

"And yet six are indifferent. My old seat is unfilled." He gestured toward the seat he'd placed the stones upon and I noticed his hands had tattoos as well. "Should those six be swayed to oppose you and should my successor choose to oppose you, the vote is split."

"It is your vote that decides, Rege, regardless of the democratic process you've asked your respected peers to engage in."

"Indeed."

His gaze conveyed seriousness but not pride, like that of an official whose new responsibility brought with it a dose of loathing. On the plus side, he didn't look like he was suffering from a swollen ego. On the minus side, he didn't look happy at all.

At first, I expected Johnny to ask him what bribe he required. The former Rege had candidly stated he would not confirm Johnny as Domn Lup unless Johnny gave him something—namely me. He'd learned of my ability to perform the spell that enabled wærewolves to retain their man-minds while in wolf form. While that deal-making had occurred in private, this Rege had his peers present to witness the proof of Johnny's power. He'd also had them vote and had had the stones tallied before everyone so he could consider his peers' opinions before making his decision.

As the silence wore on, I was glad Johnny didn't

inquire about that bribe. This Rege's thoughtfulness proved he was quite different from his predecessor. That could be good. Or it could be just as bad in a different way.

On-screen, the new Rege tapped his fingers on his thigh and said, "I confirm you, John Newman."

CHAPTER TEN

As the assembled Cleveland pack members showed their enthusiasm by howling and applauding, Johnny struggled internally to keep his poise. Always before when he transformed, even for the few noncyclical complete changes, his beast had roused and paced within, growling, but safely caged.

Not this time.

This time, his inner wolf had burst into sentience with such intensity that all his previous transformations suddenly seemed semiconscious by comparison. Though his man-mind had remained, the instincts of the beast ambushed him, enveloped him in vehement desires so powerful he could barely keep the impulses from becoming actions.

It was so overwhelming that he'd willed an immediate reversion to human form.

The wolf had withdrawn into human flesh, but it did not slumber as before.

On the screen, the Rege called for silence. "Let us talk soon about the date of your coronation. I need to assess the schedule I have just inherited, but I would like to move forward with the ceremony sometime next month. I will make the announcement later today and, afterward, make arrangements for your press conference in Cleveland on Saturday afternoon."

"Agreed."

"My Lord." The Rege gave a bowing nod and gestured. The screen faded out to the wolf rampant and shield, then faded to black.

Again the crowd howled. Gregor leaned into Johnny's ear. "Someone was spotted coming up the steps. Kirk has gone to investigate."

"Good. Where are my pants?" Johnny wanted nothing more than to vacate the room and have a few minutes alone to gather himself.

Gregor gestured and a valet hurried up with a long, thick robe. He held it open for Johnny.

Johnny didn't budge. Rage boiled up inside him instantly—in his mind he knew he wasn't even angry, but the rash, hot rage begged to be unleashed. His forearms itched. Only desperate resistance, like clenching some mystical muscle, kept his fingers from sprouting claws ready to slash Gregor for his mistake. "Dude. I said *pants*." It was a struggle to keep his voice even.

Gregor snapped his fingers and the valet scurried away. "Forgive me. As you are confirmed now, I assumed a robe would be more . . . kingly."

"I don't wear robes," Johnny snapped.

Gregor tipped his head. "It will not happen again."

The crowd quieted into the white noise of happy chatter, and The Dirty Dog—the pack's official bar—was mentioned repeatedly. Some were leaving already.

The valet hurried back with black denim jeans. Johnny grabbed them from him. "As long as I can still bend over and put my legs into my pants, I wear pants." He wouldn't admit that donning jeans in public felt distinctly undignified. "Besides, the new Rege didn't call me king."

"He won't until after your coronation. But here, to your pack, you are king already."

Johnny zipped the jeans. He wanted everyone gone. He wanted to be alone and get a grip on what was happening to him. He flung his arms up and shouted, "To The Dirty Dog!"

As expected, cheers rose and people converged on the exit. It was the quickest way to empty the room and buy himself a moment of privacy.

However, as the pack massed at the doorway, the air of the room shifted, and a distinctly *not-wolf* smell filled his nostrils again.

Red.

Johnny deserted Gregor, inexorably drawn to Persephone's aroma. It always made him want her, but tonight, because he hadn't seen her in days, her scent was new all over again. That newness made his reaction stronger. He was getting hard just thinking about touching her.

When she came into view, the wide neck of her sweatshirt slipped and his attention stuck on the pale skin of her bare shoulder. Her dark hair lay against soft flesh and he brushed the tendrils away and reached behind her neck. His fingertips buzzed with a vibration he knew was her energy—he'd never noticed this gentle and enticing sensation before.

Must be a perk of unlocking my tattoos.

She was always beautiful, but more so when all her skin was exposed and the smell of her sex mingled with his. Add this little electric feeling . . . if it was amplified when their bodies were entwined—*God I can't wait to fuck her.* He leaned down for a kiss.

Shouts rumbled at the doors.

He turned.

Voices raised in complaint as someone pushed into the room, impeding the flow of those leaving the room. In a heartbeat, his top guard appeared, towing Zhan behind him by the arm.

"Guess who thought she could sneak into the den," Kirk said as he approached. "An Offerling."

Zhan said to Persephone, "You didn't text."

"There's no reception in here. I tried. Johnny was in the middle of the ceremony, and I couldn't ask for access to a landline to call. Sorry. But I *did* tell them to expect you."

The distinct scent of ginger lingered around Zhan, with a hint of death sealed into the marks given her by Menessos. They all knew the Asian woman was Seph's bodyguard—and that his own Asian guard had ulterior motives. "Let her go," Johnny said.

Kirk gazed deeply into Zhan's eyes. "What if I'd rather hold on?" His question was seductive and inviting.

"I don't respect any man who won't follow orders." Zhan jerked free.

"I'm not after your respect, China Doll."

Johnny smelled the desire radiating from both of them—even Zhan, though she would have denied it. He didn't care if the Offerling seduced his guard or vice versa; he trusted Kirk not to reveal secrets that would get back to the vampire. What he did mind, however, was how their attraction fed his own urgency for sex.

"Red, this way." Without delay, he led her from the room. Those still shuffling out paused to allow them through the doorway. The pack members were all heading down the stairwell to their cars, but he led Seph up the stairwell.

"Where are we going?" she asked.

"You'll see." He was uncomfortably hard in his jeans. In an effort to counter this intense response, he asked, "How's your mom?"

Seph groaned.

It wasn't so different from the sounds she made when he was bedding her. "That good?" he asked. His voice sounded strangled even to him.

Seph didn't seem to notice. "Yeah. Ask me again later. What's this?" She patted the steel square to the left side of the stairwell.

"Gates. They run along the tracks," he replied as he pointed at the metal track across the entry top. Then he pointed at the floor, where a similar track was embedded in the floor. "It's like the barriers they use in shopping malls. The Omori just had it installed. We can seal off the floors individually if we need to."

"Why would you need to?"

"The half-formed wæres, mostly. Just an extra security measure."

He was climbing fast. She was keeping up, but she was panting with the effort. It resonated erotically in his ears.

"That was an impressive transformation," she said.

"Yeah."

"Yeah? That's it?"

He didn't want to tell her how he was struggling with all that was new—*Damn! The* in signum amoris! He squeezed her hand. *Red? Red, you hear me?*

She didn't answer him. He released her, hoping it wasn't too abrupt. He was aware that he had to give her some kind of answer, but like a bad joke, her mom had actually given up her right arm in the process of unlocking his tattoos; he wouldn't dare complain, but neither would he say anything that might make him sound ungrateful or imply that Eris's sacrifice hadn't garnered all they'd hoped for. "It felt easier. Much more fluid."

Emerging onto the ninth floor, he guided her toward the small guest chamber at the rear of the hallway.

"It was your first change since breaking the binding," Persephone added. "Did it feel more powerful to you?"

"Yeah." He opened the door of the small studio apartment and hit the switch for the lights, twisting the knob to dim them. "I guess." He opened the door wider so she could enter.

"You guess? I was out in the hallway and I felt it."

"Really?" Instead of letting her acquaint herself with the space, as soon as he shut the door, he seized her and held her against him. "I've got something else I want you to feel." He pressed his lips to hers roughly. "God, I missed you."

Seph kissed him back and buried her fingers in his hair.

It felt like he hadn't seen her in months, not mere days. His body thrummed with energy and ached for a release.

His tongue pressed between her lips, and he wished it was another part of his body. Her lip gloss tasted like sweet berries. He reached under the sweatshirt, pushing up tank tops to touch her skin.

That enticing resonance played across his fingers again, dripping into his palm and rippling through his body.

"Mmmm. I missed you too," she said, arms winding around his neck. Effortlessly, she hoisted herself up and wrapped her legs around him.

He carried her toward the bed in the corner and she wriggled just before he heard the thud of her shoes dropping to the floor. He laid her on the mattress and, beyond the want or need of foreplay, unfastened her jeans. She made no protest as he tore her panties and jeans away in one motion. Seph tugged her shirts over her head exposing braless breasts.

A growl rumbled up from his chest as he pushed off the pants he'd put on only minutes before, and his erection was no longer confined.

Unable to resist, he bent to kiss her breasts, to fondle and taste her—because he could. Everywhere their flesh touched, he burned, burned as if his skin had been rubbed raw and was extraordinarily sensitive—yet without any pain.

He had to be inside of her, right now. He groaned in desire as her wet warmth embraced him. It was almost too much. He reined his urgency back, using shallow, controlled strokes.

Seph gyrated under him and laced her fingers in his hair. "No," she said, her smooth thighs squeezing around him. "All of it."

He thrust deep. She moaned in approval, and part of him wished she would struggle a little, just enough to make dominating her a sweeter victory. He arched his back, gave her an extra-hard thrust. Then again. And again. The breathy uh-uh-uh sounds could have been the whimpering struggles of a subdued quarry. . . .

"Don't stop."

Don't command me. He stopped.

She ground her hips against him. "Johnny."

"What?" He pulled out of her. His tongue flicked up her neck. He nibbled on her ear.

"Johnny. More. Please."

He was in control. Not her.

"Please . . . please . . ."

The soft pleading hit him like a hard-core turn-on. He pounded into her, fucking her until he felt a fluttering energy sweep over his naked backside like an ethereal wind. She clawed him, crying out.

As she quieted, he felt her body relax into blissful serenity, and she lay, panting, but he wasn't done. It felt so good.

My turn.

His pace slowed. His fingers skimmed along her arm, lifted it slowly, gently, until her elbow bent as if she were touching her shoulder. Gently, he repeated this gesture with her other arm. Holding her wrists there, he pushed up. His weight kept her pinned to the bed.

He watched her, concentrating on what she was feeling. Her breasts rocked with his thrusts. Hot. Beautiful. Sexy.

Lowering himself to his elbows, he nibbled at her neck in small, teasing bites. The altered position changed the angle. She reacted with a lusty moan, her legs encircling him. She met his thrusts impatiently. He had her and he knew it. All he had to do was swivel his hips a little. . . .

Seph trembled and squeezed her legs tighter around him. The ghostly energy caressed him again and she cried out.

Instinctively, his mouth opened wide on her throat. With his teeth, he could feel every little movement she made. Her pleasure vibrated on his tongue.

His jaws closed a fraction.

Beneath him, Persephone's body became more rigid.

She was still climaxing, but instead of wordless ecstasy, she called his name with both pleasure and fear in her tone.

The scent of fear blossomed on her skin. Johnny's teeth closed another fraction—

What the hell am I doing?

He went utterly still, then kissed up her neck to her ear where he whispered, "You on top." He rolled, switching their positions. Now submissively posed, he splayed his fingers across her buttocks, urged her to action. Persephone needed little encouragement.

He could already tell her fear had evaporated. And that anger had replaced it. She grabbed his wrists and put his arms into much the same position he'd held hers in.

He let her have control as she rode him. He savored the feeling of her strong thighs flexing and her hips grinding as she sought another orgasm.

When the sensation crept over him, he didn't deny the release another moment.

CHAPTER ELEVEN

Y ou aren't answering," Johnny said, caressing up and down my arm.

I lay on my side. Though I nuzzled to his chest, I clutched my neck protectively. I'd been trying to remember the name of that song that had a line asking if the woman would offer her throat to the wolf with the red roses. I must have zoned out. "You didn't ask anything."

He gripped my hand and repositioned it away from my throat, gently squeezing. "Not out loud."

Right. That. "The *in signum amoris* is gone, Johnny."

"How? Why?" He sat up.

"I learned that Menessos had woven a hidden benefit for himself into it, so I unraveled his spell."

He released a slow exhalation that tickled on my shoulder. "Would that explain a headache yesterday evening?"

"After nightfall?"

"Yup."

"Yup," I mimicked him.

"What hidden benefit did he have?"

"He could hear my thoughts but block me from hearing his."

"Bastard." He smoothed my hair. "But it was kinda cool."

"It weirded me out."

He leaned down and flicked his tongue all along my

earlobe. His breath was hot in my ear as he whispered, "Yeah, but just imagine what it would've done for sex. . . ."

That might have been interesting. But I'd had enough sexual surprises for one night. I could still feel his teeth on my throat. I was all for unrestrained sexual moments, but actual fear had no place in my bedroom.

But we aren't in my *bedroom.*

We remained there in silence long enough that the afterglow's slumber had nearly claimed me when he said, "We have to go to The Dirty Dog. I need to put in an appearance." Johnny slid away from me. "It'll be three o'clock before I get there now anyway."

I stretched to slough off the sleep trying to claim me and sat up. "I haven't told you why I'm back in Cleveland."

"You aren't here just to see me?" he teased. Two paces from the bed he circled back. "Uh-oh."

"Yeah." I hadn't meant to take this long getting to the haven, though I wasn't eager to get there, either. Since Heldridge had made it to the Excelsior, Menessos's second-in-command and sometimes assassin, Goliath, would have been called back to the haven as well. Goliath had overheard his dead brother's voice emanating from my protrepticus—a magical device that, in my case, happened to be housed in a cell phone. He was none too happy thinking I had his brother's spirit trapped.

I must have been frowning at that thought because Johnny cocked his head as he asked, "What? Is Menessos in more trouble than your mother?"

"Heldridge had his audience with the Excelsior."

Johnny sat. "What's the plan?"

"Dunno. Menessos said I needed to get back to

Cleveland." I touched his chest, played with the little bit of hair he had there. "But I wanted to see you first." My gaze didn't lift to his; he'd genuinely scared me.

I could hope that it was only different because we were at the den and he'd just been confirmed as the Domn Lup. But there was a niggling little thought in the back of my mind: *What if he isn't ready to control the amount of power we unleashed within him?*

I was *sooo* glad he couldn't read my mind. I didn't want him to know I had even a small doubt in him.

Fifteen minutes later, Johnny backed me into the corner of the elevator and we made out as we rode it down to the parking garage. He was as gentle and sweet as he'd always been before. I felt a twinge of guilt over having even a mild doubt. When we emerged at the second-floor level, where there were no outer elevator doors, the cold night air rushed around us, chilling me even through my layered shirts and jacket.

Johnny wore only a black tee with his jeans. I'd been gripping his arms the whole time because I didn't trust the erratic elevator, and his skin was hot over the cords of tense muscle. Still, I asked, "Aren't you cold?"

"It's refreshing," he whispered into my ear. "I could do you all night."

I held his face. "You'd break me."

He showed me his lopsided grin, clearly accustomed to the shakes and wobbles of the machine. "That's what magic's for."

I laughed, but my mirth ended immediately when the elevator lurched to a halt. Johnny leaned in and whispered into my ear, "I can protect you, Red. From evil elevators and from whatever trouble the vamp is stirring up this time."

I squeezed him tighter.

He pulled back and gave me the most earnest countenance. "I'm . . . not like I was before, Red. The vamp couldn't kick my ass now."

I nodded, hoping he didn't decide to test that theory. "You needed to be his equal," I whispered. "And I've needed you to have this too—but I need you to *not* duke it out with fists or with magic. Okay?"

"Speaking of magic," Johnny said as he opened the rotting wooden doors, "the men are eager for the forced change spell."

I noticed he hadn't answered me.

"It could be done here Monday night," he said. "I'll check the moon position, but with roof access you should have a good view for hours."

"Depending on how things go with Heldridge and the Excelsior, I may not be able to do the spell Monday." That was four days away.

"It'll be okay." He captured my hand as we entered the now empty parking area. It stretched before us, unlit and spooky. Johnny led me to the "rock and roll" parking around the corner.

"What about Zhan?"

"I'm sure Kirk escorted her to The Dirty Dog. We show our faces for a drink or two and then the three of us can head to the haven, okay?"

"Sure." I didn't actually want to go to The Dirty Dog. My last visit hadn't gone well . . . although Cammi wasn't here and no one else seemed too upset about my arrival. Cammi was jealous of my relationship with Johnny.

Gregor had given her orders to never speak to Johnny again, so I hoped that she'd stay away and maybe I'd have a more pleasant visit to the bar tonight.

I wondered if Zhan's Offerling status was impeding her having fun at The Dirty Dog.

Johnny drew the keys from his pocket and hit a button. The lone car ahead of us chirped.

Then it hit me: "You have a car! Oooo, it's awesome-looking!" My knowledge of cars was minimal, but I was surprised he had a four-door. "I like the triton emblem. Very Poseidon-like."

"This is a Maserati Quattroporte GT S."

"Sounds fast."

"It is very fast." He opened the door for me.

I didn't need a crystal ball to predict that he'd have to show me just how fast. "Mmmm. New car smell," I said as he shut the door. The car was unfamiliar to me and the dome lights hadn't lit up, so I felt a little lost groping about for my seat belt. When Johnny eased into the driver's seat, I patted the raised block separating us. "Is this a console or a chaperone?"

"I can still reach you," he said and put the key in the ignition. Then he sniffed. He sniffed again and twisted to see the backseat.

So I mimicked him.

Someone in a charcoal gray suit was sitting with his legs stretched across the backseat. He held a thick spiral-bound notebook open across his lap. "Hello, lovebirds."

Menessos.

I glared at him. He contentedly flipped a page as if he could see perfectly in the dark. Maybe he could.

"This is very good stuff, John."

Despite the surprise appearance, it made me feel good to have them both with me. Especially with Menessos being complimentary to Johnny.

Then Johnny snatched the art pad away, shut it and tossed it on the dashboard, effectively ruining my happy moment.

"How did you get in my car without setting off the alarm?"

"How?" Menessos repeated, considering. He shrugged. "Magic."

"What are you doing here?" I asked.

"The Excelsior's people are swift, they could be here already. If they're searching for me, the last place they'd check is in the Domn Lup's new car. Nice choice, by the way. I do like Maseratis, although I've always been more fond of Aston Martins myself."

"So you're hiding," Johnny said.

In one lithe motion, Menessos swiveled in the seat, put his feet to the floor and resettled himself into the center. He leaned forward, focusing on me. "I am here to secure the safety of those dearest to me." He shifted his gaze to Johnny. "You make coupling that with self-preservation sound disgraceful. And speaking of coupling. . . ." He sniffed the air as Johnny had done a second ago, and his tone lowered. "The two of you are ready to concentrate on our mutual well-being now that your lusts are sated, yes?"

Johnny and I shared disgruntled head shakes.

Menessos sat back, hands behind his head in a satisfied pose. "Ah . . . *l'amour*."

Johnny revved the engine and backed out of the parking spot.

When he pulled out onto the road, Menessos asked, "Where are we off to?"

"The Dirty Dog," Johnny replied.

"It's a bad time for a social call just now," the vampire said.

Johnny slammed the brakes, squealing the tires. My seat belt restrained me, but I protested with a distressed "Hey!" just as Menessos crashed into the backs of our seats.

"I'm not your chauffeur," Johnny growled. "If you don't like where your hiding spot is headed, get out."

Menessos righted himself and smoothed his suit jacket. "*Touché*, John. That practically hurt. I commend you for surprising me. From now on, I'll expect your quick temper." He made no effort to leave the car. "However, I can't imagine Persephone enjoyed being thrust around like that."

"She enjoys my thrusting just fine."

My teeth ground together. The two of them embarked on a stare down.

I counted to ten. Twenty. Thirty. And I thought they'd been getting chummy. Guess not. "Guys. Enough."

"You want the protection of my vehicle, vamp? It's yours as long as you keep your mouth shut." Johnny resumed driving.

I'd honestly never seen Johnny this . . . testy.

Not soon enough we were at the bar that served as a second home to the wærewolves. If the local fire chief wanted to enforce maximum occupancy rules tonight, this would be the place to start. The whole block was lined with cars. Johnny couldn't park anywhere near The Dirty Dog.

"You'd think they'd leave you of all people a convenient spot," Menessos mused. "Or is this a surprise visit?"

I gave Mr. I'm-Picking-a-Fight the stink-eye. He winked at me.

Johnny parked two blocks away in a residential area. "I'll wait here," I told him, "but don't rush because of it. Do what you have to do. Menessos will keep me company." After a toe-curling kiss, Johnny left.

His kisses were always wonderful, but that one had had a sense of "nanny-nanny-boo-boo" to it, as if the divine depth and scope of that lip-lock had been meant to incite both my pleasure and Menessos's pain.

Men.

My gaze lingered on Johnny as he jogged up the street. At six-two his body was lean and long, but it didn't make him awkward. He was graceful no matter what he did. My breath escaped in a soft sigh.

"How is your mother doing?"

CHAPTER TWELVE

I had the urge to lecture Menessos sternly about the *in signum amoris* thing, but in fine female fashion, I decided to save that scolding for another time. "Skip the small talk and tell me what we're facing here."

He slid into the seat kitty-corner to me so we could see each other more easily, but he stared at his palms. "The shabbubitum."

"Gesundheit."

"Sha-buh-BYE-tum," he said slower.

"And that's what?"

"*They* are unique. The best description I've heard is vampire-harpies."

My stomach did a flip. "Delightful," I said morosely. In Greek myth, harpies were hideous sisters, part hag and part vulture, who were in charge of carrying souls to Hades. "What do you think they'll do?"

"They are truth seers. They will . . . reveal . . . the truth."

He made it sound like torture. Maybe these shabbubitum were more like the Siberian myth of the alkonost. Similar to harpies, alkonost lived in the land of the dead and tormented the souls of the damned. "Is it as painful as you make it seem?"

"Imagine a stranger's fingers tearing through your mind with the same hurried zeal as a thief ransacking an office while hunting for a specific file."

"Ouch."

"That, my dear, could win you the Understatement of the Year Award."

His being here was making more sense. "What are your options?"

"One, *we* could delve into the Hellish pits of the blackest magic and overlay my entire psyche with a completely new set of memories, hoping they are innocent memories and that they don't affect who I actually am. Two, I could abandon you, change my name and flee, then in a century or two reemerge and pretend to be a weak, new vampire while receiving the shelter of another master for an additional century or two. Or three, I could abandon you and crawl into a random grave and lie there starving until I become a revenant. Insane with hunger, I would lose all self-awareness, and with any luck someone from SSTIX would stake me before the shabbubitum even found out."

The Specialized Squadron for Tactical Investigation of Xenocrime—SSTIX—was the government's answer to the nationwide issue of state and local law enforcement's refusing to serve and protect where nonhumans—and greater personal risks—were involved.

That two of his options involved fleeing stunned me. And hurt me. The only choice that didn't involve him leaving sounded infinitely dangerous and implausible. *He can't just run away. He's part of this! We're not whole without him.* "What if you simply submitted to it?"

"Easy for you to say."

"No, I mean instead of resisting, what if you—" Before I could even finish I could tell by his expression that he was not fond of what I was saying.

"That is another option."

"Would they go easy on you? Would it make a positive difference in the experience?"

"No. Nor would they show any restraint on you. They are not capable of pity."

With an effort I swallowed down the big lump suddenly in my throat. *If he has to run, it will be temporary.* "Have you decided which option to take?"

He didn't answer.

In fact, he was silent long enough that my own fears ignited a fiery willingness to push. "Johnny's right, isn't he? You're hiding. And about to flee." *Am I actually selfish enough to prefer that he stay and be tortured by these things?*

"Changing my name and reemerging with another is the option that benefits you most."

"That benefits me how?"

"If I flee, it will give the impression that I have broken your hold on me. That might spare you any further entanglements."

I wasn't as worried about "further entanglements" as I was about losing him. I couldn't fulfill my destiny without him. I wanted to scream, *What about me?* Instead, calmly, I said, "What about your haven?"

"VEIN has been told that I was mastered by a witch, a witch formerly believed to be my servant. My haven is lost to me already." His voice was tight and little more than a whisper.

My heart was so heavy. This was all because of me. He'd known he was risking this, but he hadn't told me. I hadn't even considered the consequences would be this high. I should have.

Guilt and shame chilled my stomach. Fear iced it over. "You fleeing means you avoid getting killed, and I go on the shit-list, but they won't strike against me because of that 'Moonchild of ruin' business, right?"

Menessos quoted the poem:

> *Lustrata walks,*
> *unspoiled into the light.*
> *Sickle in hand,*
> *she stalks through the night*
> *Wearing naught but her mark and silver blade.*
> *The moonchild of ruin, she becomes Wolfsbane.*

"Yeah."

"That depends on whether or not you're willing to be marked by the Excelsior."

It did say *Wearing naught but her mark* . . . "If it saves our asses . . ." I started, but I really meant, *If it means you don't leave.*

"No, Persephone! The three of us are bound in a way that our respective groups dare not hope to accomplish. That we have achieved a workable union both frightens and fascinates them. Our binding to each other strengthens us, but none of us can afford a binding to anyone of higher rank, or to others not of our own kind. It would break us."

But your leaving wouldn't? I held my tongue.

"Persephone, I believe the Excelsior has only the best interests of his people at heart, but if he had control over you, it would be only for whatever benefit he could achieve for VEIN. The Witch Elder Council would not abide their Lustrata being controlled by the Excelsior."

I let my head rest against the glass, appreciating the way the coldness of it balanced my frozen stomach.

"Your current solitary status means you lack affiliation to a coven. That forces WEC to pigeonhole you into a role that reflects the disaffected segment of their kind. That already has given the Elders much to worry about—and they're so old they sleep little as it is, meaning they have vast amounts of time to plot and plan. Their designs would only worsen if they thought you were marked by the Excelsior."

I crossed my arms and moped.

"When the news of dear John's confirmation as the Domn Lup breaks, your lover will be included on, as you delightfully put it, the shit-list."

"Have we hit the worst-case scenario yet?" I was being sarcastic. Sadly, Menessos had an answer.

"The worst-case scenario," he said, "is if WEC, VEIN, or the Zvonul discover the *sorsanimus* spell that binds the three of us. We did it to keep you from being Bindspoken by the witches, but it strengthens us all. If detected, it will appear that we're preparing a coup d'état."

"Are we?"

Menessos was silent.

"If they think we're prepping for a power grab, they'll just kill us all outright. Won't they?"

"They will have to assume the three of us are sharing what confidential information we know about our respective groups. Further, they will assume that we will use the growth of our individual powers to our mutual benefit. We could all be targeted for execution, as you suggest. Or . . ." He made a visual sweep of the perimeter before answering. "They might act with more cunning. Each group has the potential to send operatives to test our loyalties to each other. Just one could pit us against each other. Dividing us would not only end the union but it would also offer that group an advantage via the information they learn in doing so."

Could Menessos or Johnny be played by outside forces?

Could I?

Wonderful. His adherence to the Machiavellian vampire stereotype was making my head hurt. I rubbed my forehead as if that might deflect the spinning-out-of-control sensation.

"What is it?" he asked.

"Congratulations. You've just made me paranoid of everyone."

He leaned forward. "I am sorry, Persephone. I truly am. That paranoia is the only thing that will keep us united and safe."

When he said my name a wave of warmth poured over me like a magical embrace. It emboldened me enough to ask, "How can we be united and safe if you flee?"

The vampire studied the world beyond the car window. "I do not want VEIN to know I am the original progenitor of the vampires. If that information is exhumed, it cannot be reburied."

He'd told me this before. A little more than two weeks ago. *Goddess, it seems like so long ago.* I'd wanted him to tell VEIN the truth so they would rally to his aid against the fairies, but he'd refused. He had been willing to die to keep that secret. And he had.

I was not insensitive to the fact that he had given the most precious thing he'd had—his very life—to maintain his anonymity, or that losing it now would render his sacrifice pointless in hindsight.

"You did the right thing, for the right reason," I said.

That mantra had bitten me in the ass a few times, but it was still, overall, a good policy.

Menessos plucked at his pant leg. "If the world learns it has someone to blame, I will become the target of every extremist group with a grudge against vampires and every vengeful person who has ever suffered because of my children's thirst."

"You're not alone in the I-Dislike-My-Exposed-Destiny Category," I snapped. "Everyone either knows or suspects I'm the Lustrata. They also seem to know more about it than I do, and have heavy expectations of me. Johnny's not in such a different position either."

He stilled, but said nothing more.

"How can that possibly scare you so much?" I asked.

He laughed, but there was an offended note to it. "If VEIN learned my secret, they would seize me and demand explanations. It could derail everything. My attention must remain fixed upon this purpose. The only thing I fear is not being able to finish *this*, Persephone, with you and John. I fear the repercussions that would befall any two of us, should the other one falter or . . . be slain."

I couldn't deny his devotion to this destiny of ours. "We must endure risks, but we all know the consequences of *not* following through get higher every day."

"Exactly," he whispered. "I can't risk not following through on what we must do because I'm distracted by the other."

"But you can't leave!" I swallowed as if I could reclaim those revealing words. Hurriedly I added, "We're all dealing with things happening that we didn't want to happen. That's part of the price we have to pay." I stared at the steering wheel because I couldn't meet his gaze after what

I'd blurted. "I didn't want Xerxadrea, Aquula, Ross, or Maxine to die. Not even Samson D. Kline. But they all did."

After the slightest hesitation, Menessos asked, "Do I not make your list of noble dead? I died for you, too."

He was right. And he repeated his dying every sunrise. It was my turn to shamefully examine the dark world beyond the car.

"Does the fact that I sit here talking to you now diminish my sacrifice?"

We were all surrendering things we didn't want to forfeit, but I still felt like an ass. "It shouldn't."

"But it does."

I whispered, "I didn't have to grieve for you, Menessos."

He shivered when his name was spoken, and I wondered if he was experiencing something similar to what I felt when he said my name. "Menessos." I said it slower, tasting the syllables on my tongue, on my lips.

He arched his back, took a deep breath, held it for a second, then sighed it away. Panting, openmouthed, he looked directly at me, displaying a sexual hunger my body reacted to—places low in my abdomen tightened.

Between the seats, I offered him my hand. "You came back. You come back every night."

"If I didn't, would you have wept for me?"

"I did weep."

Menessos wrapped both of his hands around mine. He rubbed little circles with his thumbs. "You've been away for so long."

I twisted my wrist upward. Menessos bore two of my hexes, making him the equivalent of my Offerling. He needed to partake of my blood occasionally, and it had been over a week. "Go on," I said. "Drink."

CHAPTER THIRTEEN

As Johnny strode from his car, fall air gusted behind him. Stray leaves scuttled across the asphalt as if daring him to try to catch them.

Part of him wished the wind could carry him away from everything and everyone he'd ever known, to hide from this enormous destiny, burying it in lyrics and melodies like he had before. But the bigger part of him knew that wasn't an option anymore.

It wasn't an option for Menessos, either. Seeing the vamp hiding from his troubles made Johnny's blood boil. It wasn't like Menessos was the Excelsior or anything. If Johnny had to accept being the Domn Lup, the vamp could damn well accept the responsibilities and consequences of being a Quarterlord.

Johnny wasn't going to feel guilty over lashing out either. The vamp was being a wuss and he deserved it.

Presently, that vamp was alone with his girlfriend.

Johnny thrust the thought away. He trusted Persephone. She was Menessos's master. She'd even eliminated the *in signum amoris* he had put on them.

He had to admit he was disappointed by the loss of the connection to Seph the spell had given him. And she'd undone it without asking if he'd wanted it gone.

He understood her reasons, but both she and the vamp had acted on something that affected him just as much as them, and neither had asked his permission. With the vamp it was inexcusable but expected; Persephone, however, should have known better.

When was he going to get a say in all this magic shit? Or was Persephone thinking she was his master, too?

Stop it.

His fingers raked through his hair. He was just being a dick.

She embodied the grounding sense of the future for him. The sense of family he'd yearned for, he felt with her. Living at the farmhouse with her, Nana, and the kiddo, he'd felt more complete than he ever had before.

And you called the vamp a wuss.

Johnny shoved his fists into his jeans pockets. As he neared he could see the upper floor of the bar. The windows of the apartment were darkened. Ig had lived there.

He'd killed Ig there.

At the thought, unwanted images of the scene flashed into his mind, and he could remember the taste of Ig's blood. His mouth watered.

Damn it.

You didn't tell me it would be like this, old man.

For over eight years, all he'd wanted was to know his past. Where had he lived? Who had he been before? But Ig, after learning that Johnny could transform his hands at will, had ended his search into Johnny's past and focused intensely on Johnny's future. He'd justified it by explaining that this ability was rare, and a full transformation would mean Johnny was the Domn Lup.

Ig had insisted on privately tutoring him in the responsibilities of a leader. Having so much attention from the *dirija* meant Johnny became known as Ig's "pet."

Some picked on him; others toadied to him to gain the *dirija*'s favor.

Johnny understood now that Ig had been trying to do the right thing, but at the time the exposure to politics and phony friendships had left him disaffected. He'd distanced himself from the pack, and Ig's efforts to bring him back had been drowned under the music from his band's cranked amplifiers.

He'd tried so damn hard to forget the destiny Ig had said was before him. He'd been worse than a prodigal son to Ig. He'd captured the man's kindness and hope and run away, returning only when his desire to protect Persephone had offered him no other options. He'd taken Ig's life and claimed command of the pack only to help her, not because Ig had wanted him to.

For Persephone, he'd willingly accepted his fate, but the one thing he really, truly, *desperately* wanted—the truth of his past—she'd failed to give him. Not even her magic had been able to retrieve his memories after the phoenix had clawed him . . . a phoenix he'd attacked to protect her.

Approaching the bar, Johnny could hear the thump of the bass and drums from the jukebox. The wæres on door duty bowed their heads as he passed. Inside, the smoky bar was a feast for the senses. The smell of wolf and sweat, of beer and tobacco and liquor tickled his nostrils. Disturbed's "Ten Thousand Fists" filled his ears. He pushed into the crowd.

His pack greeted him with howls.

Warm bodies danced against him. The scent of "female" overpowered everything else as the women converged on their unattended sovereign. He lifted his arms to avoid touching them, but they touched him. Hands ran over him. Hips pressed against him. His cock grew hard. For an ego-swelling moment he was immobile, fully aware of the curves they flaunted, of the heat they created, of the bare skin they displayed and how much he wanted sex again.

Clenching his jaw he maneuvered through them, touching a shoulder here and an arm there. His fingertips did more than tingle when he brushed the bare skin of a pack mate. It was like electricity crackling through him, a magnetic stirring of lust and territorial rights.

He could claim Ig's apartment and make use of his bed. God, how his whole body might react, invigorated by the potent touch of one or two or three pack bitches with their bare skin against his. . . .

As he neared the end of the bar, someone unplugged the jukebox, and the instant silence cued the pack to howl again. With everyone's attention locked on him, Johnny knew they expected a speech.

He wasn't in the mood to conduct a pep rally. He wanted to fuck—and the disregard for *who* wasn't like him. He felt dominant and invincible, but confused at the same time.

He met their expectant faces. Johnny remembered when Ig had wanted to make him second-in-command. The pack had seen favoritism and resisted the idea of one so young in a position of power. Several challenged him to fight for the position. Ig retracted his nomination, but his credibility had taken a dive. Johnny had learned that having power meant being enslaved to maintaining the trust of those under one's authority.

He pretended he was onstage, fronting a band again.

Arms uplifted, he shouted, "I have been confirmed! Celebrate with me! This isn't just my time, this is your time! The pack of the Domn Lup!" The cheers and howls were deafening.

Johnny nodded at the man holding the cord of the jukebox. He promptly plugged it back in, hit a button, and the drums of Judas Priest's "Painkiller" assaulted the bar.

Not seeing Kirk and Zhan anywhere, Johnny made his way toward the rear. He caught sight of Gregor's bulk through the doorway. He mouthed Kirk's name.

Gregor pointed up the stairwell.

Johnny remembered an unlit apartment, and could guess what they were doing. Kirk's attraction to the Offerling was obvious, but Johnny thought Zhan had more resistance. Maybe Kirk's charm had won her over. Maybe he'd gotten her drunk. He just hoped they finished up soon.

As he traveled from the front room to the rear, he saw Zhan sitting at the top of the narrow stairs. Her pose was bored irritation incarnate. Apparently Kirk's charm had not won the night. Kirk sat halfway up with his back to her. Both seemed to perk up when they saw him.

"May I leave *now*?" Zhan asked.

Johnny noted Kirk's bored eye-roll. Johnny told her, "Yes. The car's two blocks east, on Whitethorn."

"You left the E.V. there alone?" Zhan asked, starting down the steps.

Johnny shook his head. "She's not alone."

"Can I escort you to make sure you get there safely?" Kirk asked sweetly over his shoulder. He remained seated, blocking the stairs.

"All I need is for you to move your ass and get out of my way."

Kirk stood and turned as far aside as the narrow stairs permitted, but even petite Zhan had to squeeze between the wære and the wall. "If you'd give me the chance to move my ass in another way for you, you might not frown so much."

Zhan glowered; Kirk grinned. She said, "You move your mouth in an extremely undesirable way, wolf. You'll never get the chance you're hoping for." Zhan elbowed past him and stalked toward the front.

Johnny proceeded to the back room. Even without sniffing, he could detect the oaky sweetness of Laphroaig. Gregor was pouring. He offered Johnny the glass. When he accepted it, Gregor raised his own. "To your confirmation." His Romanian accent gave the words a happy cadence.

Drinking with Gregor was probably the best thing he could do. Being the head of the Omori, Gregor's reputation for brute rigidity would keep the revelers at a distance. Johnny lifted his glass in salute.

"*Noroc*," Gregor said.

Johnny repeated the word quizzically.

"It is the Romanian way of saying *cheers*."

They drank. As the liquor warmth hit his stomach, Johnny felt the beast within stretch in languorous delight. He hoped it would sleep.

They sipped in awkward silence for a long minute, then Gregor opened the steel rear door. "Shall we?"

Johnny proceeded past the screen door and onto the brick stoop outside. The chilled air chased away the lusty thoughts. Gregor followed and shut the steel door with a little thud and said, "Well?"

While he trusted Gregor enough to accept a drink

from him and let himself be herded into the dark alley, Johnny knew the Omori didn't engage in idle chitchat either. Noting that the man had kept his voice low, he hesitated.

Gregor's loyalty to the Zvonul was undisputed; Johnny's misgivings stemmed from the fact that he'd had several recent disputes with Gregor. He wasn't sure where they stood, man to man, though the offering of a toast seemed like a gesture of goodwill. Maybe even friendship.

"Well what?" Johnny asked.

"You have not smiled since you entered."

"Oh. I'm supposed to put on a fake smile when I'm in public, right?"

"I am no advisor, but even if I were, I would not advise you to be fake, my king."

Johnny wished he could toss that idea of friendship into the Dumpster at the end of the alley. The Omori were protectors of the wære hierarchy. Now that he was certain to wear the crown, Gregor was just doing his job. Johnny gulped a big swig of the single malt scotch.

"You tell them to celebrate with you, yet you do not convey a celebratory mood."

"Shouldn't a leader maintain his composure at all times?" It was something Ig had told him; he was surprised how readily those words crossed his tongue.

"He should."

Johnny hoisted his glass again. "The old Rege didn't."

"No. He often let his beast rule him."

Johnny drank again, consuming Gregor's words as well. At least he wasn't alone in this struggle, but . . . "He was not the Domn Lup."

Gregor opened his mouth, shut it again.

They stood in silence until Johnny asked, "What did you bring me out here to say?"

Gregor snorted and drew a deep breath. "For what the opinion of an Omori is worth, I think you will make a good Domn Lup."

Hearing praise when he was feeling so conflicted made Johnny doubt the words. He wheeled around. "You've observed the Zvonul for years. They're politicians. They're smooth. They've worked their way up through the ranks. I've been a *dirija* for two whole weeks. What makes you think I'll be worth a damn as the Domn Lup?"

"You killed your *dirija*—"

Johnny's spine stiffened. He was about to interrupt, but Gregor's conciliatory gesture begged his indulgence a little longer.

"It was time for a decisive action, I understand that. I have been told what you did. You did not act out of hunger for power but as an act of mercy. With a single action you ended his suffering and gave him his greatest wish: your ascension. What father could ask for more?"

Gut twisting at the memory, Johnny turned away from Gregor.

"In the gardens you could have killed the Rege. If power were all you had wanted, you would have. Instead, you stood up to me, stood up to the Rege. You gave him an opportunity to make himself lauded. He hated you for that: for seeing it and pointing it out to him. He thought you were trying to gain leverage, and he swore he would not be beholden to you for anything." Gregor scuffed the bottom of his shoe on the stoop. "You scared him. He began plotting your death. It was the only reaction he was capable of having. That wasn't a show of courage, but giving someone who'd made himself your enemy the chance to do the right thing was." He held the glass to his lips, but before he drank he said, "I am ashamed I went with him to Pittsburgh."

Johnny considered what it must have taken for Gregor to admit that, and was inspired.

"Though you lack experience, I believe you will be a good Domn Lup because your courage is unquestionable. And because you have not lost all compassion." He paused. "The old Rege had no mercy. His power made him bold, and he mistook his boldness for courage. They are not one and the same. Perhaps having power for so long, he forgot. I was beginning to."

"What do you mean?"

Gregor scanned the sky. "I've been Omori all of my adult life. I've been disposable—under the paw of my betters, their tool and their weapon. I've been very comfortable with that. Until now." He met Johnny's gaze squarely and said, "You're not like them. You make me see what the wæres could be. I don't want to be expendable anymore. I believe you're going to change everything, and I want to live long enough to enjoy it."

CHAPTER FOURTEEN

Menessos's lips hovered over my wrist. His warm breath on my skin sent a heated caress down my legs.

The barest of kisses touched me, and with it, he invoked our master/servant bond and kindled my flesh. It felt like a ghost of him was kissing the nape of my neck. My body felt lithe and warm and supple. My hips undulated and a heavy sigh escaped from my mouth.

As his fangs pierced me, a heady arousal coursed through me. It tickled the backs of my knees. It stroked under my breasts. Deep inside, it set my spine afire. I moaned softly as the fuse on my desire burned down, wondering if Menessos was getting under my skin—with more than his fangs, that is.

For a long minute the wave of bliss enveloped me, held me aloft in idyllic, aching need. I writhed in my seat, shifting my hips and feeling that if he would just give me a single caress I'd explode in ecstasy. . . .

Menessos ended his feeding as he'd started it: with a kiss. My blood smeared under his lips. He held my hand tenderly as the bleeding slowed, and his tongue flicked over my skin gently, not wasting a drop.

Coming back to myself, I discovered that we'd steamed the windows of Johnny's new car.

Then headlights shone from behind. A blue Corvette passed us and parked right in front of the Maserati.

• • •

Zhan spoke with us briefly, then returned to wait in the Corvette.

It was close to 4:00 a.m. when Johnny made it back. He was sniffing before his backside hit the seat. He shot me a quizzical look, so I said, "It was feeding time."

I showed him my wrist. It had scabbed over nicely. Johnny put the car forcefully into gear. "Home or haven?"

"Home," I said. With Menessos here there was no need to force a confrontation with Goliath. "Zhan will follow."

On the main road, he said, "Give me the details."

"We have approximately twenty hours," Menessos said. "Maybe a little more, before the shabbubitum arrive."

"Shabbubitum?" Johnny asked. Irritatingly enough, he pronounced it perfectly the first time.

Menessos set about explaining to Johnny everything he had told me before.

The information clearly irritated Johnny. We'd been on I-271 for miles and he'd been driving safely, but I could sense his tension ratcheting up.

"So because you two got busted over the mark, three vampire chicks are gonna stir up shit for me?"

"You needn't worry unless the *sorsanimus* binding is discovered."

"So what are you doing to ensure they don't?"

"I'm trying to leave, but it seems there is no viable way to claim that option. If she simply bore my mark, this would be of no concern to VEIN. The fact that I wear two of hers is everything here."

"Two?" The speedometer needle pitched to the right, and inertia snuggled me into the seat.

Shit. "Johnny."

"Two?"

I crossed my arms as if that would defend me, but I was guilty as charged. "I did it when I staked him. It—"

"You mean when you kissed him?"

I felt his words like a slap. I twisted in my seat to glower at Johnny. "I was about to kill him. He was laying down his life to save our asses—"

"Oh, well, *that* makes it the right thing for the right reason, then."

I set my jaw and continued through clenched teeth. "It wasn't a kill in haste or anger or in self-defense. It was outright murder, and I didn't want to do it. You were under the water with Fax, and I was so scared—"

"That you kissed another man." Though I'd have thought we were at top speed already, he made the engine roar and go even faster.

I remained silent for a long second. He already knew about that kiss. He'd seemed to understand before. I growled, "Yeah, I kissed him. And I staked him. Then, I put a second mark on him. It was an effort to make sure he came back because—like it or not—we need him. There was no guarantee, but I did what I thought was right, and I don't regret it. That's more than I can say for Cammi's lip-lock on you." I sat back.

From the backseat, Menessos chuckled and said again, "Ah, *l'amour.*"

The ritual, the sex, the late hour, the argument and the blood donation were a hard-hitting combo that had me yawning as we rolled up my gravel driveway. There was a glow behind the mini-blinds of Mountain's trailer near the barns, and I wondered if the Beholder—he was a once-marked member of Menessos's court—was still awake or was up early.

His porch light flickered on, the door opened, and Ares bounded across the yard. The black Great Dane pup circled the car to greet me with all the tail-wagging enthusiasm a pup could have. He tried to get Johnny to play but had to settle for some vigorous head-scratching.

By the time Mountain rounded the corner of the garage, Zhan was rolling up the driveway. The Corvette either couldn't keep up, or she didn't have the nerve to try. Personally, I doubted it was the latter.

Mountain's low voice rumbled a happy, "Good morning to you all." A hulking figure with a round face and eyes like pitch, he was formidable in appearance, but he was in fact a big teddy bear. He offered friendly acknowledgment to each of us, but the last one, for Zhan, was conveyed with something softer and more secretive. I caught the drop of her gaze in reply. She tucked her hair behind her ear, and her cheeks rounded with a small smile.

"Menessos," I said, to draw his attention and keep him from picking up on what I already knew about his Offerling and his Beholder. "There's less than three hours until you retire for the day." I kept talking as I headed for my porch. "Do you intend to head back to the haven for that? It'll shorten our time to plan."

"I will rest here."

I opened the screen door. "That's good because—" My words cut off midsentence when, before my key even neared the dead bolt, the main door swung open an inch.

"Because why?" Menessos asked.

"My door's already open," I said, backing away.

Suddenly, Johnny put himself between me and the door and was backing me off of the porch.

Menessos *hmpf*ed, pushed the door open and walked inside. "All is well," he called. The entry lights blazed.

Johnny and I moved forward as one. And stopped as one. The moment waned awkwardly, then Johnny extended his hand chivalrously and allowed me to go first. Peering cautiously inside, I discovered Goliath Kline sitting on the staircase. He smiled maliciously and waved. Then he stood and bounced on my squeaky step.

Taller even than Johnny, with a lanky scarecrow frame, he was intimidation incarnate in collar-to-toe black leather. Goliath's skin and hair were like a white palette with two daubs of forget-me-not blue, and the blue was so feral and cunning that his glance seemed more like an incision. Menessos had chosen his second-in-command and security head because he was a certifiable genius whose perfect ACT score was achieved at the age of ten. Menessos had raised him and trained him as an assassin before Making him a vampire.

And I was on this guy's least-favorite-people list.

His brother, a defunct Southern Baptist preacher, had once tried to stake Menessos and been beheaded for the crime. But apparently even brothers separated at a young age and with opposing opinions of vampires could be protective of each other. When Goliath heard Sam's voice on my protrepticus, he had grabbed me and questioned me.

At the time, I happened to have been wearing a charm that amplified my magic. He'd frightened me, and all I'd wanted was for him to let me go. In a knee-jerk reaction,

I'd pulled arcs of electrical power from him through my connection to his master and Maker Menessos. I'd put both vampires on their knees.

I'd saved Goliath's life a few hours later, but I'd never explained Samson's voice emitting from my phone. I was sure he thought I'd done something terrible like rip his brother's spirit from the ever after and forcibly bind it into the device. He needed answers. He deserved them.

Fully aware that I wasn't wearing that charm now, I closed the distance between us, flipped on the stairway light and passed him. "Follow me."

"An Erus Veneficus cannot command an Alter Imperator."

I blinked stupidly at him for a heartbeat; I hadn't known his official title.

"Besides," he added, "I've already rolled around on your bed."

At the bottom of the steps, Johnny growled.

"Goliath," Menessos said in a weary tone. "Our circumstances are far from typical. You will always treat both the Lustrata and the Domn Lup with respect, and for me, please give them an extra measure of tolerance."

"As you wish, master."

That was good enough for me. I resumed my trek to my bedroom. I flipped this light on too and rummaged through the luggage Zhan and I had dropped off earlier. Finding the cell phone, I held it up.

His eyes widened slightly in recognition.

"It's a protrepticus."

"Bullshit."

I let him see my deadpan expression.

"Samson hated witches! He would not deign to bind

his soul into a device that put him in service to you. And," he added, "you cannot exceed a certain distance from a protrepticus. This bag was here, while you were fifty miles away in Cleveland."

The latter part was true. Or it had been, anyway. I was just relieved that he knew enough about the spell to know it would require a *willing* spirit. "The spirit did not identify itself until after the spell was finished."

The vampire entered my room and angrily demanded, "Why would he do that for you?"

"I don't know what he found in the afterlife, Goliath, or how that may or may not have weighed in his spirit's decision to comply with that spell, but if it's any consolation, he *did* use every opportunity to be completely annoying. As for the distance . . ." I shrugged. "It was a triple binding, involving Xerxadrea. With her death, his spirit should have been freed."

"*Should* have?"

"When I open it, the screen stays blank, and yet it's rung a couple times since. In those instances it lights up and he's spoken to me. I can't explain it. I've asked him. He won't explain it." I tossed the phone to Goliath.

He caught it, looking confused. When he wasn't being a sinister badass, Goliath was a handsome man. For a moment, I glimpsed the vampire with whom Lorrie—the mother, now deceased, of my foster daughter, Beverley—had shared a relationship with a few years after her husband had died.

"You can use magic, Goliath. See if he will talk to you. It was never my intention to extricate him from his afterlife." I left him standing in my bedroom.

Samson's calls since Xerxadrea's death had all been

warnings I desperately needed, so parting with the protrepticus put me ill at ease, but giving the device to Goliath nonetheless felt right—and regardless of Johnny's
opposition, I wasn't going to give up my way of making
such decisions.

Downstairs, Mountain and Zhan were conspicuously
absent. Johnny had built a blaze in the living room
fireplace and was playing tug-of-war with Ares and a rope
toy. Menessos sat on my couch, his elbow propped on its
arm, and his index finger to his temple as he admired the
John William Waterhouse painting over the mantel.

Crossing my arms and leaning against the newel
post, I let the scene before me linger undisturbed. Who
knew how long the two of them could maintain such
contentedness in each other's presence?

It was a skill they were going to have to master.

Encouraged, I said, "I have to admit, I like this."

They both turned when I spoke. Johnny released his
end of the rope toy, and Ares carried it merrily around the
room and thumped down on the floor to chew on it.

"You look peaceful," Menessos said. "Finding a little
peace before the storm is enviable."

Before the storm? I've already ridden one today.

Menessos's words could have been a sincere com-
pliment, or they could have been a roundabout jibe at
Johnny to say I seemed unaffected by our spat. I uncrossed
my arms and entered the living room. "You don't seem
like you're *not* at ease."

"Thank you." His lips curved slightly. "That bodes
well, since I have just decided that come nightfall, I will
return to my haven and await the shabbubitum."

CHAPTER FIFTEEN

My spine stiffened, and any sense of peacefulness I had scurried away. Menessos was going to accept the pain and torment of being read. He was going to accept the risk of judgment.

He's going to stay.

"Why the change of heart?" I asked, keeping my voice as casual as possible.

"Escaping them is . . . improbable."

"And the ramifications you were so concerned about?"

Menessos extended his arm toward me, palm up. I walked to him and slipped my hand into his. *Can't read my mind anymore, can you?*

"I have been so focused on the negative possibilities, and on escaping them, that I had not considered how I might create an alternative confrontation."

"You didn't instantly envision every potential benefit to you?" Johnny snapped.

Menessos gripped me tighter. "This is particularly personal, Johnny."

I asked, "How so?"

"First, Heldridge is my son—the only kind I will ever have, anyway. I Made him. I watched him break free of his mortal womb and I raised him in my world. We have had our quarrels, as all fathers and sons do—"

"Quarrels?" Johnny snarled and pointed at me. "He tried to kill her!"

"Yes. Even so, it does not mean I love him less."

Johnny straightened. "You *love* him?"

"I care for all the men and women in my haven. You care for those in your pack, don't you?"

Johnny put his hands on his hips. "Yeah. Doesn't mean I'd profess to *love* them."

Ignoring him, Menessos resumed his explanation. "Heldridge broke away to become his own master and to have his own haven. He interpreted my relocation as an encroachment. Had I not been his Maker, he may not have seen it as a personal insult." He drew a long breath. "Had I not been his Maker, I would not have assumed his cooperation. I should have consulted him as a courtesy, but at the time my thoughts were not for him." To me, he said, "I am forced to admit that these events have been set in motion because I have failed as his Maker and presumed too much. For my insult, he has struck at me . . . first by striking at you, second by going to VEIN. Now the shabbubitum are being freed."

"What do you mean *freed*? They've been imprisoned somewhere?" I asked.

Intent on the flames, he told us a story.

In Babylonia, he said, the priests of Marduk were very powerful. When Nebuchadnezzar II died, his son failed to gain the support of the priests, and his brother-in-law, Neriglissar, succeeded him. When he decided on a campaign into what was known as the "rough" Cilician lands, he needed aid. Menessos was able to offer that aid—for a price: Neriglissar's eldest daughter.

He assured us that it was not like what we were thinking. She was beautiful, yes, but Menessos was more interested in her potential for magic. She had latent power attempting to awaken, but was fearful and fighting it. Menessos, who knew she could be very powerful, wanted to train her.

So he provided the assistance the king sought. Neriglissar gave Menessos a dark-haired girl, but Menessos could sense no power in her. He asked the king if he was certain this girl was his own flesh and blood. The king lied and assured Menessos the girl was his daughter. Menessos made no further accusations, but he refused to take her.

Not long after, he learned that the king had arranged to marry three of his daughters to neighboring princes in one large wedding. Menessos snuck into the girls' shared chamber. All three were primed for the power trying to manifest within them. He tapped a ley line and bespelled them, drawing a Gift into them.

I interrupted his story. "What do you mean you drew a Gift into them?"

"The fey taught me. It must be done while the power is still nascent. Though it does not often work on magic-bearing humans, the maternal grandmother of the girls had fey blood."

With pure-blooded fey, he explained, the Gift is decided by hereditary factors. When fey blood is weakened by human, a wizard must use a ley line to "jump-start" the Gifting. This enabled him to choose what kind of power they received.

Because their father had lied to him—and to many others—he gave the girls "truth-sight." By touch, they could sense the wicked truths a person would otherwise hide.

"You made them the shabbubitum," I said. To myself,

I wondered if the *in signum amoris* was anything like the Gifting spell. It had enabled us telepathically.

"Not then." He resituated himself on the couch. "I wanted them to embrace their father and to see what he was planning for their husbands. They would learn whatever nefarious plans he had in mind and that he was not the benevolent man he pretended to be. That was to be my revenge."

I was tired and wanted to sit down but was afraid that if I did, I'd be asleep in minutes. "You purposely turned them against their father?"

"I assumed they would flee from him. I could then put myself conveniently in their path and initiate their training."

"Heh." Johnny sat forward. "What went wrong?"

"I had not counted on them being their father's daughters, cunning and cruel even in their youth. I later learned they discovered their father planned to marry them off and have convenient accidents befall their new husbands, thereby claiming their lands for his own. They also learned the men they were betrothed to had similar thoughts of murdering their father-in-law."

"Oooo," I said. "Tragedy, tragedy and more tragedy."

"The more they used their Gift, the sharper it grew. They learned to detect not only the wicked truth hidden in the mind, but mundane truths and lies."

"They were mind readers?"

"Close to it."

He continued the story. The eldest sister plotted a dire course of action. She and her sisters dressed as commoners and secretly visited an old witch at the edge of town. They asked for poison to "kill the vermin in their father's barn."

The witch recognized royalty, even dressed in rags. When she told them she had no poison, the eldest, named Liyliy, grabbed the witch and read her. Liyliy learned that years before, the witch had sold poison to a soldier. Using the art of scrying, the witch eventually discovered the poison had been for the king, who'd used it to kill one of his wives—the mother of the three sisters. The witch felt guilty for her part in the fate that befell the woman and her unborn son.

"This glisten-guy killed his own queen?" Johnny asked. A sinister shiver fluttered down my spine.

"Neriglissar. He had several wives, all of them 'queens,' I suppose. His mystics had told him this particular wife would bear a son who would someday kill his father and take his throne. To avoid the fulfillment of this prophecy, he poisoned his wife as she lay in labor."

My mouth gaped open in shock and disgust.

Menessos told us the sisters had known their mother died in childbirth, and that their little brother had died with her. When Liyliy learned what had truly happened, her rage drove her mad. She struck the old witch and searched the cupboards, meaning to steal the poison. The witch called her by name and the girl was deterred, aware their identities were known.

The witch told them she knew they were up to no good and she wanted no further guilt. The eldest sister lied and said the poison was truly to destroy vermin.

The witch was not sure if this was the truth, but she agreed to make them a poison with the warning there would be consequences if they lied.

"Truth became a part of them when they were Gifted," Menessos said. "For them to tell lies was like dripping poison on their own souls. But Liyliy lied repeatedly. She lied to cover their actions, to redirect suspicions, and to protect her sisters when they accidentally revealed too much. Every time, it cost her."

She again swore to the witch the poison would only be used on the vilest vermin, and she held her sisters' hands as the witch bound them to their words. The old woman promised the poison would be ready when the sun rose.

At dawn, they found a basket at the witch's door. Inside it was a small bottle filled with liquid. The cottage was empty and the witch was gone.

During the wedding feast, the sisters served their father and new husbands wine. Liyliy poured poison into her father's cup and her husband's cup. Her sisters each poisoned their husbands' wine. The king toasted his new sons-in-law, and all drank.

The sisters' lies came to fruition and the witch's curse descended. A black halo of mist surrounded the sisters as the men died, and by it they were changed. Their beauty was stolen, their bodies transformed. Screeching and terrible, much like the creatures that were later called harpies, they flew away.

"So you didn't get to claim them and teach them after all," Johnny pointed out.

"Things would be quite different if I had."

"They did it to themselves," I said.

Menessos added, "It gets worse."

There was a price for living with betrayal and vengeance, for doling out death and despair. Bound in magic and curses as they were, the tormenting of others became the outlet for their suffering. No longer was their touch a gentle purloining of information; it evolved into a painful kind of thievery. Those from whom they were taking truths were excruciatingly aware of what was being done. The sisters learned quickly how to make the pain last. That was when they became known as the shabbubitum.

They were not immortal, but somehow the combination of curse and magic gave them very long lives. Over the span of the centuries they also learned how to change between human and bird forms.

Eventually, during the Byzantine era, the sisters were employed by a powerful Greek vampire who found it entertaining to let them read her enemies. After a decade of loyal service—and more than a thousand years of countless lies to their victims—they were Made.

The vampire had no idea what she was Making. The latent power awakened with their Gifting was scarred by their curse. Their lies infused it with madness and instability that made them treacherous . . . and in undeath, their treachery would never cease.

After they "read" their Maker to death, Menessos was asked to intervene. He chose to anchor their spirits in three of the six caryatids of the famous porch of the Erechtheion on the Acropolis at Athens.

"Those marble maidens were as lovely as the sisters once were, but I chose them because I felt they would safely exist for as long as mankind." He paused. "At the time, a friend warned me that someday the shabbubitum would serve me comeuppance."

My thoughts centered on the pagan's Threefold Law: *What you do comes back to you in triplicate.*

"Congratulations," Johnny said, his tone a little too happy. "Someday has arrived."

CHAPTER SIXTEEN

Johnny listened to the story but heard only how the vamp was setting himself up to play the wounded hero. Persephone was eating it up, too. He was going to have to apologize or something to show her he was concerned about her, too.

Then Persephone yawned.

She had given Menessos what he needed: blood. She'd given Johnny what he needed: sex. In return, he'd pissed her off. Now what she needed was sleep, and it was obvious.

Johnny rose from his seat. "Those of us who have shit to do during the day tomorrow need to go to bed." He approached her, letting his genuine concern for her show. He reached up gently and massaged her shoulders. She exhaled contentedly, so he positioned himself behind her to massage more efficiently, all the while giving the vamp, who was still holding the hand that fed him, a pointed glare.

"Indeed," Menessos said, releasing her. "You must rest."

"What about you?" she asked.

"I will ponder my tactics until the dawn forces me to retire."

"But shouldn't we—"

"No," Johnny said with a squeeze.

"The two of you must kiss and make up, Persephone," Menessos said.

Johnny felt her shudder when the vamp said her name.

"I will plan for the safety of us all, then retire here. Go. Rest."

Persephone nodded in acquiescence. Johnny guided her away from the vamp, and the two of them headed up the stairs.

Menessos called, "You will go with me to the haven tomorrow, yes?"

Johnny ground his teeth.

"Yes," Persephone said.

Johnny didn't answer. The vamp wouldn't care if *he* accompanied them or not.

In the bedroom, Goliath lay reclined on Seph's bed, toying with the cell phone. Johnny glared at him. "Out."

Silent but wearing a broad smirk, Goliath complied.

Johnny shut and locked the door behind him, then wrapped his arms around Seph and nuzzled into her hair. The smell of her was so sweet that he couldn't help tasting the tip of her earlobe.

"I'm sorry," he whispered.

"Sorry we had words, or sorry that jealousy made you act like an asshole?"

"Both." She waited expectantly, as if he should expound on the subject, so he did. "There's a whole lot of shit going on that I can't control."

"The rest of us have that too."

"I know. I know." He sat on the edge of her bed. No one in the pack, male or female, would dare presume to make a decision that affected the pack without consulting him. *But Red's not pack.* That was part of the allure and part of the problem. He wanted a similar authority over her, yet he knew he'd never have it. "You got bent when

Menessos put that spell on us because he didn't get permission, but it let us talk telepathically, and that was kind of cool. Then you go and get rid of it without asking me." He gave himself a point for keeping his tone even, and went on. "I get it that you had reason, but you did the same thing he did, and even on top of all the current hubbub, I want you to let me be part of the decision-making process."

At the last, her face fell. She sat on the bed beside him. "I did a ritual with my mom and Nana. It didn't go like I'd planned, and the short version is I ended up in meditation and I discovered what Menessos had done, and I acted while it was there before me to be dealt with. The way it happened, I didn't have the option to ask you. *But.*" She bit her lip. "You remember what I told you about Michael LaCroix?"

The name caused a new pang of jealousy in his heart. "I remember he's your ex-boyfriend from college and our adevar's big brother."

"We broke up because I wanted to be kept in the loop of his business decisions. I didn't want to make his decisions, but he opened a whole second location without so much as a 'Hey, the business is doing well.' I knew we couldn't have a future like that." She touched his leg. "I want to have a future with you. I'll consult you as much as I can, but sometimes I have to make on-the-spot decisions. So do you. I trust you, Johnny, or you wouldn't be in my bedroom right now. Don't you trust me?"

That was a loaded question. There was no way to say anything except yes. He did trust her, but the vamp would use any opportunity he could to muscle his way between them. With his self-control wavering, he wasn't sure if all these doubts were all in his head or if they were based in some reality.

Clearly troubled by his hesitation, Seph seemed like she might cry.

Johnny put his arm around her shoulders and answered, "Yes. Yes, of course I trust you."

At 10:00 a.m., Johnny's cell phone rang. He scrabbled at the bedside table, came up with nothing and figured out it was still in the pocket of the jeans he'd dropped on the floor before crawling into bed. Leaning over the mattress edge, he snatched the bottom of one pant leg and dragged the denim close enough to dig into the pocket. "Hello?"

"You asleep?" Todd asked.

"Not anymore," he told the local pack's second-in-command.

"The Zvonul made their official announcement a few hours ago. CNN picked up the story for their around-the-world snippets, and ten minutes ago they flashed your picture and name full screen. Thought you should know the world has gotten a glimpse at the Domn Lup."

Johnny grunted in reply.

Todd hung up.

"Could you do the forced-change spell for the men today?"

Persephone blinked away sleep. "Huh? What happened to Monday?"

Johnny had just finished showering. He rubbed a towel over his head and said, "I checked, and the moon will be midsky about four o'clock today. If you and the men go to the roof of the den, you could do the spell and be done before Menessos even rises. And the den is closer to the haven than here."

"Menessos said he wanted us to go to the haven together."

"No, he said he wanted *you* to go with him. Personally, I think you'd be better off to stay the hell away from the haven and the shabbubitum."

"You know I can't do that."

He knew he couldn't talk her out of it, but he had to try. "It's not safe. They're going to blame you no matter what."

"Menessos said he'd have a plan."

"I don't trust him."

"I do."

Of course she did.

"Those harpy things are coming tonight," she argued. "I need to get ready for them."

"What are you planning to do?"

"I left most of my supplies in Pittsburgh. I thought I'd run to Wolfsbane and Absinthe to restock, charge up my charms and maybe work up a potion, in case I need it tonight."

"But *Menessos* will have a plan."

She frowned at him.

"Look, you were going to do magic anyway. This is just one more thing."

She sat up, irritated. "You don't know what you're saying. The forced-change spell isn't easy or brief."

"What else would you really do? Sit around and be nervous, worrying about what might happen tonight? Why not stay busy with this?" he added. "For me."

Before him, Seph lay back. She stretched and yawned.

When the covers shifted, he pictured her naked body writhing beneath them, despite knowing she wore her shirt and undies. Desire warmed his skin like the summer sun. "Please, Red?"

She groaned. "Fine. Let's plan to start the spell at three thirty."

He jerked the covers up and kissed her ankle.

"I'll need supplies," she said. "What time do you think Beau opens Wolfsbane and Absinthe?"

Johnny lifted his phone from the bedside table. "I can find out." A few clicks later, he announced, "Noon."

"What time is it now?"

"Ten thirty."

"I'm up." She threw back the covers.

Her scent flooded his nostrils as the air of the room swirled. She was lean but curvy. She had the indication of muscle without the ripped physique of a gym-rat. It was utterly feminine, but minus any weakness the term could sometimes imply.

Having selected clothes from her closet, she headed across the hall to the bathroom.

When Johnny heard the shower switch on, he couldn't get the image of her sudsy naked body out of his mind. Unable to restrain himself, he knocked on the bathroom door and opened it before she could answer. "May I join you?" he asked.

She peered around the shower curtain at him, rubbing shampoo into her hair. "You're already showered and clean."

He unzipped his pants and lowered them enough for his erection to show. "What if I want to get dirty again?"

Persephone sized him up. "No biting?"

"No biting." *I can do this.*

"Mmmm. Well. You'd better get in here, dirty boy," she said in a sultry voice.

The water was hot and the smell of her lavender shampoo was strong as he tugged the curtain into place. Persephone had her back to him and was lathering her hair. She giggled nervously when his fingers strayed under her shoulder blades, but when he began massaging her scalp, she braced against the wall and let her head fall back.

The vibration in his fingertips was definitely milder with her than it was with the pack women, but it remained an aphrodisiac. His dick couldn't get any harder. He pressed his swollen groin right against her backside. She rubbed against him.

As he worked the cleanser through her long, dark hair, his attention caught on a group of bubbles that cascaded seductively down her spine and slid over her hips to his cock. Then Persephone pulled her hair from his grip, turned around, and backed into the shower spray.

Her expression was intent, mouth slightly open, as she rinsed the shampoo out. He was mesmerized by her, by the water dripping from her nipples. He ached to feel that carnal resonance again. He cupped her breasts.

She *mmmm*ed and arched her back. Though the shampoo was gone, she stayed under the spray, arms lifted and hands buried in her wet hair, her body undulating at his touch.

Yearning made him pull her from under the spray and crush her body against his. She responded by hitching one leg onto his hip. He held her there. He didn't kiss her, didn't do anything but stare into her eyes and feel the water sluicing over them, feel the erogenous purring created by their entwined bodies.

Desire engulfed him. Need consumed him.

"Come up here," he said.

Persephone's arms slithered behind his neck and she pulled herself up, legs wrapping around him and ankles crossing at the small of his back. As she clung to him, he reached down and positioned his cock to enter her.

"You want this?" he whispered into her ear.

"God, yes."

On impulse, he asked, "How bad?"

He felt her straining to maintain the difficult position. Standing-up sex wasn't easy if he wasn't supporting her weight by cupping her ass—and just now he wasn't. "Very bad," she said. There was a lack of conviction in the words.

He was aware that he'd scared her before. He'd seen her hesitation at his joining her here now. He had to prove to himself that he could maintain control, but he also needed her to tell him she wanted it. He needed to hear absolution in the wantonness of her voice. In barely more than a whisper, he pleaded, "Tell me."

Persephone hauled herself up higher and drew her arms tighter around him. This brought her mouth close to his ear. "I want you," she said.

He let the tip slip inside of her. "Louder."

"Yes." He heard her panting at his ear. He felt her arms trembling with the effort of holding herself up. "I want you."

He pushed his cock into her and she immediately writhed on him. He withdrew and demanded, "Mean it."

Persephone ordered, "Fuck me."

He rammed the full length of his cock into her. For all the tenacity of her command, when he gave her that thrust, her squeal and reverent sigh were the telltale signs of a satisfied craving.

He said, "The rest of the day, you're gonna know I did."

CHAPTER SEVENTEEN

Delightfully sore as promised, I stood in the kitchen making breakfast. I wore Johnny's shirt and my cotton undies; he wore only his jeans.

Just as my finger hit the button that set the coffeepot to brewing, Zhan walked into the kitchen with an envelope. My name was beautifully scripted on it. That meant this was from Menessos. "I better get some caffeine in me before I read that." I set it aside and gathered some mugs from the cabinet.

Minutes later, as the bacon Johnny was in charge of was sizzling, I carried the envelope to the dinette table, sat on the bench, and opened it.

> *My Dearest Persephone,*
>
> *Goliath has returned to the haven. You know where I am.*
>
> *I have increased the number of guards around you and your home. By the time you read this another Offerling sentinel will have arrived along with six Beholders who will maintain your perimeter. If you have not already done so, you should fortify your magical protections from the ley line.*
>
> *Even as you read this, I am negotiating for aid.*
>
> *—M*

That didn't make sense because presently he was dead. I put it back into the envelope.

"Did the vamp impart any pearls of wisdom?" Johnny asked from the stove. He fed Ares a slice of bacon.

Appreciation of his physique delayed my answer. *How can anyone eat bacon and still have defined muscles like that?* "He's sending another bodyguard and more perimeter guards. He has an idea for getting help, but he wasn't clear about whose help."

"Of course not." He flipped over the slices in the pan. "When will the horde arrive?"

"They are already here," Zhan answered for me. "The perimeter guards are set up and in position."

I leaned over the table to peer out the window.

"They're camouflaged," she said, pouring a cup of coffee. "You won't see them."

"What about the other sentinel?"

"Waiting in the car out front." She joined me at the table. "Ares wouldn't be quiet about someone new in the house, and I didn't want to wake you."

I smiled. "Thank you." Her consideration was remarkable. Well, to me it was, perhaps not so much to the sentinel stuck in the car. "Who did he send?"

"Ivanka Chernov."

The plainness of her voice was atypical. "And?"

Zhan sipped her coffee. "And what?"

"What's her story? Do you think she's a good choice?"

"She came to this country as a Russian mail-order bride. Her husband had a heart attack and died a month after the wedding. Nine months later she signed on with Menessos. That was almost six months ago. I think. Since then, she's been well trained and is *very* disciplined."

"That's a very tidy description." I smirked. "Now say what you honestly mean."

"She's scary dangerous and overbearingly stern."

"Stern?" I asked.

"She sees everything in terms of her rank, above this one, under that one, and is eager to climb up the status ladder. She's smart, but her strict adherence to the rules and regulations keeps her from seeing the bigger picture. So, she's unlikely to accommodate your 'unusual' requests unless you pull rank. And her English is pretty basic."

"She's been here over a year. Won't speaking English help her make rank?" Johnny asked.

"Yes, but she's not much of a conversationalist, so mastering the language hasn't exactly been her priority."

Johnny put down the spatula. "What has been?"

His authoritative tone stunned me. Zhan hadn't missed it either. "When you see her, you'll know."

I could feel heaviness fill the room, and the weighted silence made it hard to breathe. "Does she like bacon?" I quipped. "This could be a good time to bring her in."

Zhan opened her mouth and shut it again without answering, then left.

To avoid the pup going into a sniffing and snarling conniption, Johnny coaxed Ares into the garage with another slice of bacon. "I have to give Zhan credit," he said, putting a plate with eggs and bacon in front of me. "She's more than a pretty thug."

"Minimum IQ for an Offerling *is* two standard deviations above average."

"Intellect doesn't always mean someone is perceptive. Or adaptable."

I picked up my fork and teased, "Is the Domn Lup saying he trusts a certain Offerling?"

He brought his plate and sat across from me. "Do you remember the exchange she and Kirk had at your mother's right before the pack had to leave because of the spell?"

"Yeah. Kirk charged her with your safety. And she accepted it." It wasn't quite *that* simple, but it was an adequate summation.

"Zhan hit it on the nose when she pegged this Russian chick as a by-the-book, rank-and-rule-abiding Offerling."

"You make it sound like rule abiding is a bad thing."

"It can be. It sounds like she's a . . . a . . . drone, Red. That kind of sentinel will protect you and die for you, period. But a sentinel who can think independently, who can understand the master's bigger goal and bend the rules to be a team player in support of that goal, that's a rarer person, a rarer kind of loyalty."

A bite was ready on the fork, but I didn't eat it.

"You need to know who you're dealing with and what you can expect of them. In no uncertain terms, Zhan just told you." He shrugged. "If you expect rigid adherence to rules, you won't make a fine-line request that bites you in the ass."

We locked gazes for a moment, but when the front door opened, we both ate. Still, I watched Johnny. A few months ago, he would have been flirting shamelessly with me the whole time we were alone. Now, he was telling me how to lead people. I was proud of him, glad for his shared insight, but I was also sad for the loss of our carefree days.

A tall woman appeared in the doorway. She had short,

spiky black hair and a beautiful oval face that didn't have a brush of makeup on it. Because Zhan usually wore business casual, I had expected something similar of the new sentinel. I couldn't have been more wrong.

Ivanka wore a khaki green T-shirt and military fatigues. Add combat boots and a handgun on each hip, and the zero-percent-body-fat military bodyguard ensemble was complete. Her muscular shoulders and bulging arms dominated her appearance. She had a single backpack and a stuffed GNC bag.

It was shitty of me, but I couldn't help wondering if she'd ever been part of some Russian super-soldier experiment.

"Erus Veneficus Persephone Alcmedi, this is Ivanka Chernov. Ivanka, this is your E.V."

Ivanka set her bags on the floor, lowered herself to one knee and bowed her head. Then she stood and mimed shooting a gun. "I have ninety-eight-point-four percent accuracy with revolver." Her accent was thick. "I have black belt and run mile in three minutes, forty-two seconds."

"That's all very impressive, Ivanka."

She pointed at the nutrition store bag. "I fix own meals and clean up. I sleep little, talk less. All I ask is three personal hours every day for strength training. This work for you?"

"Yes. You'll do just fine."

After Zhan ushered Ares out to Mountain's trailer, Ivanka drove us downtown in my Avalon. She remained in the parked car.

Once we were on the sidewalk and headed for the

Cleveland Arcade, Zhan casually inquired, "May I ask you something personal?"

"Sure."

"Is Johnny okay?"

"Yeah, why?"

"He seems . . . different since Pittsburgh."

I didn't know what to say. He *was* different. Responsibility changed people, or at least when they accepted that burden onto their shoulders it did. And Johnny had accepted a burden much heavier than most. Not only had he just been confirmed as the Domn Lup— meaning he would have to step into a global spotlight— but he also had access to all the power formerly bound in his tattoos. That wasn't something I wanted to point out to Zhan, though. Saying he seemed edgy or unlike himself would imply that he was having trouble dealing with it all.

I couldn't do him that disservice.

Yet Zhan was just being my friend. After the commanding vibe Johnny had exuded in the kitchen this morning, any good friend would say something. Celia would have mentioned it sooner than this had she witnessed it.

But Zhan had shown she was willing to bend the rules. If I treated her like a confidante, like a good friend, that would put her in more danger. Not that I thought she would disclose girl-talk to her master, but if Mr. Manipulative wanted "the dirt," she could be a source of it.

Ability to see the bigger goal or not, her first and foremost loyalty isn't to me or Johnny. She serves the vampire.

We arrived at the Arcade before I had decided on an answer. Zhan hurried ahead of me to open the door. "I'm sorry, she said. "It's not my place to ask things like that. I shouldn't have."

I halted in the doorway. "Zhan, I'm grateful that you care. Answers are just sometimes hard to give these days."

"Answer or no answer, milady, don't let a beast dominate the Lustrata."

That she addressed me by my larger title, not as E.V., didn't evade my notice. Neither did the fact that she'd obviously heard us in the shower. *Darn paper-thin walls.* Warmth flooded my cheeks. I entered the Arcade.

The witch supply shop was located just inside the grand, glass-topped mall. According to the faded black and gold letters underneath the name—and the clock on my satellite phone—it should have opened five minutes ago.

I scanned around and saw no one in the balconies. The Arcade was not the shopping powerhouse it had been a few decades ago. All the warm bodies that were present were milling around in the lower-level food court.

Among them, a short man clutched a lidded coffee in one hand and a *Plain Dealer* in the other as he trudged up the stairs. His long gray beard and curled moustache identified him as much as the Ivy driver's cap of brushed twill and the bulky gray cardigan he wore over a beige button-down shirt. He'd teamed it all with khaki pants and loafers.

Maurice. Beau's hired help.

He neared the summit, and I saw the blurriness created by the hefty prescription in the wire-rimmed glasses that perched on his round nose. The crack in the left lens that I'd noticed when we'd first met was still there.

When behind the store's counter, he had the "mystical

wizard" act down pat, but he was a total fake. Anyone who had real power could tell. I didn't exactly like Maurice, but Beau was clever to have him here. It was a means to identify the clientele and gauge who should and shouldn't get to purchase items that would be dangerous to mundane humans.

Additionally, since Beau was Bindspoken, he couldn't personally touch the merchandise without causing himself physical pain.

Maurice was pretty close before he noticed us waiting by the door. He paused a few paces away. "I remember you," he said to me. "But I don't know your name."

"Hi, Maurice. I'm Persephone."

"Yes, yes. Are you here for the priapean wands?"

"No. Just some supplies. What is a *pre-a-pee-an* wand?"

He chattered a laugh and shoved his newspaper under his arm so he could dig the keys from his pocket. "I'll show you." Zhan and I parted so he could access the lock. A brass bell chimed as the door swung open, and he flipped on some lights. We followed him in. Aromas mingled, pungent incenses and spicy oils mixed with the earthiness of dried leaves and flowers, all merged with scented candles and old books to form a smell that only another witch shop could produce.

The wooden floor creaked under our feet as Zhan and I followed him past racks of pagan-oriented T-shirts and around displays of brooms and cauldrons toward the bins with loose gemstones and the display cases with wands and crystal balls.

Maurice rounded behind the counter and we waited on the customer side of it while he plodded into the back and engaged the rest of the store's lights. He brought something wrapped in tissue paper with him. "These just came in." He laid the item on the counter. "I tell you, they're going to be all the rage."

He whisked back the tissue paper, and it took me several seconds to accept what the old man had laid before us. It was a wand, sure enough. It had a six-inch wooden shaft, ending with a crystal tip secured by a metal band. The thick handle, though . . . it was a good ten inches of supersized phallic replication.

I blinked. Repeatedly. "That's—um." I squinted at Maurice and struggled for the right words.

"It's solid jade," he said, tapping the detailed tip on the counter. "Don't you think it would enhance the Great Rite?"

"I . . . I think you're a dirty old man."

He winced and tugged at his beard.

The bell chimed behind us and Beauregard entered the store. He had buzzed white hair, bushy brows, and walked with a cane. Under his brown sheepskin-lined bomber jacket he wore a black-and-red plaid flannel. His trademark cigar was not absent. The scent of peach and tobacco wafted as he neared. "Hey, doll. To what do we owe the pleasure?"

"Supplies." I passed him the list I had written up on the way here.

He scanned it. "I've got all this." He pushed the paper at his employee and noticed the priapean wand on the counter. "Maurice!"

Maurice wadded the paper, mumbled, and ambled off to collect the items.

Beau jerked the cigar from his lips and blew the smoke, staring irritably after the short old man. He flipped the tissue paper to cover the wand. "I think I know what ritual you're doing," he said quietly.

"Oh?" I wasn't worried. Since being Bindspoken, he'd forged a friendship with the wærewolves of Cleveland. He was even a regular bartender at The Dirty Dog.

"This way." He put the cigar to his lips again and parted the curtains to the back room. A small office was off to one side, separate from the warehouse area. He pulled the string on the forty-watt overhead light. I sat in the folding chair while he removed his coat and draped it on the padded wooden seat. He set about unbuttoning his flannel shirt cuffs and rolling them up to reveal the white thermal underwear shirt he wore beneath. It was his trademark style.

This was the room where he'd given me the amulet that amplified my own power and befuddled other power, making it hard to hit me with magic.

He put the cigar on the ashtray—the glass ash receptacle was fashioned like a busty woman, and the cigar lay right between her breasts. "I'm calling in my favor," he said.

In exchange for the amulet, I'd promised to come back before the full moon and hear what favor he would ask of me. I owed him. The amulet *had* saved my life, but I already had enough on my plate today. Steadying my voice I said, "Okay."

"I want you to include my son in your forced-change spell."

That wasn't an add-on to the to-do list, just an inclusion to the task already on it. *Whew.* "Sure. I didn't know you had a son. Does he live nearby? I'm supposed to do this spell at the den this afternoon."

"He'll be there." Beau puffed on the cigar, held it out as he blew smoke at the ceiling. The peach aroma was nice. "I haven't seen his face in"—he calculated—"twenty years."

My brows knit. "I don't understand." If they were on the outs with each other, Beau couldn't assume his son wanted this, and if his son didn't want this, then I certainly couldn't include him in the spell. That was a rule.

Then I noticed he was shaking. "Beau?"

"He's been half-formed for two decades."

My mouth dropped open. I'd seen the cages where the pack kept half-formed wæres. To my knowledge, there were three of them in the top of the den. "Oh. I'm so sorry."

"You didn't do it to him, doll. All I ask is that you try to undo it."

"I've never tried this on a wære who was trapped in a half-formed state. I can't guarantee—"

"Look, doll. In theory, his present state doesn't make any difference. You just stir up enough energy to kick-start the shifting process and maintain it for a full transformation. It works for the others, it should work for him."

That was true, but I would still have to give this a little more thought and consider how it might affect the spell. I had time, but it meant no potion. Not that I had an inkling of what potion I'd have tried to brew this afternoon anyway. "I'll do the best I can."

"What time?" he asked.

"At three thirty."

"I'll be there."

Maurice's voice rose from the front room. "You want me to ring up these items now?"

I nodded at Beau, but he shouted back, "No!"

"Beau—" I protested.

"You're going to bring my boy back." He stood. "It's the least I can do to give you the supplies."

"I'll wear the charm you gave me for an extra boost."

He winked. "Atta girl."

Out front, Beau told Maurice to bag the items. Without question, he began.

I roamed over to Zhan, who had found the essential oils and was sniffing deep of the scent of some small bottle. "Smell this."

"What is it?" I leaned into the bottle and sniffed. It was all vanilla, but sweeter, like it had been caramelized with maybe brown sugar. "Wow."

"I'm buying this." She carried it to the register. I followed; Maurice was almost done.

Zhan held the little bottle out, and Beau quickly handed it to Maurice. "That too," he said.

Zhan protested. "I'll pay for that."

"Not today," Beau said firmly.

I thanked Beau again. He rolled the paper top down and gave it to me, quietly saying, "Don't be nervous. You're the Lustrata."

CHAPTER EIGHTEEN

We weren't too far from home when I called my best friend since college, Celia. She was caring for my foster daughter, Beverley, while I attended my mother in Pittsburgh. After perfunctory greetings, a brief catch-up on what Beverley was doing in school, and my reiteration of how much I appreciated Celia stepping in and stepping up so the kiddo could keep her schedule mostly normal, I spilled the reason for my call. "I wanted you to know I'm back a few days early, but that Beverley should continue to stay with you until next week like we'd planned."

"What's happening now?" she asked drily.

"Menessos. Johnny. Lustrata stuff."

"The usual."

"Yeah."

"I have no problem with her staying. We've been working on the science project and I'd like to finish it with her anyway."

In the background I heard, "That's Seph? Can I talk to her?"

"Is that Beverley?" I checked the clock; it was only one fifteen. School wasn't out yet.

"Yes." Celia was quiet.

"And?"

"I wanted to hear what was up with you before telling you this. I picked her up from school today. She, uh . . ."

I heard Beverley say, "Let me tell her, please, please?"

"I'll let her tell you. But don't freak out, okay? Everything's fine."

That was a terrible thing to say. I was freaking out.

There was a rustling static, then Beverley's voice filled my ear. "Hi, Seph! Guess what?"

"What?"

"I fell off the merry-go-round and broke my arm! At the emergency room they let me see the X-ray and everything."

"Oh my gosh! You have a cast?"

"Yeah. You'll sign it, won't you?"

She sounded like it was no big deal. I relaxed some. "Sure. Does it hurt?"

"Yeah, but they gave me some medicine for that."

I spent a few minutes listening as she told me how that morning the whole class had aced their spelling test so the teacher gave them an extra fifteen-minute recess and then Bobby, the boy in her class who she had a crush on, got the merry-go-round going faster than ever before and she got so dizzy she thought she was going to throw up and when she tried to get off so she didn't "get yucky stuff on the other kids," she fell.

Finally she gave the phone back to Celia. "Is it bad?" I asked.

"No. It's actually just a crack, but technically still a fracture." She snorted into the phone and added in a whisper, "The worst of it is her mouth is running like a race car."

Relief washed over me and I fully relaxed into my seat, aware only then of how rigid I'd become. "The school called you?"

"Yeah. They couldn't get an answer on your house

phone. I'm listed as your backup. The bones weren't displaced or anything, but they knew she was hurt by the amount of pain she was having. They said she needed to be checked out, so I took her. The hospital accepted that temporary guardian form you left. They asked about insurance but happily accepted the credit card you gave me for emergencies—guess this really was one."

"I'm so sorry you had to deal with it. Did you have to cancel client appointments?" Celia was a Realtor. The market wasn't doing so well lately, so I hoped this hadn't cost her a sale or anything.

"Oh, no! Not at all. It got me out of phone duty at the office."

In the background I heard Beverley say, "I'm hungry."

An idea hit me. "Hey, why don't you two meet me at the house. I'll fix lunch. I'd like to see her for a little while—and you, of course." I didn't have time for it, but I'd make time. I wanted to see Beverley.

"Is that okay? No danger?"

"The danger isn't supposed to roll in until tonight." What if something happened to me? Who would Beverley go to? I was her legal guardian, but I hadn't adopted her. She'd go into the system . . . though I was sure Celia and Erik would step up, I should talk to them about it. *Another detail to fret over.*

"Good to know," Celia said. "We'll be there in twenty minutes, okay?"

"Perfect." I hung up and told Ivanka, "Pull in at the gas station ahead." I hadn't been home in about a week and hadn't meant to be gone this long. Any bread that remained at the house wouldn't be good for sandwiches now.

• • •

Celia and Beverley arrived just as we did.

I saw no sign of the perimeter guards, so they were still camouflaged well. The sentinels also made themselves scarce, and my friend and I set about making sandwiches while Beverley sat at the table with her vocabulary book out. Celia had suggested she do a little homework so she didn't get behind. I knew it was an attempt to keep the motormouth to a minimum.

Dressed as impeccably fashionably as always, Celia tucked her blond hair behind her ears and rolled up her cashmere sleeves, then opened the bread. "I know Theo helped you find the tattoo parlor owned by your mother, and what happened after you arrived in Pittsburgh, but how did you know to hunt for 'Arcanum'?" She dropped two slices into the toaster.

"Great El's slate."

"That Ouija board type thing in your closet?"

"Yeah." I dropped the bologna into the frying pan, where it sizzled and a delicious aroma wafted up.

"Oh, how the mighty have fallen," Celia said, crossing her arms and leaning on the counter.

"What?"

"Former vegetarian eating fried bologna."

I shrugged. "It's good."

Celia gave me a sly, sidelong glance. "Talking to ghosts on that slate led you to your mother. And a half brother you didn't know existed. Ever think of searching for your father?"

It wasn't exactly ghosts, so I skipped that part and addressed the question. "Like I don't have enough going on already?" She didn't even know the half of it.

"Yeah, what am I thinking? You never take on more than you can manage."

"Just so you know, when I used the slate, I focused it through Johnny. I wasn't after a personal goal. I was after *his* goal, so I had some distance." I flipped the bologna over. "With my father, all I have are my feelings about who I'd like him to be. My lack of objectivity would muddy up the magic, maybe even seek someone who fit the bill of what I wanted him to be and not actually find him. I do have some more photos now."

Celia was adding mayonnaise to the toast. "Wouldn't an image be enough?"

"It would be stronger with at least one concrete fact to link it with."

"Your mom has to remember his name."

Under the Father section of my birth certificate was typed UNKNOWN in all capitals to make it glaringly evident I was an illegitimate child. That wasn't a question I intended to ask Eris. She was already so possessive of me that if she thought she might have to share, she'd "forget" his name anyway.

From my dining room desk I retrieved the photo album Lance had so rudely provided. I opened it as I returned to the kitchen. In the first clear sleeve was a copy of the picture I already had of my father, only in this one, the side with my mother hadn't been ripped off. She looked so young. . . .

My father's Egyptian heritage was evident in his dark skin, black hair, and bright brown eyes. Sometimes I thought that was a happy gleam; other times I thought it was mysterious, dangerous. He had high cheekbones, and the elevated tilt of his chin suggested cultured sophistication. It was an enigma, his expression—about to erupt in joyous laughter or tumble into fury. I rubbed my finger over the amulet of Anubis he wore.

"I don't know if I'm ready to find him. Here." I offered the little book to Celia. "Little brother gave me this."

Celia put the knife down, dropped more bread in the toaster, then took the book.

I plucked the toast away from her and put the bologna onto it, cut it in half and delivered the sandwich to Beverley, who promptly put her schoolbook away.

After assembling the last sandwich, I poured us all some milk and moved everything—including a black marker—to the dinette. "May I?" I asked the kiddo.

She grinned and pushed the purple cast toward me. I signed *Seph* on it and drew a stick-figure unicorn.

"Awesome!" Beverley drank, intent on the barns. I knew she was hoping for a glimpse of Errol, a young unicorn she'd had the privilege of riding a few times.

It set me at ease to know that she was more concerned about seeing him than about the thick purple cast wrapped around her little arm.

My satellite phone rang. I jerked it from my pocket. The screen showed the call was from Nana. "Hello?"

"Johnny's picture is plastered on every news channel."

"Yeah. The new Rege confirmed him last night."

"Is that why you left?"

"No, I didn't know about that until I arrived."

"They say there will be a press conference at three o'clock tomorrow at the Cleveland Trust Bank."

"That's news to me."

"Well, that prissy reporter just announced it."

"I believe you, Nana. I just didn't know."

Beverley spun from the window. "That's Demeter? Lemme tell her about my arm!"

I passed the phone to the kiddo. While Beverley recounted her tale, I brushed bread crumbs from the counter into a paper towel, then threw it away. I put the mayo in the refrigerator and switched the bread to the other end of the counter.

Beverley shifted the satellite phone into the crook of her neck and examined her purple cast, running her fingers over my name as she told Nana that I'd drawn a little unicorn for her. Then Beverley's words tapered off midsentence. She lowered her cast. "Hold on, Demeter." She put the phone to her chest and twisted toward me. "Who's that?" she asked, pointing out the window.

I checked, expecting to see one of the perimeter guards on patrol. What I saw was a thin figure that had just emerged from the cornfield. The person was wearing a long black robe and the hood was up, hiding his or her features.

"Zhan!"

Ivanka appeared in the doorway. "Zhan showering. How may I serve?"

"Are the perimeter guards wearing black cloaks?"

"No. Camouflage."

"Then who's that?" I pointed.

Inspecting, Ivanka checked outside the window. "Hide yourselves," she said and then raced through the house, galloping up the staircase.

Hijacking the phone from Beverley, I said quickly, "Call you back soon, Nana. Bye." I ended the call and immediately hit the direct dial number for Mountain before grasping Beverley by her unbroken arm. "C'mon."

Celia was peering out the window. "I thought you said the bad guys wouldn't get here until tonight?"

"That's what I was told."

"What do we do?"

"You get to your car and get yourself and Beverley out of here." I checked again and the figure had traveled only a few deliberate paces into my yard. *Slow is good.*

Celia snatched her purse. I pulled Beverley from the seat; she dragged her book bag with her. "You gotta move fast, kiddo. Like in a fire drill." I led her toward the front door, where I yanked her coat off the peg and carried it with us rather than pause to have her put it on.

"What about you?" Beverley cried.

Mountain finally answered his phone. "What's up?"

"Someone's in the backyard," I said, hating the panic in my voice. "The perimeter guards don't appear to be doing anything about it."

"On my way."

I hung up. "I can take care of this, but you need to go," I said, wanting both Beverley and Celia to believe me. "You have to be safe." I hugged Beverley quickly and shuffled out the door with her. I saw them to the CX-7, made sure no one was hiding inside and hurried back to the porch. Celia's tires threw gravel as she backed out of the driveway.

A hand grabbed my shoulder and hauled me into the house. "Stay shielded," Ivanka scolded. The engine roared as the CX-7 rocketed up the road. I twisted out of the sentinel's viselike grip and ran for the kitchen, noting that Zhan was descending the stairs with wet hair.

The robed figure was about two-thirds of the way up my yard now. Bad thing was, whoever it was had decided to go around the west side of the house—increasing the distance Mountain would have to travel to intercept.

Then it hit me: The doors to the cellar were on the west side. The only way to get to Menessos's secret hiding spot was through the cellar.

Mine to protect.

Though Mountain was on his way, for all the brute size he possessed, running was not an option for him.

Because there was no window in the pantry, I had no view of the cellar entrance from inside the house. I scurried through Nana's new bedroom to the bath we'd added and climbed onto her sink, peering out the transom window that capped her mirror. I still wasn't able to see the metal door.

But I might be able to see someone standing there opening it.

I pressed my nose to the glass.

Don't open the cellar doors. Don't be after Menessos.

The robed trespasser stepped into sight. Closer, I could see by the way the robe lay flat against the figure's chest that this person was male.

Not shabbubitum. Menessos specifically said they were sisters.

I scolded myself for having thought it might be one of the shabbubitum.

Menessos said they were vampires. They'd be dead now anyway.

The path the robed man chose led him around the house. Though relieved, I left the window and clambered into the tub. On tiptoe to see out the window, I hoped the guy wouldn't see me. As he rounded the corner, keeping close to the house, he idly stroked the wall where I stood.

I shuddered, feeling about as violated as I would have felt if he'd touched me. My fear shrank away and anger swelled to fill the void.

Pushing past Ivanka, I hurried through the bedroom and into the living room, my gait faltering as the intruder made his unhurried way past my picture window.

Zhan, her hair wet and dressed in a short silk bathrobe, was positioned between me and the door. Ivanka was occupying a spot right at the door, but out of sight. I stood there stupefied at how my heart was racing.

Maybe it's just some freak with a leftover Hallowe'en costume. No. Some simple freak with a costume wouldn't get past the perimeter guards.

Additionally, I had wards. Wards that would keep most people away from the house. Wards I'd been warned to amp up—advice I'd foolishly put off for Johnny's task and my impromptu lunch date.

A shadow fell across the glass of my door.

I held my breath.

And my doorbell rang.

CHAPTER NINETEEN

The customized Gulfstream V-SP carrying Meroveus Franciscus had departed from Ronald Reagan Washington National Airport roughly twelve hours ago. He had retired to the windowless "black chamber" within the plane and rested as they'd flown east and into the rising sun, hours before its light would actually reach D.C. However, with the rotation of the world and the fact that Athens was seven hours ahead anyway, he had risen before they'd touched down.

A customs official awaited him when he disembarked from the plane. By the time his credentials were assessed, a limousine was idling nearby, and the chauffeur opened the door for him. According to his Rolex, it was just nearing noon in D.C. Here, it was 6:55 p.m. Darkness was settling in.

The ride was not long, and the limousine used the entrance at Dionysiou Areopagitou Street, a road running along the southern slopes of the Acropolis. With winter hours in effect, the museum would have closed a few hours ago. However, special arrangements had been made.

Arrangements like the black velvet bag waiting for him on the limo's seat.

He stared at the pouch with antipathy. Not that he was averse to the contents within the soft fabric. It was just that he was truly against the magical action he was commanded to take. Such incongruity could make for a bad spell.

When the long car stopped, Meroveus didn't wait for the driver to get the door for him. He exited the vehicle carrying the bag and strode toward the building, surveying the ruins spotlighted against the deep blue of the Greek sky. Ahead, a railing surrounded an opening that overlooked one of the archaeological digs going on beneath the museum. It, too, was illuminated, even after hours.

A man in a suit held the museum door open. "Mr. Franciscus, I am Zevon. I will lead you where you wish to go." He locked the entry after Meroveus was inside. Zevon then guided him through the glass-floored gallery to a stairway. Once they had ascended, Zevon circled around. Here was where the new Acropolis Museum housed the artifacts from the Erechtheion. Zevon gestured toward the caryatids, then he bowed and promptly walked away.

Here were five of the six caryatids, marble figures of women, which had once served as columns supporting the roof of the southern porch of the Erechtheion. Replicas now stood in their place at the site; the sixth was in the British Museum.

Legend had it the statues once protected the tomb of the ancient King Cecrops, the founder of Athens. Making a full circuit around them, in awe of their beauty, Meroveus whispered, "Shabbubitum." He remembered when Menessos had bound the sisters within. They had not gone willingly.

He also remembered telling Menessos the women would seek revenge someday. *I am not here to drink that anger for you, old friend.*

Meroveus took a moment to ground and center, to cast out his doubts and firmly set his mind to the task.

As per his request, there were three large, red apples— one placed at the base of the three most complete figures. He inspected each apple, twisting the stems to separate them from the fruit, and placed the stems in the pocket of his suit jacket.

"For centuries you have paid your mute tribute, honoring the glorious dead." He drew a red-handled knife from the velvet bag. He unsheathed the short blade and inspected the tip and edge. "And now, one of the living dead will call you forth."

Meroveus approached the first statue and sliced his index finger, letting his blood drip onto the apple's indention as he said the ceremonious words. *"Suscitatio vos ex vestry somnus diturnus. Advocare vestry phasmatis vestry somes quod vestry aeternus anima exorior universes."*

After repeating this for the remaining apples, he drew from the bag a golden necklace. The chain was made of large, irregular links, and Meroveus knew it could easily have been an artifact in this museum—it was that old. Except for the fastener, that is.

The necklace was decorated with three pieces of amber. These stones were a clear honey-gold, lightly flecked with brown. Each was as thick as a pencil, about two inches long, and bore a golden band, topped with a link that let it dangle from the necklace.

Meroveus unfastened the modern clasp and removed the gemstones. He dropped the necklace back into the bag and pulled out a square of wool. Tapping into the local ley line, under the true Acropolis, he felt the stinging, biting burn—it was as if he were shoving his fingers into a light socket. He gasped at the pain, fought the instinctive recoil, and gorged himself on the energy. As his body filled, power flowed through him to his aura, where each droplet rippled like a lover's moan, reverent and erotic.

Enjoying the sensation for three daring seconds, he impelled the power into the stones. He rubbed the first piece of amber on the wool, electrically charging the stone, then pushed the pointed end into the top of the apple, inserting half an inch where his blood had dripped.

"Electrum. Sanguinis illorum damnoris intereo sulum diluculum at revertere sulum nox notis. Mālum, Eden pernicies pomun. Effrego Veneficus Carmen quod solvo shabbubitum."

He could sense the power in the stones, ready to burst, ready to eject into the flesh of the fruit. The empowering fullness of energy was draining out of him, leaving weariness in its wake. Once all the apples were primed, he said, *"Modo."*

The temperature of the room began dropping. When it had reached that of an icy freezer, he heard the crack and rumble of stone shattering—yet the statues before him remained complete. Black haze lifted from the surface of each, surrounding them like dust being shaken off a long-dormant soul. Slowly, it coalesced until the miasma, hovering over the faces of the statues, created fluid expressions upon the unyielding surface. They were not conveying a pleasant awakening.

Six dark eyes narrowed into slits, three mouths sneered or frowned.

The murky shadows stretched forward, reaching with dark, ominous claws for Meroveus.

He placed the apple stems under his tongue and gathered the last of the energy he'd drawn from the

Acropolis ley line into his mouth. His incantation was power laden and flawlessly intoned as he informed them he was their master. *"Ego imperare, vestri victor. Vos mos concedere vel intereo."* After commanding them to concede or die, he crushed the stems between his molars and waited.

The specters hovered, claws aimed, but hesitant. *"Concedere!"*

In midair, the ghostly forms snapped like whips before being jerked into the apples.

Meroveus spit the stems into his palm, collected the fruit and knelt. From the velvet bag he reclaimed the necklace and a small leather pouch, with a flap that could snap shut. He set both the bag and the pouch aside. Careful to touch only the golden bands atop the stones, he freed each piece of amber and replaced them on the necklace. He scrutinized the gems; they were no longer translucent.

This variation on the Bindspeaking spell trapped a piece of each soul he released inside one of the stones. He didn't dare attach those pieces onto his own soul—that was tricky with a vampire at best—and he would not risk the tarnish of these wicked sisters tainting him. This gave him an access point to apply his punishment and kept him from having to physically touch the sisters. It was the best defense he could hope for. Though he would have shared this spell with Konstance if she could have saved him from having to perform it himself, it was not one he wanted others to know.

Preparing the small leather pouch, he felt the wool-lined interior, then slid the amber pendants within. He tucked the flap of the pouch over the chain and snapped it shut. The stones were now secure: hidden in the wool-lined leather, but still suspended from the necklace. He put the chain around his neck.

Holding the red-handled knife, he rolled each fruit to its side and cut it in half, then—without separating the top from the bottom—he set them aright with both pieces sitting as if uncut. This, if seen, would show that each apple's core created a natural five-pointed star. That and the severed seeds were symbolic here.

He raised the top from the middle apple and let the centermost of the three selected statues fill his sight. "I call you forth, Liyliy, shabbubitu, cursed daughter of Neriglissar. Damned bride of Belsarra-usurah."

Even as a dark vapor wafted up from the seeds, he lifted the top from the right-most apple. "I call you forth, Ailo, shabbubitu, cursed daughter of Neriglissar. Damned bride of Kurush." He repeated the gesture for the left-most apple's top. "I call you forth, Talto, shabbubitu, cursed daughter of Neriglissar. Damned bride of Ramesu."

Meroveus stood and retreated, putting distance between him and the black breath filling the space. A hand formed in the air and slender fingers stretched for the necklace he now wore, but Meroveus backed further away and hid the necklace under his shirt.

For long minutes, the energy of the ley steamed up from the apples and fed the specters, solidifying them in phases. When three enormous, ethereal owls stretched their wings, their hideous hag-faces squinted at him. They screeched, and the sound shattered the glass of a pair of display cases nearby.

Alarms sounded.

Then their bodies shuddered and thinned, becoming

nearly solid as they formed human shapes like the shabbubitum they had inhabited for centuries. But even as the flowing gowns of millennia past appeared, the fabric aged, growing tattered and gray, deteriorating like powder.

Three women stood before him, shoulder to shoulder. They were naked except for the fine, dark dust that used to clothe them. These women exuded erotic formidability. It dripped from the damp ebony curls of their hair and, trailing down their bodies, gathered that dust and created dark, wet lines that drew an onlooker's gaze away from the hatefulness stabbing outward from the depths of their black eyes.

In perfect unison, they took a slow, lissome step forward. Displaying feline agility, each shifted her weight to her forward foot and advanced again. Energy blew over Mero as the menace beneath the beauty sought a source of power and found it in the Acropolis ley line.

He touched his shirt where, beneath, lay the necklace. He was ready to jolt them, but what they drew from the line was minimal.

Sandals appeared on their feet, straps wrapping up their calves like adoring snakes. Dove gray silk materialized, rippling in a wind as it wrapped around their bodies to swathe them each in unique but elegant garments with teasingly placed patches of sheerness. Quicksilver poured impossibly up their arms, then hardened into jewelry adorning their wrists, necks. The likeness of owls formed repeatedly in the gleaming metal.

Meroveus stood imperiously as they arrived before him. "Liyliy."

She squinted in a manner both guarded and suspicious.

"*Vos es incompertus?*" Mistress of many ancient tongues, she questioned him in Latin, the language he had used in the spell to release the sisters.

"No," he said. "You do not know me." He kept his voice smooth, even. "*Venire.*" He pointed to his chest and said, "Meroveus." He walked away from them then, gesturing so they would follow. He led them down the stairs. At the bottom, Zevon was nervously shifting his weight and punching buttons on a control panel. The alarms were silenced. Zevon sighed in relief—at least until he saw the group descending the stairs.

He jogged to remain ahead of Meroveus and the women as they followed him toward the entrance.

When Zevon tried to unlock the door, he dropped the key. Meroveus and the others caught up to him. "I need your assistance, my English-speaking friend."

Zevon jumped. "Wh-what do you require? I was told I would give no blood."

"No blood," Meroveus assured him. "You need only allow these women to hold your hands."

Their young guide's attention bounced from Meroveus to the trio and back. "No harm to me? I have your word?"

Harm. Such a relative term. "You will suffer no physical injury. You will bear no visible marks. You will not be mentally damaged. Of this, you have my word."

"So specific." Zevon swallowed hard. "Tell me what I *will* suffer?"

"Pain," Mero said bluntly. "And ten thousand euros for your trouble."

Zevon stood straighter, adjusting his suit. After a difficult swallow, he held out his hands.

Meroveus motioned the trio closer to the guide. "*Percep-*

tum English lingua?" He then dialed the local VEIN embassy on his cell phone.

The women converged on Zevon. Two stroked his hair and fawned over him as Liyliy assumed her position. The sisters each wriggled a hand between his and Liyliy's palms, then laced their fingers behind his neck. Liyliy's dress slithered down her body to puddle at her feet. Zevon's sight was locked on the tips of her breasts, and he did not notice the gown reverting to mist. His mouth was open and he was panting hard . . . then the shabbubitum whispered a chant. Their voices rose, and with them, a mistlike tentacle slithered up Zevon's body and coiled around his neck.

The air crackled as their power thickened. Mero's phone burped static and he paced away to tell the assistant on the line to arrange a payment to poor Zevon. When Mero strode back, they had lowered Zevon to lie flat on the floor. He had begun to convulse. His body seized, and foam oozed from his open mouth.

The shabbubitum hovered over him; Liyliy sat on his chest. The notes they were singing ascended through octave after octave. When their voices had reached a pitch only dogs could hear, it was done. They laughed like delighted little girls.

Their guide's trembling eased. He blinked. He gasped.

Liyliy flicked the foamy drool from his chin. "Zevon," she whispered. "You are a sweet boy, untried, but with such a dirty mind." On all fours, her body assumed a position both sexual and predatory. "Oh, what I could do with you. To you." She kissed him, lightly, then rougher. In an instant she had heaved him upright by his head, squeezing him tightly to her. Zevon tried to shove her away.

Mero felt them tap the line again. This time, however, it was not a minimal touch but a seizing grasp, dark and barbed, with ravenous hunger. He brought the necklace out from under his shirt and clutched the amber-filled pouch, pouring his own power into the stones. "Liyliy!"

She released Zevon and spun on Mero. In an instant her smooth skin grew wrinkled, like crumpled paper, and—screeching—she attacked.

Pain stabbed through her body, but Liyliy leapt unfalteringly. Wings appeared behind her, lifted her into the air, then angled so she could descend and swing a foot—now a clenched talon—at this man's head. *Meroveus.* She recognized the liar. He'd been here when she and her sisters had been tricked, bound into stone. He had not been the one who'd performed the spell, but he had been part of the ruse. For that, he deserved her wrath.

Her strike connected with enough force to cast him into the air. As he was thrown backward, her head swelled to twice its size and her body transformed.

In landing, the man's ponytail was trapped beneath him. In skidding across the floor, his head was drawn back, thrusting his chin up and exposing his neck. The man's elbow smacked the floor hard enough that he released the pouch.

Liyliy pinned him with her talons around each of his biceps.

"We are hungry!" she snarled, thrusting her new owl-like beak toward his throat just as her skin prickled over with gooseflesh. On either side of her hooked nose, quill tips burst forth in large circles around her eyes, and from the deepest of her wrinkles black and gray feathers sprouted. The hair atop her head retracted into her scalp at the same time as a thick mass of feathers tore through her skin.

She felt torn apart, but his confounded expression was worth it. "We *will* sate our stomachs! On you if not him!"

Meroveus buried his fingers into the feathers upon her legs, and a surge of energy surrounded them as he channeled power to his hands and discharged it into her aching flesh.

Screeching pitifully, Liyliy beat her wings, wrenching away from him.

He grabbed the pouch around his neck once more, and as he stood, the sting of his wrath bit her again though he no longer touched her. Worse, her sisters cried out as well and fell, writhing on the floor.

Liyliy fought.

She flopped this way and that, talons skidding, wings flailing, trying to reach through the pain, to reach him and flay him with her claws, but with each attempt the pain redoubled, and her sisters' cries were like daggers in her ears.

"Release us!" they cried piteously.

Meroveus let go of the pouch and all the torment disappeared.

Liyliy thought to rip him limb from limb, but her exhausted body collapsed in a heap, and she screeched as her body reverted to its naked, human form. She didn't have the strength to even lift her head from the cold floor. She hated any weakness—and doubly so when it was her own flaw. Her sisters crawled to her and wrapped her in their arms, cooing to her.

"I did release you," Meroveus scolded them. He went to Zevon, who was still shaking. "He aided me! He gave you language! Is this the thanks we are to receive? Physical attacks?" With a steadying grip on Zevon's shoulder, he said, "They are not worthy of their freedom. Remain here. I will put them back."

"No!" Liyliy's sisters cried.

The man ignored them and reached to the pouch necklace. Turning, he walked toward the stairway.

"No, no," Ailo and Talto pleaded.

The words were foul to Liyliy's ears, and the tears on their cheeks were pollution. She would not cry. She would not beg. But she would not go back to the numb stone, either. She was smarter than that. She understood what men of power wanted. Her sisters needed her.

In a voice barely above a whisper, a voice brittle like cracked glass, Liyliy said, "You . . . you are our lord."

The haste of Meroveus's departure lapsed. He turned back, and the full measure of his suspicion was scrawled across the lines of his face. Liyliy's sisters had cradled her on the floor, but now she lifted her head. *The pouch on his necklace is the source of his dominance.* "We obey you," she said. "Just feed us."

His chin lifted. "Do you think I have not planned for your hungers?"

"You did not say as much!"

"I had to give you language first. You gave me no chance. Reckless impulsiveness is not a quality I will tolerate. I believe it is that kind of behavior that led to your confinement." He cursed quietly in the old language she would understand. "Now I cannot trust you."

"What oath will satisfy you, lord?"

Mero considered it. "Swear upon your sisters' heads that you will be obedient, Liyliy."

She hesitated for a second, knowing that responding too quickly or too slowly would send a message she did not wish to convey. "I swear upon my sisters' heads I will obey you, lord."

Seemingly satisfied, he nodded. "Clothe yourself, Liyliy."

From nothing, the gray silk writhed up and around her once more. And her scheming commenced.

CHAPTER TWENTY

It occurred to me that ringing a doorbell wasn't exactly an action I'd expect of a violent trespasser—but it could be an indication of a more despicable kind of intruder. Whoever this man was, he'd circumnavigated the wards, and I didn't want him in my house. *Wait. He did more than just get past my protections—I hadn't felt the alarm of anything triggering the wards at all.*

I strode toward the door, reaching for the knob.

"Milady!" Ivanka put a restraining hand on my arm. "Let me."

Zhan snorted and tucked her wet hair behind her ears. "Maxine and I tried that when we first arrived. The E.V. is adamant about answering her own door."

Ivanka fixed me with her "intimidating" stare. "Bad idea."

The reward for her effort was seeing my "firmly resolved" stare. "Let go."

The command made her withdraw. As I opened the door, a blast of cold air hit me like a frozen slap. My heart was pounding, and I was grateful for the separation of even a flimsy screen door between myself and this mysterious man. I said nothing.

Before me, long and pale fingers rose slowly to lower the hood of the robe.

His raven hair was worn in a non-styled manner, simply combed straight back over his head, where it hung almost to his shoulders. Add to that a trim beard, and all that darkness steered my focus to his blue eyes, his slightly sunken cheeks and a mouth that seemed a fraction too wide.

At first, I thought him bony and underweight, but as my consideration lingered, it occurred to me that he did not emit the forlorn and pitiful hunger of the emaciated. What he did radiate . . . I couldn't put my finger on. Even so—and regardless of the fact that he was dressed for a long-gone era—I found him attractive.

"Persephone," he whispered.

Granted, when most people go to someone's house, they know whose door they're knocking on. I hated being at a disadvantage with people on my porch, but that was something I was learning to accept. A lot of people recognized me since I'd been on TV. "Who are you?"

Palms out in a benign gesture, he said, "Call me any name you find worthy of me."

I blinked. "Okay. Henceforth you shall be known as Creepy."

His only response to my sarcasm was the corner of his mouth crooking up.

Mountain arrived and assumed an intimidating pose one step from the porch.

"Why are you here?" I asked Creepy.

"A friend told me you might be in danger. I am here to provide protection."

Peripherally, I noticed Zoltan, a young dragon, slithering silently along Mountain's path. "What friend?"

"Menessos."

It surprised me so much that I winced.

Mountain crossed his arms over his broad chest as he

spoke. "He's not someone most people want to claim to know, let alone be friends with lately." Zoltan slithered to Mountain's side and hissed. *So much for "surprising" strangers with our pet dragon. We need to work on our offensive tactics.*

Creepy perused the dragon without any of the astonishment I expected. In fact, he sounded convincingly bored as he answered, "I care little what people choose to think."

"Why were you in my cornfield?"

"The vortex was the easiest way to arrive."

He rode a ley line. Fairies rode ley lines, and if any fey remained here on earth, they couldn't get home because of my actions. Probably not something anyone left behind would be happy about. "Get off my porch."

At my words, the tension radiating from Zhan, Ivanka, and Mountain ratcheted up a notch.

He made no effort to vacate the porch. "Have I offended you, Persephone?" His voice was husky, but sounded sincere.

My perimeter wards were specifically set to keep fey out. If he was fey—even in part—he should have at least set the wards off. Pondering this, I had to admit that fairies didn't get as tall as this guy. Also, none of his features had the distinctive curves and points of fairies. He was all straight lines.

"If I have interrupted something, I assure you it was not my intention."

"What is your intention, then?" Going forward, I pushed on the screen door, confident it would force him backward, toward the edge of the porch.

He still didn't budge.

Just as I thought the door would smack into him, his crooked smile grew and the door slipped *through* him.

I gasped.

Before I could even form a thought about the possibilities of him being a ghost, the door swung back, but this time it did not pass through him.

"My intention . . ." He reached toward my cheek.

His hand hovered above my skin. Though the temperature outside wasn't much above freezing, I could feel the warmth radiating from this man and a fine trembling all around him. Then he touched me with the gentlest of caresses.

His countenance blossomed with wonder. "I can feel the storm within you. The burning blaze and the flood, too. You are so close . . . so very close."

Ivanka's big, silver gun slid into my view, business end about two inches from Creepy's nose. "Retreat," she snarled. "I ask only one time!"

Without looking at her, he said, "No."

Even as she fired, the screen door moved through him again. I backed away *and* sidestepped, nearly tripping over my own feet. I covered my ears too late, but I kept Creepy in my sight. The bullet zinged through his incorporeal form. He reached for Ivanka, ripping a giant hole in my screen as he solidified and grasped her wrist.

My ears were ringing from the gunshot, but I heard him growl, "I have stated that your master sent me, Offerling." He squeezed and jerked.

In my whole life I had not been so close to someone as their bones broke. The sound was as sickening as seeing her forearm bend in the middle.

Ivanka screamed and her knees buckled. She cracked

her head on the lower portion of the door, which was still partially open. He released her as she collapsed, smoothly stripping her of the gun. "The effrontery of your actions is unacceptable."

For all the horror of the last eight seconds, the sound of his calm, sad and melodic voice soothed my aching eardrums.

Creepy's gaze fell to the weapon in his hand.

Zhan and Mountain closed in.

He did not grip the gun as if he might threaten us with it, let alone fire it. His finger was nowhere near the trigger. I signaled the others to quell any rash actions.

Ivanka whimpered at my feet and spewed several angry phrases in Russian.

Holding the gun by the barrel, Creepy thrust it through the torn screen and offered it to me. "I have no need of this device. Since you carry no weapon, I assume you will show more discretion with this."

I didn't need to be told twice. Keeping my eyes on Creepy, I fumbled the weapon into my grip. It was heavier than I expected, and I clicked the safety on and aimed it at the floor. "Did Menessos mention who I might be in danger from?"

"Strangers," he whispered. "I will not let any harm come to you."

The stalker possessiveness in his tone sent a twinge of fear through me. My fingers yearned to tighten around the handle of the gun, but I'd just seen how ineffective it was. "And what if it's my opinion that *you* are harming me?"

His expression became one of wounded disappointment. "I would never." It was a whisper, but it sounded like a vow to my stalker-cautious ears.

Since he was going for heavy, I kept my tone light instead of accusatory. "You just broke my sentinel's arm. That damages my security, and I consider that personal harm. And you busted up my door."

"She provoked me by firing. As for the door . . ." He scanned the screen up and down, and the wires began knitting together.

My jaw dropped. I poked at the mesh. This wasn't an illusion. It was tangibly repaired.

I hadn't even felt a tug on the ley line.

Clues clicked into place. Not a ghost. If not fey, he had to be a witch . . . a sorcerer.

"Say you forgive me," he whispered.

Instead, I said, "Anyone who bothers with the news knows I'm connected to Menessos, so dropping his name around here isn't going to earn you any trust, respect, or anything else, for that matter. Injuring my people actually puts you on my shit-list. So, Mr. Creepy-Who's-Supposed-to-Be-Providing-Protection-Not-Diminishing-It, you've got my attention. Now what are you going to do with it?"

He scanned around, gestured toward Mountain and Zoltan. "Your dragon's horns have not sprouted."

My fingers impatiently tapped my thigh, but I held my tongue, waiting for him to go on.

"Can you predict when they will?" Mountain asked with a chuckle. "Just name the day and the hour, then you can go home and we'll call after that to let you know how much credibility you've earned."

"There is no predicting to it," Creepy replied. "His transformation will begin the moment you take the action that causes it."

Transformation? I recalled that Hecate's dragons had had four limbs *and* wings. I asked, "What action?"

"The dragon must be poisoned." The hint of a curve strayed to his lips. "She Who Walks Between Worlds should know that."

I don't like being scolded. I like it less when a stranger is doing it. But I learned something new about myself: When a creepy stranger who definitely knows I'm the Lustrata scolds me and also suggests I poison a pet, I loathe it.

Despite the narrowed eyes and crossed arms that signaled my annoyance, Creepy came right up to the screen. "Do you have any seeds of the *Strychnos nux-vomica* tree?"

I'd not heard of the vomit-tree, but the other part was obvious enough. "You mean strychnine? No. I don't keep poisons around the house."

"No matter." He lifted his empty hand toward the edge of the porch, palm up, closed it and reopened it. It was full of dark coins.

Zoltan's nostrils flared and he slithered forward.

Creepy let the dragon close in on him.

Those aren't coins.

CHAPTER TWENTY-ONE

Zoltan, no!" I shouted, pushing on the screen door. Creepy blocked it with his foot, but I was too late anyway. The dragon's tongue had licked over Creepy's hand, and the odd seeds were gone.

Mountain scrambled forward even as Zoltan crunched and swallowed. His big arms circled the dragon's body. "No! Spit it out!" He squeezed, as if doing the Heimlich maneuver, but who knew exactly how high or low a dragon's stomach was? Suddenly Zoltan was choking. I couldn't be sure if it was the seeds or Mountain's actions, but I was betting it was the former. Zoltan flopped to the ground, pinning Mountain. Behind me, I heard a window open. I saw Zhan's foot as she slipped out.

"Bastard." Creepy didn't even bother to acknowledge me, captivated by the creature's spasms. I smacked the door angrily. He wasn't going to let me out, so I tore a hole in my just-fixed screen and shoved the gun through, whacking his still-solid head with the handle.

The sound it caused made me smile.

At least until he glared at me and his irises flashed red. "That. Hurt."

I withdrew my arm from the mangled screen. "He's in pain because of you!" I glanced at the writhing, eel-like dragon. Zhan had helped Mountain get free, and he had scooted a few feet away.

When I spied Creepy again, he wasn't solid. He was

halfway through my door. "Hey!" I retreated, mad at myself. Creating a distraction was a standard bad-guy tactic, and this arrogant ass had told us what he'd do.

Ivanka made an awkward grab for his leg. While her broken arm was held tight to her chest, her uninjured arm swung through him. She kicked to no avail.

"In the fey world the dragon had no access to such trees," Creepy said. His voice was ethereal at first but changed as he solidified. "Dragons crave bitter tastes, bitter like those seeds, for a reason." He kept coming toward me. "The seeds stimulate his spinal cord."

"He's convulsing!" I kept retreating. This hall led to the kitchen. There were knives and things to throw in there.

"Yes. He will have violent convulsions."

I spun and ran for the kitchen, hoping to find something that would make a more useful weapon than a gun I had no intention of firing. Maybe salt. Maybe the silver-plated holiday turkey-carving set. As I arrived in the kitchen, though, I saw Creepy was already there. In fact, I ran right into his solid arms. "Do not fear," he said, wrapping me in his embrace. "It is no different than a wærewolf's transformation."

I struggled; he released me. His words sank in.

"There is so much I want to tell you," he whispered.

A roar trumpeted outside, so loud and so strong that the dishes in my cupboards rattled. I stood there blinking, stunned that he'd let me go, and stunned by that sound, until I noticed movement in my yard.

The rest of the dragons were slithering across the rear lawn.

I ran for the front, where Ivanka was getting to

her feet. I shoved the screen door open. On the porch, however, my gait slowed, and I arrived in the yard flabbergasted at the not-so-small dragon. Zoltan's smooth skin now rippled with scales. He had a gleaming spinal ridge and a crown of ebony horns upon his head. He sat on his haunches, his tail wrapped around him. His neck was curled down, his snout snuffling his new claws. "No wings," I said.

"Five claws," Zhan mumbled beside me, adjusting her robe. "He has five claws!"

"Does that mean something?" Mountain asked.

"In Chinese legend, the five-clawed dragon is the symbol of an emperor. Being a black dragon, he is a king of deep, numinous waters." Her teeth were chattering. Mountain put an arm around her and pulled her to him.

The other dragons slithered around Zoltan and released cheerful bellows.

From directly behind me, Creepy whispered, "I can help you, Persephone. More than you can imagine." He then advanced on Zoltan. Reaching up, he boldly seized the rhinolike horn that had sprouted from the dragon's snout. "I charge you with the safety of this estate and the woman Persephone. Your life will be forfeit to me if she is harmed during the hours that Menessos is absent. Do you agree to this, dragon?"

"Wait a minute," I tromped off the porch. "We don't even know who the hell you are!"

Creepy released Zoltan and spun toward me, laughing. "You dubbed me Creepy. That is who I am."

"There will be no deal-making—"

Zoltan lunged forward and shoved his head between me and Creepy. Using his long neck like a restraining arm, Zoltan kept me back as he nodded at Creepy and warbled.

"No!" I protested, ducking under Zoltan's neck and coming up right into Creepy's hands.

He held my face tenderly in his palms as he said, "It is difficult for me to find time to be away from home . . . so much to do, you know, but I have provided you with protection as I said I would. Now I must go." Creepy strolled away, toward the grove where the ley line crossed my property.

I crossed my arms and glared after him. Maybe he could feel it; he put his hood up.

Letting my arms fall loose at my sides, I asked the dragon, "What have you done?"

He blinked big green eyes at me and flicked the gill fins at his throat.

"Get inside before you freeze," I said to Zhan.

"I have to check the perimeter guards first."

Mountain led the dragons back to the barn. The eel-ones slithered readily away. Zoltan walked. I couldn't help laughing as he tried to figure out in which order his legs were supposed to lift. He tried one at a time. He tried front two, stretch, back two. He tried left side, right side. By the time he made it to the barn he'd figured out that right front and left rear, followed by left front and right rear, worked best.

I found Ivanka sitting at the dinette in a cold sweat and murmuring about "vahnting votka." She had splinted her own arm with wooden cooking spoons and duct tape. I didn't have any vodka, so I found the ibuprofen and sat four pills and a glass of water in front of her. "Double dose."

She frowned at the little pills. "Votka better."

"Probably," I agreed.

She jostled the pills into a pile in her cupped palm. "Bullet not much bigger."

"Ivanka."

"I pulled trigger." Still staring at the pills, she shook her head. "I shot him."

"You did the right thing."

"I know," she said unremittingly. "But I miss."

After she swallowed the ibuprofen I said, "You need to go to the hospital."

"*Da.*"

Heading upstairs, Zhan called out, "The perimeter guards were unconscious but are waking up and appear unhurt."

"Could have been much worse," Ivanka murmured.

Minutes later, as Zhan came downstairs dressed in her usual casual suiting, Mountain entered, too. He said, "Zoltan now fills up what spare room the dragon barn had to offer—which wasn't much."

Zhan added, "That man better not feed any other animals on this property or we'll need more barns."

"If he comes back and even so much as tries to feed one of the animals," Mountain said, "I'm tackling him. Ghost thing or no."

"What was he?" Zhan directed her question at me.

"I don't know." I wasn't going to mention the red flash. "But Ivanka needs to get to the hospital."

"Da," she repeated. "Sooner is good."

"After what just happened, I'm not leaving you," Zhan declared. She told Mountain, "You take her," then asked me, "would you like me to call Celia and tell her all is well?"

"Yes, please." Zhan was as good a sentinel as I could hope for. Better, even. She felt like a friend. That made what I knew I had to do even harder. "I need you to stay here."

"Menessos gave direct orders that you were not to go anywhere unescorted."

"They could be at the ER a long time. I don't want the elementals to be here alone."

"The perimeter guards—"

"The animals don't know them. They know you."

Zhan unhappily capitulated. Mountain backed slowly away, saying, "I'll get my truck."

"Guardians of the element of water, I consecrate these items."

Standing before my bedroom altar, I dipped a pine sprig into a bowl of hallowed water and let my trembling hand shake drops from the leaves over the items I'd been given this morning at Wolfsbane and Absinthe. I'd already said the verses for earth, air and fire. "Banish the energies of previous owners or those who have made or touched these items. Purify them with your fluid force. Charge them with your liquid energy that these tools may now be sacred."

Some items were best blessed under certain moons, but since Johnny wanted me to do the spell in about an hour and a half, the current waxing moon phase would have to do. Palms hovering above the items on my altar, I added, "May all astrological correspondences be correct for this working."

I thanked Hecate and the elements, and then extinguished the candles.

In ritual, concentration is key. Being in full control of the conscious mind and silencing the random thoughts, the doubts and worries, is essential for successful magic. Not surprisingly, self-discipline is one of a witch's best assets. I'm usually pretty good at maintaining concentration. Today, however, that proved a struggle. I'd paused and put a barrier up with my ritual circle to help keep anxiety out of the magic working. As I released the circle, all my worries flooded back into the forefront of my mind.

The shabbubitum will be here in a few hours.

I have to do the forced-change spell on the roof of the den and get Beau's half-formed son back to normal.

Menessos sent Creepy here, and now Zoltan is a five-clawed emperor dragon.

I was eager for Menessos to rise so I could interrogate him, but there was a whole lot of magic to be done between now and then.

My satellite phone rang. I checked the display. It was my mother calling.

CHAPTER TWENTY-TWO

Eris snorted as Persephone's voice rattled out a standard "please leave a message" recording. She hung up and immediately went to her "woogie room," her magical supply room. She kept her ritual gemstones in stacked compartmented plastic cases, in alphabetical order. Setting them aside until she had the right case, she put it on the table and opened it. The case wasn't easy to open, but only because her thumb wasn't accustomed to the dexterous little flick that it required. She reached inside for the petrified wood and noticed her opals were gone.

Puzzled, she selected the stone she was after and shut the lid. She replaced the cases as they should be. She rummaged through her runestones and chose Dagaz—the one like a letter X between two bars, and Ehwaz, the one like an M.

Spiritually, the former rune was associated with awakening and awareness, and the latter with movement and change for the better. The petrified wood was ruled by spirit, by Akasha. Eris dropped the stone and runes inside a small plastic cup, added a white candle and a lighter and carried them to her room. Persephone didn't have to answer her phone, but Eris was going to enlist some help getting Persephone to come to her senses.

Johnny sat in a white office with his hands in his lap. It felt like being in a principal's office. But he was on the wrong side of the desk—as in behind it.

The wide mahogany desk had lots of drawers. Matching filing cabinets were positioned conveniently behind him. There was a computer, a planner, stapler and a blotter. A metal cup contained a dozen ink pens. All the stuff a desk-jockey would need.

But the worn leather seat he occupied had long ago conformed to someone else's body.

Ignatius.

This was the office of the *dirija*. Formerly, Ignatius Tierney sat here. For now, this was Johnny's office, and presently Todd, the second-in-command of the pack, and Chris LaCroix, the regional *adevar*, were seated across from him. Todd was blathering on about a meeting they'd just had with the Ohio Department of Transportation. ODOT had put a new compensation package on the table concerning their bid to buy and tear down the Cleveland Cold Storage building for the new I-90 project. Johnny had opted out of the meeting because he hadn't been to any of the previous meetings, but Todd had attended them all. Besides, after the coronation Todd would become *dirija*, and whatever decision they came to would affect his rule.

"Can you believe it?" It was evident that Todd felt the city was trying to bully them into accepting the bid. "If they think Ig was the only one with balls around here, man, are they in for a surprise."

The adevar, a Zvonul agent in the wærewolf version of the IRS, had journeyed here with the former Rege. He had searched the pack's financial records on that Rege's order, and when he'd been made aware of this matter concerning the building, he'd sent a formal inquiry to ODOT, which had clearly made the area reps nervous. This new deal was part of the result.

A typical visit from an adevar was like being audited. They were accountants with all the authority of a governor, should they choose to exercise it. According to Todd, this particular adevar, Chris LaCroix, was the "least prick-ish" one he had ever met. Todd had told Johnny that they'd "lucked out" getting this guy, but Johnny wasn't as impressed. He knew Chris was the little brother of the one major boyfriend Persephone had had in college.

He wondered if Chris had told his big brother that he'd run into her.

"What do you think, Mr. LaCroix?"

"I contacted Celia Randolph, a local Realtor and member of this pack. According to her report addressing real estate in this area, and considering the age of the structure and the revenue from the billboards, ODOT's offering what this building is worth. But."

"But?" Johnny prompted.

"That can't even begin to cover the cost of purchasing an existing building in the area and making the necessary modifications, nor can it cover the cost of buying land and building a new structure. The mayor threw in some tax breaks, but it doesn't provide what we need to relocate this den."

"Options?"

Chris said, "I've sent a complete dossier about the matter to my *diviza*."

The door to Johnny's office was open, and in the room beyond he could see Kirk's feet propped on the desk. A few other wæres were also lounging out there, listening to iPods or watching movies on their cell phones. Then Kirk's feet plopped down.

"You told ODOT this?" Johnny asked Chris.

"Yes."

"You should have seen their faces!" Todd sneered.

"I imagine in the next few weeks the *diviza* will visit Cleveland to negotiate."

Kirk appeared in the doorway. "She's here. Parking lot cameras showing Persephone and two idiots wearing field-camo who came in just behind her."

"Send our men to the roof. Tranquilize William and transport him. I'll bring her." Johnny stood. "Chris, if you'll excuse Todd and me, we have something to attend to."

"Of course."

Johnny walked out of the office and entered the elevator. During the descent he reached up to grip the upper edge, stretching to loosen stiff muscles. The contraption lurched to a stop just as Seph shut the door on her Toyota Avalon.

"Where's Zhan?" he called.

"Unhappily left behind." Seph pointed at the Audi parked on the far side of her. "She made these guys follow me." She opened the trunk. As she bent and reached inside, the hoodie-blazer combo slid up her hips, and he admired the curve of her backside. Desire flickered within him.

"What can I carry?" he asked.

Seph handed him a duffel bag and a cardboard box. Two men sat in the Audi, wearing camouflage, just as Kirk had indicated. They weren't going to blend into the concrete here. "What's with them?"

Broom in hand, she shut the trunk. "Perimeter guards. This reassignment was unexpected. I told them that since they had to stay in the car, their duty here was going to be very boring and they might as well nap. I promised to wake them when I'm ready to leave." She dropped her keys into a side pocket on the duffel. "Shall we?"

"No." Johnny studied her. She squinted just slightly, as if she were in pain. "What's wrong?"

"As always, there's a lot going on."

"What else has happened?"

"I'll tell you on the way up," she said as she gestured at the elevator. "It'll keep my mind off the rickety ride."

"Ig had everything mechanical regularly serviced," he assured her as they approached it, "and the Omori updated everything after they assessed the security system around their Domn Lup. I swear to you: The elevator is safe. It's just the wood gate that's rickety." He patted it as he held it open for her.

"Why keep such a rotten gate if safety really matters?"

"It's a deterrent. Works brilliantly on non-wæres. As you know."

Seph boarded the lift. Johnny lifted the false top and put his thumb to the real control button. The scanner quickly read and approved his print, and they started to rise. She asked, "How are you going to make sure the wolves get to their kennels after they've changed?"

"I'll herd them into the stairwell. Remember the gates you noticed last night? They are at each level. A few of the men who aren't going to be involved in the spell are going to lock all the gates except the uppermost and one of the kennel levels. Then they get as far away as they can."

"So you'll only be able to get to the levels with kennels. Will they all know what kennel to go to?"

"Yup."

"Beau's son hasn't been kenneling with the rest of them."

"Good point, but they aren't territorial about their

kennels, and it's routine to be in them when transformed. Those not involved are supposed to head back in an hour to check on everyone. They'll handle it if William is stubborn." He added, "Don't worry."

The elevator shuddered. "Easy for you to say."

"Those little bounces are no different than a car hitting a pothole."

Seph crossed her arms. "If a pothole knocks a tire off my car, I won't plummet twelve stories."

"You won't plummet here either." The elevator doors opened.

He led her past the cages where the half-formed wærewolves were kept. On one of them, the cage door was open. "One last flight of stairs to the roof." At the end of the hall they made a right, went under an arched entryway, and saw a wide set of metal steps rising through the ceiling. Johnny opened the door at the top and propped it open with one of the cinder blocks he'd had brought up just for this purpose. Here was a cold brick room with glass-block windows and a gritty floor. "Almost there," he said, proceeding to the final door. "Ready?"

"Yeah."

"You sure? You avoided telling me what was up."

"Later. Let's just do this."

"Any last-minute messages for the men?" Johnny asked as he picked up the other block.

She considered it. "Stay together."

Johnny opened and propped this door as well.

Atop the main building were two structures other than the one they were emerging from. The others were also brick and glass-block and, additionally, they bore colorful graffiti. In the center of the roof was a big formerly black water tower—formerly because it too wore the spray-painted lettering. The building was tall enough that drivers on the highway wouldn't be able to see them, and far enough from downtown that people in the taller buildings wouldn't be able to either.

Three dozen men stood gathered around the base of the water tower. William, half formed, was sprawled at the edge of the group, unconscious.

"There's more of them than I expected," Seph said.

"The Omori all wanted in on it."

"They know their man-minds won't be immediate? It'll happen with their next cyclical change?"

"They know."

She glanced up at the sky scattered with gray clouds. "All right. Have them gather in that far corner so the water tower doesn't block the beam."

Johnny directed them where to stand, then had Gregor and Kirk move William. Johnny wasn't standing with them, however. When they were in position, one man noticed and asked, "You are still going to go through it with us, right?"

Johnny blinked. "Yup." He'd promised to go through it with them to assure them that it was not some witch trickery. *I can handle it. I'll just change back when it's done.*

"Of course he is," a voice from the back said. "He won't let his woman see all of us naked without putting himself front and center of her view." The men chuckled.

Johnny stood at the front with his best men: the Omori, Kirk, and the men who'd volunteered to stand with him and face the fey on the shores of Lake Erie. While they undressed, Persephone used her broom to sweep a huge circle enclosing them all. She called the elements and used candles in tall beakers of colored glass. Then she said,

> Persephone and Isis, goddesses whose names I bear,
> Artemis, Inanna, and Ishtar, your lunar purpose I share.
> Hathor and Hera, be present here this hour,
> Hecate! Come now, lend my rite your power.
> Encourage the elements to participate
> As we seek their man-minds to liberate
> Reward the courage these men have shown
> I beseech you, O wise and wonderful crone.

With her arms over her head for the last line, she formed a triangle with her thumbs and index fingers. She lowered her arms so she could see the moon through that open triangle, and remained thus for a long minute. Then she sang strange words.

Energy stirred around them and Johnny detected the men shifting uneasily behind him. He saw second thoughts betrayed in some eyes. "Steady, men. I feel it too," he said to them calmly. "This is normal. She must call the power and contain it away from us until there is enough to fully change us all. Only then will that power descend."

He saw one man's mouth open, ready to ask for reassurance, then he clamped it shut, thinking better of letting his peers know he was worried.

Johnny added, "She is able to hold that much power, and more. Otherwise I wouldn't allow this. I stand with you." *But I will change back as soon as I get you all to your kennels.*

His skin abruptly itched, like he'd been dipped in

icy water and coated in sand. *She's tapped the ley.* He remembered that when she'd transformed him and Celia and Erik and Theo, she'd sung this hauntingly beautiful song, and her power had erupted as her voice had found the high note of the melody's crescendo. She was building to that note now.

He rolled his shoulders. "Relax, men. Don't fight it."

"Look up," someone whispered.

Everyone turned their faces skyward, where, ten feet above their heads, a mass of energy was forming. It swirled, shimmering like glitter on waves of heat. As the mass developed color, four arms stretched downward, one to each candle. When the energy-arms reached the candle flames, the center above them exploded, and that energy snapped into the candles like a tape measure recoiling.

Then, except for the single note Persephone was sustaining, there was silence.

Johnny remembered what Menessos had said during the first spell. He'd whispered, "Rise cone of power. Rise to our call. Deliver lunar energies, to one and all."

In the sky, the exposed moon flashed, and a focused beam of reflected lunar light fell, encompassing Persephone's circle. Her voice wavered. Her knees gave.

Johnny felt his skin crawl, felt it scrub against his raw muscles like coarse sandpaper. His beast growled savagely, exultantly, as it burst through his flesh.

His change was fluid and fast, and he stood on all fours in a beam of cold light, while the others' transformations were more prolonged. He felt electrified and invigorated, yet a hunger gnawed at him, a hunger that had nothing to do with his stomach.

Change back.

He sniffed the air. He could smell well with his human nose, but with his wolf nose—it was like every molecule in the air was amplified, akin to a blast from an aerosol spray. So many compelling scents mingled at once.

Change back.

Nostrils flaring, he stared down his elongated black nose and sorted through the smells.

Human. Wolf. Sweat. Rooftop. Brick. Metal. Cotton. Candle wax. Fire. Car exhaust. Lavender.

Persephone was on her knees directly ahead and leaning to one side, unsteady in the buffeting wind. Her hair flapped about. She pitched forward—caught herself on her hands.

Change back.

He could smell her sex. He recalled their shower, the bubbles cascading over her ass, the water dripping off her tits. He'd made her writhe and scream when he'd been inside her. He'd made her wear his scent. He could smell that too.

Change back now.

The beast whimpered, stationary and ready to withdraw . . . then a new scent filled his nostrils. A scent that seduced him. A scent that seized his ambiguous hunger and made his jaws drip saliva. A scent that stupefied his man-mind, silencing his thoughts and leaving only the beast that quavered with a raging appetite.

He smelled blood.

CHAPTER TWENTY-THREE

The charm Beau had given me made a real difference.

When I'd held the lightning energy, I'd felt ready to explode. The volume of ley energy I'd briefly contained was threefold—ley energy scalds in the first instant and settles into a heady buzz, like an addict's high. The ley and lunar energies had swirled within me, rather like oil and vinegar refusing to mix. Stormy and volatile. I'd tried coaxing the powers, folding them together like cake batter and foamy egg whites. Still they had resisted. So I'd gone bully. I'd used the Reese's Cup-size charm like a blender, cramming that energy through the charm, whipping it into a frothy force, and then I freed the energy, refiltering it through myself.

A witch releasing energy was like any human body expending energy. In about twenty seconds, my body was convinced I'd just finished a hundred-kilometer marathon and celebrated by going a couple rounds with Rocky Balboa. Containing the power, filtering it, targeting it, and releasing it used nearly all of my own energy, and after my already stressful midday, I felt woozy and weak.

I collapsed to my knees in exhaustion. The dizziness made me pitch forward. The rough rooftop tore at my palms, ripping runnels that filled with warm blood.

I was so tired I didn't care. I just wanted to sleep.

The beam dissipated to a chorus of wolf howls.

Beau's son? I checked where the half-formed wolf had

lain. A full-formed wolf lay there now, unconscious. *I did it.*

A pony-sized black wolf stood stiff-legged at the edge of the pack. Beyond that dark wolf that I knew to be Johnny, I saw wolves begin padding away from the group, spreading out.

I sat back on my heels, fingers curled to favor my wounded palms. Softly, I said, "Keep them together, Johnny. Lead them to the kennels."

The black wolf's yellow eyes remained steady, and he persistently sniffed the air.

Wolves loped around me, circling. There were so many of them. . . .

"Johnny."

The black wolf lowered its muzzle. It shook itself.

"Johnny?"

He stepped in my direction.

I swallowed. Hard.

Slowly, I put my knuckles down and very, very cautiously pushed to get my feet under me. Very, very cautiously I stood. The black wolf kept easing forward. I stood my ground for a heartbeat or two, then I couldn't suppress the need to retreat.

The black wolf paused, sniffing where I'd fallen. Its pink tongue licked where my skin had torn. Where I'd bled.

Oh shit.

Behind me, a wolf growled.

Before me, the black wolf continued licking the roof. I trusted the Domn Lup to rule his pack and protect me, but the growl to my rear came again, nearer. Still the black wolf did not react.

I dared a quick scan behind me. The other wolf was gathering itself, preparing to leap.

"Johnny!"

The black wolf's nose came up, but his head stayed low, nostrils quivering and yellow gaze locked on me. Its posture was entirely animal-on-the-hunt. "What's wrong with you?" I whispered.

He eased forward with deliberate, stalking steps.

Heart pounding, it took everything I had to not run for the door. "Domn Lup! Herd your pack down the stairwell. Do it now!"

Behind me the other wolf snarled. The black wolf viciously snapped its jaws at the other wolf, which then whimpered and retreated from me.

Thinking—hoping—that he was sending me down the stairs first, I shifted my retreat toward the door he'd propped open.

The black wolf made the same jaw-snapping growl at me, lunging and forcing me away from the safety of the room beyond that door.

As I quickly backpedaled, I tripped over the duffel with my spell supplies. As I fell, even as I thought to brace against the fall, I saw the black wolf leap.

Time slowed down. Instead of throwing my arms back to catch myself, I reached forward and buried my fingers in the fur on the sides of its head. With a feral snarl, the wolf's hot breath blew over my cheeks. Those long fangs were just inches from me, and we hadn't hit the roof yet.

I had only one choice: I called on the ley.

Stinging energy answered. It ripped into me as my back hit the rooftop, and I rammed it down my arms, ejecting it right into the black wolf. Unfocused and unpurposed, the energy was raw and shocking.

The wolf yelped in pain, jerked and leapt away from me; tufts of black hair stuck to my bloody palms. My head bounced on the rooftop, hair catching in the rough texture and yanking out.

The wolf landed a few yards away and twisted back, a wicked rumble rising from deep in its chest. My hands went to the rooftop, ready to launch me up again, but I felt the smooth broom handle. Gripping it, I rolled, straddling it as I said, "Awaken ye to life." It boosted me into the air and shot forward as the black wolf closed in again.

Johnny.

What have you done?

The wind over the city tore the tears from my eyes before they could spill to my cheeks.

Johnny had attacked me. Attacked *me*.

What's wrong with him?

But in my heart I knew. I'd ignored that nagging little fear, and it had been right.

His beast is loose.

If I hadn't burned up the *in signum amoris*, I would have known that something was wrong before Johnny's man-mind had been highjacked by the beast, caught in the throes of bloodlust.

He'd broken my trust in his beast, and I wasn't sure this could ever mend. My tears flowed faster.

Miles away, something else hit me: His best and bravest were with him, and for now, they were all feral and would follow the dominant male among them, even if that wolf was leading them to trash their own den in order to get out and find meat.

No one was supposed to return to the den for roughly another half hour. What if they weren't in their kennels when the other wæres showed up? The others would know something wasn't right with their Domn Lup.

Worse, what if the pack was able to break the barricades? If the three dozen fully formed wæres escaped the building and were loose in a city completely unprepared for them—right before the Domn Lup was supposed to have his prestigious press conference—it would mean disaster for Johnny.

His disaster would mean the ruination of our trio *and* the failure of me and my destiny.

I couldn't allow that to happen. No matter what.

My speed slowed. My phone was in my purse, locked in the car. My keys were in the duffel on the rooftop. There was no one I could call and no time to wait for someone else to go and make sure this didn't escalate into a multilevel tragedy.

I circled around and headed back.

CHAPTER TWENTY-FOUR

I circled the Cleveland Cold Storage building and saw only one wærewolf on the rooftop. By the placement of this wolf, I knew it was Beau's son. Still unconscious, he hadn't moved so much as an inch. It was cold, so, despite his being covered with fur, I collected the other men's piled clothing and covered him up with several T-shirts, topping that with layers of jeans.

I spiraled down the building and flew into the parking area. The guys in the Audi were still asleep.

At the stairwell, I could hear grunts and snarls of wolves, far, far up. The sound wasn't getting closer or louder. Only two questions remained: Would the gates continue to detain the thirty-some wæres tearing at it, *and* could I coerce them to their kennels? If the others figured out Johnny's man-mind wasn't dominant, they'd suspect this whole thing was my wrongdoing.

Hovering away from the stairwell, I noticed the elevator wasn't here. I opened the bug-eaten gates and peered up. The carrier was dark up in the shaft, but it was nowhere near here. The last wæres out must've left via the stairs as Johnny escorted me up in the elevator.

I intentioned the broom into the metal and cement tube and slowly rose to the fourth floor. Forcing the doors open a crack, I listened. From the sound, the wæres were blocked just around the corner. They were none too quiet, so I forced the doors wide enough to let me dismount the broom.

I'd been here before, when the Omori had first arrived. The *dirija*'s office was on this floor, as was the big gymnasium-sized meeting hall.

Cautiously, I skimmed along the wall between the elevator and the stairwell. When I was able to see the gate, my stomach almost dropped out of me. Wæres were crammed against the iron bars and shuffling around each other and upon each other, more irritated by the lack of room than organized about destroying the gate.

With man-minds, they'd be out by now.

But with man-minds, they'd be immune to bloodlust. That wouldn't take effect until the next transformation under the full moon.

I backed slowly away, leaned on the elevator door, and ran fingers through my hair.

My head was bleeding. Or it had been. When I'd fallen backward on the rooftop, I must have split my scalp. Flying just afterward, the cold November temperature and the rushing wind probably helped me not notice, cooling the blood on my skin and crusting it before it had a chance to run down my neck.

I brushed the flecks of dried blood from my fingers.

When the first wære snorted, I understood how thoughtless that action had been. The dozens of wærewolves around the corner intensely sniffed the air. And the iron bars creaked like they were bending.

I had to do something.

Straddling the broom and ready to hover into the elevator shaft, I firmed my resolve and intentioned the broom to hover, then slowly descend. How was I supposed to get them to their kennels? *All they want is meat.*

Or blood.

By the time I got to the bottom, I had an idea. Then I shot it down.

They'll smell me. Those noses will detect me and they'll be after me and there's no way out except the stairwells and elevator.

I flew up to the roof and landed to assess what magical items I had with me. The stones were hematite, green aventurine, bloodstone, and coral. Coral, if worn where all can see, is broadly protective. It can guard against simple things like accidents or violence, or it can ward away demons. Hematite was great for healing purposes, but it was also grounding, as in attuned to the physical plane. The aventurine was a lucky stone. I could use luck, but it was also noted for increasing perception, and I didn't want to bring it near the wolves and chance that they'd be more inclined to see me. Bloodstone lends courage and . . . *when smeared with heliotrope, affords the wearer invisibility!*

But where can I get heliotrope in the next minute?

My breath caught. My gaze slid to the duffel.

Caramel-sweet and vanilla.

I pounced on the duffel bag and clawed through it. Pushing aside the flask of crystal water I'd used when calling the element of water, I found it: the little bottle of essential oil that Zhan had been so keen on.

Beau had dropped it into the bag with the rest of the items. I'd blessed it with everything else, distracted by my visit from Creepy. I twisted the small bottle to read the label and about choked.

Heliotrope.

Thank you, Hecate!

Another thought popped into my head: *They may not see me, but they'll still smell me.*

Even if I had enough of this oil to bathe in, I'd not

change my scent, I'd just temporarily mask it with something else they'd detect and know was unusual. I scanned around. And again.

I didn't have anything that wouldn't alert the wærewolves to something "other" being close by.

My gaze caught on William.

Smell like one of them.

Scurrying over to him, I stole about ten hairs from his furry head and scrambled back to the duffel bag, where I opened the Baggie of salt I'd used when calling earth. I threw a sprinkling of it around me in a circle. After speaking the swiftest of invocations, I chanted. I opened the essential oil bottle, smeared the bloodstone with dabs of oil and envisioned it cloaking me in invisibility.

I wasn't literally capable of pulling an Invisible Man act, but this was just enough that the wolves would fail to notice me should I be still and far away.

Invoking Beau's charm, I made doubly sure of that.

Then I wrapped William's fur strands around the stone. They stuck readily with the oil coating. And I envisioned the wolfish scent of William surrounding me. Using magic directly on a wærewolf in wolf-form was as dangerous as using it on one in human-form . . . but I wasn't using it on him. I was actually drawing a tad off him and wrapping myself in it.

I put the stone in my front jeans pocket.

I was about to end my quickie ritual, but when I spied the water flask I had another idea. I unscrewed the cap, then dug my fingernails into my hair, dragging my nails over the clots of dried blood in my hair, being careful not to reopen the wound. Then I scrubbed the globs from my fingertips on the edge of the flask so it all fell into the water.

I replaced the lid and gave it a good shake.

Saying a brief but heartfelt thanks to the deities and elements I'd invoked with the first spell, I jogged a widdershins path and released the original circle and the smaller one I'd just employed. Truly, the first ritual was ended and this was mostly irrelevant, but it was the right thing to do. Farsighted Hecate had influenced Zhan this morning. All the more reason for me to spend a few seconds honoring the blessings I had before leaping into the wærewolves' den.

CHAPTER TWENTY-FIVE

I walked into the little building atop the Cleveland den. My ears rang, now out of the open wind of the roof, and my stomach gave a flip as I peered down the stairs. My feet would be seen by any wærewolves down there before I'd see them.

Waiting, I listened. Being bound to Menessos had given me better-than-average hearing, but still I worried. At a measured pace I descended. Once in the room, I made my way out into the hall. There were two other half-formed wæres in cages up here, but they were behind barred doors and didn't show themselves.

I sat on the broom again and glided to the stairwell, where I descended half a level, rounded the landing, and eased down the other half. Here, the room beyond was empty.

This reminded me of when I'd climbed through these levels after escaping the Rege. I'd taken a baseball bat to the head and, disoriented, had been thinking "up" meant "out." I'd never been to these parts of the den before, so I'd been utterly lost.

Now, however, I knew where I was and what was waiting for me.

There were more wærewolves in the Greater Cleveland area than they could kennel on one floor. Since this group had been blocked at the fifth floor, I knew there were kennels on five. And on six. There had been no kennels on eight, where the confirmation meeting had taken place, but I was hoping they had built them on seven as well. I wasn't sure I could sneak past the wæres crammed into the stairwell if I had to go to six.

On seven I found kennels and was so happy the broom intentioned in a spin that was rather like a happy dance.

There were probably eighty kennels here . . . I only needed them to use half that. I flew to the kennels farthest back.

Another fragment of recollection crossed my thoughts.

The memory that Johnny had given me was one that had happened here. His first change after learning he was a wære. He'd kenneled with the rest of the pack . . . Beau had locked all the doors with a key. . . .

They don't self-lock?

This plan can't be ruined by this flaw after all the effort!

I tried to swing shut one of the doors. It was heavier than expected, and I had to throw my weight onto it. It clanged quietly as metal hit metal.

Click.

I pulled on the bars.

I yanked.

It didn't open.

That was good, but there would be no shutting them sneakily if they all needed this much effort. I rolled my eyes—and saw there was a little cylinder atop the door. It was similar to the spring atop my screen door that made it snap shut, but this was hydraulic, and I could see the barest hint of wires, fed from it into the metal bars.

They'd upgraded the doors. *Johnny told me the Omori had upgraded the den security and more. Both he and Renaldo activated the elevator with their thumbprints.* I scanned around for the master switch for these doors and found a key-code pad attached to the wall near the stairwell, and the tube that encased the wires running from it connected to the cages.

Yes! I opened the flask. With one swinging gesture, I splashed the bloody water in a half dozen cages. Another swing, another and another.

I was running low, but I had enough to splatter droplets into enough cages and drop a puddle of it leading from the main aisle to the stairwell.

The ruckus below had lapsed into the same grunting it had before, but as I hovered in the stairwell, chancing to inspect the key-code pad and hoping there was a marked Close button, the intense canine sniffing began again.

I flew up and around the landing, out of sight. "C'mon." My heart was threatening to beat itself out of my chest as I waited, listening so hard, ready to bolt up and around another flight of stairs, ready to flee if I had to.

I heard one wolf, then a few more, and then suddenly they all had the scent. They rough-and-tumbled their way into the kenneling area, following the scent of blood to find the source. I peered around the edge, letting only the smallest part of my head show . . . but none of the wolves were aware of me. Their noses were on the floor. When about half the pack was in the kenneling area, a familiar black wolf crowded past the others.

I waited as they spread out, sniffling paths to the rear.

Johnny paced back and forth, on the trail, but not entering a cage. Every time I thought he was about to enter one, he backed out and searched for the scent elsewhere, found it.

They all had to be inside a cage. Some were grouped, sniffing in twos and threes.

The broom floated me forward, into the stairwell and then into the room with them. I hovered beside the device. I had to figure out how to work it. The buttons had numbers and letters, like a phone. There would be a code to close them. A code to open them.

And those codes could be anything.

Then Johnny entered a cage.

I punched in the numbers correlating to the word *close*. Nothing but a quiet beep. *L-O-C-K.* Quiet beep. *S-H-U-T.*

The doors swung closed.

I sighed in relief.

Too soon.

Upon hearing the little motors whir, most of the wærewolves backed deeper into their cages and away from the metal.

But not Johnny.

He thrashed and squirmed until he broke through his door, causing the little motor to grind and give.

"Shit." I sat very still. *Don't see me. Don't see me.*

He reviewed the confined state of his pack and studied the doorway. He broke into a gallop.

"Shit. Shit. Shit." I swung the broom into the stairwell, twisting up it as fast as possible. When I burst into the hallway of the topmost floor, he was right behind me. He leapt. His paw knocked the bristles of my broom and caused me to swing slightly sideways, but that actually helped me get through the turn to the room with the steps to the roof.

I was up and out on the roof before he'd topped the stairs.

Leaning down, I snagged the strap of the duffel, where

I'd shoved what ritual items were still usable. Flying out over the edge of the roof into the open air beyond, I twirled around.

The big black wolf put its paws on the raised edge and snarled and barked and growled at me. "You're going to have to figure out what to tell the rest of them," I shouted, not sure he'd even understand me. I'd done all I could.

I dropped down and entered the parking garage. I unlocked the trunk and put everything inside, including the stone wrapped with William's fur. The guys in the Audi were still asleep. I knocked on the window and woke them as promised, and was about to get into my Toyota Avalon when a Hummer rolled up the ramp, followed by a Magnum and a white delivery van.

Hector, the former *dirija*'s assistant, was driving the Hummer. I recognized him by his size and his trademark Hawaiian shirt.

Seeing me waving him over, he cruised close and rolled down his window. "How'd it go?" There were three other men with him.

"Good, but I need to ask you something. Privately."

He put the window up and parked. The others who had ridden with him wandered over to talk to the wæres climbing out of the other vehicles, but Hector came to me. "What is it?"

"There was a situation," I said softly. "I think a surge of bloodlust hit some of the wæres. How do you deal with that?"

"There's a small meat locker on four. Beau usually supervises us on full moons." He frowned. "I don't know what's in it, we haven't had newbies in a while and it's usually just the newbies that act up."

I acted casual. "I guess the spell must have made them sensitive."

"That happen before with this spell?"

"Actually, yeah. One of the wæres that changed the first time tried to attack me." It had been Erik. Johnny had intervened.

"You all right?" Hector asked.

"Yeah. I'm a little shaken up, but . . . I'm fine."

Beau hurried around the end of the Hummer. "How's William?"

"He's fully wolf—"

Beau hugged me and danced me around in a circle in the small space between cars. "I knew you could do it! I knew you would!"

"Beau." I pulled away, too sore for such antics. "He's still on the roof, he's still unconscious and . . . Johnny's with him."

"Watching over him! What a fine Domn Lup."

"Yeah, but you should be cautious approaching him. He's jumpy, okay?"

"We will be." Beau walked away. One of the others had pushed the button to bring the elevator down, and everyone was assembling near the gates.

I grabbed Hector's arm. "Seriously. Be careful. You understand?"

He caught the worry I was conveying to him. "We're wære too."

"Still."

With concern darkening his features, he nodded.

CHAPTER TWENTY-SIX

I n Saranac Lake, New York, SSTIX Investigator Kurt Miller eased his Ford Crown Victoria into the garage and cut the engine. He hit the button to lower the garage door and sat checking the emails that had rung in on his Droid phone during the drive home.

He entered his home via the laundry room, greeted by the mingling scents of "sunshine fresh" dryer sheets, pot roast, and the bread machine. *If she keeps using the bread machine, I'll never again run a mile in under eight minutes.*

At forty-three, though, do I need to run a mile in under eight minutes?

He plopped his briefcase onto the folding table by the dryer and hooked his coat on a peg. He smoothed his hair, trying not to think about how thin it felt.

"Brenda," he called as he continued on to the kitchen. "Something smells wonderful."

A woman wearing tan khakis, a tight-fitting periwinkle sweater and pot-holder gloves came into view. She was placing a large pan on the stove. The curly brown hair that draped down her back had few grays in it.

"Hello, beautiful."

She used her foot to shut the oven door and flashed a perky smile at him as she tossed the pot holders to the counter. "You have a good day?" she asked as she wrapped her arms around him and kissed his cheek.

God, I'm a lucky man. "As always," he said. "You?"

"Mmmm-hmmm. Diane and I went to the furniture store. They have this gorgeous bedroom set. I want you to see it this weekend, okay?"

"Sure," he said. He sorted the mail on the built-in desk. *Phone. Cable. Ah . . . Premier Interior Designs.* P.I.D. had just finished remodeling their kitchen two weeks ago. He glanced around the updated and expensive environment and sighed. It made Brenda happy and helped compensate for the time his job often took him away from her.

"But I do have some bad news. We have a change in plans for tomorrow night." Brenda's chipper demeanor dimmed considerably.

"Oh?" Kurt kept his expression blank while he wondered what they were supposed to have planned on doing.

"We aren't going out with George and Diane tomorrow."

Kurt hadn't remembered, but he was as disappointed as his wife. Brenda and Diane had been best friends since high school. Similarly, he and George had been pals. "Why? George didn't put his back out at the gym again, did he?"

"No. Diane is babysitting for Toni this weekend." There had been another couple who had always run around with them, Antonia and Andy. A heart attack had killed Andy about ten years before. The two women had made sure Toni still felt welcomed and included her in their socializing, then tragedy had struck again a few years back. Toni's daughter had died and she'd been left raising a grandson, Evan, on her own. They'd all remained friends, but Toni no longer went out much. To need a babysitter for an entire weekend was unusual.

"Why?"

"Toni's going out of town. She's leaving tonight."

"Why?"

"Hey, Mr. Specialized Squadron Tactical Investigator, my kitchen is not an interrogation room."

He laughed softly at Brenda's often used phrase: *My kitchen is not . . .* "And what a beautiful kitchen it is." Kurt coerced her away from the stove and into an embrace.

"Indeed." Brenda kissed him, then gently departed from his arms.

He could understand her being saddened by a change in plans, but this was a little much. "We'll reschedule."

She said nothing as she collected the plates and flatware and set the table.

It wasn't like Toni to do something that impacted other people's plans. She'd known they were all going out. Kurt hoped the three women hadn't had a falling-out. "Bren, what is it?"

"Toni won't give me a straight answer about why she's leaving and where to."

"Maybe she's going to Vegas. You know, what happens in Vegas . . ."

"Kurt."

"What?" he asked. "Andy's been gone ten years and things have only gotten worse since. She's allowed to go to Vegas. Maybe she's embarrassed." Poor woman. Toni's parents had been killed in a car crash her senior year in high school. Pregnant shortly after, she and Andy had gotten married the day before graduation. They'd done well for themselves and their daughter. Little Francine had everything a girl could want until her dad died when she was fourteen. After Andy's death, Toni couldn't afford the big house and downsized to something more modest.

Brenda opened the bread machine and removed a round loaf. "She's not going to Vegas."

"Are you sure?"

"Yes. She's going to Cleveland." She set the bread on a cutting board. "Of all places, she picks there. There! And on a bus, no less. She'll be riding more hours than she'll get to stay in the city. For all that trouble, if I were her, I'd be going someplace *warm*."

"Does she have family there?"

"I don't think she has any family at all, Kurt. Just Evan."

"Damn. Whatever she's doing must be important if she's willing to ride a bus."

Brenda placed the serrated knife by the loaf with more force than was necessary. "Quit it. This isn't funny."

Kurt pulled her into his arms again. "I just want to see you smile."

Brenda laid her head on his shoulder. "Kurt, have you *seen* her lately?"

"No," he admitted.

"She looks awful. She doesn't get her nails done anymore, and half the time she doesn't even bother with makeup. She always used to fuss over the details, and now . . . she doesn't. It's not like her. She needs to go somewhere and relax. Diane and I have been telling her that for months."

Maybe a long, arduous bus ride would be relaxing after taking care of that kid. "Maybe that's what she's doing."

"Yeah. That's what she said."

"So why aren't you happy?"

"I pressed her and she gave me the name of the spa she was going to. It doesn't exist."

It wasn't like Toni to lie. "So, we're back to Vegas and embarrassment."

"No, Kurt."

He rubbed his wife's shoulders. "She'll tell you when she's ready." She arched into the impromptu back rub. "If you and Diane have been telling her she needs a vacation, why is Diane the one who gets to look after the boy?" *Babysitting would do her good. Maybe it will get that mothering need worked out.*

"Because George actually *likes* kids. Unlike someone I know . . ."

Kurt realized he had given her an opening to lead this into another conversation about adoption. Kids weren't Kurt's favorite portion of the population. Loud, spoiled, tantrum-machines. He and Brenda couldn't have kids. For him, that was the end of the story. Not for her.

Leaving his arms again, Brenda selected a bottle from the new little wine refrigerator, and leaned against the counter, downhearted but not sulking. "Diane asked if we would come over to their house for dinner, but I told her you would rather reschedule."

"Smart woman. Diane better not take her eyes off that boy."

"Kurt."

"He's a brat."

"Kurt!"

"Am I wrong?" The last time Kurt had seen the kid, probably two years ago, he'd tried to be tolerant, but the kid made him nervous. Evan was into cars, so Kurt thought seeing the flashing red light mounted to the dash of his car would be fun. The kid had been delighted, but he'd proceeded to push every button and flip every switch in the car *and* in the house.

Brenda sighed but said nothing. She slid the wine and the corkscrew toward him, and then carried the meal to the dining table.

Kurt made a mental note to check the bus schedule.

It was well after nine when Kurt switched on his home computer. Though the evening was far from over, the world was dark, and Brenda was presently soaking out her worries in a cherry-blossom-scented bubble bath.

He checked the online schedule and found that the local terminal would have a bus leaving tonight at eleven twenty, and, with all the stops and connections, it seemed that someone could arrive in Cleveland as early as one in the afternoon tomorrow.

That is a long ride. It was definitely out of character for his wife's friend.

He opened his briefcase and plucked out a key to a certain filing cabinet. Inside, the rearmost files comprised his personal copies of a particular cold case from his days as a local small-town cop. He drew out the one marked *Hampton, Elena A.*

He opened it a fraction and saw a candid photo of a positively gorgeous young woman. Black hair, long and straight and thick. He remembered how sleek her hair used to feel when he ran his hands through it.

Guilt twisted in his gut.

He'd cheated on Brenda. They hadn't been married yet, but he'd still been unfaithful. After high school, he'd gone away to college. She'd stayed home to attend the local community college. They maintained their relationship long-distance. Then he'd met this girl . . . Elena. They had a math class together. Deliberating for all of August and September, he built up his nerve and asked her out. Throughout October their romance had been torrid. He'd even considered breaking up with Brenda, but resisted. Then Elena abruptly broke it off with him the day after a wild Hallowe'en party they'd attended. She said she was transferring to a college closer to her hometown in Montana and stopped talking to him.

Kurt never saw Elena again until her file crossed his desk. She'd ended up in Saranac Lake, working at the federal prison as a guard. *Did she know I was here?*

He closed her file, set it aside and pulled another. *Burdette, Doug R.*

This file he opened fully. Photocopies of news clippings lay on top. *Deadly House Fire.* There was a picture of the remains of a house, below the date May 20. The next clipping had bold letters stating, *Gruesome Discovery in the Ashes.* The next, *Authorities Suspect Murder, Arson.*

Behind that was the official documents, then a photocopy of a work ID. Burdette had been an HVAC mechanic at the prison. Next was the autopsy report. Kurt scanned the highlighted words: "*. . . in approximately twelve pieces found on the stairs and in the upper hall*" and "*. . . claw marks consistent with those of a large animal.*" The official cause of death was listed as exsanguination.

"Kurt?" Brenda called from the hallway.

"Yeah?"

She appeared in the doorway. "It's awfully late for work."

He let the pages slither through his fingers to lie flat on the file. "I think I've got a break in this case. . . ."

"I took some melatonin," she said. It was her natural sleep aid. "I'm going to bed."

"Good idea." Kurt rose from his seat to go and kiss her. She hugged him tighter and longer than usual. "Toni will be okay," he whispered.

Brenda left him there. "Good night."

Sinking behind his desk again, Kurt flipped to Burdette's autopsy. Under that was a list of driving citations—speeding, DUI, hit-and-run damage to other vehicles. There was a rap sheet, too. Assault and battery, destruction of private property, various domestic violence crimes. There were also charges of possession, contributing to the delinquency of a minor, and a dropped charge of rape.

Since these files first crossed his desk years ago, Kurt had always wondered how a sweet, straight arrow—never even a parking ticket—like Elena could have been with someone like Doug Burdette.

Doug had been a less-than-model citizen, but he'd been alive when someone—some*thing*—tore him limb from limb. Burning the house down had not been able to disguise that.

Kurt closed that file and slipped Elena's to the top again. After mustering his resolve, he opened it. Except for her picture on top, it had the same organization: articles, ID, autopsy. He reread part of the report. *Cervical vertebra 1 and cervical vertebra 2 fractured, allowing for the odontoid process to sever the brain stem. This severe hyperextension of the head and neck is consistent with a forward fall down the stairs.*

Her body had been found at the bottom of the steps.

Something had entered Elena's house. It attacked

Doug and ripped him apart. Elena must have stumbled in her attempt to get away. The fire, deemed to be a result of a cigarette meeting alcohol, had either forced the killer to leave before it could tear into her, or the killer had set the fire to destroy evidence. Kurt had his opinion about which it was.

She shouldn't have died like that.

He reached into the filing cabinet again and brought out a third file. This one was marked, *Hampton, John C.*

Inside, an enlarged photo from the local high school yearbook showed a sophomore with longish black hair, blue eyes. Beside it was written: *John Hampton. Dated Francine Brown. Missing since fire.*

Under that was a report Kurt had filed himself. But Kurt didn't need it to vividly recall that night. . . .

He was driving like a maniac, speeding under street-lights, following a teen who was on foot but ran like a startled deer. Kurt would gain on him, then the kid would race down a side street, forcing him to slam his brakes and squeal around a curve. He thought the kid must be on drugs; he should have been getting tired.

At the end of the road sat an abandoned mechanics garage. The kid kicked down the door and ran inside. Kurt left his patrol car. Drawing his gun but keeping it lowered, he jogged to the doorway and shouted, "Come on out, son. I just want to talk to you."

"Leave me alone!"

"You know I can't do that."

"Go away! I have a gun!"

Inside, Kurt crouched behind a stack of bald tires. Three days ago this kid's house had burned down with his mother and her boyfriend inside. "I know you've been through a lot. Let me help you."

"Nobody can help me!"

"Let me try!" Kurt shouted.

"Just leave!" Gunshots sounded from the far corner. Kurt aimed through the space between tires and fired. He heard a scream and a growl. He heard metal crunching like cars colliding, and then silence.

When he inspected the far corner, he found only a pile of clothes, a gun with the barrel bent under and a giant rip in the steel wall. Outside, the only prints were those of a large dog.

Kurt had put two and two together and formulated a good guess as to what had torn Burdette apart. Everyone in the office had said he was crazy—neither their shootout nor the murders had happened under a full moon.

The crime had never been solved, and in a village like Saranac Lake, there weren't enough resources to keep the investigation active. He'd moved on himself, started working for SSTIX. Maybe the incident more than eight years ago had inspired his interest in xenocrime, but the federal wages and benefits, as well as the chance to stay in Saranac Lake and still remain in law enforcement, had been the deciding factors in taking the job.

The old case could only vaguely be deemed SSTIX territory, but his personal interest—in Elena, in Toni's connection to John Hampton, in the mystery of that night—remained.

Have you finally found him, Toni?

• • •

Kurt collected some clean clothes in the laundry room and shoved them into a backpack, then scribbled a note to Brenda:

> *Something came up with that case. May be gone most of the weekend. So sorry. Go ahead and buy that bedroom set you wanted. We'll break it in when I get back.*

With the case files in his briefcase and the backpack over his shoulder, he left the house as quietly as possible and drove to the bus station. He parked a short distance away, close enough to see the station clearly but far enough away that he wasn't obvious.

A few minutes later, a cab rolled up and Toni Brown got out.

Using his Droid, he found the location of the Cleveland Greyhound station and programmed it into his GPS. He'd arrive in eight hours. Plenty of time to get there, sleep a while, and get into position to continue surveillance.

CHAPTER TWENTY-SEVEN

Twenty-five minutes away from home, I nearly drove into a ditch because I felt Menessos rise. I wasn't ready for the intensity of the sudden sensations that rocked me, or the awareness of his painful awakening. At least the sentinels Zhan had ordered to follow me in the Audi stayed off my bumper after that.

Twilight had fallen when I put the Avalon in park in my driveway. The guys in the Audi parked alongside me. With everything that had transpired in the last hour and a half—and now that road safety wasn't a concern—I wanted a few minutes to just shut everything else out and piece together my thoughts.

Yeah, that would've been nice, but I wasn't going to be that lucky.

Before I was even out of the car, the front door opened and Menessos appeared on my front porch. His hair was still shower-damp, and he had not yet donned his suit jacket.

Leaving the duffel in the passenger seat, I got out and shoved my keys into my pocket, thereby rediscovering how much my hands hurt.

I'm tough. If I focus on getting back to the haven and dealing with the shabbubitum, I can break down later. Just not tonight.

As I stepped onto the porch, Menessos said my name softly. He reached out to touch my cheek and asked, "What's wrong?"

I don't know why, but when I'm fighting tears, if

someone is kind or empathetic I immediately lose the battle. With Menessos being both kind and empathetic, it instantly dissolved the mental plugs crammed into my tear ducts.

I fell into his arms, sobbing. I didn't care that I seemed weak. I didn't care that the men in the Audi could see me. I didn't even care that Menessos would use this to get his way about something someday. I just had to release some of my grief or I'd explode.

The vampire held me so tenderly, smoothing my hair and patiently letting me cry it all out. In his embrace, each breath seemed easier, the flood of tears tapered to a trickle, and the burden on my hurting heart grew lighter.

When I finally stopped, the world was darker. Colder. And his curls were dry.

"Oh, Persephone."

I met his eyes.

This was his time, the night. This was when the life vampires knew was regained, and his gentle embrace imparted to me a piece of the promise inherent in his preternatural existence: *You will carry on.*

I accepted that quiet strength. "Thanks."

He kept one arm around my shoulders, guiding me as he reached for the screen door. "Let's get you inside where it's warm, shall we?"

In the living room he saw me to the couch, then stood awkwardly nearby as I wiped my cheeks. He said nothing, so I asked, "Where's Mountain and Ivanka?"

"Still at the ER, I'm afraid. Ivanka is having surgery. Screw, plates, and whatnot." Seeing my shock and concern, he added, "She will be fine."

"Zhan?"

"I sent her to lie down."

He fed from her.

He sat next to me. "I'd offer to make you coffee, but I must confess I do not know how."

I tried to smile for him. It was a weak and watered-down version. His attempt to express contentedness was much more successful. He stroked my hair and tucked a lock behind my ear. "As an alternative, may I pour you a drink?"

I shook my head. "Not a good time to start drinking."

"*Au contraire.*" He gave a little tug on my hair. "I know what you need."

"Let's just get to the haven, okay? You drive." I offered him the keys.

He waved me off. "I don't drive much."

I thought back. He'd always been chauffeured in a limo or a cab. Or he walked. "You don't know how."

He sat straighter. "I do so."

My stare remained steady.

"You are simply more experienced," he said reasonably. "And we have little time."

Right. Break down later. "Fine." I stood. "But while I'm behind the wheel you're not allowed to ask me what happened."

He stood too. "I did not intend to ask, dear master. You may tell me when you want me to know. Or not."

On I-71, I set the cruise control at a modest seventy-two miles per hour.

Menessos busily sent and received messages on his satellite phone. He seemed calm, but I didn't recall any other time when he'd been so enamored with messaging.

I wasn't surprised he had things to take care of, but I wondered why he didn't just make calls. Then it hit me: I had already shown him I'd been pushed to the edge of breaking down. Whatever he didn't want me to overhear must have been info that would have added to my anxiety.

My line of reasoning added to it anyway. My stomach was in knots by the time he was finally finished texting. Directing my thoughts away from the mind-rape he was going to endure, I said, "So. Who was the creepy dude you sent to the house?"

He fidgeted but didn't answer.

"Menessos." My firm tone had some effect, but not the kind that won me an answer.

"What did you think of him?"

After being too stubborn to answer, his question was far too casual. "What part of 'creepy' didn't convey what I thought of him?"

Menessos gave a short laugh. "Well, I was hoping you might go into detail."

"Funny, I was hoping the same thing."

We sat in silence while two mile markers passed.

I broke. "At least give me a name."

"Creepy is more fitting than you know."

"Then *what* is he? He freaking dematerialized himself."

"Really? That's quite interesting."

My voice was low and my lips hardly moved as I said, "Menessos."

He shivered. "Zhan told me what he did to the dragon, and how Ivanka's arm was broken."

"Yeah, and your note said you would send help. Ivanka could have avoided her injury if the person you chose to send possessed *less* apparent stalkerishness and *more* tact." I waited for him to offer something. He didn't.

Johnny's attack had just royally screwed up my ability to trust him, and now Menessos was withholding important information. So my next tactic was a low blow. "Well, at least the shabbubitum will figure out what the big secret about this is. I hope I get to hear it from them."

"Persephone."

Apprehension sucked. Anger felt much better, so I went with it. "Drop the difficult act and tell me who the creep you sent to my house was!"

"I cannot."

"You mean will not."

"No. I *can*not."

"*Riiight.*" I could justify my antagonism because it felt like it was accomplishing something, which I preferred to the sedentary and stagnant nature of worrying.

"I know in my heart who he is, and yet his name evades me. He's bound me against it. My tongue cannot speak his name, my hand cannot write it, and I daresay even the shabbubitum will not be able to draw it out of me, as I cannot even think it. Though they would surely find great pleasure in the pain I would suffer as they tried." He paused. "I cannot even describe him. I would doubt my sanity if not for my certainty that he bound me against this knowledge. Can you even imagine it, Persephone?"

That was a seriously intense kind of binding, but then Creepy had displayed great wizardry skill. He'd even teleported himself from one end of my house to the other. "Wait a minute. This guy put a binding upon you, my dear vampire? I don't think I believe that. I'd have noticed *something*."

"The binding was placed during my awakening this evening."

"Oh." I *had* almost put the car into a ditch. "Okay, I did feel that, but are you saying you don't object to some weirdo binding you from telling me his name as he offers to help?"

"I thought the assistance of strangers equaled some assurance of their quality."

"Maybe for a *random* stranger. Someone you send isn't in the same category. And what about the spiel you preached at me over not binding ourselves to those with higher rank or not of our own kind? This creep is sooo *not* a vampire."

"This is an exception to that rule."

"Menessos."

His eyes fluttered shut for a second or two. "Must you know the name of everyone who offers you aid?"

I considered it and groaned exasperatedly. "No. I understand he has some reason to hide his identity, but that doesn't inspire my trust."

"People trusted Superman without knowing his true identity."

Stunned, I stared at him, then broke away only because I could tell the Avalon was drifting into the adjacent lane. "One, I can't believe you just referenced a comic book superhero. Two, that was fiction. And three, Superman earned the trust of those who witnessed his actions. Creepy's actions included trespassing, personal assault, and the poisoning of my pet."

"Ivanka will heal, and the protection I sought for you and your property was granted in the conversion of the dragon. Besides, my note said I was getting help.

Since I sent him and told you, the claim of trespassing is excessive."

I ground my teeth. "Strangers on my property, crossing my wards without invoking them, can expect to be considered enemies. Even if they drop your name."

"Under normal circumstances, a wise approach, but our circumstances are far from normal. And speaking of the unusual, you did bring your broom tonight?"

"It's in the trunk." My fingers tapped impatiently on the steering wheel, and more grinding of teeth ensued. He wasn't able to give up answers, so he was opting for a subject change. But I wasn't giving up. Maybe I could pry some clues out of him. "Maybe, as the Lustrata, I should be greatly offended by this binding upon my Offerling. I'll work on severing it ASAP."

"Unnecessary."

"I'll be the judge of that."

He gently stroked my arm. "Persephone. Do not attempt to sever this binding."

Thinking of what I'd done in my meditation world, I felt confident I could find a way to disengage the binding, though I wasn't sure I wanted to visit either Menessos's or Creepy's meditation worlds. "Don't worry. I'm experienced at removing binding spells."

"I don't doubt you. I just *want* you to leave it alone."

"Oh, well, that's different," I said sarcastically. "He said he could help me more than I could imagine. With your endorsement, I guess next time I'll just ask Mr. Exception-to-the-Rule to move in and set up shop."

"Persephone!" he said exasperatedly.

His power tingled through me, but inside I gave a little cheer.

"In case you've forgotten, *I* presently have need of aid as well," Menessos grumbled. His expression was that of a gambler suckered into a game of Russian roulette. "Assistance of his caliber comes with a price. That binding was part of the terms."

My inner cheer turned into an aggravated scream. Anyone who was willing to help Menessos in exchange for keeping their real identity a secret from me was someone whose help I had to be wary of. I knew Menessos was desperate . . . but what had he done, and what would it cost us?

CHAPTER TWENTY-EIGHT

Heldridge Ellington had been confined to a holding cell. It was little more than a tiny room with a narrow bed, but it was dark and windowless, and when the day dawned he'd rested without fear. Upon arising this night, he was promptly given a pint of blood through a small receptacle on the door.

Though confined, this was preferable to the moist, earthy tombs he'd been hiding in lately. With Goliath Kline hunting him, his options had been few.

He drank and lay down, sated.

I wouldn't have tried to kill her if I'd thought there was a chance of claiming her and making her my witch. That would have galled my former master, had I bested his witch and forced her to free him. He would have had to concede her to my court then. Taking his queen for my own, making myself the commander of her power, he would have respected me for that. It would have elevated me in his mind, and in everyone else's.

His lips formed a thin, hard line. *But I am without magic.*

No matter what might have been. What is, is, and surely the Excelsior has chosen a course of action. One more night, maybe two, and they will come to me and tell me that I was right, that my former master is under the thumb of a witch. They will be grateful that I saved them from the embarrassment of a Quarterlord being made an informant for WEC.

Unless releasing the shabbubitum requires a certain moon phase. If that's the case, I could be in here for weeks.

Or, to confirm my truthfulness, they may bring the shabbubi-tum to me first.

Neither of those were welcome thoughts. Heldridge wished he understood the implications of magic better, but he had been unable to master the magical arts. He hadn't the talent for it.

He remembered when Menessos had found him after the Great Chicago Fire in 1871.

Orphaned, homeless, cold and starving, Heldridge had roamed the ashy streets seeking shelter, friends and food. He'd seen no one he knew. One day, he saw a man beat a baker unconscious and steal a bag full of bread. He secretly followed the man and discovered he'd been hiding in the basement of a burned-out house.

Heldridge had waited until dark, tiptoed down the partially charred staircase and stolen the bag of rolls. As he'd made his surreptitious departure, one of the boards broke and Heldridge fell. The noise awakened the man.

Heldridge raced away. The man gave chase, but the boy—slighter and more agile—scurried through the remains of buildings that the man dared not enter.

When he thought he'd escaped, Heldridge sat down to eat. The man appeared out of nowhere and hit Heldridge so hard the boy couldn't think straight. Then the man unfastened his belt. He crouched over Heldridge and pulled off the boy's pants.

The next thing Heldridge knew, the man was screaming . . . then he wasn't.

Heldridge gathered his wits and picked himself up to see Menessos wiping his mouth as he stood.

"He bloodied your lip, mister," Heldridge recalled having said. He hadn't understood then what he'd been saved from or what Menessos had done to rescue him.

"Yes," Menessos had replied. "I believe he did. But he won't hurt you anymore, son. Why don't you hurry on home."

"Don't have a home."

"Then get back to your parents."

Heldridge had dropped his chin down.

"That wasn't your father, was it?" Menessos's voice had sunk deeper.

"No. My pa's dead."

"I see. And your mother?"

Heldridge shook his head side to side.

"Why don't you come with me, then?"

"Who are you?"

"My name is Menessos."

"That's a funny name. Is it Polish?" Heldridge recalled his pa always complaining about some Polish men in their neighborhood. They always seemed to have strange names.

"No, it isn't Polish." Menessos picked up the bag of rolls.

Heldridge thought this funny-named-man would claim them, but he surrendered the thin cloth bag back to him. "This way."

"Where we going?"

"To my home. It isn't burned." He'd walked away.

Heldridge had followed. "What are you doing out here if you have a home that's not burned?"

"I have a crew of men who can rebuild homes. In the evening, I inspect the work they did during the day, and see where else I can send them so they get paid. What's your name, boy?"

"Heldridge."

"That's a funny name. Is it Polish?"

"No." He tore greedily into the roll, chewed. "One of my grandpa's last names is my first name. I'm Heldridge Ellington."

After that, he'd stayed in a modest house with a polite woman, Miss Babette, who cared for him. She even started schooling him. Menessos visited every evening, and Miss Babette gave him a report of Heldridge's day.

Eventually Menessos asked the then twelve-year-old Heldridge what he wanted to be when he grew up. Heldridge had thought hard about his answer. His father had been poor. He'd worked on the docks. But there were men in fine suits around town. Men who rode in carriages.

"I want to be a businessman," Heldridge had answered.

"Then you shall be," Menessos said.

Arrangements were made and Heldridge learned from the best tutors, but at various intervals—sometimes months, sometimes years—Menessos would show up and ask him strange questions and would require him to say odd phrases in Latin.

He knew now that these had been tests of his magical abilities.

He had failed them all, but he'd learned to be a savvy businessman. Eventually Menessos rewarded him and Made him. With his help, Menessos had built a strong and prosperous haven.

Then the day came when Menessos brought in another child. *Goliath.* This weak mortal's intellect had captured his master's interests.

His master fostered the child much the same as he had

fostered Heldridge, but Menessos's interests had been keener because the seed of a witch was sprouting within this child.

You were ready for me to leave, Menessos. Ready for me to be my own master so you could name Goliath your Alter Imperator. I could accept that my failure to manifest magical talent meant I was not what you wanted in a son. But you didn't have to bring your haven to Cleveland. You could have relocated your Lustrata to Chicago. No one there would have been watching you in your city. But in my city, I was watching, and I recognized what she did to you.

Yes, I took action. Yes, I told. You've gone soft. It was no less than you deserved.

Now they're waking the shabbubitum. I remember what you told me. "They are more dangerous than anyone could have realized."

You should have left me alone. Now we'll see how you manage—magic to magic.

The door of the holding cell opened, jarring him from his thoughts. A sentry gestured for him to come out.

"Where to?"

The vampire did not answer.

Having little choice, Heldridge walked from the cell and was escorted by twelve sentries to an elevator where another vampire waited. The vampire had a shaven head and wore a collarless shirt that had only the bottom half buttoned. It could have been a fashion statement but for the obvious scars on his neck. Once upon a time something had claimed chunks of his throat. His expression was one of disgust and contempt, and worse, the vampire had flat, lusterless eyes.

That was a bad sign.

During his century-plus of unnatural life, Heldridge had seen such before. Some of the younger undead had developed this phenomenon, recovering their life at sundown to bear the awful weight of their dead hours in their gaze. They were the vampires he knew would not long survive their new life. He had learned why the selection process for Offerlings was so intense and why their service was required for various lengths of time before being Made. It was not so much exclusive as it was merciful.

"Who are you?"

"I am Giovanni Guistini, advisor to the Excelsior."

Heldridge was stunned. Listening to Giovanni speak was like hearing the hiss of an old steam locomotive, adding in a scratchiness so one could make words of it. With such a voice, his words would have to possess serious insight for anyone—much less the Excelsior—to suffer employing him for his *spoken* opinions.

Four sentries stood in the elevator. Giovanni stepped in with them. The sentry behind Heldridge poked him in the back; he joined the group. More sentries piled in behind him.

They rode downward in silence and Heldridge considered Giovanni.

An advisor to the Excelsior would not be a young vampire. It was different when the suspiciously cruel eyes were on an older vampire. Heldridge had learned that when seen on a haven master, this symptom meant the vampire was *not* likely to expire, but those around him or her definitely were.

He decided to regard Giovanni as extremely dangerous and unforgiving. It meant Heldridge wouldn't dare to give these vampires any resistance or trouble.

The elevator doors opened on an underground parking garage. More sentries waited there and led the group to an idling black limousine. "Get in," Giovanni said as a sentry opened the door. Eagerly, Heldridge did. Four sentries were waiting inside. Heldridge sat in the center of the rear and was relieved to be out of the presence of the scarred and raspy advisor. Then Giovanni joined him. Heldridge scooted to the far door. "Any chance you'll tell me where we're going?"

"None."

CHAPTER TWENTY-NINE

By the time Menessos and I arrived at Public Square, I had accepted his assertion that he couldn't tell me about Creepy, and my thoughts circled around the impending threat. My hands were shaking. In front of the haven I hit the hazard lights. "What can I expect of this shabbubitum reading of you?"

"It will be nearly as painful to view as it will be to bear, but you must not interfere." Menessos couldn't have exited the car any faster. A doorman from the haven hustled to the driver's side so he could park it for me. I popped the trunk lever. After grabbing my overnight bag and broom from inside, I said, "What if—"

"Not under *any* circumstances, Persephone." Menessos straightened to his full height as he spoke so that he might look slightly down his nose at me.

"But—"

"No buts. Do not interfere."

I kicked at the sidewalk. I hated not getting my thoughts out, but I hated the implied helplessness ten times more. I blurted, "As the Lustrata I should do something."

"You will. You will observe without acting."

"That's not helpful." Neither was the chill in the Lake Erie breeze that was blowing my hair around and hiding my frown.

"Actually, it is. However, if you mean it's not 'heroic,' that is true, but trying to be heroic tonight would be . . . unwise."

I glowered. "How is it *helpful*," I snarled, "to stand by while someone is tortured?" I stamped the bushy end of the broom stubbornly. "What am I here for, if not to aid you? You did say they might try to kill me."

Menessos was very still. "You must be seen here at my side in court. Until the instant that they say you are my master, everyone in this haven must believe you are not."

I swallowed hard. *He wants me to flee, but only after it's confirmed that I'm the bad guy, once every member of his haven knows what I've done and then hates and resents me like some of the pack hate and resent me being with Johnny, and like some of the witches hate and resent me.* I didn't like being put in danger, especially when it seemed like danger for the sake of being in danger. This witch wasn't an adrenaline junkie. *If he just wants me to see him suffer for more of my pity—* "What's the payoff for you in that?"

"If you are absent, your guilt appears evident. If you are present, it appears you are innocent. I mean, if you *were* my master, logically, why would you wait around knowing they would be obligated to seize you?"

"Exactly," I said insipidly. The need to "sell" the notion of being innocent, I could understand, but that seemed thin considering just how guilty I was.

Menessos gently smoothed my hair into place as the wind died down. "The additional benefit is that VEIN will be assured my people were unaware of it. All of my people. Even Goliath. They will not be read or censured for their silence."

Crestfallen, I let my shoulders slump. "Oh." Accepting a personal risk to ensure others didn't have to suffer what the shabbubitum did to read them . . . that was danger that had a noble purpose.

He had me where he wanted me and he knew it.

"You're betting my life," I said, "on your ability to twist things."

He tilted his head and peered at me softly. "You can't deny I'm good at it."

Seduction. Now? Suspicious, my chin levered up as I considered that. "What are you up to?"

He tweaked my chin and grinned mischievously. "Trust me?" It was a breathtaking smile. The smile of the fantasy King Arthur of my girlish dreams. "Yes."

He leaned in and put a quick peck of a kiss on my cheek. The brush of his short beard was soft and warm. "Perfect." He walked away. "You will keep that broom Xerxadrea gave you handy, won't you? I suggest you keep it right beside your stage seat."

Inside the haven, Beholders were setting up brass posts linked with velvet ropes as if preparing for an exclusive evening. Seven met us in the lobby carrying a roll of blueprints and a flat carpenter pencil. Her blue-black hair was gathered up in a high ponytail. It made her beauty sharper and her turquoise eyes brighter.

She was just leaving the work-in-progress dance club that was set to become a source of haven income, so the construction boots and jeans she wore didn't surprise me, but the low-slung leather belt laden with dirty, well-worn tools did. Seeing us, she advanced. "Boss. Erus Veneficus."

"How is it coming in there?" Menessos asked.

She offered him the blueprints. "Ahead of schedule."

He *tsk-tsk*ed her teasingly. "And you thought they would lose a whole day without you." He unrolled the paper.

"I never said they'd be a whole day behind, and for the record, your secondary request ate up my first two hours of the night. I just got back." She pointed to a few places that had markings in red. They had a brief discussion concerning changes to the original plans.

Menessos approved of her solutions and rerolled the paper for her. "Did those two hours pay off?"

"VEIN's biggest jet is scheduled to arrive at Dulles in D.C. for refueling, then is heading for Hopkins. Arrival is set for twelve twenty." She checked the display on her satellite phone. "About five hours from now." She paused. "Ivanka?"

"Mountain messaged me that she was in recovery. He will let me know when she's able to be released."

"They won't keep her overnight?"

"They might, but I want her brought here."

"Her quarters are ready. As are the rooms of the Erus Veneficus, per your request." She gave me a look that was happy, but with an undertone of sneakiness.

"Thank you, Seven." Menessos strolled away.

I didn't follow. Seven was the previous Lustrata. I had so many questions, but I hadn't had a chance to speak to her since she'd told me her true identity shortly before the battle with the fairies. I switched the grasp on my broom and offered her my hand to shake. "I hope we'll have a chance to talk again."

She wrapped her arms around me. "It's good to have you back," she whispered.

"Persephone?" Menessos called.

She released me and I joined Menessos at the elevator.

"She likes you," he said as we rode down.

"I'm glad. I like her too. Would like to know her better." She was, after all, Cleopatra VII, as in *the* Cleopatra. Who wouldn't want to ask her a million questions? But, since she went by the name Seven now, it was easy to assume that she didn't want to be known for her past.

With that thought, I gained a little insight as to why Menessos didn't want the world at large to know his own past. *He wouldn't be seen as who he is, but as who he was.*

That drew my thoughts to Johnny. I wanted him to be who I knew him to be. *But he isn't himself since we unlocked his tattoos.*

Maybe I'd been hasty in getting rid of the *in signum amoris.*

Am I doubting Hecate?

I followed Menessos from the elevator, down the stairs of the theater, up the ramp and across the stage. I situated my broom to lean against my seat, noting the Beholder on his knees a few feet away from Menessos's throne. He was wiping what appeared to be a new decorative inset in the floor. Someone called out, "Testing the light," and a glow rose up from under the stones the man was wiping clean.

Rejoining Menessos, who had waited for me, we wound our way through the backstage area to where our separate rooms were located. I started up the stairwell that led to my rooms directly above his.

"Do you wish to freshen up and then join me? Or may I join you?"

Halfway up, I turned back with a telling sigh. "Promise no funny business?"

"I am not a comedian."

"But you *are* who you *are*."

"Indeed."

At least I knew what to expect with him. And after thousands of years, he didn't bother denying it. As I watched him ascend the stairs I wondered if he'd wrestled with it. I wondered if he'd won. Or if he'd lost and come to terms with it.

I punched in the entry code, Beverley's birthday, and entered to find my quarters were candlelit and a fire blazed in the double-sided hearth. The warmth that greeted me, the sweet gesture behind it, almost spouted the waterworks again, but I kept the tears in check. Hearing Menessos arrive at the door behind me, I said over my shoulder, "This isn't a strategizing setup."

"Just now, you require a soothing environment."

On my way inside I stripped off my blazer-hoodie combo. "You have a plan, don't you?"

He appraised my face, my body. "Indeed."

Noting the double entendre, I clarified. "For the shabbubitum."

"Them, too."

I carried my coats toward the bar, intending to hang them across the seat. "Tell me." Then I noticed how dirty and torn the back of my blazer was. "Shit." The den rooftop had ruined it.

"I can get you a new jacket. Any kind you like."

"That won't gain you the favors you're after."

Menessos entered the kitchenette and opened the refrigerator. "It can't hurt my chances."

Admittedly, I examined his backside as he leaned down and rambled around a shelf. He had a very nice, round ass. When he stood straight, I inspected the rip on my blazer more studiously. "Tell me your plan."

"It begins with these." He held up a bottle of wine and a small plate bearing slices of marbled cheese, salami, and little crackers. Seeing my dubious expression, he added, "Fear not. You do not overindulge, and I am not a lecher, so getting you drunk and taking advantage of you is not part of my plan, though it is a wildly good idea that I have entertained. Tonight, however, your shaking hands belie a need that I am well acquainted with. A drink would help." He retrieved a glass from the cupboard and set about uncorking the wine.

"Telling me what your plan is *not* is not telling me your plan."

"True." He poured. "You are not materialistic, so pretty things will not sway you, but I will woo you with time, Persephone." He set the bottle aside and presented me with the glass. "It is the one thing I have that dear John does not."

Johnny. I did not accept the slender stem. *Could I ever trust Johnny again?*

I relived the rooftop attack.

After scenting my blood, his beast had conquered his man-mind. But even in human form, he was losing control when we had sex at the den. He'd recovered, but. . . . *Do I want to bear the scars—both the emotional and the physical ones—of him relearning his self-control?* I had to believe that he *could* regain control.

"Persephone." Menessos put power behind the whisper and warmth fluttered down my spine, down my legs, and echoed back up with a fine resonance that hinted at the kind of thrills this vampire could induce. "Drink the wine."

I drank the wine.

CHAPTER THIRTY

Meroveus Franciscus sat separate from his guests aboard the plane, assessing them. Aware that he would need someone to give the sisters use of a modern language, he'd reviewed the files on their colleagues in Athens on the plane before the dawn had claimed him. He'd wanted someone who was generally naïve, who served with an excessive amount of adoration, and who had more than average debt. Zevon was part of the arrangements that had been made.

In addition to language, the sisters now knew what Zevon knew of the world.

He hadn't wanted them to know too much. Zevon did not have much use for current events, international politics, or the names or locations of world leaders. It would not bode well for the shabbubitum to know such things. Their reputation indicated they could not resist powerful temptations . . . so, better to shield them from it.

But he could not shield them from the novelty and comfort of a limousine. He could not keep them from seeing the modern city of Athens or the ruins that made them cry. He could not keep them ignorant of the machine that carried them into the air, or the impressive nightscape of New York City as the Gulfstream landed.

He could, however, make them remain on the plane while it refueled.

Mero checked his messages. An assistant had left him a lengthy voice mail about the Zvonul having announced the confirmation of a Domn Lup, and followed it with the public details. *Not good for Menessos if Giovanni has his way.*

Minutes later, the shabbubitum grew excited as lights streaked toward the plane, and they chattered to themselves seeing that it was another limousine. It was no surprise when the cabin door was opened and Giovanni boarded.

He had to see. Like a child, he must poke at the dead things he has found.

The sisters remained in their seats, attentive but quiet as they considered Giovanni. Ailo and Talto reacted to his exposed scars and warped skin with unmistakable revulsion. Liyliy's expression revealed only a wary curiosity.

Giovanni visually inspected them as well, obviously noting with predictable male appreciation the curves beneath the gray silk. His gaze lingered on the eldest. "What is your name, my beauty?"

At the sound of his voice, her curious expression fell into a repulsed sneer. She stood. "I am Liyliy."

Giovanni's admiration dissolved with her revulsion. "Has Mero told you the purpose of your freedom?"

"He speaks little." She lifted her chin. "But he is more pleasant to hear."

Features hardening into a scowl as rigid as the flesh of the disfigurement he flaunted, Giovanni spun to the doorway behind him and barked, "Bring him."

Mero knew what was next. He wanted to deny Giovanni, but showing a discord between them would only give the shabbubitum something to work with. He held his tongue, but it was not easy.

Heldridge joined them.

The sisters had a completely different reaction to the broad-shouldered and handsome vampire. Ailo and Talto came to their feet beside Liyliy. Chests heaved and fell as adoring sighs were cast into the air. Mero could not deny the smirk that crawled over his mouth when he saw Giovanni's jaw flex angrily while the females admired Heldridge.

Giovanni saw Mero's sordid satisfaction and growled to Liyliy, "Read him. Tell me if he believes the Northeastern Quarterlord bears the mark of a witch."

"Who are you that I should obey your order?"

Giovanni glowered.

"Liyliy," Mero said, "tell us if Heldridge sincerely believes the Northeastern Quarterlord bears the mark of a witch."

"Gladly." Liyliy strode forward, circled Heldridge once as she appraised him. Before him, her silken gown faded into a puddle of mist at her feet. Her sisters joined her. "Give us your hands."

Heldridge swallowed hard. He had feared the Excelsior would require that he prove the truth in his words. No matter how gorgeous these women were, he knew that what was going to happen to him would be terrible. He'd heard Menessos's tale.

But my former master, my Maker, will get what he deserves.

He offered them his hands.

The most beautiful one touched him. "What is your name?" he whispered.

"Liyliy." As soon as she had answered, she began whispering a chant.

Her clothes had dropped away and he was mesmerized by her voice, her pert breasts. Her sisters whispered, too, and in seconds the mist swirled like a tentacle around his neck. He had only a moment to worry about it, then that mist surrounded his head like a mask and thickened. As he smothered under what now seemed like cloth, instincts overpowered him. He shook his head as if that could loosen the fabric—but it couldn't. Then he felt them, thousands of . . . somethings . . . like tiny mites marching across his face, crawling under his eyelids. They surged into his ears and up his nose. They tunneled into every pore. He screamed and they flooded into his mouth.

It was like being eaten alive.

Suddenly his lungs were full with them, each one now like an atom of oxygen racing into his bloodstream and being carried throughout his body. Worse, the tiny assailants burrowed through his skull. His head felt perforated, as if he would crumble in on himself at the slightest touch. If he'd had the breath to scream again, it would surely have killed him.

Then these tiny *things* slithered into his brain like electric eels, jolting him, sinking barbed teeth into his memories, then twisting without letting go, wringing every thought he'd ever had and drinking up whatever spilled.

Mero had witnessed the method of information transference before, so instead of observing the shabbubitum at work, he watched Giovanni. He wanted his coadvisor, who had been so eager to unleash this trio, to be sickened by the scene, to be horrified by the screams and disgusted by the red foam that bubbled up from

Heldridge's throat onto his lips. But Giovanni seemed to notice only Liyliy's writhing nakedness.

When it was done, Liyliy languished in her position atop Heldridge, arching her back and stretching her arms up high. The tentacle of mist that had coiled around Heldridge's head retreated from the vampire and slithered up to form black satin gloves on Liyliy's upraised arms.

It could have been a beautiful display, but the vampire's screams of pain were still echoing about the cabin as she topped that sound with her own throaty, maniacal laughter.

Her sisters traded glances and joined her in the sinister mirth, wrapping their arms around her waist. Liyliy's arms fell about her sisters, and the disturbing joy continued into awkwardness for those around them.

Mero understood what had spawned the sister's reaction, though he doubted Giovanni did. Menessos had given these women power that led to their self-destruction, then Menessos had confined them in stone. Now, Heldridge had demanded they be set free to judge the very vampire who had imprisoned them.

Moreover, the treacherous sisters now had the not-so-naïve knowledge that Heldridge possessed. That data would contain inner workings of the vampire power structure as it existed today, as well as U.S. and international politics that affected the haven Heldridge used to master.

The fool has no idea how much he has increased the difficulty of my task. Or maybe he does.

Liyliy laughed. Heldridge had lived a long, long time. The information she and her sisters had just gained from him was much more complete than poor nonstudious

Zevon's. A vampire's longevity provided a depth of knowledge that a young mortal man could not fathom. The industry and mechanization of the world had changed radically under his watchful eyes, and now she understood this marvelous age more thoroughly.

"Well?" Giovanni demanded, interrupting her amusement.

Her mirth faded. "Yes. He believes that Menessos has been marked by his Erus Veneficus. A fairy told him as much, but events he has witnessed and conversations he has overheard support the claim."

And now I know why we were brought back. Now I know that the one who released us, this Meroveus, though he worked with the one who imprisoned us then, he is now reprimanding our jailer.

Giovanni extended his hand to one of the vampires who had escorted Heldridge aboard. A leather case, much like a sealed quiver for arrows, passed into Giovanni's grip. He tossed this to Mero, who caught it and set it aside.

Wondering what was in it, Liyliy stood. She eased away from Heldridge and toward Meroveus. *He's giving me one of the two things I want most of all—the vampire who caused our tragic curse. Eventually I will get the necklace away from him too . . . maybe even right now. . . .*

Her black gloves faded to mist, which reappeared around her body as she crossed the small space inside the flying machine—the jet airplane. When she arrived before him, the mist had made a revealing gown of black lace that accentuated the size of her breasts and was translucent in all the right places. "You are taking us to Menessos. You want us to search his mind for the truth. Correct?"

"Yes."

The corner of her mouth crooked up sweetly. "Allow me to show my gratitude." She reached for him.

He swatted her wrist away, then backhanded her across the jaw.

"*Numquam tangent vester dominus!*" In English he repeated, "I am your lord. Never touch me. Dare you even try that again," he spat, "and I'll bind you into the stones of the nearest urinal." He looked past her. "Giovanni, get Heldridge off the plane."

CHAPTER THIRTY-ONE

I stared at the plate of food. I was hungry, but my hands were gross with scabs matted with wolf hair. I turned on the faucet. When the water was warm, I started washing with the hand soap from the counter. It stung like hell.

Menessos disappeared into the back of the apartment and returned with a small first aid kit. He set it aside and reached for my hands. "Allow me."

"I can do it."

"And I allowed you to tend my wound once. Please be so kind as to allow me to return the favor?"

Long ago—well, it seemed like a long time ago—Samson D. Kline had nearly staked Menessos; I'd cleaned the gash, put antibiotics on it and bandaged him up. Of course, he'd promptly quoted poetry and come on to me, too. Sighing, I sidestepped to let him close.

We were silent for a long minute as the warm water ran and ran. The static sound of its flowing became musical as he continuously rubbed my skin with gentle, diligent strokes. His every rhythmical movement was made with such tender purpose that I was spellbound by it all. His thumbs slid over the grooves in my flesh, and the sensation was exhilarating—it took my breath away but it wasn't pain, no, it was rapturous and left me gasping. Though I detected a stinging ache, it seemed far away from my body and inconsequential . . . so long as he did not stop.

"Do you remember when we met?" Menessos asked as he sat beside me.

I blinked as if just waking from a dream. I recalled him patting my hands dry and wrapping gauze loosely around the backs of my hands, and I remembered eating three meat-and-cheese-topped crackers, but I did not have a recollection of planting myself in the very corner of the black leather sectional couch. Yet, here I was.

"Do you?" he repeated.

"Yeah. What does that have to do with your plan?" I drained the last of the wine from the glass.

"Everything."

As the effects of the wine loosened the tension and soreness in my shoulders, I twisted and propped my feet on the end of the sectional away from Menessos. Candlelight and wine. I could guess what *he* wanted. But what *I* wanted was a nice, hot bath with enough bubbles to make me forget what had just happened on the rooftop of the wærewolves' den. However, I was betting that the bubbles the wine produced in my brain had a better shot at achieving that.

"Do you recall the stake that was on your property?" Menessos asked.

"I do." His former and estranged E.V. had made and enchanted a stake to keep Menessos away from her. She'd used a little of the home earth in his dirt-bag mixed with her own blood—which was bound to him—and Blessed Water to create it. He had not even been able to be in the presence of the stake. I'd destroyed it.

"Once I'd marked you, it hurt you to be near it, though more subtly than it hurt me. And when I was near it, I could convey some of the pain it caused me onto you."

"Yeah, so you could threaten Johnny." He'd let me bear *all* the pain. Damn near killed me, but also enabled me—and Hecate—to flip the mark back onto him, though neither of us had known it at the time.

"Exactly. It was . . . self-preservation."

"Something you lacked on the beach." I leaned forward and put the empty wineglass on the floor. When I sat up, Menessos scooted closer.

"The beach was different."

His whisper was imbued with such sweet resolve that I couldn't argue. I could only stare and relive the moment I'd staked him, then rewind and relive kissing him.

Would I be better off in his arms instead of Johnny's? Would I be safer?

I held my breath.

How can I even think this? Am I so tired I've gone fickle?

My gaze dropped to my twice-wrapped palms.

I knew exactly how I could be thinking what I was thinking. But it hurt so damn much. Like the shabbubitum, I'd done this to myself. I'd given Johnny what he needed to be Domn Lup: his wolf unbound. But I'd also created a situation that undermined the love that had prompted my actions.

There's that stupid L word again.

Menessos slowly lowered his lips to my wrist, giving me plenty of seconds to protest. I didn't. When his fangs pierced me, I barely felt it. He didn't go deep, but he didn't need to.

With his teeth just under my skin, he kindled my flesh, raising heat throughout my body. Gooseflesh followed. The hair at the nape of my neck prickled and a deep sigh drifted from my lips. My sternum burned within me. My nipples hardened and I yearned to be touched.

But he held only my wrist and sipped of my blood.

So I touched him.

The fingers of my free hand stroked his head, combed slightly through his walnut-colored curls. His hair was so soft. When I caressed his earlobe, he shuddered, and I felt the needle-tips of his fangs leave my flesh. He kept his head lowered as the kindling died slowly away, but I could hear his breathing had accelerated.

He sat up slowly and released my wrist. "There, my master. That should be better." He freed one of the bandages.

He'd pushed some healing into me. A week or so ago, after the Omori had hit me with a baseball bat, Menessos had fed and the goose egg on my cranium had disappeared. Now, the cuts on my palms were more like scrapes, and the sore puffiness was gone. I wasn't as tired, either. "Much," I whispered.

He relaxed into the couch and stroked my cheek, then his hand fell to his lap.

Zhan could have told him that my afternoon was spent with the wæres. From that, and my weepy arrival, he could infer a lot.

Menessos is the master manipulator. If he's sitting here being so gentle and sweet, he has a reason. Maybe Zhan even told him how Johnny was acting, what she overheard.

"How does the stake connect to our dilemma now?" My voice was still husky with desire.

"I can still transfer my pain."

Aha. "To your master."

"Yes, but you are here and expected to be seen. If you

fell into agony, it would give away what I was doing."

This wasn't going where I thought it would.

"But if I move it via my soul . . ."

I blinked. "You mean you'd send it to Johnny. Through the *sorsanimus*." Was he testing me, to see if I felt vindictive? "Why not just spread it out over your people? The whole haven will be here."

"I can and will . . . they will be expecting that. But since Johnny could endure a lot of pain, I would give him a large chunk of it, and meanwhile, as I pretend to be in pain, I'm actually still able to function secretly."

"Is this what you and Creepy worked out? Torturing an innocent in your stead?"

"Johnny is hardly innocent."

I tilted my head forward expectantly. "Elaborate."

"Your hands have been torn open, and his fur—I could smell him—was stuck in your dried blood. Follow that with your tears and I don't need you to tell me what happened, sweet Persephone, because I can guess."

I swallowed hard. I expected him to ballyhoo about Johnny being dangerous and to boast how he was fully able to control himself. But he didn't crow about his merits at all.

"I have to keep some of the pain." He shook his head side to side, as if his body were trying to refute the notion. "The shabbubitum are skilled mistresses of torture. They would know if I was completely faking. So our new ally taught me to think through the pain. I know what they will be asked to find, and I will make that easy for them. But I suspect they will dig deeper for information, information they want personally that has nothing to do with the request being made of them and everything to do with how to hurt me most. It is that which I cannot give them . . . so I must give them a lie."

"But they will know."

"As they increase the misery to find what they seek, I will defer more pain to Johnny and maintain my own ability to think. I will guide them to the knowledge they think they want. All I need is for you to call dear John and tell him what to expect. Receiving the news from you will be less irritating to him, despite whatever has happened, than if I delivered it myself."

The mere idea of calling Johnny inspired an Olympian amount of grumpy anti-enthusiasm, and some angry little part of me did think the idea of Johnny getting a whopping dose of out-of-nowhere pain was something he had earned. *Shut up, little angry part. That is not the person I want to be.* "Won't the shabbubitum know you're deferring the pain?"

"Not with the aid I have secured."

"What did it cost you?" My arms crossed over my chest. Again, it felt way better to argue about this than to accept the anxiety over the idea of talking to Johnny.

"Much. But less than it would without his assistance."

"Menessos—"

"Shhh." His finger touched my lips. "I have already torn my soul and given my life for you, Persephone. Comparatively, what Creepy asked is a small price to pay."

I uncrossed my arms, batting away his gentle touch, and then scooted around on the sectional in a huff. With my feet on the floor, I glared.

"What?"

"My mother is already using what she's lost in an effort to control me. I don't need you doing it too."

Menessos blinked, rose from the couch, and left without a word.

I remained where I was, feeling like an ass.

The guilt wasn't enough to keep me from sleeping, however. Or maybe the drowsiness was a result of the wine. Whatever the case, Risqué woke me hours later, banging and kicking on my door. When I opened it, the red-eyed whatever-she-was stood there pout-frowning at me. She wore a pink tank top and matching ruffled boy-shorts with her clear platform heels. Not unexpectedly, she was toting a garment bag. "Boss says it's time to play dress-up."

Privately, I worried. Menessos had less than practical tastes in clothing for me. With him leaving pissed off, I was sure there would be little to the outfit and that it would have matching shoes with heels ridiculously high.

I motioned her inside. "Show me."

Risqué set her makeup case down and draped the garment bag along the couch. She unzipped it and held up the gown. It was white satin covered by an outer layer of something crimson and sheer and meant for bedroom clothes. The style was elegant, and though the dress was empire-waisted, the length was tight through the hips, with a very, very high slit on one side.

I grimaced.

"Your garter must show. It is the symbol of your status in the haven. Get used to the high slit."

"And the shoes?"

She laid the gown over the back of the couch, rambled in the garment bag bottom, and presented me with a pair of shiny patent-leather shoes that resembled scarlet ballerina toe shoes—if toe shoes had five-inch spike heels thinner than pencils. "What do you think?"

"I think that purchasing those should include a three-day wait period in which time changes are made to the phrasing of the accidental death clause of the wearer's life insurance policy."

"Boss said you'd say something to that effect." She dropped the shoes aside. She reached into the bottom of the bag again and produced a pair of standard, peep-toe crimson pumps with a sturdier three-inch heel. In a bored tone she asked, "Will these do?"

"Absolutely."

I showered so that Risqué could perform her salon magic on my clean hair. My injuries had not healed completely, so I warned her about my scalp wound mostly so she would be gentle—*as if!*—and partially because washing it had reopened that wound and I was bleeding in a vampire haven.

She inspected my scalp and told me that there were three cuts on the lump, but only one of them needed stitches. I wondered how bad they had been before the kindling. As it turned out, minor medical care was another painful service she offered. I tried not to be alarmed she had such supplies in her cosmetics kit.

Risqué put the final touches on my makeup and hair, and promptly gathered up her cosmetics while I dressed. She zipped me up and headed for the door, golden curls bouncing. Girl-chat was not something we could pull off. "When it is time, Mark will usher you to the stage."

"Thank you."

She snorted and the door closed behind her.

In my bathroom, I flipped on the lights and regarded myself. It was not to inspect what Risqué had done. She was an expert beautician and loyal to her "boss." My purpose here was to affirm to myself, "I can make the call."

Trembling, I dialed Johnny's number.

"Hello?"

It wasn't his voice. "Beau? Is that you?"

"Yeah, doll, it's me. Thank you. I can't say it enough! Thank you, thank you, thank you!"

"Are you drunk?"

"No, silly dame. I'm delighted! My son is wholly a wolf. In the morning, I know he'll be a whole man again. I'll have him back. And it's all because of you, doll. I have my boy back."

"You're welcome, Beau. Where's Johnny?"

"Oh. He's still furry."

He hasn't reverted yet? I clamped my jaw against the tears and fought them back by telling myself how pissed Risqué would be if she had to come back and touch up the makeup.

"Gave Hector and the boys some grief getting him into a kennel, but a side of beef did the trick. Why are you calling? Something up?"

My boyfriend was eating raw meat and chewing on cow bones. I felt nauseated. *He could change back if he wanted. If he was man enough to know what he wanted.* "Beau, I have to tell you something. Johnny is going to have a bout of severe pain tonight."

"Because of the spell?"

"No, no. It's nothing to do with the spell. It's something else."

"I'm leaving here shortly and I won't be back until morning. You better talk to Hector."

I heard the phone being shifted around, then Hector said, "Hello?"

"Hi, Hector. I need to let you guys know that Johnny's going to have a fit of pain tonight. He may writhe and howl and carry on, but there's no need to worry. It shouldn't last long, less than twenty minutes."

"What's all this about?" His suspicion was thick.

"I can't tell you more than I have, Hector. Please understand."

"It's magic, isn't it?" Softer, as if he didn't want others nearby to hear, he asked, "Is it a side effect of the spell?"

"No. This is something only Johnny will experience. Whether he is in wolf-form or human-form. The others won't feel it at all. Just don't be alarmed. Like I said, it shouldn't last long, and he'll be fine when it's over."

"So he knows about this?"

If I said no, then the wærewolves could see it as a strike, just like the vampires saw my hexing Menessos as a strike. *Did I trust Johnny to have my back when his man-mind did return?* "Yes," I lied. "He knows."

CHAPTER THIRTY-TWO

Mero and the shabbubitum gracefully emerged from the limousine. The people on the sidewalk were few. They held back and paused, curious. Some lingered across the street to watch. The limo drove away. Mero firmed his grip on the round leather case that contained the Excelsior's formal document commanding Menessos to submit to being read by the shabbubitum.

With their arms linked, the women surveyed the scene of the Cleveland Public Square with awe, murmuring to each other. As Mero brought up the rear, he noted the May Company building that housed the haven. Prime real estate in the heart of the city; it was very Menessos.

He hoped the location and grandeur were indications that Menessos had not changed.

Inside, there was a cherrywood kiosk in the middle of the room, a ticket booth from ages past. To either side of this wooden structure, velvet ropes blocked passage. Just behind the ropes, two guards waited with their hands clasped before them.

Inside the booth stood a vampire with golden brown hair secured in a curly ponytail. He left the booth with the air of an undergraduate who'd rather be playing drinking games at a frat house than playing the part of the haven concierge. "Meroveus Franciscus, Advisor to the Excelsior, and party, welcome to the haven of the Northeastern

Quarterlord. I'm Sever. We've been expecting you," he said. "If you will follow Sergei?" He gestured to one of the guards and unhooked the velvet rope to allow them through.

Mero detected the true life around Sergei; an Offerling. He led them to an area out of sight of the main doors and to some fine leather seating near the elevators. "Please make yourselves comfortable. Your escort will join you shortly." The guard excused himself to a position politely far away, but kept them in sight.

Mero sat on one of the leather chairs with the case upon his lap while the women discussed Sergei's and Sever's merits. The modern world had them enthralled, as did nearly every male their eyes beheld, but Mero was wary. He could not allow himself to think he could anticipate their behavior, or expect their compliance.

Also weighing on his mind was Menessos. It had been a long time since they had last seen each other. The world was so different. From the recent reports to VEIN, he had reason to think Menessos was perhaps very different as well. Mero did not want to make an enemy of him; yet with the duty set before him, it seemed impossible to avoid.

The elevator gears hummed. The bell dinged to announce its arrival and the doors opened. A raven-haired woman with stunning blue eyes strolled out. A beaded teal dress clung to her every curve, and he could not fail to recognize Seven. She assessed the group as she neared. Mero stood. She bowed her head. "Greetings, Meroveus Franciscus and honored guests. Welcome to the Quarterlord's haven. I am Seven and will accompany you to our Lord."

He knew she knew him, but she introduced herself just the same. Perhaps because he did not greet her by name on sight. *Better to play this cool and distant.* "Of course."

Seven walked toward the stairwell and said, "If you will follow me."

Following Seven, Mero led his group down the grand stairwell. Behind him he heard the light footfalls of the shabbubitum, the heavier tread of Sergei. When they arrived at the great doors, Seven brought them forward.

Directly around him was a railed reception area with a DJ station. Music was playing softly, but at a signal from Seven, the DJ lowered the volume even more.

Before him, stairs led down to the expanse of a theater house that was no longer sloped and filled with rows of seats, but level and filled—like a nightclub or restaurant— with tables and gilt chairs. Mero noted that, modern clichés created by famous authors notwithstanding, Menessos had managed to find and convert an underground theater into an elegant new haven, one that brilliantly, dramatically, unquestionably reflected Menessos.

And there he was. Menessos sat enthroned onstage under flattering lights. Goliath Kline sat to his right, and the E.V. to his left. To either side, the fanged symbol of the haven floated across a series of large screens.

The house lighting lowered. A spotlight illuminated Seven where she stood just in front of them. "Meroveus Franciscus, Advisor to the Excelsior . . . and party," she announced. She stepped out of the light, allowing Mero and the shabbubitum to replace her in the glow and on the screens placed to either side of the stage.

He felt the scrutiny of the haven members from the

darkness below them. Seven gestured for him to descend the steps. Mero preceded the women down into the midst of the haven members at their tables, crossing the floor and pausing before the stage. He admired the setup. Most havens he'd seen of late positioned the master on a dais of some kind, but this, this was tactically superior. One had to climb a ramp to get to the otherwise railed-off stage. Retreating would involve ascending the equivalent of three flights of stairs just to make the hallway.

And anything could be behind those stage curtains.

Knowing what he had been sent here to do, and how outnumbered he was, understanding the security and the location of exits was necessary. There weren't any good, immediate options . . . but Menessos was in attendance. *He has to know why I'm here. Whether he fights this or not, he must know there is only one way for this to end.*

Mero stopped a few yards away from the ramp that led to the stage. "Greetings, Quarterlord, and Hail to thee, Menessos, Magus Periti Nocte." Mero bowed low, as did those with him, as the formal greeting between wizards was spoken. The wizard greeting was not required, but it would force Menessos to greet him in kind, and that would make everyone here know that Mero was a magical force equal to their esteemed master.

"Hail to thee, Meroveus, Magus Periti Nocte. I extend the greetings of this court to you, Advisor to the Excelsior, and to your companions."

Mero tilted his head in acquiescence of the greeting.

"What brings you, Meroveus Franciscus and party?"

He noted that Menessos had also carefully avoided acknowledging him as a friend from centuries past. At least Mero had some time to play diplomat and consider what that meant. "The Excelsior has noticed that your behavior has had a rebellious flavor of late."

"Rebellious?" Menessos's mouth crooked up on one side. "Have I . . . provoked . . . our Excelsior with such actions?"

The emphasis gave Mero a clue. They used to play such games in the courts of deviant masters. One of them would infiltrate the haven, suffer the rise to some authority. When the other would appear, the first engaged him in a fiery debate in court. They emphasized certain words to signal each other on how to respond or to conduct an underlying conversation that others were oblivious to. Sometimes their purpose was best served if the newcomer lost his temper, and sometimes the newcomer had to incite the mole. It was a ruse that required deep trust between the two of them.

But this was Menessos's haven. The authority was his, so . . . *Do I trust him that much still? Would he use our past to play me? Is he this far under the thumb of his witch?* "You didn't seek the Excelsior's . . . consent . . . before relocating your haven." His timed glance toward the witch meant his single word was a question about her. He hoped Menessos recognized it as, *"Do you consent to her?"*

"It is *my* haven. To do with as I see fit."

Mero understood that to mean that Menessos was still the master here, and that whatever show was to occur would be for the benefit of his haven. Or his witch.

Mero nodded once, shutting his eyes to indicate he understood the message.

In a monotone, Menessos added, "Chicago had become tedious."

Speaking without inflection and using a plain verb like "had become" instead of something more telling meant the message was complete. Mero continued, ready to provoke Menessos. "The Excelsior expects to be apprised when his Quarterlords make such changes."

Menessos waved dismissively. "I sent him a change-of-address card."

Quiet laughter swept through his court.

Mero waited until the crowd had quieted once more. "Indeed, but only after this property was purchased and renovations had begun."

"Ah . . . had I asked the Excelsior to bankroll the move, then I would have needed his permission. As I require no financial sponsor, I personally paid the expense of all aspects of the relocation. Therefore, I am at liberty to do as I please."

"To do as you please?" It was a striking statement; repeating it made the crowd stir uncomfortably. Mero knew when talking with Menessos it was he who did all the conversational navigation. Mero just had to keep up and do his part.

"Within my jurisdiction, of course. Cleveland is well within the borders of my quarter of the United States."

"That is true, but a decision such as this forces the Excelsior to ask what other broad decisions you might see fit to—"

"Do you mean to imply that a Quarterlord has not earned the right to make such broad decisions? Does the Excelsior plan to micromanage the Quarterlords now?"

"No, my lord. I mean to imply only that the Excelsior finds the relocation of a Quarterlord's entire haven to be noteworthy *prior* to the move."

Menessos was quiet for a heartbeat. "Have you come to censure me, Meroveus Franciscus?"

"I have." He opened the case and produced a scroll.

Menessos gestured for him to ascend the ramp.

Mero obeyed, but he could not resist the temptation of assessing the Erus Veneficus seated beside Menessos. *The witch who hexed the great Menessos. The Lustrata?* She wore a regal gown made with a sheer layer of red over white satin. The skirt was slit high, and her scarlet garter encircled her shapely leg. A broom was propped against her chair. Mero paused several paces away from Menessos and lowered himself to one knee as he offered up the scroll.

Menessos motioned for his witch to retrieve the scroll.

Mero was ready. He whispered, "*Aspicio.*"

As she advanced, the fluttering sheer fabric of her gown mimicked the flow of bloody water and interfered with his visual scrutiny. However, his aural assessment was unhindered, and the energy that surrounded him tasted of that energy surrounding her.

Such a vibrant life force. Inherent power. Residue of the ley line . . . not just a witch but a sorceress. Glowing silver mantle . . . a warrior? A badge embossed with the symbol of balance, a pair of scales. Mero began to believe it. *This is the Lustrata.*

Her slender arm swung gracefully forward to collect the scroll. He released it into her grasp, scanning up her body to her eyes. Brown and gray, they were not wanton, not waiflike or unsure.

This woman was not material for a voluptuous centerfold on paper. Hers was a majestic beauty, the kind meant to be captured in more permanent media, like the canvas of centuries past. *Or imbued with the ceaseless life of the vampire.*

She expressed no emotion in her other features and said nothing, but she did not have to. Her gaze conveyed wariness, protectiveness, and a silent warning: She promised him ruination, should she find it necessary.

Taking her to the Excelsior will not be an easy task to accomplish.

CHAPTER THIRTY-THREE

I carried the scroll, a roll of thick parchment sealed in its coil by a fat daub of scarlet wax, which was embossed with a seal: an *E* with a single fang stabbing through the uppermost horizontal line. I offered it to Menessos.

He accepted it without averting his attention from the advisor. He certainly had perfected every aspect of the mien of a haven master: command and carriage, the promise of power, and the threat of his wrath.

Goliath, on Menessos's right, sat silent and still but nonetheless exuded intimidation. I could feel the rage vibrating in his aura, and see the rigidity of muscles tense and ready to spring upon prey. It was Goliath being a perfect Alter Imperator, but it also had a quality that, just then, reminded me of Johnny.

The predator within wants out.

As I sat again, I heard the wax seal crack as Menessos broke it. He sniffed as the page unrolled. The writing, what I could see of it, was in a beautiful script, in a language unfamiliar to me, and the author had used a red-brown ink. I understood why the vampire had scented the page. *It's written in blood.*

Menessos handed the scroll to Goliath, who stood and read aloud, translating.

By order of the Excelsior, the vampire Menessos, Quarterlord of the Northeastern United States, is

hereby required to submit to the shabbubitum for
a truth-reading, that it may be determined if this
Master Vampire has been bound not simply to his
Erus Veneficus, but . . .

There, Goliath faltered. He faced me with all the
vehemence and hatred he could express.

"Read on, Goliath," Menessos said gently.

"Master?"

"Read on."

. . . that it may be determined if this Master Vam-
pire has been bound not simply to his Erus Veneficus
but by her.

Audible gasps were heard. A giggle emanated from
one of the three women that had accompanied this
Meroveus Franciscus. Introductions weren't necessary; I
could guess who they were.

"Let the shabbubitum ascend the stage," Menessos said.

The three women strode up the ramp with all the
pomp and circumstance they had, and they had a lot.
Every eye in the room was on them as they strutted in
perfect unison. Their similarly styled dresses of gray silk
flowed like quicksilver as they moved. Either this trio was
as well rehearsed as any Top-40 girl group, or they were
just naturally ethereal.

Halfway up the ramp, their gowns became mist.
Pieces fluttered away to form globes around every light.
What was bright grew dim; what was already dim lost
all illumination. The formal court ambience of the room
disintegrated.

As the stage fell into murky shadows, the women's clothes re-formed. Their chins lowered, warriors marching into battle, mouths opened to show threatening, bared teeth, and dark eyes glittering with the promise of bloodshed.

By the time they reached the stage, the front-most of them was dressed to kill—if she'd been going to the Dragonslayer's Ball, that is. Her tight leather jacket was darkest gray and had spikes protruding from the outer forearms. Her pants were poured-on leather, and her heeled boots had silver embellishments on the shins, like owl heads with their wings wrapping around the back of the boot. It was beautiful, except for the fact that the owls' hooked beaks protruded as spikes. Chains draped the top of her foot and ankles, securing spurs shaped to mimic very pointy owl talons.

The pair behind were attired much the same.

Mero asked Menessos, "Do you willingly submit to this as your Excelsior commands you, Quarterlord?"

For a tense moment, Menessos said nothing.

The air in the haven was too thick to breathe. His people were here, on edge with the dramatics, and ready to act should he give the word. I had no doubt that they would all fight for him and attack a vampire wizard without showing any fear.

He would never ask that of them.

I wanted him to run. But I knew he wouldn't. Couldn't.

This had to be done.

"That is," Menessos finally said, "exactly how I wanted it to be." He stood and stepped off the dais, setting his feet upon the newly inlaid circle, a pattern of yellow sphene, bright green emerald and the blue-purple tones of fluorite. It was lit from beneath, and the glow brightened as he spread his arms wide. I was sure Creepy's advice had something to do with this newly added embellishment.

"I am ashamed of nothing," he said. "Come, Liyliy, cursed daughter of a foolish father. Bring your sisters and your vengeance, and let this be done."

A voice lifted from the back of the hall and cried, "Wait!"

CHAPTER THIRTY-FOUR

Liyliy's sisters spun toward the back of the hall. She heard the assembly shuffle around. She saw Menessos, his Alter Imperator and his Erus Veneficus all rush to identify the interrupter. She, however, did not turn. She remained intent on Menessos. The speaker's voice was unmistakable.

"Giovanni," Mero whispered. He cleared his throat and announced, "Giovanni Guistini, Advisor to the Excelsior."

Giovanni spread his arms, widening the gap of his shirt to display his scars. "I trust I am welcome here, Quarterlord? Your doorman wasn't so sure."

Menessos glanced toward Mero, but Mero did not acknowledge it. Liyliy wondered what Menessos was hoping to read on the other advisor. Since it was apparent that Menessos did not intend to try to escape as this interruption weighed on, she spun in time to see the concierge limp and stumble into view behind Giovanni. His nose was a bloody mess. Had he not been all the way across the room, she would have been tempted to taste him.

"Join us, Giovanni. Share the stage with me." Menessos made it sound like a threat.

The scarred man swaggered his way to the stage. Liyliy thought him an ugly creature, parading as if the world saw majesty in him, but arrogantly unaware that he was not only atrocious but pitiful as well.

"Just in time," he rasped as he ascended onto the stage. He claimed a position beside Mero and clapped the man on the arm. "I decided I couldn't miss the show," he said. With a gesture at Liyliy he added, "Proceed."

Disliking him, Liyliy asked Mero, "Do you give the word, lord?"

"Proceed," Mero said.

She smiled at Giovanni's sneer.

She and her sisters approached Menessos. At the same instant, both his Alter Imperator and his Erus Veneficus stood. Liyliy halted and assessed both of them, concerned there might be a threat. She had good reason to be suspicious. No one on the stage was powerless— except Giovanni. In the information she'd gained from Heldridge, she knew Goliath was powerful and that Persephone was something special called the Lustrata.

Believing that neither of them would make the first strike, Liyliy proceeded. "When last we met, Menessos, I promised that I would drink of you . . . that I would bleed you dry."

"Rash promises from a woman should never be taken seriously."

She slapped him, but instead of following through, she jerked her arm back and sliced the side of his chin with the spike on her sleeve.

Another round of gasps claimed the audience at her insult, but Menessos, damn him, did not react. Liyliy snickered. "You bleed before me. Tasting will come next."

"Liyliy," Meroveus said warningly.

Menessos ran two fingers over his wound, then reached out slowly to wipe it on Liyliy's lips. "Taste," he said. "I do not fear you."

She sucked on her bottom lip, then let it slide back into its pouting place as she *mmmm*ed seductively and batted her lashes. "Delicious . . . I can't wait for more."

Unmoved, he offered her his hands.

Irritated that he showed no fear, Liyliy snatched them viciously. In position on either side of her, the sisters placed their fingers between the other's joined hands, then grasped behind Menessos's neck. Liyliy's leather jacket disappeared, forming a tentacle that wrapped around his neck, and she whispered a chant. Her sisters murmured along.

The tentacle flattened and thinned until it covered Menessos's face. Though her pleasure in this moment was obvious, she seemed irked when he did not fight her veil. Menessos simply inhaled. Almost all of her mist disappeared inside him in one inhalation; his chest rose with the depth of that single, fearless breath. It angered her, but she knew she was infesting him. She had only to wait for it. . . .

"You know what I learned from Heldridge?" she whispered. "I learned how you shattered him, rejecting him when it became clear he had no magic. I learned how it broke him. He wanted nothing more than your love . . . because he loved you more than his mortal father."

Menessos gagged and coughed and wheezed for want of real air.

Liyliy guided their chant into a melodic song. Through the notes she sang, pieces of her aura traveled over the thresholds of the mental doorways opened by her mist, and she crawled around inside of him.

As one, she and her sisters lowered Menessos's now

rigid form to the floor so that he rested with his waist between Liyliy's feet. She crouched over him.

The light shining up from the floor underneath him brightened. Yellow and blue and green shone up from around his torso, around his neck. She sensed the magic of the colorful stones, but it was too late. She was in a million pieces, in a million rooms of memory inside his mind. . . .

No!

Every room was empty.

Her chanting song changed in pitch and she rocked forward onto her knees—the spikes on her shins forced her to keep her toes flexed, but she had anticipated he would fight back. Without releasing Menessos or her sisters, Liyliy bucked and her body lifted into a handstand. Then she slammed the two-inch spikes on the front of her boots onto Menessos's thighs.

He groaned under her and gritted his teeth.

You cannot hide the truth, Liyliy thought. Her legs straightened, slicing him open.

He screamed.

The tang of copper filled the air. As Liyliy sang on, her will filtered into the air and mingled with his blood. Inside him, she tore down the walls, until only framework and connecting wires remained. Tearing on these wires, she ripped them in two and sucked on their sparking ends—his memories exploded into her like lightning.

It jolted. It hurt. It burned her alive and it devoured her. She loved every second of it. No matter the aching cost, this revenge was bliss.

A thousand pieces of her swarmed into the room of his marks. He was hiding the memories she wanted, so she burrowed into the walls and found hundreds of thousands of wires interwoven like threads of madness. Gnawing on the tangled knots, she tasted of dozens of memories at once, duplicating their essence, always searching deeper, farther, wanting information that would hurt him or destroy him.

Every detail she could use, she consumed.

CHAPTER THIRTY-FIVE

When Liyliy spoke, a wisp of power fluttered at the nape of my neck and I thought, *Get ready, Johnny. Here it comes.*

When the mist covered Menessos, when he gagged on it, I realized that I was holding my breath. A heartbeat later, his body trembled, then seized. It was unbearable, so I concentrated on Liyliy. She reacted to his suffering with vengeful glee.

Menessos had predicted this would be as painful to watch as it would be to bear. *And he said not to interfere under any circumstances.*

Giovanni, the newly arrived advisor, laughed out loud when Liyliy sliced Menessos open. He lay there helpless, wounded and bleeding, pouring out his life to defend me, to protect our trio. Despite my earlier wounds, my fists were clenched at my sides and I found myself contemplating the murder of this advisor.

He stood rapt in deviant delight as this gruesome scene played out. Of the non-haven members on the stage, only Meroveus appeared to have any distaste for the activity before us.

My vision grew blurry with tears I didn't want to shed, but I was aware when Liyliy's head suddenly snapped up in my direction. Peripherally, I detected Goliath also facing me. I blinked to force the tears out. The disbelief and confusion were so plain in his expression that I could see his self-questioning begin as he relived a few choice memories and searched for the clues he'd missed.

Menessos groaned in anguish, drawing my attention back to him . . . and Liyliy. Her eyes were condemning slits.

"Tell us!" Giovanni demanded.

She wrenched free of the others and pointed at me. "Twice-marked he is! By her!"

I spun to grab the broom leaning against my seat. Menessos had also told me to be ready to flee, and I was sooo out of here. "Awaken ye to life," I whispered as soon as my hand was on the broomstick.

Then Goliath's hand was on mine.

With a shocked gasp, I tried but couldn't wrench free. "Strike me," he said softly. "Now."

I blinked stupidly but saw Giovanni heading toward me.

"Make it good, Lustrata, while I can still be of aid."

I yanked free and smacked the handle of the broomstick across his forehead. He stumbled back.

I lowered my grip on the broom and swung it at him, connecting with the side of his head. Off balance, he tumbled off the dais and right against Giovanni. Both fell down hard.

"Restrain her!" Giovanni croaked.

Liyliy struggled to her feet—her footwear wasn't making it easy.

Frankly, straddling a broom in a hurry wasn't easy. Doing so in a dress was worse. The dress's high, high slit made the straddling part easier, but actually sitting the broom with my feet tucked up behind me and my toes curled over the dried and dyed-black straw was completely immodest. Everyone could see my undies as I flew up and across the former theater.

I heard Mero say, "Get her, Liyliy. Bring her to me."

A screech—a terrible, grating and inhuman sound— filled the theater. Over my shoulder I saw Liyliy's body transforming, becoming something owl-like. Something with wings.

Shit.

I intentioned the broom faster, hunkering as I shot past Sever and through the double doors of the theater entrance. The broom skidded sideways in the hall. Accustomed to flying in the wide-open sky, I meant to use more speed than was wise. I needed to maneuver, and there wasn't enough room to accelerate.

At the bottom of the staircase, I could hear the sounds of giant wings struggling with a space not large enough for them. A shriek of frustration chased me up the stairwell, but so did the crack of splintering wood. Liyliy wasn't giving up.

On the ground floor, I turned toward the ticket booth, shouting, "Open the doors!" to the guards ahead. The vampire on duty did as he was bidden, then—bless him—recognized that he'd be in the way. To his credit, he hit the ground and propped the door open with his torso.

I intentioned the broom up and avoided the people on the sidewalk just beyond the haven's entrance. The abruptness and manner of my exit caused people to point and shout. Heading due north, I looked back and saw Liyliy crash through the haven doors, shattering them. The people's shouts changed into screams. She had become a giant black owl, stumbling about on her talons before her flapping wings caught air.

Intent on my escape, I wondered where I could go.

Not the den. Wait! I have a dragon at home.

As I sped up and into the night, I passed over the Cleveland Memorial Shoreway and wondered if I could ask that much of Zoltan. He had no wings. Sure, Creepy had transformed him for the purpose of my protection, but leading this harpy to my house meant putting all of my animals and Mountain in danger. A standoff wouldn't be pretty even if I did win, and, worse, she could use everything there as leverage.

Where would I have an advantage over a giant, pissed-off owl? Certainly not high up in the wide-open sky. Maybe I could outmaneuver her. Just as I was closing in on the water of Lake Erie, I intentioned a hard left and zoomed south around the backside of the Rock and Roll Hall of Fame. Skimming the North Coast Harbor walkway, I heard a screech and shot upward, rocketing over the dome of the Great Lakes Science Center and heading for the turbine.

Owls are renowned for their specialized feathers that afford them nearly silent flight, so I kept checking behind me. Liyliy had been gaining, but my evasive spin cost her. She was pumping her wings hard.

CHAPTER THIRTY-SIX

Meroveus Franciscus knew Liyliy was transforming to pursue the Erus Veneficus. "Bring her to me," he commanded. Her answer was a scream as her body warped. Her nose elongated and curved sharply down like a beak. Her pouting pink lips grew thin and faded to white, becoming a crooked line with drooping ends. It was nauseating to see her skin swell and sag, beset with wrinkles, as that cracked topography replaced her lovely face with sunken ravines and bruised slopes. When the feathers burst forth, she screeched again, revealing two rows of little pointed teeth in her hideous mouth.

As the eldest of the sisters took flight, her wing brushed his chest and a gust of wind hit him hard enough to force him a single step backward. He visually followed her departure, but as soon as she was out of sight, he realized, *The most dangerous of the three just slipped away.*

Perhaps I should call her back.

He reached to his chest to touch the necklace—and discovered it was gone. Instantly, his jaw clamped hard and his hand curled into a fist. *So clever! She's stolen the only means I have of controlling them—but her sisters do not know that.* He collected himself and smoothly flattened his fingers on his chest as if merely smoothing his shirt.

Movement on the stage drew his attention. Giovanni shoved the Alter Imperator off of him and lurched onto his feet. "You idiot!" he shouted at Goliath. "You let her get away!"

Slowly, and with some graceless difficulty, Goliath got his feet under him. He shook his head, dazed.

"Liyliy will bring her back," Mero said calmly. With the necklace gone, however, he was sure Liyliy wouldn't bother chasing the Erus Veneficus. She would simply flee, but no one else knew she had that option.

Giovanni stared down at Menessos, who was in shock and bleeding profusely. Liyliy's sisters were lapping at the blood on his thighs. "Damn, this is sweet," Giovanni said as he crouched. "You're ruined. And now the Excelsior's wrath is yours. Let's drain him dry, ladies." He dropped to his knees, and, mouth wide, fangs gleaming, aimed for Menessos's throat.

Goliath ran forward and kicked Giovanni in the head. The blow had enough force to send Giovanni sprawling backward. His nose gushed blood. Across the theater, Sever was heard emitting a triumphant, "Yes!"

Giovanni threw his arms up and trembled with rage, screaming as he gathered himself to stand.

Goliath straddled his wounded master and glowered at the sisters, who scurried away to sit at Meroveus's feet like dogs.

"You dare!" Giovanni bellowed. "You dare strike me? You're in league with him! Has she marked you as well?" Giovanni spun to Mero. "Tell them to read him!"

Meroveus shrugged. "When Liyliy returns. Perhaps."

"Mero!" Giovanni shouted.

"Unless I am presented with a sealed document of kill-authorization from the Excelsior," Goliath said through gritted teeth, "none of you bastards will touch my master."

"I bear no such document," Mero said. He knew his son would not sign such. "Do you, Giovanni?"

The other advisor's answer was a wordless growl. He stomped from the stage and away toward the theater entrance.

Mero wandered closer and scrutinized the Quarterlord. He had seen Menessos at his best; this had to be his worst. It pained him to know that he had delivered this trouble to the great Menessos. "Call your Offerlings to the stage," he said softly.

The Quarterlord's mouth worked, but no sound came out.

"Offerlings! Attend your master!" Goliath's voice boomed into the stunned silence of the theater. People rushed up the ramp. Offerling blood was imbued with the essence of their master, twice the amount Beholders had. Drinking of them provided him sustenance greater than the blood of the unmarked.

Twenty minutes later, Goliath instructed Beholders to bring a stretcher. They conveyed their master offstage to his personal quarters. Mero followed. Goliath blocked him from entering. "You will let me by," Mero said.

Goliath shook his head. "No. I won't." Behind him, Seven and Mark hurried into the back chamber. A woman with blond ringlets and red eyes directed the Beholders as they carried Menessos in after the pair.

"As senior officer representing the Excelsior, I could have denied him the sustenance of his people and kept him virtually incapacitated while my investigation continued."

"It was your bitch who did this to him." Goliath's features hardened. The corner of his mouth crooked up and the mask of a criminal contemplating wickedness was complete. "So your token gesture means shit to me."

"Goliath!" Menessos's voice wafted from deep in the chamber. "Bring him to me."

The Beholders emerged from the back room, leaving with the stretcher. One of them said, "Risqué asked that you give her a few minutes before bringing the guest in." Goliath allowed the Beholders out, then he gestured Mero and the two women begrudgingly toward the seating area in the front room.

Mero ordered Ailo and Talto to sit at the leather in-the-round couches, and the three of them waited until the Offerling had tended her master's legs. Carrying the remains of his torn pants, she left. Goliath, Seven, and Mark remained with him.

Through the door the Offerling had failed to close, Mero heard Menessos saying, "You need to go, to keep the others calm. Assure them I am fine, that all will be well."

"But—" Seven began.

"Do as I ask. Do it now."

She and Mark departed, the former casting a worried glance at Mero on her way out. Mark called out, "I'm on door duty, Goliath."

When the outer door shut, Mero stood, anticipating that he would now be allowed to see Menessos. As he neared the entry, Goliath asked, "When did she mark you? How?"

Mero stepped into view. Menessos was on the bed, covered by a sheet, but he was sitting up and in the process of unbuttoning his shirt. "Perhaps it is best if he not answer," Mero said.

Goliath spun and gave him a scathing scowl.

"The less you know, the better it will be for you."

"You don't scare me." Goliath's voice was low, like a warning.

Menessos pulled his arms from the suit shirt casually, but the note of his voice was urgent as he said, "Goliath, the Advisor and I must speak privately."

The Alter Imperator's struggle with this request was obvious, but Goliath bowed slightly and said, "As you wish, my master."

"Entertain the ladies for me," Mero said as he passed.

Goliath did not answer, but shut the door behind him.

"His loyalty to you is impressive." Mero appraised the room's size, the stones of the wall broken only by a thick, rough-hewn mahogany mantel that encircled the room at chest level. Trinkets were set upon it here and there. Furniture was sparse, and a large mahogany poster-bed swathed in black silk dominated the area.

"Indeed." Menessos tossed the shirt to the floor. "It has been too long."

"I wish the circumstances were better."

"I wish you had left the shabbubitum in their stones." He groaned and rolled each shoulder as if to loosen stiff muscles. Under the sheet that covered him, his legs stretched, testing. "Their inquiry hurts like hell."

"Sorry about Liyliy's boots."

"Easy for you to say."

Mero spread his arms slightly. "I figured interrupting her at that point might be dangerous. My concern might have been misconstrued."

Menessos conceded both points with a tip of his head. "All things considered, I am glad you remembered our old game. Bring the chair." He gestured toward the far corner.

Relieved and assured that Menessos was not changed for the long years since they had last spoken, he reached for the chair, then froze and assessed its nearby mate. "Are these—?"

Menessos nodded. "The castle in Caernarvonshire."

"I heard they had sold everything a few years back." Mero gaped at the high-backed William and Mary seats.

"I had them reupholstered. Come."

"Amazing." He carefully lifted the antique, carried it to the bedside and sat. That Menessos cared to hold on to trinkets from the past was another sign that encouraged Mero. "I hope whatever you have in mind is worth the damage you just took."

Menessos affected a calm demeanor. "I relinquish my status."

"A new Quarterlord will be appointed."

"Goliath will have my haven."

"He is too young—!"

"I'm not saying he will be Quarterlord, but he *will* have my people. This will become the Cleveland haven and Goliath will become the haven master. Whoever the Excelsior appoints as Quarterlord can move their haven to Chicago. My old building remains empty."

Mero shook his head and sat forward. "You know what will happen. Goliath will be challenged by older vamps who long for such status."

"He can take it."

His old friend seemed to have it all worked out. Yet he had the distinct feeling this conversation was being steered as well. "Are you certain?"

"Absolutely."

Mero sat back. "I will do what I can."

"How did you secure the release of the shabbubitum?"

Without giving Menessos the exact details, he answered, "I filtered their souls through apples and amber, trapping a piece of each in the gemstones. Via the stones, I can exert my will."

Menessos considered that. "Was it your idea to release them?"

"No. Heldridge requested it."

"Damn that fool." Menessos rubbed his temple. "Deric went for it on his word?"

"Not his. A clever bit of vengeful redirection swayed him."

Menessos was silent, then said, "Giovanni."

"His grudge is as ugly and as permanent as his scars."

"He should be dead. That he is not should make him grateful enough to get over it."

"Time does not heal *all* wounds."

Silence followed, then Menessos broke it by casually asking, "So your son did not send you here with a stake in addition to that scroll?"

Mero shook his head side to side. "No stake."

"And what of my witch?"

Mero tilted his head, curious. The underlying intensity in those words made him think this was the point they'd been coming to all along. "That is more difficult to say."

"Call Liyliy back." It was not a request.

"I cannot."

The air crackled between them and Mero felt the other vampire tap the ley. Menessos leaned forward, sneering. "If Persephone is harmed, the scope of my wrath will surmount any torment you've ever known."

The threat was frightening, but it was equally telling. "She's more than just the Lustrata to you."

"Mero." Menessos's voice was like a taut string, ready to snap. "I heard you tell Liyliy to bring her back. You did not specify 'alive.' Call. Her. Back."

"It is not that I am unwilling to call her back, I am unable." Mero stood, paced away. "On her way out, Liyliy stole from me the necklace bearing the amber."

"You fool!" Menessos threw the sheet back.

Before he could get up, Mero placed a restraining hand on Menessos's shoulder. He said, "Stop," but Menessos threw him off and thrust his legs over the side of the bed. Spreading smears of red appeared on the bandages. "Stop!" Mero shouted. "You're not ready to be up yet."

The door opened and Goliath stood there waiting for his master to give a signal.

"Your wounds are deep," Mero said. "She practically cut you to the bone." Feeding on his Offerings would accelerate the healing process, but it was not instantaneous. If Menessos was able to walk around without ripping his stitches before the dawn, he'd be very lucky. "Please, sit back and allow me to explain," Mero said.

A tense moment passed before Menessos gestured at Goliath, who demonstrated his reluctance in the slowness with which he shut the door.

As Menessos reclaimed his former position, Mero sank into the seat. He rose again to retrieve the silken sheet that had slithered to the floor when tossed aside. "Your witch is in no danger," he said, spreading it over Menessos's lower half. "Liyliy has the necklace in her possession. She's just going to flee. It is the confinement of her sisters we must worry about. They don't yet know the necklace is gone."

"You don't know Liyliy," Menessos argued. "She won't

simply run, encumbered with the safekeeping of that necklace. She'll want the thing destroyed, and she knows that Persephone—if caught—will be in a bind herself. She'll use that leverage to make my witch destroy it." Menessos shook his head. "You worry about rebinding the sisters. I want my people out searching."

Mero saw the other vampire's hands clench. He knew Menessos wanted to be out searching personally.

A commotion in the outer room had Mero heading for the door. Goliath and Mark blocked the doorway, then he heard Giovanni's voice saying, "I am an Advisor to the Excelsior, and as such, I demand you let me pass!"

"What do you want, Giovanni?" Mero asked.

"I have news."

Mero asked, "What news?"

"I've spoken with our Excelsior." His grin was as malignant as his tone. "He's named me the Interim Quarterlord." Snickering, he added, "The documentation to prove it is on its way."

CHAPTER THIRTY-SEVEN

I flew between the blades of the hundred-and-fifty-foot-tall turbine. Liyliy was so focused on me that she must have misgauged the rotation of the huge blade. I heard her cry out as it came down on her head.

Taking advantage of the opportunity, I sped around the south side of the Cleveland Browns Stadium.

Seconds later, Liyliy still wasn't behind me.

Just as I released a sigh of relief she dived from the opening in the upper section of the southwest corner. Apparently being smacked by the giant metal blade of a wind turbine wasn't enough to hurt her.

I intentioned for speed, and Liyliy's talons raked through the broom's straw. It caused the top of the broomstick to point up and I was carried once again into the sky. Below, Liyliy hit the ground but immediately flopped and flapped to gain altitude.

Though my heart was racing, the cold wind was becoming more than a mere annoyance. This gown had zero warmth, but I had to escape. With a thought, I hit the open air and asked the broom for sixty miles per hour. *Seventy. Eighty.*

The wind was such that I found myself again wishing for a pair of goggles like I'd seen other—albeit *older*—witches wear. My eyes were watering and forced shut. I managed a forward peek every few seconds to ensure that I wasn't about to fly into a cell tower or something that might sneak up on me, though I was relatively certain that that wasn't going to be a problem while skimming the shoreline of Lake Erie.

The harpy was far in the distance, but not giving up.

Ninety. A hundred.

The skirt of my dress was flapping so hard that I heard it begin to rip. The sheer outer layer couldn't withstand this kind of abuse. Neither could my skin; I was so cold. My body ached with exhaustion again.

Cedar Point Amusement Park appeared when I was peeking. Behind me, I saw nothing of the owlish figure, so I dropped low and slowed, halting on the far side of the Sky Ride.

I was panting like I'd run a race, but I hadn't. I was just so tired. Ready to blame it on an adrenaline rush bottoming out, I thought of something that I hadn't considered before: How does a broom fly? It's a magical item with the specific capability of flying, but what fuels it once it's in the air?

There was only one answer that made any sense. Me.

I just fueled a broom for triple-digit speed. After being drained during the forced-change spell, I didn't have much to spare.

Apparently, the intentions were only as good as the stamina the riding witch had to offer. I could refuel from the line, to a point anyway, but my pursuer would likely sense that and locate me, so for now, I resisted that urge. Finding cover was priority number one. The harpy might have been gone, but I needed a warm place to hide and recover. I surveyed the darkened park. There was no getting into the stairwell that led up to the ski-lift-like Sky Ride. The doors were of course locked.

Directly across from me was the Jack Aldrich Theatre. To the north, I saw Point Pavilion. That would provide overhead cover at least. I flew under the metal roof and put my feet down atop one of the picnic tables.

I'd just begun to feel a noticeable reduction in my pulse when a shrill screech echoed over the park. I flew to the end of the row, then crawled under the end of the farthest table and slid the broom with me. The scuffing sound of it made me grit my teeth and hope that Liyliy hadn't heard.

Talons clacked on the metal roof as it creaked with the weight of something large.

Shit, shit, shit!

Stock still, I held my breath.

It seemed a long minute ticked away before I heard the scrape of talons leaving the roof.

Relief flooded over me—too soon.

Liyliy, in human form, dropped to the ground midway of the pavilion, clothed in a sheath of gray silk.

She'd be waiting for a shift of shadow to give me away. So I remained frozen in place and watched her from the space between the seat and the underside of the table.

Her silk fluttered into mist, stretching, searching.

She was going to find me no matter what.

I dropped to my stomach and rolled from under the table on the far side, dragging the broom with me and intending it up even as I rolled atop it.

Liyliy screeched, jerking her misty-parts back to her and shifting to owl smoothly. The broom carried me over the wall to back of the pavilion area and toward the roller coaster there. Liyliy was right behind me. I swerved into the coaster's supports, darting through where she was too big to follow. There were larger spots that accommodated her easily, though. She angled up and shot through one, stretching down as soon as she passed through.

I zigzagged and zoomed underneath the coaster. She was above, and the track provided me cover. I followed the twists and spins, feeling the whoosh of air as talons reached for me if I drifted to one side. Again and again, she tried to find purchase in my skin. I slowed down for sharp curves. I sped up for the few straightaways. I was so tired, I tried to tap a ley line. *Where is one?*

The chase made it difficult to feel for a line, and when I did find one, I absorbed a sip here and there—more of the biting shock of initiating such a connection and not so much of the actual transfer. The swift curves of the coaster made it impossible to maintain the link to the ley line.

Defeating her would require more than speed and maneuverability. I was going to have to use magic, but this was happening too fast to think of a focusing rhyme.

Her talons touched my back.

I screamed.

The broom veered down and right, keeping the swipe of claws shallow, but I no longer had the coaster track giving me cover. I tried to swerve back under, but Liyliy anticipated the direction of my veering, and my rebound. She dived again, forcing me in the opposite direction.

A talon closed around my biceps and heaved upward.

My arm wrenched and I screamed again. Still holding the broom, I kicked and swung the bristly end at the harpy's beak with all my might. As my efforts made me twist in the harpy's grip, I felt the bones of my shoulder grind out of the socket just as the stiff straw jabbed into Liyliy's big, round, yellow eyes.

She screeched and released me. I fell past a sign for the Raptor and landed on a bed of mulch, twisting so I didn't land on my arm. Still, it slammed against my side as I collided with the ground. The pain was a white-hot spotlight inside my head. The whine that emerged from my lips was the last thing I heard as that white light darkened.

Liyliy landed beside the unconscious figure and resumed her human form. She straddled the fugitive Erus Veneficus and grabbed her hands. As her clothes melted into a wispy tentacle she said, "Let's see what's in your mind."

She chanted and the tentacle dipped toward Persephone's neck.

When it touched her, a glow emerged around the E.V. For an instant, Liyliy saw silver-white armor. In an explosion of light, Liyliy was thrust backward.

She rolled end over end and came up panting and swearing.

CHAPTER THIRTY-EIGHT

A s Interim Quarterlord," Giovanni said, "my first action is to declare Menessos unfit for leadership. I assume control of this haven—"

"That duty has already been assigned to Goliath," Mero interjected. "I was sent here to conduct this investigation—"

"And as the Interim Quarterlord I am assuming control."

The tension in the room ramped up. Goliath was shaking with fury. Mero knew that if the situation exploded, irreparable actions would commence. He also knew that his son was a master strategist. He'd given Mero an advantage, if he needed it, and the option to back down if that was what he needed.

Mero put a hand on Goliath's shoulder and the lanky vampire withdrew to one side. Mero entered the outer chamber. "Since you have declared yourself the Interim Quarterlord, Giovanni, you will of course understand that my rank as Advisor trumps yours. If you cared to be a part of the investigation instead of running off to beg leverage of the Excelsior, you would have already known that I relieved Menessos of his position and bequeathed this haven to Goliath, dubbing it the Cleveland haven. It is no longer a Quarterlord's haven, so you have no one to command here. However," he gestured ceremoniously to Goliath, "I trust you will be compliant with the Interim Quarterlord's requests. Should you have any concerns,

I will be available to hear them and mediate without hesitation."

Goliath bowed his head respectfully.

Mero approached Giovanni. Quietly he said, "Your personal grudge against Menessos is a veil before your eyes. I will not be able to judge your motives kindly if you are not carefully impartial in how you progress from here, *Quarterlord*."

Giovanni backed away, making sounds like a vicious dog. "I want the shabbubitum sisters sequestered in an interrogation room. I want to question them immediately."

"I know just the place to conduct that," Goliath offered and headed toward the door.

"Ladies, please follow Goliath. Your compliance is expected." Mero patted his chest as if to remind them the necklace was under his shirt. They followed Goliath out.

Giovanni hesitated long enough to glare, then trailed the group. Mark, who was still on duty at the outer door, shut it after Giovanni. "Mark," Mero called before it had completely closed. When the man responded, Mero added, "I believe your former master would like a few words with you."

When Menessos saw Mark, he motioned him close. "Get a search party assembled. Every Beholder and Offerling we can spare needs to be on the streets. I want to know in what direction Persephone flew off. I want them to find witnesses, to report in what they learn from them, then to follow up all leads."

"What about the harpy? Won't she bring her in?"

"No. We cannot rely on her. Our people should not confront her; she must be treated with caution. Appoint someone here to coordinate via phone. That way we can combine the efforts if needed and call it off when Persephone's found."

"Is the court witch a traitor, Boss?"

"No."

"It won't be easy to convince the Beholders and Offerlings of that just now."

"Don't worry about that. Just tell them Persephone must be brought in unharmed. Tell them Goliath has been appointed Haven Master and that the order comes from him."

Mark bowed before leaving.

Mero resumed his bedside seat. "Their continued loyalty is a tribute to you."

"As is yours. Thank you for trumping Giovanni."

"It felt good," Mero said as the door opened.

Goliath rolled a cart bearing a television into the rear chamber. He powered the system on and left.

In a conference room, Giovanni paced. The sisters were seated at a large cherry table. The décor was all dark browns, leather and wood and a few items of deep green. From the aim of the shot, the lens of the camera had to be hidden in the upper corner.

"We saw many things," Ailo was saying.

"Tell me all of it."

"What we see is . . . voluminous. We could discuss it for weeks," Talto explained. "The images convey so much meaning, books' worth of words into a snippet of memory. And it darkens with time."

"If you have a specific area to focus your curiosity, ask questions," Ailo suggested.

"Both the sound and picture are good," Mero observed.

"Yes," Menessos said. "The microphone is encased within the scrollwork of the torchiere floor lamp."

"What of the witch?" Giovanni demanded. "Is she the Lustrata?"

"She is the bearer of the Lustrata's mantle. Her powers are not yet complete, but she is getting close."

"Did Menessos willingly accept her hexes?"

"Not exactly."

"What do you mean?"

"She bore his mark, and then that mark was flipped."

"Flipped?"

"It was overturned and the connection that was once his binding upon her, metamorphosed into her binding upon him."

"How did she accomplish this?"

"She did not. A goddess did."

At that, Mero faced Menessos with the question plain in his expression.

"The Lustrata has Hecate's favor."

Mero wanted to know more, but the interrogation continued.

"A goddess." Giovanni crossed his arms. "A goddess."

"No mortal can sever such a mark. Only divine intervention could have achieved this." Talto's tone was utterly serious.

"You do not have to believe or enjoy what we claim to have seen, but you would be a fool to discount our words," Ailo said. The warning in her tone was not hidden.

"The second hex?" Giovanni prompted.

"He was nearly dead," Talto said.

Ailo clarified. "She had staked him."

Again, Mero faced Menessos in disbelief. He whispered,

"You covet a mortal woman who drove a stake into your heart and forced a hex upon you?" This intimate revelation declared the complexity of the vampire that had Made him. "Why?"

Menessos remained intent on the screen and made no attempt to answer.

Giovanni, too, was astonished by this. "She staked him in order to hex him," he repeated. "How did he survive?"

"The stake was extracted."

"Is Menessos aware of her political intentions?"

"From what was in his mind, she appears to have no aspirations of power and authority."

"Appearances can be deceiving," the advisor snapped. "The attempted murder of a Quarterlord to secure dominion over him is an act of war in and of itself." Giovanni began pacing again. "She has used her sway over him to blind him from the truth."

"That is not true," Menessos said to Mero. "I placed a small binding upon her, disguised as a bond between her and her lover. It enabled me to see past any personal barriers. There was no trace of what Giovanni suggests."

"Was," Mero said to emphasize that was past tense. "When was that and what about now?"

"That small binding has been removed, but you would be wise to not doubt me when it comes to her merits."

On-screen, Giovanni said, "The Domn Lup cannot be subjected to her magic, as wærewolves cannot abide those energies . . . and that explains why she is his lover. The seduction subdues and sways him." He paced continually as he considered this news. The sisters sat in silence.

To Mero's disappointment, Menessos was keeping his face carefully blank. But Mero knew his friend's thoughts were racing. An enemy was tying together the threads that would enable him to make a case for the elimination of the court witch who had clearly won so much more than Menessos's admiration.

"Do you want to know what we saw of you in his mind?" Ailo asked conspiratorially.

Shoulders squaring and jaw flexing, Giovanni snapped, "What did you see of me?"

Talto clasped Ailo's hand. Ailo said, "You were a charismatic captain of men . . . and seven hundred professional soldiers followed you to Constantinople—a mission you undertook only after Menessos recommended it based on the glory you could attain there." Her voice was enthralling, all dulcet tones and hypnotic inflections.

"She's using the ley," Menessos said.

"Bespelling him?" Mero stood. They were about to take action—

Menessos motioned him back into his seat. "I have seen them play this game with non-magic-using vampires before. They do not like him or his questions, so they toy with him."

"You were defending the wall when a debilitating injury forced you to leave your post," Ailo said. "Because of your departure, many gave up hope and fled. The enemy observed the panic that beset the guards in your absence. His redoubled efforts conquered the Byzantines. The Queen of Cities fell."

Color drained from Giovanni until he was pale even for a vampire. He backed up until his spine was against the wall, as if memories were playing out before him—he stared in horror at nothing.

"But your injury was not a mortal wound," Talto said.

Ailo whispered a chant as Talto continued. "A single crossbow bolt and shrapnel from the Ottoman cannon . . . but not as life threatening as initially believed. And yet it was too late. Panic had swarmed the troops and the men had fled. Days later, finding the weakness you had displayed inexcusable when paired with the devastating cost, Menessos took your throat."

Giovanni's fingers skimmed over his neck. Talto rose from her seat and, with a gentle touch, caressed his cheek. She took up the whispered chant and let Ailo speak: "It was another vampire, Konstance, who saw in you a mighty captain worth saving. As Menessos protested her actions, she fed you her strong blood and worked the change upon you. Though your death was not averted, she welcomed you into undeath."

Giovanni blinked and seemed to recover himself from far away. Seeing Talto, who was chanting still, he balled his fist and struck her. She was flung across the room. "Never touch me! Never!"

She screamed and leapt to her feet, crossing half the distance. "For this you hate Menessos?" Talto asked. "You hated yourself for the failure wrought in your absence. You wanted death. He gave it to you. Konstance is the one who brought you back."

"She loved me!" Giovanni shouted. "And Menessos poisoned her mind against me."

CHAPTER THIRTY-NINE

Why does Deric keep him as Advisor?"

Mero shrugged at Menessos's question. "He plays the devil's advocate very well. It is better to keep someone who is that bitter and conniving nearby rather than monitor them from afar." A long moment later, Mero asked, "Now that your people are searching, will you help me rebind the sisters so they pose no threat?"

"I'll help you," Menessos said, "but only if we bind them to me—not you."

"Bound to *you*?" Mero was so surprised that he was out of his seat before he realized it. He paced away, then back. "Your haven is lost, the power of your people will be transferred to Goliath and you will not have the means to contain these sisters," Mero argued.

"Liyliy outwitted you, Mero."

"It was not as bloody as what she did to you, and still you insult me."

"It is not my intent to insult you, my friend."

"But you do, and *after* I have done all I can to minimize the tragedy here."

"I am grateful for that," Menessos said, "but I have spoken truly. She stole the necklace from you. I will bind her sisters more thoroughly. . . ." He sighed. "It is no less than I deserve."

"Deserve? As a penance?"

Menessos said nothing.

"You can't mean to make them your own? It would make them stronger!"

"Through the connection forged in the blood exchange, a deeper binding could be placed upon them. One that would ensure their loyalty."

Mero was incredulous. "Their story is sad and you feature in it more than most know, but this . . . error . . . is not your doing. It is mine. If either of us must suffer that solution, it should be me." A deep breath could not counter the fearful tightening of his chest that the mere idea inspired. "They would have to accept it, and as they loathe you already they would surely not accept such a binding. Their former master tried as much. You know how that ended." They had read their former master into madness and death. "I stand a better chance of gaining their acceptance."

"You cannot risk this, Mero. Your son needs you. If you succeeded, Ailo and Talto would require too much of your time, and I apparently will have plenty . . . without the duties of a Quarterlord to perform. Besides, with Liyliy absent, they cannot conduct the kind of reading that the three of them can do together. And   "

"And what?" he demanded. He knew Menessos's expression indicated fast thinking and serious risks. "What are you thinking?"

"When Giovanni is through with them, they will be tired. If you bring them here, one at a time, I can seduce them into the blood exchange. Then . . . the rest is just binding their flesh." He paused and lowered his voice. "They need not agree."

Mero sank onto the edge of the bed. "A black binding? Are you mad? Performing it would corrode your soul—"

"Some souls aren't affected by the black arts."

"You've made mistakes, but you're no demon."

The corner of Menessos's lips curled. "This will work best if done while the sun is risen."

Connecting the clues, Mero whispered, "A black binding with the sun up means you and the sisters would be dead flesh, making this black necromancy . . . are you saying you have a demon?"

"I do."

All magic had an element of danger to it. All bindings were to some extent evil. But this . . . magic used on the unwilling was vile and twisted. Moreover, Menessos was shackling them to him *forever*. As endless as vampires were, committing centuries to each other was not uncommon. Even millennia could be achieved when the bonds of friendship were strong—Seven and Mark were evidence of that. But Ailo and Talto were wicked, and they hated Menessos.

Mero couldn't allow him to do this. "This is too dangerous."

Menessos crossed his arms. "Then suggest something better. Something sure to work."

Mero had nothing better. He stood and paced away.

On paper from the bedside table, Menessos wrote up a list. He then sent for the Offerling who had tended his wounds, and upon her arrival he gave her the paper. "Bring these items as soon as you can. Then we'll discuss what I want you to do with them."

Mero watched her leave and marveled that he had not identified her before—the red irises should have been a giveaway, but demons were rare and red contacts were not.

"She is half-human," Menessos explained. "Her mother did some very bad things. Her father was one of them."

Flashing a smile at his Maker's wit, Mero said, "Risqué has the better half on her exterior. She's beautiful. No tail."

"She has a tail, a short one. The ruffles disguise it."

"Do you truly trust her?"

"Yes. Her mother gave her up at birth. I saw to her upbringing, so I trust her implicitly," Menessos added.

"You taught her magic?"

"Of course. Demon father, witch mother. It was necessary for everyone's safety."

"And she is powerful enough to do what you suggest?"

"If I was not certain, I would not allow her to work magic on my corpse."

Mero was growing weary with the impending dawn before Giovanni released the sisters from his interrogation. There was no time to discuss what Giovanni might have asked them. Mero asked Menessos, "Where might the two shabbubitum secure their rest?"

"Take my bed for the coming day," Menessos said to Ailo and Talto. He had risen from his bed an hour prior and slipped into silk sleep pants. Although his movements were stiff and slow, his injury was clearly mending. He gestured to the rear chamber. "Here you will have privacy."

"We are honored by your gesture," Ailo said and directed her next words at Mero, "but our sister has not returned."

"She will," Mero assured them, patting his chest. He gestured her nearer.

"What if she does not appear by first light?" Ailo asked, verging on tears. Behind her, Menessos led Talto into the back chamber.

Work fast, Menessos. Still touching his chest, Mero closed his eyes, as if he were contacting Liyliy in some manner. He maintained it for as long as he dared, murmuring, "Her chase of the Erus Veneficus carried her far away." He dragged out his act for another minute, then ended it. "She has found a safe haven for the day already. She will rejoin us come nightfall."

His performance satisfied Ailo, who wandered toward Menessos's private chamber. "Ah good," Menessos said as he opened the door. "I was just coming to get you. Your sister said you would want to hear the history of these antiques. . . ."

Mero inched closer. He heard Ailo's stifled scream as Menessos attacked. He watched as his Maker drank from her. Ailo struggled. She tried to beat at him with her fists, but Menessos restrained her. She tried to transform, but Menessos tapped the ley line and prohibited her. He drank until she was weak enough to comply. Then he Marked her and put her to bed beside her sister.

Minutes later, Menessos created a magic seal on the shut door and, licking his lips, said to Mero, "It is done." He sauntered toward the seating in the round. "Mark!"

The door opened. "Yes, Boss?"

"Bring two beds to this outer chamber for the Advisor and myself."

"I'm on it, Boss."

"And Mark?"

"Yes, Boss?"

"You'll have to quit calling me Boss."

Mark stalled. "Yes."

Menessos opened the door again within minutes for two burly Offerlings. Mero was glad Menessos did not cling to the coffins many vampires preferred. Instead, the men brought in two modern versions of old-fashioned closed beds, the type with bifolding doors to allow access and provide privacy. Narrow enough to fit through the wide doorway, they were each sized for a single occupant to lie comfortably.

As he climbed into the bed, Menessos said, "If you leave your clothes on the floor, you will find them cleaned and pressed upon waking."

"Wonderful." Mero undressed. "Are you not nervous?"

"I die easily, Mero. It is the return that I find difficult."

"Not for the dawn. I meant, aren't you nervous about the black binding that will be placed upon your body while you are elsewhere?"

Menessos considered it. "No. I trust Risqué. The only unease I feel stems from not knowing where my Erus Veneficus is."

CHAPTER FORTY

Johnny was dreaming. He was racing across white sand toward a giant clock. As he neared, he could tell the brass disk at the bottom of the pendulum was taller than he was. He gauged the swing of it. The ticktock beat was much too fast, cluing him in that time was running out as more and more sand gushed from the base of the clock, raising it higher, farther away. He had to get through!

Only a few feet from the pendulum, he felt the rush of wind in its wake. He planted his foot and it sank in the sand more than he expected. He had to lift his other leg high and fast to step up onto the clock's base. The ticks and tocks were so loud here.

Momentum carried him into the path of the pendulum—

His eyes opened.

He still heard ticking.

His nostrils filled with the scent of the cement beneath him. *Cement?* He was in the den. In a kennel. Memory of the rooftop rushed back to him. *Red*—

He sat up—and spotted the source of the ticking.

A woman was striding toward him, carrying a file. The tips of her heels were clicking on the cement floor. She was blond and wore a trim lavender business suit with a too-short-for-the-office skirt. She had shapely legs, and her pace was lithe and unhurried.

She also smelled of wærewolf.

Johnny stood.

"Good morning, sire. I'm Aurelia, your assistant and Zvonul liaison."

Her voice was warm and friendly. Too friendly. She assessed him up and down, and Johnny became more aware of his nakedness.

"You had a rough night." Her gaze fell to something in the cage behind him.

The remnants of a side of beef lay on the floor. The hay that was supposed to be in this kennel was piled up at the edges, pushed into the adjacent kennels.

He remembered agony, a pain like he was being eaten alive from the inside out. He recalled thrashing about and howling. *What the hell?*

Red!

Mind racing, he recalled all that he'd done and her reaction. *I've fucked everything up. God damn it. I knew I shouldn't trust myself. . . . I've failed. I failed me, but worse, I failed her.*

"Let's acquaint ourselves in your office," the woman said. "After you're dressed."

Ten minutes later, Johnny had collected himself, mostly, and entered his office, dressed in black jeans and an Ozzy Osbourne concert tee. A tray rested on his desk, a plate with an insulated cover not restricting the aroma of the bacon and eggs underneath. There was also coffee, milk and orange juice.

He ignored it all, sitting and picking up the phone in one motion. He was punching in Persephone's number when his new assistant walked in. "Aurelia—"

"You may call me Aury, if you like."

"I have a few things to take care of first. Then I'll see you."

She sat across from him. "I can wait."

"Do it somewhere else."

Aurelia crossed her long legs unhurriedly. "You want to make sure that I understand I am not your top priority. I get it, Mr. Newman. But please try to remember I work for the Zvonul and am here to aid you."

He tore his eyes from her thighs and said, "Aurelia, I don't play games. If I say I have other things to do, I do. It's not a show meant to put you in your place."

"Then you need me more than you think you do."

Johnny shoved the receiver onto the cradle. "You *will* wait somewhere else."

"Pout, pout." She strutted out.

Kirk appeared in the doorway but directed a whistle after the leggy blonde who'd just passed. "Dude. It's good to be the king."

Johnny couldn't stifle the single laugh at the movie reference. "What do you need?"

"It's William. He's awake, but he's not responding. Beau's calling an ambulance."

"Send someone with him."

"Renaldo is still here."

"He'll do."

Kirk left, calling out, "Hector wants you to call him."

Johnny picked up the phone again and punched in the number for Seph's satellite phone.

She didn't answer. When the voice mail picked up, he couldn't bear to leave a lame recorded apology. He hung up and dialed the house number.

No one answered that either.

Jaw clamped, he dug out his cell phone and found the number for Menessos. He couldn't call that—the sun was up and the vamp was tucked in with his dirt bag—but a secondary listing was that of the haven. He called that number.

It rang and rang without going to any kind of message service. Pissed and worried, Johnny let it ring. There had to be some Offerlings or Beholders around somewhere.

Finally, someone picked up. "Hello?"

"Ivanka?"

"Da."

"This is Johnny. Where's Persephone?"

"Who?"

"The Erus Veneficus."

The heavy sigh that answered him made his stomach ice over. "I know the shabbubitum were there last night. What happened, and where is Seph now?"

"No idea."

Great. I need to know what's happening and I get the one person in the haven who can barely speak the language and isn't big on details. "What do you mean you don't know? What happened?"

"She mark our boss two times. She Make him like Offerling to her."

An awful thought occurred to him. "Did the shabbubitum take her?"

"They try."

"Ivanka. Tell me what happened!"

"She fly away on broom. Creature pursue her. Neither come back."

He stood. *Damn this den for its concrete walls that block cell phones! I could be on my way to my car—* "Who's out searching for her?"

"All Beholders. All Offerlings."

"Did they check her house?"

"Mountain already there."

Right. Duh. "Write down these numbers . . . ready?"

"Wait . . ."

Johnny groaned impatiently.

"My arm broken. Be patient or I no write number."

Be nice to the Offerling you want to call you if they find anything out. "What happened to your arm?"

"Strange man at E.V.'s house. Bastard snap like twig."

"When? Yesterday?"

"Da."

No wonder Red was acting so weird when she came to do the ritual. Then I— The guilt he felt was so sharp he cut off the words before he could even think them. He gave Ivanka the numbers. "Call if you learn anything, but I'm on my way over there. I'll get some of my men organized and we will help with the search."

"No. Stay away. Forget her."

"Ivanka—"

"E.V. betray us. She betray you, too."

The phone went dead.

This wasn't right. He had to do something. He had to go and find her—

He couldn't ditch the press conference. The Zvonul had set it up, and if he was a no-show he'd be getting his "kinghood" off to a terrible start, discrediting the Zvonul and making wærewolves everywhere look unreliable.

I have a few hours. I can search a while and then go to the announcement.

He had just hung up the receiver when Aurelia reappeared in the doorway with her arms folded over her chest, the file dangling to the side by her fingertips.

"It's nine o'clock. We have six hours until your press conference. We have to find you a suit and write a brief speech. We have to have your security team assembled and briefed. We have to scout the location and pinpoint the best positions for security placement *before* the reporters begin arriving, and they do tend to be early, vying to gain the best vantage point for their cameras. So can we get started while there's still a chance to pull this off and look professional?"

CHAPTER FORTY-ONE

I became aware.

I opened my eyes as if I'd been sleeping, and I think I had been, but there was nothing to see but blackness so all-consuming that not even an indication of shape pierced this dark.

My mouth was full of salt. Spitting, I reached up—*pain*.

It ricocheted around my body with more force than I'd put into the attempt.

A full minute later the pain had subsided enough that sense returned and I could contemplate the state of my own body. I was lying on my side, I was cold, and my wrists and ankles were tightly bound. A length of rope connected the two bindings, further limiting my ability to move and forcing me into an uncomfortably cramped position. Every breath made my shoulder prickle. It remained out of socket. My right fingers were numb and I continued to spit salt. On the plus side, I still wore the dress and shoes.

I blinked and blinked but couldn't get used to this dark, couldn't cut through it. *As black as the inside of a cat, as Nana would say.*

Unwilling to move my body, I used the only other thing I had: my head. Rubbing my cranium against the ground, a feat my neck complained mightily about, I burrowed my cheek into it. What I felt was like sand, but the overwhelming smell of salt in my nostrils made me believe I was lying on a mound of salt.

"Help!" My throat was dry. My call was little more than a whisper. I tried again, putting every effort into projecting my voice. "Help me!"

Not only did the vibration of my voice do terrible things in my shoulder but my words echoed back to me, metallic and dry. I was enclosed in a space that was very big and open and dark.

As long as it's not Tartarus, I'll be okay.

Concentrating, searching for a ley line, an intangible part of me reached forth—and instantly recoiled, as if shocked or burned. It made me physically jerk, and the pain made me whimper, but I determinedly tried again, more gently.

The result was no different.

A power barrier.

I couldn't be Bindspoken. What had Liyliy done?

Hungry, in pain, and pissed off, I decided not to lie there and do nothing.

In movies, people put their out-of-socket shoulders back in by hitting them on something.

I tensed, pouring every effort into rolling onto my stomach.

Searing pain ripped a scream out of me and I threw myself onto my side, as I had been.

That was stupid. A mountain of salt isn't a firm surface. Being tied up like this ruins the leverage.

My small efforts had won me a cold sweat and a constant throb in my shoulder. I couldn't fail. Not here, not now, not like this. I didn't want to be the one to blame if our tripled union collapsed.

I thought of the *sorsanimus*. Could I reach beyond this veil prohibiting magic by reaching inward to my soul? I thought of Johnny. *I need you to find me. I need help.*

Exhaustion overcame me, and I was lost again to sleep.

CHAPTER FORTY-TWO

Johnny tried to get a sense of where Persephone was, but he couldn't seem to incite the *sorsanimus*. After what he'd done, she must be blocking him. He couldn't exactly blame her.

Presently, he sat in the back of a rented limousine, between Kirk and Gregor. He wore the suit Menessos had given him to wear at the haven. Five Omori and Aurelia sat inside the limousine with him. Two more limos accompanied them, one preceding, one following, bringing the rest of the security team.

"Why the Cleveland Trust Bank?" Johnny asked, scanning the world outside the darkened windows to keep from ogling the cleavage exposed by Aurelia's low-cut blouse.

"It is ideal," she answered.

He looked at her, expecting her to go on, and after his gaze dropped to her chest, she did. "Impressive, isn't it?" Aurelia's lips twisted in a happy little smirk.

Johnny faced the windows again, swearing to himself.

She added, "It's a structure everyone can get to, but it's not so easy for the media to park close. That keeps their equipment to a minimum, and since we search them upon entering, that's kept short. As a perk, since it is presently vacant we won't be disturbing any county offices like we would if we did this on, say, the courthouse steps."

Their planned route had them travel Third to Carnegie

to Ninth. As they drew close, Johnny told Kirk to switch with him so he could have the window.

The Cleveland Trust Bank was a big gray tribute to Italian Renaissance architecture on the V-shaped corner of Euclid and Ninth. As the limo sat waiting for the light that would allow them to use the Euclid entrance, Johnny let his eyes be captured by the structure, as they always were when he visited downtown. This spot was a strange mixture of ancient and modern times, and oddly enough the sleek towering skyscrapers, the streetlights, and even the asphalt street with the covered bus shelter right in the middle of the road all seemed out of place. Not the bank's columns.

The building was constructed in a style so beautiful it had endured for millennia, with four sets of paired fluted columns supporting a very Greek pediment complete with grand figures. Just above and behind, the crowning dome could be seen. He'd always wanted to see the inside.

Today, announcing that he was Domn Lup to the world—*the world!*—he would.

Red should be here.

He retracted the thought as soon as it was formed. He couldn't blame her.

But after what he'd done, not being out there looking for her right now tore his heart into pieces. He should have been looking for her, but he couldn't get out of this, either. *Afterward,* he promised himself. *Afterward I'll find her.*

A short, fat, balding man unlocked the doors of the bank as Johnny and his entourage approached. "You're early." His frown was deep.

"We specified that we would be," Aurelia said.

"You didn't specify *when*."

"A matter of security. Can we get off the street, please? There are many tall buildings around. A sniper could be lurking in any window. . . ."

The fat man hurriedly opened the door. "Of course."

In passing, Johnny assessed the man's expensive suit and knew this wasn't just a doorman. The interior drew his attention while he remained aware of what was going on around him.

"You are . . . ?" Aurelia asked.

"Leo. Leo MacPhearson." He relocked the door. "I'm the building supervisor."

Aurelia opened her file, flipped through pages. "Yes, here you are. Okay." She pointed to a pair of the Omori. "You cover these doors, you the Ninth Street side."

When she indicated, Mr. MacPhearson gestured into the bank. "This way." He hurried to stay ahead of the group. "Much of what you see here is priceless," he said. Leading them into the rotunda lobby, he pointed to a carved wooden embellishment that ran all the way around the circle that was open to the next level up. "Such as the craftsmanship shown here in the underside of the first mezzanine level."

Johnny noticed two things: The place was as elegant as he expected, and it stank of stale air. It was a shame such a place was sitting idle. His gaze was drawn upward by the beige pillars that supported the second mezzanine level. They had gilded tops and even more elaborate ornamentation above them.

"On up, you'll see murals that were painted by Francis Davis Millet, who subsequently died on the *Titanic*."

MacPhearson continued his tour-guide spiel. "Crowning the rotunda is the stained glass dome, sixty-one feet across and eighty-five feet up, which, contrary to popular belief, is not a Tiffany glass piece. It merely follows the style of Tiffany."

Johnny rotated on a circle of brass in the center of the rotunda and studied the overhead panes of glass in hues of blue and yellow and green, then asked, "Why is it empty?" Around him, the members of his own pack and the Omori halted as well.

A few paces ahead, "tour guide" MacPhearson realized he wasn't being followed. Warily, he scanned the group, as if conducting a head count. "The city acquired the building and the tower attached for new government offices, then those plans stalled. So here it sits until they decide what to do with it. And it's my responsibility to make sure this structure remains intact—a responsibility I take very seriously. So, if your security has reason to believe we may have a situation here today, I need to know about it."

Gregor drew nearer and said, "This is all standard procedure, Mr. MacPhearson. We've not acquired any intel suggesting adverse events today. We just take our responsibility very seriously as well."

MacPhearson studied Gregor for several seconds. "I'll permit a few of your men to access the first and second mezzanines, so long as I send one of my men for every one of yours."

"Agreed," Aurelia said. "Where is the podium to be placed?"

"Podium?"

Aurelia shuffled her papers.

Kirk stepped up beside Johnny, and as he looked at his sharpshooter, he recalled the man's attraction to Red's bodyguard. He leaned in, "Do you by chance have Zhan's cell number?" he asked in a whisper.

Kirk gave him one solemn nod, but his wordless answer told Johnny that this was a secret. He pulled Kirk aside. "I need you to contact her. Coordinate with her to find Red."

"She's missing?"

Johnny nodded.

"I'm on it," Kirk said and left.

"Page three of the contract the Zvonul offered—where are you going?" Aurelia snapped.

"I gave him an errand," Johnny said smoothly.

She gave him a nonplussed stare, then turned back to MacPhearson. "Page three of the contract states that we require a podium 'designed to denote some level of status.' It also serves as cover should shots be fired."

"I don't have anything to do with the contract, just the building." MacPhearson took a phone from his pocket, punched a number. "Do you know anything about a podium in the contract? Page three?" he said into the phone.

Johnny's phone rang. It was Hector. Kirk had told him to call and he hadn't. "'Lo?"

"Hi, John . . . I mean, sire. Sorry."

"Don't worry about it."

"I need to ask you something. Not on speakerphone, and not where others can hear."

Johnny drifted away from the group. "Go ahead."

"Were you expecting that . . . fit . . . you had last night?"

A flashback of writing in his kennel hit him. He remembered seeing Hector beyond the bars. Not far away, Aurelia dropped her file and bent to pick it up. Her ass was so damn nice—he turned away. "Why?"

"John, please. Put aside the authority and the need to know my motive before you reveal anything. I get how the politics make life difficult; I was Ig's assistant for years. Just, right now, be the guy Ig and I used to drink with. Be straight with me. Did you know?"

"No."

Hector swore.

"Why?"

"Ig knew people. We have sources inside the haven. We know what happened. Your girlfriend called your phone last night, early. She warned me you were going to have a fit. She said it wouldn't last long and that you'd be fine. She said you knew about it, and you didn't. She lied, John. She lied and she did something. Something magic. You need to know what it was."

"I'll find out. I'm sure it's fine."

"She'd marked the vampire. Twice. She had control of him, you understand? The haven was essentially under her control. We can't afford to have that happen to our Domn Lup."

"Hector, I can handle it."

"I bet the vamp said that, too."

CHAPTER FORTY-THREE

I woke up. My body still hurt, but there was light on my face.

Johnny's here.

I blinked until things came into focus. Well, not things, but thing: the small black candle about two feet away from my head. It was dripping dark wax into the powdery white salt. The little flame was reassuring. It meant that someone—

"You're awake."

I recognized that voice. It wasn't Johnny. *Oh hell.*

With his knees bent up and his arms clasped around them and the long sleeves of his black robe covering him, Creepy had completely blended into the background, which seemed to be iron. The meager illumination didn't stretch very far.

It seemed my call through the *sorsanimus* had worked and been answered, by Menessos anyway. I lifted my head; it wasn't easy with the crick presently in my neck. "Untie me."

"I cannot."

"What? Menessos sent you to—"

"Menessos did not send me this time."

Exhaling slowly, I let my head rest against the salt again. *This is where Menessos's nondisclosure deal starts biting me in the ass.* I wasn't entirely certain I wanted to know the answer but asked anyway, "Then why are you here?"

He pitched forward onto his knees. The salt—there had to be tons of it here—shifted as he disturbed it. He repositioned the candle so it was a foot or so away from the crown of my head. Then Creepy lay down in front of me, mimicking my pose exactly. "My eyes are addicted to your beauty." He reached for my cheek. "And my hands yearn—"

"You have to untie me." I didn't have time for this, and I certainly didn't want to know more about his yearnings.

His touch trailed to my neck. "I don't *have* to do anything," he whispered. "I don't even have to be here. . . ." His fingertips glided so softly over my shoulder.

Every nerve was hypersensitive. Pain jolted through me. I gasped and tensed and shouted, "Don't!" That only made it worse. Tears welled in my eyes.

"Your flesh is heated and swollen, so tender."

"My shoulder's out of socket," I said through clenched teeth. "Don't touch me."

The next thing I knew he was wiping my tears. Then, as if sampling the most decadent confection, he licked his fingers. "I cannot bear to see you in such pain."

"Then help me," I pleaded. Even Creepy's help would suffice.

With purpose, he sat up. I was grateful for his change of heart—until he grabbed my shoulder. I tried to scream *no* or *don't* or *stop* or any other cease-type command, but as he shoved the bone into place what left my mouth was a wordless and primal expression of agony.

The sharp intensity disappeared, but an awful ache remained as I tried to relearn how to breathe.

"There." Creepy's fingertips brushed my cheek and he lay down again. "That's better, is it not?"

When I could speak, I said, "Please untie me."

"I told you I cannot."

"If you can repair a screen door, you can make a rope untie itself."

"Yes. I am capable of that."

"Then what are you waiting for? Help me!"

"It is not that simple, Persephone."

My stomach gave a little heave as I recalled Menessos saying *our* new ally had taught him to think through the pain. My knee-jerk reaction was to not make any deals with this man, but I was not in a position to negotiate. "Explain," I growled.

"Liyliy needs you to do something."

Fuck her. Luckily, before the thought became words that escaped my lips, I decided expressing negatives to the one person—well, whatever Creepy was—who might get me out of all this was a bad idea. "What would that be?"

"She will tell you when she rises at sundown. That is why I cannot untie you. If I did, then you would not be here when night falls. Tied up, you will stay *and* you will be motivated to do what she asks of you."

"What do you care if I do what she wants me to?"

"I told you I could help you more than you know." He drew very close to me, almost nose to nose, and caressed my cheek. "You need to know that you can do this." His fingertips slid to the back of my neck and held me as he kissed my forehead. When his warm lips abandoned my skin, he whispered, "*Malek tsalmaveth. Basilissa nekros.*" He released me and blew out the candle.

I blinked in the sudden darkness, waiting for his touch to resume, waiting for him to do something I'd protest. He did nothing. "Hey," I said.

Nothing.

"Hey!"

He was gone.

CHAPTER FORTY-FOUR

T he press conference would commence at three o'clock, with security in place to Gregor's satisfaction. Mac-Phearson had acquired a podium to Aurelia's satisfaction, though MacPhearson had fussed at the men bringing it in, warning them not to scuff the floors if they valued their jobs. Johnny sat in a room down a hall off the rotunda and listened jealously as the crew performed a sound check on the mic.

Things were so much easier when all I wanted to be was a rock star.

On the cell phone he hit the autodial for Seph, again. Still no answer. He called the haven again. After five rings Ivanka growled, "Da, Johnny. I am here. I have no news. Stop calling!" She hung up on him.

"Silence that phone," Aurelia said on her way to the door. "It's time."

Johnny set the phone to vibrate and followed her out into the hall.

"You wait here. I'll have everyone's attention once I begin, so you can come to the head of the hallway after I'm talking. Wait there until I introduce you."

Johnny noticed Gregor watching her strut away and remembered that Gregor had been the guard of the Rege in the Courts of the Zvonul in Romania. "You already know her."

"Aurelia Romochka. Press Secretary to the Court of

Zvonul. Very good at her job. They couldn't have sent you a better liaison. She's great at managing the media, organizing social events and the like."

Johnny rolled his shoulders to alleviate the tension. He was anxious and a tad shaky. A few cleansing breaths helped. "Not an easy task, to gain any kind of rank being a female under the last Rege."

"How do you think she gained her rank?" Gregor asked gravely.

"Under the Rege?"

"Under his fists." Gregor added, "He broke many females. He didn't break her. She's strong."

In the main room her voice boomed from the sound system. ". . . thank you to all the media here today. We are delighted to have you join us. . . ."

Johnny walked toward the head of the hallway. A curtain had been placed there for privacy. He waited and listened until he heard ". . . and now, it is my great honor to present the Domn Lup."

Once he was in position behind the podium, Johnny scanned the prepared speech that was waiting for him. Having power such as that being given him meant many things. Chiefly, bearing the burden of maintaining the trust of the people under his authority. He'd previously thought of it as a kind of enslavement. He didn't disagree with that notion now, but he knew the words on the page, and he deemed them good words. Honest words.

He wasn't here for the power. He wasn't here to become a dictator. *I will not be like that,* he vowed silently. *Not because I am better. Better men than me have succumbed to the seductions of leadership, perks that are not lacking in the role I am about to embrace.* He glanced at Aurelia. *The difference is*

I see the danger, even here at the outset. If I remain mindful of it, I will not fall.

"Hello," he said. "I am John Newman."

Flashes blinded him.

"As I ascend to the rank and privilege of the Domn Lup, I find myself inspired by the responsibility I am about to embrace. . . ." The speech was short, and he followed it by inviting questions. None were unexpected. He responded appropriately to each.

Aurelia leaned over and touched Johnny's elbow. "The next question is the last," she said softly, making a point of checking her wristwatch for the assembled media to see.

Johnny smiled at the crowd. "I'm told there's time for only one more question."

There were hands raised, and he tried to find someone he hadn't yet called on. "You, with the green tie."

"Where did you grow up? What can you tell us about your human background?"

Cameras flashed again.

Johnny shrugged. "I don't know. I can remember the last eight years only. Prior to that is gone."

"Why?" the man in the green tie asked.

Others shouted questions like "Did you have a head trauma?" or "Were you attacked by a wærewolf then?"

Aurelia cut between him and the podium. "I'm sorry, that will be all for now."

Gregor clasped Johnny's arm and led him along the velvet rope that not only cordoned them off from the media and the public at large, who had crowded closer, but also led directly to the hallway they had emerged from. "There is a limo waiting, sire." He moved to switch their places so he was the one nearest the velvet rope.

Before Johnny was out of reach, a woman leaned and reached, snatching Johnny's wrist between both of her small hands. Her grip was viselike; he paused. Cameras clicked relentlessly around them.

"Ma'am—" Johnny began.

"We have to go, sire." Gregor's voice was stern. "We have to leave so that the media can wrap up and the building can be emptied."

The woman said, "I knew you before you were a 'new man.'"

Gregor reached toward the woman's fingers. "You have to release him, ma'am."

"Wait," Johnny said, his free hand slapping onto Gregor's chest.

"What does an old woman know?" Gregor whispered.

She fixed Gregor with an unwavering stare. "Enough to bring me over five hundred miles," she said. "On a bus."

CHAPTER FORTY-FIVE

Kurt Miller had followed when Toni Brown had hailed a cab from the bus station. As a SSTIX agent, he'd been made aware of some hubbub about the wære's Domn Lup, but as the regional agent for upstate New York, it had been of only peripheral interest to him. Listening to a local radio station, he learned a major announcement by the wæres was being made at the Cleveland Trust Bank. When the cab dropped Toni off in front of an impressive building with columns, he read Cleveland Trust Bank along the top. *Why does this matter to you, Toni? Is he supposed to be here?*

Kurt drove slowly and saw her leave the cab and head inside; he also glimpsed security using metal-detecting wands to check the people going in. He found parking down the block on the opposite side of the street, then jogged back. It bothered him to leave his gun in the car, but he'd not get through security with a weapon.

As he waited for his inspection at the checkpoint, he scrutinized the security staff. None of them fit the description of the person he suspected she was looking for. He also worried that Toni might see him as he waited or as he entered. It was a risk he couldn't dodge.

Inside, he searched for a few moments before finding her. The place was thick with media people, and Toni was shorter than most. Her silver-blond hair—too silver for her age—helped him locate her in the area to the side of the podium, right along the velvet ropes. It was not a prime press spot, but it was obviously the entry and exit for those making the announcements here today.

He had to give her credit; Antonia Brown was many things, but stupid wasn't one of them. Positioning himself in the crowd about ten feet behind her and away from the podium, he was confident she wouldn't catch a glimpse of him.

Once the Domn Lup was brought out, however, Kurt was stunned. Tall, lanky, with black wavy hair and a cleft chin—this had to be Elena Hampton's son, John. *He's the Domn Lup. Change at will? That explains everything. God, tattoos on his eyelids? That had to hurt like a sonofabitch.*

After the announcement was made and the pretty speech given, this "Johnny Newman" allowed the reporters to ask questions.

Detective Miller considered what plan Toni might have. She had positioned herself where the Domn Lup would see her, but he hadn't recognized her on his way out. Then the final question was asked and he claimed he had no memory before eight years ago.

If that's true, he won't know you at all, Toni.

Kurt worried that if she acted in some rash and desperate manner, the security here would respond. They couldn't hurt her in public, but Kurt didn't trust wærewolves, even when they were being honest about what they were.

When John Newman left the stage, Kurt was relieved the security started to change places with John as they neared Toni's spot.

Then Toni very nearly leapt forward as she grabbed at the Domn Lup. There were gasps and flashes, and the noise level of the media side rose as they compressed the area, straining for pictures and trying to hear.

In the shuffle, Kurt surged toward Toni. He couldn't let anything happen to one of his wife's best friends. He was right behind her when he heard her say, ". . . on a bus."

It seemed the whole room stilled, like someone had stopped time. Then John Newman said, "Let her through. Bring her with us."

The brawny security man unhooked the velvet rope and let Toni through, his glare enough to keep anyone else from trying to pass through. He snapped the cordon back in place and followed John Newman out.

Bring her with us. Bring her with us?

Kurt had to get to the parking garage *now*.

CHAPTER FORTY-SIX

Three limos pulled into the parking lot of the Pilgrim Congregational Church. It was well out of downtown in Tremont, and was the location the wæres often used for meetings they wanted off-site of the den, especially if they wanted to avoid vamps.

Gregor had insisted the old woman not ride in the same vehicle as Johnny. He'd put her into the first car and ridden with her. When Gregor got out, Johnny, who was sitting by the window of the middle car, hit the button to lower the window. "Well?" Johnny asked. "What did you find out?"

"She's a stubborn woman who is apparently not intimidated by riding in a limo surrounded by wæres," Gregor announced, clearly frustrated.

"What did she *say*?" Johnny clarified.

"That she will only talk to you."

For the entirety of the fifteen-minute ride, Johnny's emotions had swirled. He wanted to hear what she had to say, and he feared it. *Who was that woman? Not my mother, surely! She would have said something different, right?* Now he intended to talk to her, and he didn't want everyone else listening in. He opened the car door. "Then let her talk to me. Send her inside. Alone. And send the rest of the men home." He approached the church.

"Sire—"

"You heard me." Johnny kept walking.

He pushed open the great doors, walked into the theatrical interior. Here, there was real Tiffany glass, a dome and columns as well. He sat in a pew near the front and viewed the pulpit.

The answers I sought were locked away. I didn't know when the phoenix taloned me that it would cost me any chance of that knowledge. Don't let this be a hoax.

He heard the outer door open again. Momentarily, quiet footsteps entered the chapel. The woman sidestepped into the pew just ahead of his and kept her distance.

He observed her as she stood looking up at the dome then at other architectural details. She didn't seem nervous; she seemed very much at ease. Her silver-blond hair was short, and she was dressed in a gray pantsuit made of a material that didn't wrinkle. He recalled her saying she'd ridden five hundred miles on a bus. That would explain the strange mingled scents around her.

Finally, she sat down in the pew, keeping her spine straight, shoulders squared. As she turned to face him, he noticed she'd tried—without complete success—to apply enough makeup under her eyes to hide the dark circles. She didn't sleep well, he guessed, but she wasn't as old as he had first thought. The preponderance of silvery white hair on her head belied age—or hardship. She did emit a profound tiredness.

"You certainly picked a beautiful spot to talk," she said.

"What's your name?"

"You used to call me Toni."

He regarded her, repeating the name over and over to himself, but he had not even a hint of recollection. "Do you dislike wæres?"

She shrugged. "I don't know any. Or I didn't until now. I liked you well enough before."

"How do you know me?"

"Indulge an 'old' woman for a moment, will you?"

He felt only impatience, having waited eight years already, but he forced the hastiness aside and unclenched the fists he hadn't consciously made. Gregor had surely insulted her when he'd called her old. Wanting to ease that offense, Johnny deliberately relaxed his shoulders and nodded.

"What is the date of your earliest memory?" she asked.

Suspicion filled him. "Why?"

"Everything else I think I know hinges on this time line."

"Because you're a fraud who wants information to twist into your lies?" Johnny sat back with a tired, regretful exhalation. "Tell me what you came here to say, or get out of here," he whispered.

Toni fixed him with the look that cross mothers wear.

He could force her to tell him. It probably wouldn't take much to make her talk. A wave of shame rushed through him. *What's wrong with me?* He'd lost it last night and he might have lost Persephone forever, but this impulsive carelessness wasn't *him*.

Johnny raked fingers over his scalp, as if he could harvest a good idea that way. He stood and paced out into the aisle, ready to leave before the beast inside him did something horrible.

He couldn't abandon this chance. Staring straight ahead into the darker depths under the choir loft, he was overwhelmed with the need to know and the understanding that this was his chance. Maybe his only chance. He couldn't live with himself if he didn't master himself, sit his ass down and find out.

As he turned back, he felt more in control.

"My first memory is of waking naked in the Cleveland Metroparks. That was actually roughly eight and a half years ago. In June."

"June," Toni repeated. She scooted over in the pew. Patting the space she'd just opened, she said, "C'mon." He sat. "What happened to you then?" The empathy she conveyed wasn't false.

"I ended up at the hospital. I didn't know my name and couldn't remember anything. They called me John Doe but couldn't find any head injuries. I was released to social services. The police assisted them in a missing persons search. Found nothing. By then I was used to being called Johnny, so I stuck with that, but the name Newman fit because . . . I was a new man." He snorted. *Let's see if she knows what I know about the tattoos.* "Teenage punk, all tattooed up."

"The last time I saw you was in May. You didn't have the tattoos then."

That was a relief. He knew Eris had given them to him after he'd been abducted. Facing Toni squarely, he said, "There's a giant hole in my life. Can you start filling it in now?"

Toni reached into her purse and produced a small brown diary. The lock on it was broken, and a thick rubber band was keeping it shut. She plucked the stretchy plastic ring away and opened it, then handed him a school photo of a pimply teen, maybe fifteen.

Johnny's breath caught, recognizing his own face, minus the tattoos.

His thoughts were racing, so many, jumbled and frantic. This was him. Toni really did know him! He checked the back of the photo. It was blank. "What was my name?"

"Ironically enough, your name *was* John. John Hampton."

Elated, Johnny grinned as he repeated the name to himself many times. As he did, his gaze fell to the diary, and he wondered if that was his, if his own thoughts had been recorded there. "You're not my mother, are you?"

She laughed. "No. But I suppose I fed you more than she did there for a while."

"What's her name? And my father's? What were they like?"

Toni raised her hand as if to say slow down. "I don't know."

Johnny's grin disappeared. Desperation roiled up. He snapped, "What do you mean you don't know?"

Toni shook her head and muttered, "This isn't going to work." She also stood. "You've a temper, John. That's something I never could abide." She left from the opposite end of the pew.

Johnny nimbly leapt to the seat of the next pew and jumped into the aisle to block her. "Oh no, you're not leaving *now*."

"I've given you a name. That was more than you had before, and you don't intimidate me, John."

"I haven't tried yet." His beast snarled inside him.

Toni leaned against the pew and crossed her arms, still clasping the diary. "Well, go on then," she challenged. "Do your worst."

The beast slavered inside him. It wanted free, but Johnny fought. *I am in control. Me. The man, not the wolf.*

But the wolf was strong.

Johnny's fingers itched. He threw off his jacket, tore the tie loose, and ripped the shirt, sending buttons flying. His fingers elongated and, even as dark hair sprouted from his skin, his nails darkened and sharpened into points. He lifted the black claw between them, and, when Toni did not react, he let the dull edge slide across her cheek—without pressing. "What do you mean you don't know?" he asked again.

"You didn't talk about them," she said calmly, "and if you want to scare me, you'll have to do much more than that." She curiously perused the tattoo on his chest.

Johnny couldn't smell any fear radiating off of her. It made his anger swell. He wrapped his hand around her throat, still without pressure. "I can do much more."

Toni simply blinked at him, no trace of fear anywhere.

It reminded him of Ig . . . Ig hadn't been afraid to be mauled either. He'd been dying anyway.

The thought of his father figure hit him like a jab in the gut. That emotion weighed upon the beast until its grip weakened. Johnny felt control become fully his once more. But a disturbing idea had occurred to him.

Concentrating, Johnny induced the transformation through his whole upper torso. His grasp on her neck was loose, even as his snout elongated and his nose grew infinitely more sensitive. She did not shrink away as he leaned in close, sniffed. Closer, he put his nose into her hair, against her neck . . . there. There it was, embedded in her scent. *Disease.*

He released her and reverted, feeling the defeated whine of his beast. He retrieved his shirt from the floor and punched his arms into the sleeves. "How long do you have to live?"

Toni's eyes widened, then she set her jaw. "Maybe six months." She bent to pick up his jacket and tie.

"What do you want?" he asked. "Treatment in exchange for your information?"

She transferred the garments to him. "You can't buy me any time, John."

"You can beat the disease if I infect you. Is that what you want?"

"Hell, no!" She sank onto the pew as if her knees were suddenly weak.

The buttons were gone, so he couldn't keep his shirt closed, but he still donned the jacket. He folded the tie and leaned against the end of the pew. "Then what do you want from me?"

Toni opened the diary again and retrieved another picture. In this one he was younger.

Johnny studied the mixture of innocence and mischief in that youthful face. "What grade was I in here?"

"That isn't a picture of you, John. That's my grandson."

CHAPTER FORTY-SEVEN

Kurt Miller followed the three limos as they departed downtown. His GPS was still on, but he was very aware that if he needed to make a hasty exit, he didn't know this city at all.

Based on the security the wærewolves had shown at the press conference, he made sure to keep back as much as he dared, yet, not knowing the city, he couldn't lag behind too far or else he might lose them. Soon they were on West Fourteenth Street, and the limos gathered in the parking lot of the Pilgrim Congregational Church.

He drove on by, made the first right, circled the block, then parked his Crown Victoria up the street and kept his distance. The brawny guard was marching away from the middle limo, and the Domn Lup entered the church door alone. The guard opened the door on the first limo and Toni climbed out. The guard raised his arm to gesture her into the church.

Out of habit, Kurt reached for the old worn file stamped COLD CASE on the passenger seat, opened it to a page for notes in the back, checked the time, and wrote:

3:40 p.m. I witnessed Antonia Brown entering the Pilgrim Congregational Church of her own accord seconds after the man just named Domn Lup of the wærewolves entered.

Using his BlackBerry, he accessed the internet and searched for images of the new Domn Lup. Flipping the page in the worn file to the picture of a very similar, youthful but untattooed face, he whispered, "Gotcha."

He noted the men around the building, guards, like wærewolf secret service. "But how do I actually getcha?"

Sitting at the dining table in the combined living-dining room, Eris held seven cards. She laid them down, drew a card, and had to sort through them to put the right three together and make a spread.

Playing cards had been Demeter's idea, and Eris had agreed before she realized she wasn't able to shuffle. Demeter had to shuffle for her, but she made Eris deal when it was her turn.

Eris discarded, then maneuvered the four remaining cards into her grip again. Outside, the Slut's rumble sounded. Lance was home from the college classes he attended at the Art Institute.

Nana drew a card, laughed, laid down a three card spread and discarded. "Rummy."

"You win again." Eris laid down her cards, glad it was over.

Lance charged up the stairs, rattling them so they could be heard inside. The door opened. As soon as he entered, he noted that the television had the news on, reporting on the Domn Lup and showing Johnny's picture. "The press conference is over. Why are they still going on about him?"

Demeter answered, "A Domn Lup's big news."

"We're not wæres. Why do we even care?"

Eris said, "Because he's your sister's boyfriend."

"Half sister," he corrected.

"Lance."

He groaned exasperatedly and stomped away. A second later, music blasted from his room.

Embarrassed that he would act this way in front of his grandmother, Eris shoved the cards into a pile, disregarding that they weren't all facing the same direction. "I pushed him hard. He's way ahead of his peers, in college at only seventeen. Some days he doesn't appreciate that."

Demeter sat back and propped her leg on the chair adjacent to her. "You abandoned Persephone—"

Eris stood abruptly, her chair squealing on the floor. "Mom. Not now."

"If not now, when?"

Eris stomped over and switched the television off. It was awkward working the remote with her left hand. *I didn't ask for this.*

"Never? If that's your answer, that's too late."

"Fine. You want to do this to me now? Have at it." Eris flopped down on the couch. The force of the action resonated up into her sore shoulder and she tried to keep the pain from showing.

"That is exactly what I'm talking about. If 'I want to do this to you now.' Do you think I'm out to get you?"

"Feels like it."

Demeter hobbled over to the opposite couch. Again, she propped up her leg, using the length of the cushions. "All this self-pity you're wallowing in—"

"I'm not—"

"Yes, you are!" Nana shouted. "And you're pressuring Persephone, trying to guilt her into loving you. She doesn't love you, Eris. You've given her nothing but abandonment, and followed that with a guilt trip."

That's ridiculous. "I'm her mother. And I saved her boyfriend's life!" She had expected her actions would buy her daughter's love. That her sacrifice hadn't simply filled Persephone with compassion and devotion pointed out a flaw in Persephone's character. Eris had begged Frigg, the Norse goddess of motherhood, to prod Persephone into recognizing that fact . . . but it seemed Frigg was not inclined to aid her.

"Yes. You saved his life," Demeter said. "And you could have saved your arm if you had gone to the hospital with the medics."

At those words, Eris's stomach formed a molten ball. *I didn't ask for this!* But Eris knew in her heart that she had. No one knew about the countless times she had thought to herself, *I'd give my right arm for another chance. . . .* "The spell needed finishing."

"It *could* have waited. You were impatient for the benefit, eager for Seph to see you as not giving up. You chose not to go. You chose to threaten Zhan's life in order to stay and finish. Did you think that would erase the past? Do you think Persephone owes you now for those choices you *freely* made?"

Yes. The word almost slipped out, but Eris bit her tongue. Demeter was twisting it all around just like— "You've been scrying!" That's where the opals had gone. Her mother had always been perceptive; her scrying ability was unmatched. Growing up with her had been a nightmare. Demeter could use the magical properties of opals to combine scrying with a form of astral projection. This was a skill Eris had never completely understood, but it busted her in lies, skipping school, underage smoking . . . so much more. Demeter could use it to pick up information that was, for lack of a better term, psychic. *She knows. Frigg help me, she knows.*

Demeter didn't deny it. She put her leg down and sat forward. "You saved a life, Eris. You're a hero. So act like a hero. Not a martyr."

Tears welled up and fell before Eris could think to fight them. Demeter sank onto the couch next to her. She squeezed Eris's hand. "There's a boy in there who loves you and needs you, and he's afraid he's losing you to a sister who's never been a part of your lives until now."

Eris sniffled. "He told you that? Or did you scry that up too?"

"Neither. It's written all over him. You're not seeing it because you're so wrapped up in Persephone. I know your daughter. She won't be pressured or pushed into your life. Focus on Lance now and let her go. I promise she'll come back."

Risqué worked by candlelight at the altar table in Menessos's private rooms. She was unperturbed by the fact that his corpse and Meroveus's lay in closed beds nearby. Her makeup case was on the floor at her feet. Another case, similar in size but filled with magical miscellanea, was beside it.

Her master had inspected the items she'd brought to fulfill his list. He'd explained what he wanted her to do with them. It was a difficult task, brilliantly plotted and full of risks.

Risks. Perfect for me.

She began,

> *Necklaces two, I now make,*
> *With spell-work meant never to break.*
> *With carnelians and malachites,*

The wearers are stable in their human hides.
Birch, iron, and silver wire,
This spell will never expire!
Iron lockets open wide,
These I now place inside:
Dragon's Blood, powdered fine,
Mandrake root, and turpentine.
One dark hair from the Lustrata's head,
This binding you can never shed.
Vampire wizard's blood—two drops!
Now this binding cannot be stopped.
Sealed with fire, hot as the sun,
This binding cannot be undone.

Each necklace was placed into a basket. She laid the jewelry carefully, as one link in the chain of each was yet open. Carrying the basket and a bucket with welding supplies, Risqué stepped to the back chamber door. She declared her mortality and opened it without trouble from the spell her master had placed upon it. Still, she felt the compulsion he'd placed. The seal would not keep an immortal from leaving, but it would cause him or her to linger within.

Risqué lit candles around the bed where the two dead shabbubitum lay, then called a circle encompassing Menessos's large bed.

Crawling onto the bed, Risqué sat straddling Ailo's corpse. She lifted Ailo's head, put the necklace under her neck and replaced her head on the pillow. Laying a heavy welder's glove across Ailo's throat, Risqué hooked the open link atop the glove, satisfied that it was a tight fit. Donning protective goggles, the half-demon fired up the small torch. Clasping the link with long-nosed pliers in one hand, the torch in the other, she chanted, "I bind you Ailo to Menessos and Persephone."

When the link was secure, she did the same to Talto. By the time she had taken up the circle, the iron was cool enough that she could retrieve the gloves that had protected the sisters' necks. She removed also a few hairs from each of their heads.

Crawling onto the bed between them, she tied the strands together in knots, chanting, "Ailo and Talto, you are henceforth bound to Menessos and Persephone." When the hairs were well knotted, she dropped them into a thin cotton pouch. She clipped the sisters' fingernails and toenails and added these trimmings to the pouch. After she cut a fingertip of each and squeezed out blood to stain the sides of the pouch, Risqué left the rear chamber.

She let the candles continue burning; the undead liked to awaken with a dim light waiting.

Returning to the altar, she burned the pouch on charcoal, then gathered the ashes. She put half in a glass vial. The other half she stirred into a lotion she'd made with oil, beeswax, a few drops of water, orrisroot and buckthorn bark.

After lighting candles all around the outer chamber, she opened the door to Menessos's closed bed. She repositioned a pedestal to be nearer and placed a candelabrum on it so the black tapers could light her endeavors. The glass vial, an ink pen, surgical gloves, a knife, a needle with two colors of thread and the little bowl with lotion from the altar were placed with Menessos, then she undressed and crawled inside.

Sitting atop his body, she opened his sightless eyes and

murmured lovingly as she drew symbols on his forehead. She drew symbols on his cheeks and down his sternum. Still chanting, she drew an ankh on his throat. Donning the surgical gloves, she rubbed the lotion where she had drawn, chanting, "Ailo and Talto are yours to command," following it with the seething words of a far fiercer language in a voice that was not entirely her own.

What flicker of energy she felt as she worked she believed to be of her own making, and she did not know that a hooded man had appeared in the chamber, standing on the other side of the enclosed bed. She did not know he placed his palms upon the wood and spread his fingers wide. She did not know how he smiled, listening to her.

When the symbols were smeared and all of the lotion absorbed into Menessos's skin, Risqué clutched the knife. The words of her staccato chant had a dark cadence as she placed the tip of the blade just lower than his sternum. With an ecstatic cry and a flick of her stubby tail, she cut a deep, three-inch line.

Wedging the gash open with the knife tip, she poured the ashes from the vial inside her master's body. As she sewed black and red stitches into his skin, she chanted, "Sealed within you, their binding will never be undone."

CHAPTER FORTY-EIGHT

Toni's words didn't sink in at first. When they did, Johnny's lungs expelled all oxygen, as if he'd just been kicked in the gut and a terrible weight had crashed onto his shoulders. His bones felt too fragile to bear it.

"I remember the first time I ever saw you. You and my daughter were teamed up for a class project. I'd just gotten home from work, and you arrived shortly after. I'd passed you on the road and thought, 'What's that kid doing out now?' It was cold and night was falling. Then you showed up on my porch. My daughter brought you into the kitchen to introduce you, and I thought, 'That poor kid.' You'd walked in the snow in your sneakers. Your jeans had holes in them and were wet from the knee down. Your hair was a mess—it still is, I see—and you barely made eye contact. I set out some cans of soda and a bag of chips and started dinner. You finished off the chips and paid very little attention to the project."

Johnny's legs had become gelatin. He staggered into the pew and sat.

"It was a subject she struggled with, and she was frustrated with your half-ass effort. I remember her words exactly. 'Maybe nothing matters to you, but this grade is important to me, so either man up and help or go home.' You stood up to leave. As she saw you to the door, I heard her tell you that she was going to do something with her life, she was going to college and needed a good high school record. She said she wouldn't let you ruin her GPA so she'd just do the whole thing and put your name on it, too. You answered with a sarcastic 'Gee, thanks.' She said you should thank her, because it'd be the best grade in your whole high school career." Toni shook her head at the memory. "I didn't like the idea of you walking home in the snow when you'd barely just arrived, but I was so proud of her, standing up and fighting for something she wanted.

"You see, after her father died . . . she'd been lost for so long. But she'd fought above her sorrow and depression, and she had goals again.

"I told her how proud of her I was. She said you were a loser anyway." Toni tilted her head. "Then the doorbell rang."

"I came back?"

"You did. You promised you'd man up. I could have cried, because I knew whatever you had at home, it was worse than the wrath my little girl had just poured on you. The next time you showed up to work on the project, you had nicer jeans on, though still wet to your knees, and your hair had been combed. The time after that I gave you a ride home and was appalled at how far you had to go. You said it was shorter to go through the woods. It explained why your pants were wet up to your knees."

"What kind of house did I live in?"

"A modest older two-story on the side of a hill. It was an odd little place, kind of in a hairpin curve of the road. There were no houses around it, and the woods stretched right up to the back door."

She knows where I lived. "What city? What state?"

"Saranac Lake, New York."

He shook his head. "I don't remember. Even hearing it, it sounds foreign." He paused. "What's your daughter's name?"

"Francine. Her daddy called her Frankie from day one, and I always said he would have gotten such a kick out of the two of you, Frankie and Johnny."

"Do you have a picture of her?"

Toni flipped into the book again, offered him another photo. This one was not from school. It was of a girl curled up in a recliner with a book. She was looking into the camera as if to say, *You're interrupting a good part.*

Frankie was beautiful. Her light brown hair was straight; it hung to her shoulders, and wisps curled lazily under her chin. Her skin was pale, and her blue eyes were like deep seas. "Where is she now?"

"She's dead."

"Dead?" Johnny repeated, head snapping up.

"Three years ago, some of her high school friends had come home from college for the weekend. They were about to graduate and wanted to go out for Cinco de Mayo. Frankie wasn't going to go—"

"Wait, her friends came home? Wasn't *she* in college?"

Toni shook her head. "She didn't go. She was hired as a cashier at the grocery and stayed home to raise Evan."

Johnny swallowed hard. *Evan.* His gaze fell to the picture of the boy. *His name is Evan. . . . He's . . .*

"She wasn't going to go," Toni said. "You see, she always thought about you on Cinco de Mayo."

"Why? Am I Mexican?"

Toni almost smiled. "Not that I know of. Eight years

ago on Cinco de Mayo I was working late. You weren't supposed to be at my house, but teenagers don't listen to those kinds of rules when a school project has blossomed into first love. Shortly before I was expected home, you left . . . your usual route of going down the road then crossing into the woods as always. You were attacked, and somehow, you made it back to the driveway and collapsed. That's where you were when I pulled in. We called an ambulance. You were in the hospital for three days. Frankie was guilt-ridden because she hadn't known you'd been lying there in front of our garage—injured. She wouldn't leave your side. They said it was a wild dog or a wolf. It was too soon to do a check for the virus, but they had you tested for rabies and signed you up to get tested for the wære virus before the next full moon."

A shadow of painful memory shaded the woman's face. "So, five years later, when her friends wanted to go out, she was reluctant, and I knew she was thinking of you. I encouraged her to go." Her expression hardened, fell. Tears welled up. "Four of them went out dancing. Only two of them survived when a drunk driver hit their car on the way home."

Toni tugged a tissue from her purse.

She shoved the diary at Johnny. "This was her diary. She kept it sporadically during high school. It tells the story of you 'the loser' becoming you 'the boyfriend' across the spring, and there's more after . . . after you disappeared." Toni swallowed and crumpled the damp tissue. "She didn't know she was pregnant until after you were gone. She was so scared when she told me. Evan was born on Valentine's Day." She valiantly met his eyes and said, "He'll be eight this February. It's the last birthday of his that I'll see." Tears rolled down her cheeks, and she dabbed the tissue at them again. "Then he'll have nobody, John. Nobody but you."

Suddenly the puzzle that was his past had new pieces that changed the picture entirely. With all the instincts he'd been struggling to control, Johnny sat there oddly aware of the absence of them. He was numb.

He made himself think the words: *My son.*

Was it possible? Comparing his school pictures and this child's, yes it was. Not just possible, but probable.

So why didn't an immediate course of action spring into his mind?

I'm not father material.

A wanna-be rock star lived a selfish kind of life. A wærewolf could be dangerous. A political leader lived with constant danger.

I should tell her to put the kid into children's services. Let a normal family raise him.

His heart skipped a beat at the thought.

He'd only traveled his rock-star path searching for a sense of belonging, and didn't family provide that? He knew plenty of wæres who were fantastic parents. Who were the political leaders trying to make the world better for if not their own offspring?

All he'd wanted since waking in the park was to know his past and to find his family. *This* wasn't a possibility he'd ever considered, but he had some leads now that could help him find his parents.

That was still a goal in his heart.

Recognizing that, he knew that his own need to find that truth would never leave him. He couldn't leave this kid—his kid—to grow up with the same need to know.

He couldn't let him grow up without real family. He couldn't cut him off like he'd been cut off.

Johnny stood, and his voice was as unsteady as his legs. "Toni, if you'll ride back to the den with me, I'll get my car and drive you home." He tucked the pictures into the diary and put it in the inside pocket of his sport jacket.

"It's a very long drive."

"I want to meet him."

CHAPTER FORTY-NINE

I'd drifted in and out of sleep so many times and was so hungry and thirsty that I couldn't be sure if only minutes had passed, or hours. My body was stiff and sore, and my shoulder still felt hot and swollen. My right fingers, however, weren't prickly like before.

I hadn't felt Menessos awaken, so it must not be night yet . . . but with this barrier up, I might not feel him rise.

If Liyliy's sisters killed him . . . would I be able to tell the difference in the ache a master feels and all the pain I feel now?

Damn it, what if he's gone? Johnny can't help me.

I'm all alone.

Something creaked overhead and suddenly half of the ceiling slid open, retracting into itself with a terrible metallic clang. Dim evening light flooded into the darkness. I'd begun to think maybe I was in one of those domes where the Department of Transportation kept salt for the roads, but this was not like being inside of an upside-down bowl. In fact, the walls actually sloped in at the *bottom*.

I took in my surroundings. The place was a long rectangle with metal supports placed at regular intervals along the walls like ribs in—a ship? *A cargo hold!*

I wonder if she read me while I was unconscious?

Welded onto the far wall was an odd ladder with half-moon footholds. It rose toward the catwalk below the roof-door, where the silhouette of a giant owl suddenly appeared and dropped through. As she landed, Liyliy tossed a plastic bag to the side and resumed her human form. Her silken gown flowed down to her ankles. Quicksilver flowed and formed an owl-motif bracelet. She extended her arm, pointing a finger at me as she advanced; a crude knife formed in her grasp.

I said nothing as she neared. Creepy had said she needed me to do something; I had to assume that meant she needed me alive. I'd be doing very little if I was incapacitated any further, so I managed to counsel myself and keep my fear in check.

Until she poked me with the knife tip.

The first two or three pokes I could ignore. "You are brave," she whispered, and jabbed harder. I felt the skin on my forearm tear with the fourth. She hovered over me to lick the blood. The tips of her hair brushed my skin, and even that was painful. I sucked air through my teeth.

She laughed and slapped the flat of her blade on my shoulder.

I screamed.

Liyliy dropped the knife behind me. "Now your blood has the flavor of fear and pain." Her hands sank into the salt as her lips touched my skin, skimming between my neck and my swollen shoulder. When she bit me, there was no euphoria easing the sharp sensation, as when Menessos fed.

Menessos.

I hadn't felt him rise. She had risen, so surely he had too. Unless they staked him.

Have I lost them both? Is our triangle well and truly broken? Loss and despair crept over me.

Liyliy drew back and licked her lips. "This is the side he feeds from, isn't it? I can taste him."

She hadn't drunk much, but my energy was as low as my mood, and I was famished and dehydrated. The world swam before my dizzy eyes.

Liyliy grabbed up the knife again and I whimpered when she jostled the rope and began cutting. It occurred to me she hadn't yet touched me with her hands. In fact, it seemed like she was trying very hard to touch only the rope, but then she was probably trying to keep from draining me too much.

When she had finished cutting, she backed away, keeping the knife pointed at me.

She'd severed only the portion of rope connecting my bound wrists to my equally secured ankles; I wasn't free. In the dim light, I noticed the rope had silvery threads running through it. Remembering the pieces of her and her sisters that had floated up to cover the lights at the haven, I wondered if these were also portions of her, like the silver that adorned her leg.

"Sit up. Slowly."

Keeping my arm against my body, I sat stiffly up. The light-headedness made me fear toppling over, and sitting made me aware my dress was a dirty, tattered ruin. Seeing it, I couldn't help trying to smooth my hair. After a hundred miles an hour on the broom—*where is my broom?*—my hair must have looked like a fright wig.

My muscles complained and threatened to cramp; I lowered my arms. I swallowed hard. "When I blacked out at the amusement park there was enough night remaining for you to drag me back to the haven. Why didn't you?"

She studied me but said nothing.

"If you didn't need me for something, you would have drained me."

"You should be grateful I did neither of the things I could have done."

"I am grateful." A wave of dizziness struck me and I leaned too far and nearly fell over. "I just want to know why," I said firmly, as if I hadn't just almost fainted. "It wasn't an act of kindness."

From the bag Liyliy produced a bottle of Coke, a Snickers candy bar and a bag of Sun Chips. She dropped them beside me. The Coke fizzed inside the bottle. "Eat."

Famished and fully aware I had only myself to get me out of this mess, I worked at the bag of chips, holding it with my teeth and pulling. I was bearing the brunt of the lifting in my left, compensating to minimize the motion of the right. I poured a few chips into my mouth, where they promptly turned pasty with my great thirst. As I chewed, I wedged the bottle between my knees, slowly opened it and drank. It was warm, but it was liquid. The caffeine and sugar would help, too.

Liyliy paced about. "You are an Erus Veneficus who mastered your master, so you are very powerful. Having mastered Menessos, I count you doubly powerful." She took a pose before me. "He believes you are the Lustrata."

I had the distinct feeling she was waiting for me to confirm or deny it. "Look, I have to be honest. If we're trading flattery here, I'm gonna have a hard time coming up with compliments for you."

She leaned in close, squinting evilly, and smacked my shoulder.

I screamed again and fell over on my side.

Liyliy pounced, punching her fists into the salt on either side of my head. "He could be wrong. You don't seem like much of a threat." Underneath those slitted lids, her eyes yellowed, grew bigger and rounder. Her nose elongated like a beak.

Putting every ounce of confidence I could muster into my tone, I said, "Okay, I'm intimidated already. Just tell me what you want me to do."

She tossed her head like she was flouncing her hair and sat up. Her face resumed a human form. Reaching back and under her hair, she produced a golden necklace with a small pouch on it. It didn't seem like much, but then neither did the charm Beau had given me. In magic, the shiniest wasn't always the most powerful.

"Unmake this."

CHAPTER FIFTY

Mero awoke with an agonized groan. If he remained completely still, the pain would subside faster. However, a few feet away, Menessos screamed his way into life.

Mero opened the door of his bed and climbed out. A servant had lit candles around the room, and, as promised, his clothing had been cleaned. He tugged the elastic band from his long hair, finger-combed his dark curls and regathered the ponytail.

Menessos was still panting from the pain of transfer, so Mero tried to be quiet as he dressed. *For all the torment I experience, torment he never warned me about, there is no comfort in knowing his is worse.*

When Menessos emerged from his bed, he was still panting. "Have they found Persephone?"

"I don't know," Mero answered. "How are your legs?"

Menessos ignored his question and pointed at the altar near the main door to his chambers. "The table. Is there a note upon it?"

Mero stepped closer to inspect. "Four bottles, a few candles, no note."

"Damn it!"

The mournfulness of his words struck Mero. "If she is the Lustrata, my friend, she will be fine."

"I have taken a risk, Mero. A terrible risk. But it had to be done."

"What did you do?"

Menessos stared at the floor. "There was no other way."

"Menessos?"

"I exposed her to . . . to someone far more dangerous than Liyliy."

"Who?"

A cry resounded from the rearmost chamber. The sisters had awoken as well, and were quite unhappy about something.

"I cannot say." Menessos moved somewhat stiffly, but he managed to dress quickly. His legs were obviously well on their way to being healed. Bestowing two of the bottles on Mero, he carried the other two and walked to the wide door at the rear chamber. He spoke a chant to nullify his spell. Mero followed him inside; this room also had candles already lit. The sisters were seated on the bed.

When they entered, Ailo stood and demanded, "What are these ugly things?" The mist that became clothing for them was a vapor lingering around her neck, trying to slither between the necklace and her skin, but power radiated like a breath from the links of the chain, and the mist could not waft close.

Menessos offered Ailo one of the corked bottles. She snatched it away. There was no pride in Menessos's voice as he said, "The power Meroveus once held over you now belongs to me."

"Betrayer!" Talto cried, spitting at Mero as he tried to offer her one of the bottles.

Menessos, whispering, made a fist and squeezed it so tight his hand shook with the effort.

Talto collapsed in pain and curled like a fetus as she cried. Ailo thrust the bottle back into Menessos's arms, forcing him to release his magic. She wrapped her arms around Talto. Though she glared at Menessos, she said nothing.

"I would have you consider your words more carefully, Talto. Meroveus is our guest, and he bears your dinner."

Talto continued to cry, and Menessos set the bottles on the mantel and drew close to them. "You were both weak and tired after your long interrogation last night. I drank of you and let you drink of me . . . do you remember?"

Ailo frowned as she thought back. "You mesmerized us! You made claim to us!"

"I did."

Talto wailed. "We did not want this," Ailo said.

"You are mine now. I will protect and provide for you. Be obedient and you will find that I am a just master."

"Our sister will come for us!" Talto cried defiantly.

Menessos sat on the edge of the bed. Mero was surprised by the calm reassurance of his manner. "Your sister stole Mero's means of binding you three, and she has not returned, Talto. Because of her thievery, you were re-bound to me. Liyliy is a thief who stole her freedom and yours, and fled. She has abandoned you. In her stead I have made the pledge to care for you. If you call anyone 'betrayer,' it must be Liyliy."

Talto's sobs shook the room.

Mero sat on the leather seating in the round. The enclosed beds had been taken to the rear chamber, and all of them had fed. Though electric lights provided illumination, a few bergamot-scented candles were burning. The citrusy scent had been Seven's suggestion, an attempt to instill the sisters with calmness and peace via aromatherapy. Presently, Mero listened as Seven gave Menessos a report.

"The Interim Quarterlord is unaccustomed to the actual duties connected to the job that has just been bestowed upon him. And it seems that the Columbus and Cincinnati havens are disputing territory in Dayton. Remember, we thought their feud was just achy evidence of old wounds? Apparently the ailment is a disease that is no longer in remission. He's finding it difficult to deal with the phone calls."

"Seven," Menessos said with dismay. "I've managed to keep them at the negotiating table for weeks, and that has not been easily achieved. What have you done?"

She put a hand on the back of the couch and leaned in. "I want that man out of my haven and out of Cleveland."

"Seven."

"They intend to fight, so let them—while *he's* in charge. Let him show his leadership skills if he has any. It will keep him busy."

"He won't tolerate their squabbling and he won't consider their havens should he supply an active resolution."

"Exactly." She stood straight and crossed her arms. "Leonard of the Columbus haven will go over this Interim Quarterlord's head in a heartbeat." She shot a pointed glare at Mero. "And I'm sure the Excelsior will be delighted to have to intervene."

"Seven," Menessos said again. This time his voice was tight enough to snap.

She uncrossed her arms and let her soft touch drop onto his shoulder. "You have other matters that require your attention. Allow me to handle this." When he opened his mouth to argue, she sternly added, "I know how to handle

petty men with their eyes on power that is not their own."
Her expression dared him to argue that fact.

Menessos conceded. "What of our search for Persephone?"

"Everyone we have has been out all day searching, and
they plan to take shifts throughout the night, but they
have to rest, so there won't be much getting done here on
the nightclub."

"She must be found!" he whispered. He clutched his
stomach, as if he were in pain. Seven noticed, and she
seemed about to inquire, but Menessos said, "Go on."

"Ivanka said she was hounded by calls from the
Domn Lup until three o'clock—at which time his press
conference began. She hasn't heard from him since. The
event was recorded and I have it cued up if you would like
to see it." She offered her master an open laptop.

"Later," Menessos waved it away. "Are they searching
for her too?"

"The den claims they do not have her and are not
looking for her, but I suspect something is going on. They
would not let me speak directly with the Domn Lup."

Menessos considered it. "Send Zhan. She and Kirk have
an understanding."

"Zhan is at the farmhouse assisting Mountain. It will
be an hour before she can get there, but I'll convey your
order." Seven paused at the door. "Anything else?"

"Just find her."

"We will, Boss."

Though Mero hung on their every word, he wasn't lax
in his observation of the sisters, who sat huddled together
in the corner, whispering and crying.

From the relative safety of her sister's arms, Talto

spoke. "The witch mastered you. Why do you agonize over her disappearance? If she is not here, she cannot be your puppeteer."

Menessos rose and proceeded to the corner. Talto made to cower, but he sat on the floor with them. "Is that the way your former master treated you, Talto?"

"Yes!" she snapped. "Read this one, torture that one. Night after night after night. So much horror and despair. We wanted to be free of it. We killed Rouma, and I bear no regret."

The threat and warning in her tone were not hidden. Mero thought that Menessos would surely wield his power and double her over in pain again. But he didn't. He simply said, "Rouma? I meant Liyliy."

CHAPTER FIFTY-ONE

The sun had set as Johnny and Toni emerged from the church. Toni preceded him into the limousine. As he sat, Aurelia reached to shake hands with Toni. "Hi, I'm Aury. And you are?"

Toni didn't take the proffered hand. "Nobody you need to know."

Aurelia pursed her lips in irritation. Johnny shook his head once to indicate she should back off. It was a silent ride to the den.

When they arrived, Johnny held the door for Toni and pointed at his Maserati. "Wait over there." She walked slowly away. He led Gregor aside. "Get my car keys and my wallet from my desk, and the gym bag under my desk. Toni and I are going for a drive." Gregor nodded.

As the rented limo drove away, Aurelia watched the men trudge onto the lift but did not join them. "Are you coming, Aury?" Gregor called.

"Go without me." When they were out of sight, she set down her attaché and drew closer to Johnny. "What's going on with the woman?"

"Nothing I can't handle."

Her lips pursed, then stretched as they rounded. "Oh, I'm certain that you can handle a lot." She cast a fleeting look toward the car and the woman standing beside it. "Did I hear you say you were going for a drive?"

He crossed his arms and glowered down his nose

at her. He knew what she was up to. "If you were eavesdropping you did."

Closing the slight distance between them, Aury tossed her head, and her long, pale hair spilled behind her shoulder, revealing the best contours of her swan neck. "I'm a tenacious woman, sire. That rubs some men the wrong way . . . and I only want to rub you the right way. I trust you can see that my persistence doesn't have to be a bad thing." She spread her arms just enough to make her blouse stretch tighter across her chest.

She had to know what she was doing, exposing her beautiful flesh to him. Johnny wanted to ignore her, but he was mesmerized by her tone, her scent, and the eagerness in her body.

"I mean . . . diligence can be very rewarding, and . . . well," she mimicked his pose in a manner that deepened her cleavage. "I intend to give you my every effort." Her voice dropped at the end, and the sparkle in her eyes was full of carnal promise.

Her breasts were nearly touching his folded forearms. Just the slightest forward lean would break the ice and establish a basis for further contact. He had only to reach out and instigate it—an accidental touch, a fond caress . . . and he would trigger a compulsive, consuming, crushing landslide of passion.

He kept his arms firmly crossed, grasping his own elbows. The self-imposed physical restraint allowed him to resist the overwhelming urge to touch her. Without it, his hand might have raised of its own accord. He said nothing aloud, but repeated Persephone's name to himself silently.

Behind them, the elevator clanged and whirred as it descended again.

Aury wasn't done. "You were fabulous today, sire. How about when you're finished with your drive, you and I celebrate?"

Johnny knew he should tell her no, but his mouth wouldn't open and refuse her. The elevator arrived.

"Think about it," she said as she retrieved her attaché and strutted to the elevator. Gregor delivered the gym bag and the key to Johnny. "I dropped your wallet inside."

"Thank you."

"Should I follow?"

"No. I do this alone."

"Sire, wait."

Johnny spun, ready to chew Gregor out—then he saw the cord Gregor was holding. The phone charger for the car.

"Since your gym bag already has a change of clothes, I assume you won't be back tonight. Keeping your phone fully charged and answering it might calm the others should they become nervous over your whereabouts."

The tension drained off Johnny. "Thank you," he repeated, recalling that Gregor had heard her cite how long she'd been on a bus.

It was a five-hundred-and-sixteen-mile journey; according to the GPS, a full eight hours. Three hundred and twenty-eight miles of it was I-90—which the Maserati covered in just under four hours as Toni slept. Johnny did eighty-five while she slumbered, enjoying the music of the engine, lost in his thoughts.

That was a long time to think.

In the first hour, he'd considered how aggressively

he'd been behaving and wondered if the longer he was in human form, the more the wolf-effects wore off . . . but in the second hour he'd contemplated what it meant to be human. He wasn't fully either, and the time of overlap would be most sensitive.

By the third hour, he'd concluded that hunger, dominance, fight or flight, and sex were all linked to both his human and his wolf. Basic instincts of mammal life. Emotion, however, was the province of only the human animal. Like rage. Rage inspired murder, whereas wolves hunted and killed only to eat.

Since meeting Toni, most of the factors that affected both sides of his nature had been quiet. With the exception of the moments in the den parking garage with Aury and Gregor, he'd felt more in control of himself than he had in days. But in the garage, it had been lust and anger —both very much human territory—that had sought to rule him. Even at the church, it had been his anger and fear that had made him aggressive.

So, emotion could numb him. Could damn near immobilize the bestial side of him, if he was able to be vigilant with his feelings. His emotions could buoy him above the wolf in all the ways that man was meant to be more than an animal, like courage and compassion, and in none of the ways that man's superiority became man's shortcoming, like rage and greed.

It was just after ten o'clock when they picked up I-81 north at Syracuse.

Toni awoke. They agreed on a burger joint for a food and facilities break, then were back on the road. Johnny kept the speedometer at seventy-five.

"What's he like?" Johnny asked.

Toni smiled. "He's all boy. He can't sit still. His mind is on anything but his schoolwork. He climbs everything. He catches frogs and digs up worms. He's full of energy and he's . . . he's just vibrant!"

Johnny realized he was smiling.

"He's got a mouth on him, though. I should be tougher on him than I have been, but . . . he lost his mother. I lost my daughter. Spoiling him helped us both get through it."

"Does he remember her?"

"Oh, yes. There's a picture of her beside his bed and he . . ." Her voice thickened, cracked. "He kisses Mommy good night every night."

Johnny didn't have to see her tears to know she was crying.

"Where is he now?"

"With some family friends. I'll call them in the morning and go get him." She resituated herself in the seat. "I was thinking, once we get to Saranac Lake, I'll show you where the house is and you can drop me off. I'm sorry, but I don't have a guest room. I don't even have a couch, just a short love seat—"

"I don't mind staying at a hotel."

She sighed gratefully. "Thank you."

"No, Toni. Thank you."

CHAPTER FIFTY-TWO

I studied the necklace dangling from Liyliy's fist. It was a reasonable guess that since she wanted it gone, it represented either some danger to her, prohibited her from something, or had some power over her. Testing my theories, I reached my bound hands up to accept the necklace.

She lurched away, then tromped angrily around me, saying, "You will not touch it!"

It has some power over her.

Liyliy was kicking granules of salt all over me. I rolled to my back, blinked repeatedly and shielded my face to try and keep it out of my eyes. "How am I supposed to destroy it without touching it?" I demanded.

"Destroy? I did not say destroy!" She kicked me in the shoulder and I rolled, screaming in pain. Staring down at me, she growled, "I said unmake."

Panting, I laid my head on the mound and concentrated on getting this salt-flavored air in and out of my lungs. *Correction, that thing must provide the bearer some control over her.* Thinking back, I recalled that when I'd accepted the scroll from the advisor Mero, I had glimpsed something around his neck; I'd wondered then if he'd been wearing a magical amulet or pendant.

Aha.

So she needed the Lustrata to unmake the necklace.

"I trust you know the difference."

"I do," I said. Simply destroying a magical item could either break whatever spell it housed or seal it, depending on the item. The stake I'd burned in my hearth—*just over six weeks ago!*—had been made of wood and blood and mud. The spell-work attached had not been able to hold onto ash. As the wood had been consumed, the magic had evaporated, released in fiery transmutation.

Magic in metal was not so easy. Metal didn't transmute when superheated; it could become molten, but it was still metal and the spell wouldn't release. Unmaking a necklace of what appeared to be gold would be no small feat.

Or maybe the spell wasn't attached to the metal.

The pouch would burn, but I was betting the important stuff was within. If it had stones, crushing them would seal the magic in place. A major counter-spell would then be required to undo the magic—with no guarantee of success, let alone permanence. "I have to know what I'm dealing with. Are there stones inside the pouch?"

Liyliy retreated to a safe distance and opened the pouch. Her wings sprouted and hoisted her toward the open top. As she hovered, the blustering air flung salt every which way, and I had to shield my eyes again. When the rush of air diminished, she was standing, wingless, before me. "There are three. Amber."

Those stones would burn and transmute.

Liyliy, apparently, understood all this. If I tried and "accidentally" cracked the amber, she would surely kill me.

My only experience with unmaking anything was the *in signum amoris.* That had been a spoken spell sealed in actions and energy—it had existed like worn jewelry, attached to me, but not a part of me. Burning a fence in my meditation world had removed it in much the manner of losing jewelry down the drain. That was substantially different from unmaking physical matter in this world. I'd also had Hecate's help.

Why would Creepy want me to know that I can do this?
He knows Menessos and Johnny can't help me.

I scratched my head as if I was still thinking. I had to either do this impossible thing, or get it away from her.

I couldn't fight her physically; my shoulder injury was too fresh for me to expect to make much of a show as an opponent. But. Even without access to the ley line, I had power within me. Although most of my energy was depleted, she had brought me food . . . with more I could reenergize myself. Maybe enough to make one lucky strike, claim the necklace, and flip the balance of power here.

I could hope.

Donning an expression of an idea that had just struck, I sat up and clawed through the salt for the candy bar she'd dropped. "I need more food." I opened it and devoured a bite. "What you want me to do requires a lot of energy, and if you won't let me tap the ley line, I need some other way to fuel it. Bring me water, energy drinks and any power stones you trust me to have."

She warily assessed me as she thought it through. Providing me energy that I might try to use against her was a risk she had to take. She couldn't expect me to succeed without it.

Finally she said, "Then you go back into the dark."

• • •

After the overhead door shut and darkness surrounded me again, I waited long enough for Liyliy to leave. Then I reopened the Coca-Cola and splashed a fizzy circle around me.

Mother, seal my circle and give me a sacred space.

I need to think clearly to solve the troubles I face.

I could usually slip into an alpha state like flicking a switch . . . but not today. I tried again.

Grounding and centering myself didn't work. Something was wrong. It wasn't me, either, all injuries aside. This salt-and-iron environment was interfering. Since meditation had nothing to do with outward magic, my contact with this stuff had to be to blame. Venturing a guess, I'd have bet that Liyliy had done something to this salt and that was keeping me from tapping the ley.

Salt as mere salt couldn't stop me. Iron couldn't either, but apparently both in the high amounts found here, and mixed with whatever empowerment Liyliy had worked, was enough.

She'd even gone so far as to stuff my mouth with salt.

Thinking about that made me thirsty again; I gulped another drink of the Coke and visualized the caffeinated beverage burning the salt out of me. That gave me an idea.

Pushing my aura to include what was directly touching me—I didn't have enough energy to spare for cleansing the tons of it that was here—I said,

Mother, cleanse this salt and give me a sacred space.

I need to think clearly to solve the troubles I face.

That did it. In seconds, I sat on the shore with a lake lapping quietly before me, a willow tree beside me and crickets singing in the darkness. My bonds and wounds did not go with me, though the torn and ragged dress did. I stood, searching all around.

A shadow crossed the inland darkness, a shadow with ears pricked.

For a single heartbeat, it seemed like a dark wolf racing toward me, attacking—but I knew this was not true. The shadow was too small to be Johnny in wolf form. It was Amenemhab, my jackal totem animal, who was approaching.

He padded close and sat. The crescent moon above us silvered his back and darkened his muzzle, but his tail wagged happily—a good sign.

"It's good to see you."

"Likewise," he replied. "How's your mother?"

The last time I'd chatted with him, it had been about her. I filled him in on the events since then.

"So she does care and she has learned," he said.

"Yeah. I guess." I hadn't believed this was possible when he'd suggested it. "She's trying to guilt me into reciprocating, but that's not why I'm here."

"It isn't?"

"No." I explained that Liyliy was holding me hostage, and that she expected me to unmake a magical necklace without allowing me to touch the necklace or to tap the ley line for power.

"Hmmm . . ." he said.

I remembered that Creepy's visit might be important too, but before I could speak, Amenemhab said, "And yet the two are not so dissimilar."

"Huh?"

"As Liyliy is keeping you from the freedom you want, you are similarly holding your mother hostage from your love, which she wants."

I frowned at him, but he was undeterred.

"Liyliy wants you to unmake the necklace and will restrict your freedom until you do as she wants. You want your mother to change, and you restrict her access to your heart until she does as you want. Are you following me so far?"

"Unhappily, yes."

"Liyliy refuses to give you access to the item of power, but this complication makes winning your freedom more difficult for you, and because Liyliy does not trust you, this undermines the success of her goal. Care to outline how this is reflected with your mother?"

I crossed my arms, not that a physical show of being "blocked off" would have any effect on a totem animal. "I refuse to let her into my heart, but my standoffishness makes her more stubborn, and because I don't trust her, all this undermines my chance of eliciting a change in her behavior."

"See? You do understand." He flashed the jackal version of a grin. "As Liyliy denies you access to the ley line, she lowers her chances for a satisfying outcome. As you deny your mother your love, you do the same, and it is a shame, for that is the one thing that *can* change her."

"Okay, I get it. I see it. Life is wildly synchronous. But I can't do anything about my mother if I don't get away from Liyliy. So help me out here. How do I unmake this thing?"

"Why would you?" Amenemhab stood and paced back and forth before me. It was unnerving, since that was exactly what Liyliy had done. Just as I was about to say something about it, his tail dropped down. "Unmaking a spell of this magnitude, which was never part of you in either the making or the receiving, is interference with karmic repercussions. If you do this, you will bear an iron chain. It will have to be abolished if ever you are to reach your destiny, and nullifying it in this lifetime would be very difficult indeed." He bowed his head.

"Then I have to get the necklace away from her, which will be next to impossible."

"Is she so fierce?"

"She's very capable and there, my right arm is injured."

His snout lifted. "You've been tested. Those tests were not given you simply to strengthen you. In passing them you earned power and were afforded privileges and opportunities . . . such as unmaking that which was unjustly wrought upon you. But to balance the success of an opportunity, there comes a challenge."

My shoulders squared. "So what do I *do*?"

He cocked his head. "Have you evaluated where you are in your cycle?"

"You want to talk about my period?"

"No. Your *life* cycle," Amenemhab laughed. "Birth. Life. Death."

I scratched my head. "I'm pretty sure I'm well past the birth part and into the life part, and hopefully none too close to the death part."

"Each facet of life can also be gauged upon its life cycle. Like a love affair. Some are born quickly, live briefly and die in flames."

Johnny. My stare dared the totem animal to make that connection.

"It is the way of existence—and your existence as the Lustrata is no different. What is birth?"

"Birth is creation, beginning, initiation."

"And life?"

"Life is development, growth, progress."

"It is time to evolve, Persephone. Time to take what you know and all you have earned and unite it." He held his head high. "Embracing the goddess whose torches light your path and whose grace protects you is easy. Embracing the goddess who would set you aflame, who would drown you and cast your body soaring wingless into the sky . . . is not easy, and yet you embrace Her still. Some would let fear immobilize them, yet you just accept what She asks of you and do it. That sets you apart, Persephone."

I hadn't thought to "blame" Hecate for the close calls during my tests. Though I hadn't grasped it during the first test—I'd been naïve, but I'd come to understand that danger was to be expected when a deity assessed a mortal.

"Your devotion and loyalty shine like bright beacons that declare you ready for the more treacherous journey along the deeper path."

I cast my eyes toward the island that resembled a spearhead jammed into the middle of the lake. I'd seen the giant steps to Tartarus inside there. I didn't want to go back.

"I cannot tell you the answer," he said softly, "for these things of which I speak are uniquely yours, as will be the manner in which you combine them."

"If I have so much, why isn't the course of action obvious to me?"

"Being the Lustrata is no simple honor. It will only get harder."

Delightful.

"You have a decision to make, Lustrata: *Cor aut mors.*

I leave you to it." He turned to leave, then stopped. "My time with you is growing short, Persephone; I feel another totem will soon replace me."

That made me sad.

"Be at peace, Persephone. When things change here, it is evidence of evolution." Amenemhab trotted away.

I awakened inside the cargo hold. Not wanting Liyliy to find the wet circle of salt and become suspicious, I wiggled around and hoped it disguised my actions.

"*Cor aut mors*," Amenemhab had said. It was Latin for "heart or death." It meant a choice between the morals and loyalty of the heart, or the insignificance and disgrace of death.

Of course I would choose "heart."

C'mon, Snickers bar, and kick in. I have a karmic suicide to avoid.

CHAPTER FIFTY-THREE

In her suite at the Cleveland Renaissance Hotel, Aurelia emerged from the bathroom carrying an empty goblet. She wore a thick terry robe, and her towel-dried hair was combed straight. As she crossed the living room to the table, where an uncorked bottle of wine rested on a bed of ice, she paused to dig a small portable radio from her pocket and place it on the damask-covered fainting couch. She poured herself a second glass of wine and watched the city below.

Cleveland was nothing like her Bucuresti. Though the cities were nearly the same geographical size, there were far fewer people in Cleveland. Also, this city's nickname, her research had revealed, was "Forest City": A motto adopted in the 1830s, it made no sense in the present day. There was no forest here; not now, anyway. It irritated her that the phrase was utterly inaccurate. Continuing to pay homage to an outdated vision, she felt, highlighted the lack of forwardly mobile thinking that would be needed to make this city great and prestigious again.

Her home was known as "Little Paris," and with its beautiful architecture, its universities and theaters, cafés, and museums it was, indeed, an eastern version of that grand city. The Dâmbovita River was far more beautiful than the Cuyahoga.

"What's he like?" Johnny's voice emitted from the little radio.

Aurelia left the window. "Finally." Since the Domn Lup had fled Cleveland, he and the woman had spoken little. The woman he called Toni had said she needed a nap, and the silence had ensued. Hours of it.

"He's all boy," Toni answered. "He can't sit still. . . ."

Setting her goblet on the table, Aurelia lifted the little radio, holding it tightly as she reclined on the fainting couch and listened via the bug she'd planted in the Maserati's key fob.

Detective Kurt Miller knew when the Maserati hit I-90 north that the Domn Lup was escorting Toni back to Saranac Lake. His Crown Victoria couldn't hope to keep up with a car like that, but he didn't have to now. When he arrived in his hometown just after 2:00 a.m., he drove slowly past Toni's house. The lights were out. There was no fancy car parked in the driveway, either. He cruised by the area hotels and spotted the sleek vehicle at Gauthier's Saranac Lake Inn.

He called in a favor from his old friends at the village police department and had a cruiser sent to stake out the Maserati. The assigned officer was to call him if anyone used that car, then he was to nonchalantly tail it.

Kurt stretched. He was ready to go home and sleep in his own bed.

Johnny walked into the lobby area of the hotel. A man with a bushy moustache emerged from the back room. "Hello. Welcome to Gauthier's. Would you like a queen or a king? I have a suite available."

Johnny dropped the keys on the counter and readied his wallet. "Nothing fancy," he said. "Just a room to sleep in."

The man swiped the credit card and gave it back, then asked him about the make and license of his car, which brought an impressed whistle to the man's lips. "Are they really all they're cracked up to be, the Maseratis?" the man asked. "I mean, you can get more horsepower for less money in a Corvette Z06." He slid the room key across the counter.

"I drove a Z06," Johnny said, retrieving his keys and the room key. "I opted for the Quattroporte. I just . . . liked it more."

"Ahh," the man smiled. "You must be a family man, going for the four-door."

Johnny's chest swelled. "Yeah."

"Your room's on the second level, all the way down on the right."

After showering, Johnny crawled into bed with the diary in his hand. He read entries about Frankie missing her dad, about how her mom cried at night, and about her mom struggling to pay the bills . . . but it was the entry about her hating her father for leaving them that struck him hardest.

Will Evan hate me for not being there?

He read about a fight Frankie had with one of her friends, about a crush on a boy who never acknowledged she existed, and about trials with a monster math teacher. Then she documented his "loser" appearance. Toni had glossed the story over, but after an hour of reading, he had a grasp of who Frankie thought him to be, and how that evolved as she grew to know him, love him. She'd drawn a whole page of hearts and written "Francine Rosalee Brown + John Curtis Hampton" inside them.

She mentioned that he said nothing of his home life

except to mumble that he hated his mom's boyfriend and couldn't understand what she saw in him. There was no other insight to his family. Frankie said she pitied him, and she had been perceptive enough to understand she was pinning on him all the love she could no longer give her father.

He had the feeling they could have made it work, high school sweethearts, together forever, because each would fit perfectly into the hole in the other's heart.

But Frankie was gone. Soon, the kid would be alone.

No. No, he won't be alone.

CHAPTER FIFTY-FOUR

Sitting in the utter blackness of the cargo hold, I clenched my hands. I said, "Heart," as if hearing my own voice would make everything comprehensible. When it didn't, I whispered, "*Cor.*"

Core.

Soul.

The *sorsanimus*.

I couldn't tap Menessos or Johnny under this confinement, but I knew neither of them would give up if they were in my situation. I would not be the weak side of the triangle.

But how am I supposed to "evolve" when I'm tied up and imprisoned? Evolving sounded like it should be a very active process.

To the darkness, I said, "I asked once for the wisdom to keep my feet upon this path, to be what You had made me, Hecate, and to accomplish the goals You set before me, to be Your instrument, humble and just, and fulfill my purpose. Well, here I am. Show me Your bright torches."

I waited.

And waited.

"Just a little illumination would be helpful."

The glowing armor that was the mantle of the Lustrata began to shine around me.

Thank you, Hecate. She had bestowed this upon me

when I'd accepted the name, rank and responsibility of being Lustrata. It had glowed around me when she'd given it to me, when Xerxadrea had outed me to her personal coven, and when I'd been in the darkness of the Hall of Tartarus.

Its light was reassuring, and I kicked myself for not thinking of this earlier.

This beautiful silvery armor had gleamed to identify me and light my way, and yet its brilliance had surrounded me on one other occasion, unbidden: when I'd forced the former Rege into a half-transformation. It had been a desperate action for me, but apparently a moment of judgment, as well. *To be Your instrument.*

Was that my evolution, to be more than a woman who stepped up whenever Chance lay at my feet, an occasion when some action of mine could make a difference? Was I to go from being defensive but proactive, to being offensive and aggressive?

Still bound, I couldn't attack Liyliy. At least not physically.

That left magic, but I couldn't tap the ley.

Creepy had said that I needed to know I could do this. *This what?* Amenemhab had said to combine what I have.

Feeling stupid and helpless and disliking every second of it, I consoled myself with the perks. I was bound to two powerful men. Hecate was on my side. I'd passed tests of fire, water, and air.

Wait. Creepy had also said, *"I can feel the storm within you. The burning blaze and the flood, too."*

He'd pointed out that I had the fire and flood and storm within me. Three elements. Three tests. And here I sat on a mound of salt, which represented earth—the one element in which I had not yet earned anything. And yet, iron represented fire. Air was in abundance, and if this was a ship, then there was water nearby.

How could I combine fire, air and water? Fire and water canceled each other out—or fire caused water to transmute and combine with air . . . *steam*!

What could I do with steam?

I had to get off this salt.

Wriggling and dragging myself across this would take forever. Without my hands free to balance, hopping or crawling was out. I figured rolling would be the best way—and most painful. Gritting my teeth and tensing to restrict some of the movement my shoulder was about to endure, I made the first and second rotations. I had to catch my breath, then I made two more. Following this pattern, I neared the wall quickly.

Guided by the light of my mantle, I sat up and scooted into position by the ladder. I lifted my arms and, using only my left, levered my feet under me. I stood—too fast— and had to grapple for the higher half-moon rungs to keep from keeling over. Holding on, I shook off as much of the salt as I could, then slid my foot into one of the half-moon openings. They were too far apart for my bindings to reach both, so I had to settle for having only one foot bearing me. Like an inchworm moving one end, then the other, I eventually had myself three rungs from the level of the salt.

After securing my balance with my knee, I reached around the support bracket, placed both palms against the iron and focused my will.

> *Metal, iron, smelted ore*
> *Element of fire in your core*

That heat within, I bid it rise
Release it now, these ropes incise!

My thumbs tingled, and I felt a jolt like I had when under my mother's truck trying to get the tire. *What the——?*

My thumbs! Mudras! Of course!

In yogic theories, the mudras were various hand gestures and positions that awakened the kundalini, or the corporeal energy. Each finger represented a different element. Thumbs represented fire, and metal represented fire, which explained the charge I got under the truck and here!

Bending my thumbs back to touch the rope as much as I could, I pressed the outermost loop against the edge of the bracket. I smelled smoke. Maintaining my single-mindedness, I rubbed the rope against it and snorted against the stink of burning fibers.

Incredibly, the silvery threads I'd noticed in the rope before were some type of metal—and the metal was part of Liyliy. It liquefied and re-formed as barbed wire, cutting into me as I applied pressure to the rope.

I had to work fast—surely Liyliy knew I was doing something now.

Increasing the pressure of the rope on the heated bracket, the sharp barbs of the wire broke my skin, and the wire heated. As the rope burned, so did I.

Grinding my teeth, groaning through the searing pain, I kept pushing.

The rope severed. I jerked from the bracket, steadying myself with my knee, and flapped my hands so the rope would unwind itself—but the wire did not fall away. In fact, the weight of the rope seemed to push the barbs deeper.

I used my thumbs to touch the bracket and thrust the wire against the edge directly. The wire fought, tightened, and tore my skin before the heat melted it through. I pulled free of it so fast I probably did more and unnecessary damage, but I didn't want to risk the stuff re-forming.

I leapt down to the salt. I had to get my feet free now; Liyliy was surely connected to this stuff and knew what I was doing.

The knot in the rope around my ankles was in the back, so I couldn't see it well. Additionally, my thumbs were numb from directing so much of the fire element through them, so I dug at it with my fingers. Messing with it caused the wire in it to grow barbs as well. These seemed to spring up everywhere I reached—until I dug my thumbs under the wire. "Fire!"

The wire melted around my touch and fell into the salt.

I rolled away from it and worked at the rope. Where my thumbs touched, the fibers burned. Knowing what to do now, I touched my thumbs onto the rope—on a spot not in contact with my skin—and burned through.

Kicking free of the coils, I tore off my shoes, climbed to my feet and reached for the ladder.

CHAPTER FIFTY-FIVE

Mero, Ailo, and Talto were being given a tour of the haven by Menessos. "And concluding our little tour, this is the Haven, with a capital *H*. There is already a national buzz about this nightclub, and it is expected to become a destination for those who would seek a place in our nocturnal culture."

Mero was impressed. "It will support the entire group?"

"We believe so. There will be plenty of job openings for my . . . I mean for Goliath's Offerlings and Beholders there, as well as at The Blood Culture."

"What is that?" Ailo asked.

"It was Heldridge's brainchild. An ingenious combination of business and strategy, The Blood Culture is a bar located between the Cleveland Clinic and University Hospitals. It is also right on the Health Line, a designated transit that connects them. Local healthcare professionals supplement their income by giving blood, as do the many area college students. Then the bar sells it to the local vampires."

"Do they cater to a mortal clientele as well?" she asked.

"Of course."

"And your local government does not object?" Mero asked.

"Only the local Red Cross was bothered. We made a

deal with them. They have their people collect the blood, and we donate half of it to them. We had a surplus anyway."

A silence lingered, and Menessos gestured them out of the construction zone and back into the haven. "Do you mind if I make a call?" Mero asked, getting out his cell phone and putting it to his ear. "My reception isn't the best below."

"Indeed," Menessos said. "Ladies." He gestured again, and they preceded him to the stairwell. The elevator dinged and opened as they started down.

"There you are," Giovanni exclaimed. "I've been looking everywhere for you!"

Mero kept his phone at his ear, as if he were continuing to talk to someone, even though he'd halted his call when he spotted Giovanni. He listened as Menessos asked, "What can I help you with, Giovanni?"

"Not you. Meroveus." Giovanni spotted him and aimed his course right for him.

"I'll call you back," Mero said and shut his phone.

"Yes?"

Giovanni opened his mouth and shut it again.

"What is it?" Mero asked.

"I need a favor."

It evidently cost him to say the words, so Mero responded benevolently. "What is wrong?"

"I loathe the paperwork of a haven. I am no businessman. And I am no mediator, either. I am a warrior, I settle disputes by killing my enemy. And I now long to slay both the masters of the Columbus and the Cincinnati havens."

"But of course you cannot. What can I do?"

"Talk to the Excelsior. Have him revoke my status as

Interim Quarterlord and call me back to Washington."

Mero put a hand on Giovanni's shoulder. "I will see what I can do."

After speaking with his son, Mero returned to the lower levels of the haven. Just as he drew near to Mark, who was again guarding the door of Menessos's private rooms, Seven came running, her phone in her hand. Mark kept Mero back with one thick arm and opened the door for Seven smoothly with the other. She entered without breaking stride.

Mero and Mark crowded the doorway behind her.

"Boss. Just got a call."

"And?"

"Privately?" She flicked a glance toward the sisters.

"Outside."

Mero and Mark backed up. Seven and Menessos left next. Mark shut the door.

"Well?" Menessos asked.

"One of the Beholders on patrol spotted Liyliy entering a convenience store. Said she was filling a basket with candy bars."

Menessos grabbed her arms. "Where?"

"I've called for your car to be brought. I'll explain on the way there." She led him away.

Mark remained by the door, but Mero followed. Menessos held his stomach, jogging to keep up with Seven, who said, "I have the Beholder's location—are you all right?"

"Yes. Please continue."

"I have the location. I sent a call for everyone else to form a grid, stationed on every street corner expanding away from her location so we can register her movements in any direction."

"Seven, I could kiss you."

"Save them for her, boss."

Menessos gave a snort. "You must quit calling me that."

Seven flashed him a smile as she ran. "Never."

CHAPTER FIFTY-SIX

I couldn't reach the overhead door from this ladder, but the catwalk had a secondary ladder. I had to swing my leg over the railing and climb it from the outer side of the catwalk, but after climbing as high as possible, I wrapped one leg around the ladder to steady myself and shoved at the hatch cover. It was too heavy for me to just slide this panel into the next. Rising another ladder rung, I gained some leverage. Pushing with all my might, I managed to open it two inches. I wasn't sure I could gain enough leverage to open it far enough to crawl through.

Then air swirled in around me.

Putting one knee over the rung to balance myself, I lifted both arms over my head. My shoulder ached, but I pressed my index fingers—fingers associated with air—against the metal roof.

> Breath and breeze and gusting wind
> Element of air bluster in!
> Eddy and churn, swirl and sigh
> Take this door and open it wide!

I've heard wind howl beyond my windows. I've heard it rush through the trees. Neither of those sounded anything like the screaming force that answered me. Salt whipped into the air and scoured my skin. I shut my eyes and fought to maintain my position.

The roof creaked like a door slowly closing, then the sound escalated. With a *whoosh* it was shoved open.

I climbed free of the cargo hold.

Standing on the deck, I looked around. The city of Cleveland lay beyond, all aglow.

Closer was the Rock Hall to my left and the Great Lakes Science Center just ahead. I was on the *William G. Mather,* the steamship that built Cleveland—now a museum.

I laughed, delighted to be free. *How do I get off of here?*

A shrill screech in the sky stole my good humor.

With a frustrated groan, I straddled the railing. I had to touch the water to invoke it.

Then my attention caught on the water. This was going to be cold.

I leapt.

It was more than cold. I surfaced, shivering and treading water. The mantle remained around me, and its soft glow helped Liyliy locate me. I couldn't release it; only with it active could I access the elements. My teeth chattered as I gathered my will. I pointed with my pinky fingers while still paddling the water with my hands. Liyliy was diving in, talons forward.

> *Stream, river and beautiful lake*
> *Element of water, crest and break*
> *Froth and splatter, splash and spray*
> *Reach and cast my enemy away!*

The calm water stirred around me. Waves built and crested over me. The current carried me away as the owl was slapped with a mighty wave. With a flap of her wings she gained altitude and circled back.

Again she made a try for me, and again an uncanny wave rescued me.

Dawn was a long way off. I would succumb to the cold long before the sun rose.

I swam closer to the ship. Because of the inward slope of the ship's hull, she couldn't dive at the same angle. She adjusted, preparing to swoop in straight at me. She might drown me, or squash me against the side of the ship. There were many possibilities, but it was unlikely letting me live was among them.

As I was heading toward the rudder, thinking that there was more cover there, it hit me—

Combine what you have earned.

Splashing forward, I put my thumbs against the ship's hull, pointed up with my index fingers and kept my pinkies in the water. And I kicked like hell to stay afloat.

> *Element of fire, give me heat!*
> *Element of water, boil and seethe!*
> *Element of air, combine with these . . .*

Over my shoulder I watched the dark form descending. I focused, hard. I reached deep within me, and I finished,

> *Lake Erie, arise, and give me steam!*

The talons gleamed in the moonlight, silver and sharp. The owl wings spread, adjusting her aim. A sharp cry of triumph exploded from her beak.

Air swirled behind me. About three yards away, a blast of boiling water burst free of the surface. Pulled into the whirling wind, it was transmuted by the touch of wicked air.

The owl crashed into the thick veil. She screamed as it hit her huge eyes and blanketed her fleshy talons. She screeched and flapped and stumbled through the air. She lurched out of my sight, and it sounded like she crashed into the hatch and was flopping around on the deck.

A wave of heated water flowed over me, and I was grateful for its warmth.

I heard an awful screech, then a dark shadow flew away over the lake.

I swam toward the rocks of the North Harbor. With my arm feeling so bad, "swimming" was actually more like floating on my back and kicking to propel me in the proper general direction.

As I neared the steep slope, the large, slimy rocks ahead made me wary. I wasn't fondly anticipating that climb barefoot, and I wasn't hankering to be dripping wet in the cold night air as I made my way downtown, either, but here I was.

Wading out of the water, I saw a flash of light above, but it disappeared. I tried to wipe the silt from the shreds of my gown. I'd ruined two nice dresses in seventy-two hours. Laughing at myself, I scrambled on, slipping but determined. I was halfway up when I heard someone say, "May I help you?"

I looked up.

Menessos.

He's alive.

Of course it was him. My Arthur, I could count on him.

His shoulders lowered. His eyes softened, expressing the relief that filled him.

I offered him my hand.

CHAPTER FIFTY-SEVEN

Liyliy could barely see out of her filmy eyes.

Consumed with a bitter, malefic rage, she flew. In time, pain wore her down. She tapped a ley and healed herself enough to keep functioning, but some of the damage was permanent. She feared returning to her human form, feared knowing what new curse was hers to own.

The revenge she would reap upon the Lustrata would have to be profound.

Another thought occurred to her.

She would need help . . . and she knew exactly who would want to help her.

Giovanni.

At the hotel, despite checking in so late, Johnny was showered and dressed by 7:00 a.m. The gym bag had held dark blue jeans, a white tank undershirt, and a button-front shirt. It was black and had silk-screened eagles and guitars on it. The short sleeves barely hid his armband tattoos.

He shoved the suit into the gym bag and, in the lobby, used the available computer to search the internet. First, he did a local white-pages search for the name Hampton. Among the fewer than six thousand residents of this city—according to Wikipedia—there were no Hamptons.

My mother has moved away. Or married. He had no hope

of finding her on his own, but a private investigator could search the records.

Undaunted, he began his second search, perusing articles about boys raised without fathers, about absent fathers reappearing in their sons' lives, and the challenges these men and their sons faced.

The statistics were discouraging, the facts heart wrenching, but Johnny vowed to not screw this up. To be better than the data he'd found.

At 8:45, he checked out, and the guest services lady suggested the Blue Moon Café for breakfast. He thanked her and wondered if she had any idea she'd been talking to a wærewolf.

Sitting in his car, his phone beeped. He had a text from Kirk. *Your GF was found safe. Where R U?*

Johnny sighed, eyes shutting momentarily with relief. He'd been so consumed with all that had happened to him in the last twenty hours that Seph's danger had slipped his mind. He fought back the twinge of guilt with the knowledge that she was okay.

He texted back: *Alls well. Should return l8r 2day. Let u kno when I kno.*

Saranac Lake wasn't very big, but it seemed like a nice place to grow up in. *I must have grown up here. In the Adirondacks. With all these trees.* He recalled Toni saying the kid was a climber.

What if the kid doesn't like me?

What if I don't like the kid?

What if I do?

The café on Main Street was easy to find. When Johnny parked and walked into the café, the people there quieted. He wondered if they did because they'd seen the news yesterday, or if they just did that to all strangers.

Sitting at the counter, he ordered the Café Steak-and-Eggs and a Tupper Stack of pancakes with two glasses of orange juice. By the time his food was served, the chatter had picked up again, and as he ate, he heard whispering about his car.

One old man wondered too loudly, "Maybe it's stolen."

"Stolen?" another questioned.

"A cop's pulled up to the curb. He's just sitting there."

The other man scolded the first, "There's all kinds of fancy cars 'round here during skiing season."

"But it ain't ski season yet. Did you see that fella's face? He's got tattoos around his eyes! That's a shady character, there."

He glared openly at the man, who hunched into his seat. Johnny shook his head and resumed eating. He was nearly finished when his phone rang. "'Lo?"

"John," Toni said. "You can head over now."

Johnny downed what remained of his juice, placed a fifty on the counter and headed out. He noted that there was a police car up the road, but it didn't follow him. A green Crown Victoria seemed to trail him out of town, but it turned off before he arrived at Toni's house.

Will the kid be scared of me with all these tattoos?

From the driveway, he studied the house. In the morning light, the beige aluminum-sided ranch, with black shutters and a brick-red front door, seemed smaller than it had in the dark last night. It was cute and well kept; the many trees were bare, but the lawn had been raked and the leaves tended. The bushes were trimmed, the flowerbeds mulched and ready for the snow that would soon fall.

He shut the car off and dropped the keys in his pocket.

Toni opened the front door before he could knock. "Have a seat. I'll get him."

Johnny entered a modest living room with two chairs and a small love seat, as she'd said. All were dark brown and worn. He sat on one of the chairs and noticed that the oval coffee table showed signs of wear and tear on its edges. He understood why when he saw the bin of Hot Wheels under the coffee table.

He swallowed, hard.

"Evan! Come here," Toni called.

"I'm playing!"

"There's someone I want you to meet."

"Who?"

"Come here and I'll introduce you."

Silence.

More silence.

Toni rolled her eyes and started forward, but Johnny touched her arm. "May I?"

She blinked. Nodded. "Sure."

Johnny walked down the hall with his heart pounding. The walls and ceiling seemed to be closing in on him, though he told himself it was just a small house. The *vroom-vroom* sounds of a boy at play met his ears, and he eased into the doorway as if his world was in slow motion.

The room was a sunny yellow with framed posters of sleek cars. The twin bed was primary red and shaped like a Ferrari. The bedspread was also red. Though there was beige carpeting, a small area rug, made like a city with roads, lay next to the bed. It seemed the rug city was under construction—dump trucks and backhoes were placed along the streets.

The boy lay in the middle of the city on his stomach, feet kicking up and one sock half off his foot. He was positioned away from the door, his attention riveted to some Hot Wheels setup. The boy—*Evan*—was guiding cars into a motorized area that caught the cars and sent them speeding through loop-de-loops. When the cars crashed, he laughed delightedly. "All right!"

Maybe this will work out after all.

"So you like cars?" Johnny asked.

At his voice, the boy turned, and his big brown eyes started at Johnny's shoes and rose unhurriedly upward. "You're really tall."

"Yup."

"Why are you wearing makeup?"

Great. "I'm not." He pointed at his face. "These are tattoos."

"Why?"

"Because I used to be in a rock-and-roll band."

The kid hit a button that switched off the motorized part of his toy. He sat up, cross-legged. "Who are you?"

"My name's John. You're Evan?"

"Yeah." He scratched at his brow. "Why are you here?"

"I . . ." Johnny's mouth opened and shut. He couldn't just blurt out *Because I'm your dad.* "I heard you like cars."

"So?"

Johnny bent and picked up one of the cars. "This one. Do you know what this is?"

Evan studied the car. "Ferrari. Like my bed. Only that one's light blue."

"What do you know about Ferraris?"

"They're cool and they go fast."

Johnny dropped to one knee. "This one happens to be a 599 GTB Fiorano. Do you know why they go fast?"

Evan blinked.

"This Ferrari has a V12 engine. That means it has twelve cylinders. . . . Do you know anything about engines?"

"No."

Johnny asked, "Would you like to?"

"No." Evan jumped up, snatched the car from him and left the room.

What did I do?

Evan dashed straight to Toni in the living room.

Johnny followed behind him.

"Who is that guy, Gram?"

Toni glanced past Evan to Johnny. "He's someone you need to know."

"I don't want him touching my cars."

"Then, just say so," Johnny said.

Evan spun around, and in doing so, he scanned the front picture window. His head snapped back to the driveway. He eased forward and put his nose on the glass. "Whoa. . . . Is that your car?"

"Yup."

"Wow. What is it?"

"It's a Maserati Quattroporte."

"Does it have a twelve-V engine, too?"

Johnny laughed. "No, it's a V8. It only has eight cylinders."

"It still looks cool."

"Would you like to go for a ride?"

Evan's eyes lit up. "Could I?"

"If Toni says it's okay."

"Can I, Gram? Can I? Can I?"

Toni regarded Johnny steadily. "Can I talk to you privately?"

"Sure."

"Evan, go to your room."

"But Gram—"

"Get your shoes," she said. Evan scurried off. As soon as he was out of carshot, she seized Johnny's arm. "Don't you dare try to take him from me yet!"

"I wouldn't!" Johnny realized what she'd thought. "I wouldn't steal him. He doesn't even know me yet."

She released his arm.

"I don't know where to start. He obviously likes cars. So do I." He shrugged. "You can come with us."

Toni sat in a chair. "No," she sighed. "Go for a drive, just the two of you."

Evan returned with his shoes on, laces flopping. "Tie those or you're not going," Toni told him. "No speeding." She pointed her finger at Johnny. "And he has to sit in the back."

"We'll be back in twenty minutes. You have my word."

After letting Evan sit in the driver's seat for a few minutes, Johnny told him to get into the back—Evan crawled over the console—and put on his seat belt. Johnny revved the engine a few times while in the driveway, and Evan giggled gleefully.

He backed onto the road and headed back the only way he knew to go. Soon, Evan was begging, "I want to go fast!"

"Toni said not to go fast."

"She said no *speeding*. The speed limit is higher on the highway. That's why they call it the *high*way. Geez."

Johnny saw a sign for NY-3. He followed it, heading west. He punched it up to the allowed forty-five. "So, tell me a little about yourself, Evan. Do you get good grades in school?"

"School? Bleh." Evan stuck his tongue out. "Can we go faster?"

"No."

"Not even just a little?"

"Well. Tell me about school and I'll go a little faster."

"I like recess and gym. Art class is fun."

"What else?"

Evan sat up like he was trying to see the speedometer. "Are we going faster?"

"A little."

"How fast?"

"Forty-eight."

Evan sat back in his seat with arms crossed. "That's not fast."

"I'll do sixty-five in a straight stretch if you tell me about your spelling tests."

"I do okay. Not As, but no Fs either."

"What about your teacher?"

"Seventy-five?"

"Your teacher is seventy-five years old?" Johnny asked incredulously, teasing.

"No. Can we go seventy-five?"

A straight patch stretched before them and there were no other cars around except the one about eight car lengths back, so Johnny slowed down to thirty, then punched it so it would feel more dynamic to hit seventy-five.

CHAPTER FIFTY-EIGHT

I nvestigator Kurt Miller was following the Maserati as nonchalantly as possible for a quiet Sunday midday. Most folks were in church now. The roads were empty.

And it seemed John Hampton was heading back to Cleveland.

Kurt followed him, wondering if he could even make an arrest based on a warrant for a suspect identified as human. He decided to leave that to someone else to decide. The real question was, *How am I going to stop him while he's still in my jurisdiction?*

Then the fool gave him cause. He did a quick stint of seventy-five in a forty-five.

Kurt rolled down his window, slapped the magnetic base of his police beacon on the roof, and flipped it and his siren on.

"Your grandmother is going to kill me."

Johnny's voice grumbled from the radio. Aurelia had been making notes, and perked up.

"What?" the kid said.

Then Aurelia heard the siren.

"Cool!" the kid said.

"Not cool," Johnny said.

"You're pulling over? This car could outrun the cop's car! C'mon! C'mon!"

"No," Johnny said firmly.

Aurelia picked up her phone.

The Maserati drove onto the shoulder in front of Kurt, who waited. He wasn't in a uniform, but he had a badge and handcuffs. The warrant for the arrest of John Hampton had been issued years ago, but warrants never expire.

Would he resist? What if he secured him into the cuffs *and* into the back of the car, then he did that at-will transformation thing? Kurt had no other choice.

Kurt Miller got out of his Crown Victoria and, with his hand on his weapon, he approached the car. Two good paces from the driver's door, he halted, set his feet and drew the gun. "Step out of the car, now!"

Nothing happened, so he repeated himself.

The door opened.

"Keep your hands where I can see them."

John Newman, or Hampton, eased from the car, with his palms outstretched. "I know I was speeding," he said. "It was stupid. I was showing off for the kid."

"Kid?"

John motioned with his head toward the car interior. Kurt peered through the back window and saw Evan worriedly watching him. *Damn it!*

"Since you're not in a cruiser or a uniform, could I see some ID, Officer?"

"I'm a SSTIX investigator." Kurt tossed his badge wallet to Johnny.

John caught it, examined it. "SSTIX? Since when did they make arrests for traffic violations? And do you always draw your gun on speeders? Or do you enjoy scaring kids?"

"Put your hands on the roof of the car."

John did. Kurt put the gun into its holster. As he frisked him, he noticed that John focused on the Crown Victoria. "You were following me earlier."

Kurt slapped the cuffs onto the tall man's wrists. "You're under arrest for an outstanding warrant. Your cooperation won't be as scary for the kid as your defiance would be." He then recited the Miranda warning. It surprised him that John didn't resist at all.

"What warrant? And how do you even know who I am? You haven't asked me for my name yet, and I don't even live here."

Kurt steered him toward the Crown Victoria. "Maybe not anymore, John, but you used to." Kurt gave John a push to indicate he should go toward the green car.

John proceeded as bidden, silent for the distance. *Maybe he's stunned.* After shutting the Crown Victoria's door, Kurt returned to the Maserati. He retrieved his badge wallet from the roof of the car, then opened the door closest to Evan and, crouching down, showed the badge to him. "I'm Kurt Miller, a federal investigator," he said. "We've met before. I'm a friend of your grandmother's."

"Are you gonna cuff me too?"

"No. But I do need you to get into my car with your dad so we can go to the station."

"My dad?" Evan's mouth hung open.

They haven't told him. Double damn it. "Sure. If he's driving and you're in the backseat buckled in, that means you're his son, right?"

Evan's face hardened and he stared at his shoes. "He was only speedin' 'cause I begged him to 'cause it's such a cool car." He crossed his arms. "It's not his fault. It's mine."

"You need to come with me. At the police station, we'll call your gram. She'll pick you up." *She may never forgive me for this.*

Evan slid out, shut the door.

Kurt offered him his hand.

"I'm not a baby," Evan said.

They walked toward the Crown Victoria on the side that was furthest from the road. "I'll move my files and you can sit up front in my car."

"No. My gram says I always hafta sit in the back."

"Does your gram tell you to obey officers of the law?"

"Yeah. And she says it's a law that kids sit in the back."

Kurt ground his teeth. Evan was still a brat. He didn't think that John had any reason to hurt the kid, but letting Evan sit in the back might give John an opportunity should his cooperation fail out of desperation.

Evan suddenly rushed to the car.

"Hey!"

Before Kurt could get there, Evan had climbed in the front and slammed the door. He sent files skidding to the floor as he twisted and hit buttons, partially lowering windows and successfully locking the doors.

Kurt glowered through the window at him and demanded, "Unlock these doors, now!"

"No!" Evan stuck out his tongue.

CHAPTER FIFTY-NINE

Johnny sat in the back of the Crown Vic wondering what he'd done to end up with a warrant. It didn't matter, really. This detective plainly knew something about him, something that could provide information that would lead him to his family. He was willing to go to the station . . . or wherever a SSTIX agent took you . . . to find out. He was confident that the Zvonul could get him out and cover the incident if necessary.

Besides, he didn't want to give Evan the impression that breaking the law didn't have consequences.

Suddenly the boy scurried into the car and locked the agent out of his own car.

So much for that idea. "What do you think you're doing?" Johnny asked.

Evan turned the car off and grappled to get the keys out of the ignition. "I'm helping you."

Johnny shook his head. "This isn't helping."

Evan crawled into the back beside him. "There's got to be a key to the cuffs on here. Then we can drive away!"

"You're pretty smart to figure that out."

Evan beamed.

"But breaking the law and messing with a detective isn't smart."

"Not in the least," the detective confirmed. He stood near the barely open passenger rear window with his arms crossed, obviously pissed off. His gun was still holstered at his side.

Evan flipped the keys around on the ring.

"Evan," Johnny said. "Stop."

Evan blurted, "Are you my dad?"

Johnny felt like he'd been punched in the gut. *I'm sitting here handcuffed. Now is not the ideal time to admit this.* But he couldn't lie, either. Johnny dropped his head down, ashamed. He'd wanted to tell him in a happy setting, not one that said *Hey, I'm a criminal.* Staring at the seat, he whispered, "Yeah."

Three heartbeats later, Evan said, "You don't want me, do you?"

Johnny's head snapped up. His mouth opened, but nothing came out.

"You don't." Evan threw the keys into the front, where they skittered across the dash to the windshield. He flopped back in his seat, spilling tears.

"Evan . . . I don't know you—"

"But you don't like me!"

Johnny hesitated, shocked at the quick hurt and quicker anger in the boy's tone. He recalled some of what he'd read online earlier, about fatherless boys feeling unwanted. "Don't put words in my mouth," he said firmly. "I didn't say that. If I don't know you, how can I know if I like you? You don't know me, either. Can you say you like me?"

Evan sniffled. "You like cars."

Johnny was silent as an easy smile claimed his face. "Yeah. Yeah I do. You probably get that from me. And check me out, sitting here in handcuffs. I must've done something bad. I did speed . . . I suppose you get your fast thinking from me too. But getting the cuffs off and driving away from here won't solve the problem, Evan. It will make it worse."

Tears rolled from Evan's eyes. "I don't want them to take you away! I just . . . I just got you."

Johnny concentrated, shifting just his forearms, pushing them into slender paws and slipping from the cuffs. He kept this all confined behind him until he was certain that he was completely human again, then he reached over and pulled the crying boy into his arms.

Beyond the window, the detective stooped to get a better view inside the car even as he reached for his gun. Johnny waved him off. "It's okay," he said, to Evan and to the officer.

"No, it's not," Evan cried.

It hit Johnny that he was holding *his kid*. The tears of *his kid* were wetting his shirt, like a soothing balm and a fierce binding in one. Though he'd never seen Evan as an infant, had never diapered him or fed him or taken him to the school bus, this moment of simple human contact and affection was mightier than hearing the Rege confirm him. "Evan, he says there's a warrant for my arrest. If I did something bad, the consequences of it are mine."

"What did you do?"

"I don't know."

Evan sat back, sniffling. "How can you not know?"

"I don't remember anything about my life, except the last eight and a half years. I was . . . I was abducted . . . kidnapped . . . and my memories were wiped away. I don't remember your mother, and I never knew she was pregnant with you."

"That's why you haven't been with me?"

"I didn't know you existed, Evan. I swear it. Or I would have been here."

Evan threw his arms around Johnny's neck and held him so tight Johnny could scarcely breathe.

Listening to their conversation, Kurt was awed. To an eight-year-old, that almost insignificant connection of "liking cars" was enough. Enough to build on, enough to start a relationship.

He listened as John was firm with the kid and used logic that a youngster could follow, and Evan, potential future hooligan that he was, settled right down, compliant.

Kurt recognized that this kid *wanted* a father, *wanted* to be led and loved.

It was a revelation to him, to find that a brat like Evan yearned for the love of a father.

When John escaped his cuffs, Kurt was ready to draw his gun to maintain control of the situation, but John waved him down. As Kurt observed what was transpiring in the back of his car, the emotion on John Hampton's face couldn't be disguised by the tattoos. Kurt had seen all kinds of men as a cop. He recognized responsibility when he saw it.

He realized, too, that John "Newman" could have touted his status as Domn Lup, or even gone into a full-out transformation to avoid being captured. He had done nothing but shun his cuffs to console his crying son.

Minutes later, John had Evan crawl up front and unlock the doors.

Kurt slid into the driver's seat.

"Evan," Johnny said, "tell the man that you're sorry for locking him out of his car."

"I'm sorry for locking you out of your car."

Kurt said sternly, "Don't ever do that again."

"I won't."

"And I'm sorry for removing your handcuffs. If you need to put them back on me—"

Kurt shook his head. "No. There's obviously no point. Besides, if you were going to try and flee, you've had ample chance."

"Can you tell me more about the warrant? What am I supposed to have done?"

"You really don't remember, do you? That bit in Cleveland wasn't just a cover-up."

"I don't remember, but I want to. I don't even know who my parents were. I just learned last night that my birth name was John Curtis Hampton. And . . . I would be grateful for anything you can tell me."

Curtis? Kurt leaned and gathered up the files that Evan had kicked to the floor. He lifted the file marked "Hampton, John C." *Curtis with a* C. *Damn it, Elena . . . why'd you give him my name?* He'd never before even considered what John's middle name might be. He flipped through the file; there was no mention of the middle name . . . but the birthday . . . July twenty-fifth. *About nine months after the Hallowe'en party.*

Kurt's hand covered his mouth, rubbed across his whole lower jaw. *He could have been born prematurely. He could be another man's son.* His gaze shifted up to the rearview mirror. He resembled Elena. But that height, that cleft in his chin . . . *Those could be mine.*

This can't be. It can't.

If Brenda found out I cheated . . . I can't lose her.

John was whispering reassuringly to Evan, "It'll be

okay." He looked askance at Kurt. "Right? He'll get back to his grandmother, and you and I will go clear all this up at the station."

I'm an officer of SSTIX. I let my private pain over Elena's death feed a hate for wæres, and now . . . now I find the Domn Lup is likely my own son. I can never speak of this, never let it get out. It would ruin my life in every way.

"John Curtis Hampton, you say? I'm very embarrassed to admit this, but I believe I've made a terrible mistake. . . ."

CHAPTER SIXTY

As Johnny drove into the driveway, Toni rushed onto her stoop, cheeks flushed with anger. "I think we're over that twenty minutes I promised her," Johnny murmured to Evan. "Don't forget our promise."

"I won't tell her about the cop, Dad."

After a high five, they got out of the car.

Arms crossed, Toni said, "You're late!"

"We . . . got a little carried away."

"Gram!" Grinning from ear to ear, Evan ran from the car and clasped her in a big hug. "He's my dad!"

"You told him."

Johnny nodded. "That's okay, isn't it?"

Toni assessed Evan's giant smile. "Yes," she said. She hugged Evan back. "Yes."

Kurt Miller parked his Crown Victoria in the garage. Once he'd stuffed the files into his briefcase, he left the car. Inside, he heard the treadmill motor running in the basement. "Honey?" he called.

"Down here!" she called, slightly breathless.

Kurt descended sluggishly. His mind had been rolling for the last half hour as he'd driven around, thinking. Brenda already knew for certain she couldn't have kids. A uterine problem. In vitro was out. Neither felt surrogacy was an option, so his fertility had never been tested. They had accepted they could not have children. But now he knew: He could father a child. *How would it make her feel?* She'd already dealt, years before, with feeling "flawed." *Would this bring that pain back?*

At the bottom of the steps, he stood and regarded her.

"What?" she asked and let loose a self-conscious giggle.

He said nothing.

"Kurt? Is it the case?" She powered down the treadmill and walked toward him. "Is everything okay?"

He wrapped her in his arms.

She laid her head on his chest. "Kurt. What's wrong?"

"Nothing's wrong."

She didn't argue, she just let him hold her.

This is who she is. Patient. Loving. I've been so selfish for so long, thinking I could never make a real fatherlike connection to some kid I didn't know. It seemed an insurmountable mountain, but he'd seen two strangers conquer that slope in the back of his car today in a few minutes, under less than perfect circumstances. Sure, John was Evan's biological father, but as any law enforcement officer saw daily, fathering a child didn't make a man a parent.

He sucked down a breath. With his mouth lightly touching the top of her head, he whispered, "I want us to make an appointment with that adoption agency you found."

EPILOGUE

I woke up clean in my comfy bed at the haven. The clock read 1:30 p.m. A fire was burning low, providing just enough light for my drowsy eyes.

Menessos.

I still have Menessos.

My satellite phone rang. Grabbing it from the night-stand, I saw it was Nana. "Hello?"

"Everything going well with your critical situation?"

"Yes, I think it's resolved. For now. How's your knee?"

"Gonna be fine." She paused. "Your mother's a piece of work."

"Yes, your daughter is."

I heard her marked exhale. "You smoking?"

"No, but Goddess I want one."

"You coming home soon?"

She paused. "Yes. Yes, I am."

"Good."

There was silence on the line, then she said, "I love you, Seph."

"I love you too, Nana." We hung up.

I thought back over last night.

Without speaking much, Menessos had wrapped me in his jacket. He had held me all the way here, and ushered me quickly to my rooms so I could shower and change—two things I'd been eager to do. It had required a lot of conditioner to convince my hair to comb out, but eventually, and with the aid of hot water and ibuprofen, I felt human again.

A hot meal had been waiting for me after I showered. Chicken noodle soup, no less.

The broth had had a delicious hint of rosemary, and the fat noodles must have been homemade. There had been gourmet crackers as well; they'd been buttery and sprinkled with rosemary, too. After eating, I had felt restored, and sleepy.

Unable to get my mind off the fight we'd had before the meeting with the shabbubitum, I'd felt guilty. It hadn't exactly been a fight, but I'd shouted at him and told him I didn't need him exploiting what he'd given up.

I had to admit that my venting might have been more about the state of my relationships with Johnny and my mother than it had been about Menessos. Feeling remorseful about it, I'd gone down to his chamber wearing my thick terry robe and a sling for my arm. Mark had been sitting in a comfy chair outside his door, playing a game on his cell phone. "May I?" I had asked.

He'd said, "Of course." I'd knocked.

"You should be resting," Menessos had said. He'd shut the door behind him, but not before I'd seen the advisor and Liyliy's sisters in his chamber.

"I want to apologize."

Mark had abruptly excused himself and meandered toward the stage to give us privacy.

"There's no need—"

I'd put my fingers on his lips to shush him. "Yes, there is. Friday night, before the advisor arrived . . . I . . ." I hadn't been able to tell him that Johnny had attacked me. He'd claimed he'd known, but I hadn't been ready to talk about that yet. Just thinking about it generated burning tears. "I wasn't myself. I appreciate all that you do for me, all that you have done and sacrificed for me. And I thank you for it."

I had opened my arms then and, awkwardly, we'd embraced.

"Oh, Persephone. I just want . . . to keep you safe." I'd shivered when he'd said my name, and he'd broken the embrace too soon. "Go now. You must rest." He'd put on a brave countenance, but something sad had been lurking beneath.

I'd caressed Menessos's face and pulled him to me. I'd kissed him, tenderly, sweetly, and he'd let me. Then I'd flicked his lips with my tongue. He'd sighed. He'd trembled under my touch and his arms had snaked around me to clutch me close. I'd tasted him and explored his mouth, indulging in his cinnamon flavor, kissing him as a lover would.

Later, in my safe and warm bed, rousing to a lazy Sunday afternoon, I remembered all this, and anticipated Menessos waking less than four hours from now.

Nothing will ever be the same.

My satellite phone on the bedside table rang. Ozzy Osbourne's "Bark at the Moon" flooded my ears, and I knew exactly who was calling.

Johnny.

Fantasy.

Temptation.

Adventure.

Visit PocketAfterDark.com, an all-new website just for Urban Fantasy and Romance Readers!

- Exclusive access to the hottest urban fantasy and romance titles!

- Read and share reviews on the latest books!

- Live chats with your favorite romance authors!

- Vote in online polls!

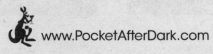

www.PocketAfterDark.com

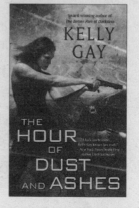